A JOURNEY INTO WAR

A JOURNEY INTO WAR

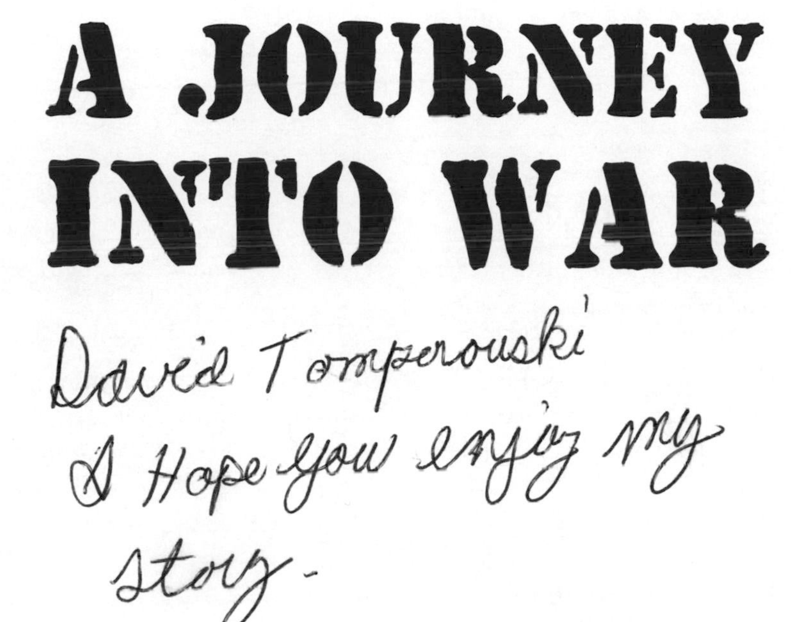

GERRY FELD

November

worked with cousin Jerry Tomporowski at the Correctional Facility in St. Cloud!

Library of Congress Control Number: 2017900912
ISBN: Hardcover 978-1-5245-7814-5
Softcover 978-1-5245-7813-8
eBook 978-1-5245-7812-1

Print information available on the last page.

Rev. date: 03/06/2017

To order additional copies of this book, contact:
Xlibris
1-888-795-4274
www.Xlibris.com
Orders@Xlibris.com
756083

CONTENTS

DEDICATION

IT WOULD NOT BE PROPER TO WRITE THIS NOVEL WITH OUT DEDICATING IT TO ALL THOSE WHO HAVE FOUGHT SO GALLANTLY TO KEEP OUR COUNTRY FREE THROUGH OUT OUR NATIONS HISTORY. THEY WERE TRULY MY INSPIRATION FROM BEGINNING TO END.

AND TO MY WIFE JOANN, WHO ENCOURAGED ME ON SO MANY OCCASIONS WHEN I HAD GIVEN UP ON THE PROJECT. WITHOUT HER COAXING I WOULD HAVE NEVER COMPLETED THE MANUSCRIPT. THANK YOU FROM THE BOTTOM OF MY HEART.

AND TO MY SISTER CAROL, WHO BEGAN PROOF READING MY MANUSCRIPT AND COMPLAINED WHEN THE STORY TOOK UNEXPECTED TURNS THAT SURPRISED HER. REGRETTABLY SHE NEVER FINISHED PROOF READING AS THE MANUSCRIPT WENT IN AND OUT OF STORAGE SO OFTEN, SHE PASSED AWAY IN 2015.

PREFACE

As a young boy I was completely enthralled with World War Two. There was nothing about the subject that did not fascinate me. Luckily, I was surrounded by my Father and all his World War Two friends, who shared many stories with me. I always looked at these men as my super heroes.

Unlike other children my age, I never read novels if I could help it. I consistently sought out historical accounts of the war. It became my passion. In high school, the late Father Allen Spicer was my instructor in American History. As we studied the war, it did not take him long to discover my passion for the topic. Understanding the depth of my passion, he continually challenged me to delve ever deeper into all aspects of this monumental struggle.

Keeping true to Father Spicer's challenge, I never quit studying or digging out the small facts that made this war all the more interesting. Two of my favorite subjects became Pearl Harbor, and European Airborne Operations. So in 1977, when I decided to write the great American War Novel, I struggled on which aspect of the war to write about. After much thought, I chose the war in Europe. The time line of the war and major battles are one hundred percent accurate. During the writing, I always had a mountain of reference books aside of me, where I could look up dates, names, or other facts I felt were important. On describing battle scenes, I have taken literary license. There were hundreds of small unit actions through out the war that have never been written about. So I put together combat scenes that could very possibly have taken place.

I wanted the reader of my book to understand what the main character was about, and what drove him to succeed. After speaking with many Veterans' from my home state of Minnesota, I decided this was where my story must begin. In that light, I not only created a main character, Steven Kenrude, but also his family, love interest, and hometown of Glendale Minnesota. Through out the book, I bounce back and forth between the war and Glendale. It was imperative to me for the reader to understand how the war affected not only the fighting soldier, but his family and loved ones back home. This war was not easy for anyone on the home front. I tried in many ways to describe some of the struggles, and challenges that were such a major part of every day life.

There were several times I decided to quit writing this book. At times it was frustration, other times it was just lack of quality time to work on it. In the early eighties, I actually tossed it into a file cabinet slamming the door shut. There it lay for nearly a decade. Finally in the mid-nineties I completed the book or so I thought.

After finding no one interested in publishing it, I relegated it back to the dark drawer of my file cabinet. Again, it sat until the winter of 2011, when my wife, Joann convinced me to take another look at it. To be honest, I never liked the original ending. So it was obvious, I would need to reconstruct that part for sure. Nevertheless, as I started reading on page one, I came to realize quickly, the book was not a quality piece of work. It truly was in need of work.

So I started over rewriting the book from cover to cover. However, as the summer of 2012 arrived, once again it was shoved into the drawer. I just did not have the quality time that was necessary to work on it. As planned, I resumed work as winter finally set in. After finishing the book, with a completely new ending of course, I once again started over. I went through the book line by line to ensure I was presenting a quality book in the best possible way.

I even considered taking out some or all of the gritty, hard core language I use through out battle scenes. However, refusing to acknowledge the stress, anger and heartbreak of battle hardened Veterans' pushed to their breaking point, would have lessened the impact of this novel. I decided if the book were going to be realistic the language needed to stay.

Once again in 2017, I went through the book page by page. I felt one more time around was essential.

I was totally surprised when Steven Ambrose's Band of Brothers came out. Although his book is factual, it paralleled many facets of my fictional story. I did not use any parts of his book. Any similarities are purely coincidental, as my battle scenes had been completed well before his excellent work hit the shelves.

This work has been a labor of love, sweat, toil and tears. It has been a long road since I first put pen to paper. In fact that is the truth. I began writing all of this long hand on legal tablets, before typing the first108 pages on a Smith- Corona type writer. Those pages were eventually retyped to a computer with the rest of the manuscript. A computer with word processing was a real God send to help bring this novel to completion.

I hope you enjoy this story I have created. Through out this process, Steve, Harry, Franny and the rest of my characters I wrote about became good friends of mine. Now I would like to share all of their strengths, fears, love, hopes and dreams with each of you.

GEN. GEORGE S. PATTON JR. ONCE SAID

"IT IS FOOLISH AND WRONG TO MOURN
THE MEN WHO DIED. RATHER WE SHOULD
THANKD GOD THAT SUCH MEN LIVED."

AS PLATO POIGNANTLY BELIEVED

"ONLY THE DEAD HAVE SEEN THE END OF WAR"

LET US NOW BEGIN OUR JOURNEY INTO WAR

CHAPTER 1

THE SAMUEL EVANS

The North Atlantic was exceptionally rough this Sunday morning, as the sturdy Liberty Ship Samuel Evans crashed through ten foot foam covered waves, as she made her way toward New York. Her cargo on this voyage was a thousand homesick soldiers, all veterans of the brutal war that had devastated Europe. Many of the hardened combat veterans cooped up below decks in tight compartments, cursed every swell that rocked the Samuel Evans. Sea sickness as horrible as it can be, was exasperated by stagnant air, crammed tight conditions, and overflowing toilet facilities. If the rolling of the ship did not affect you, the combined odor of fuel oil, vomit, and raw sewage could finish off the best of men. Men took turns seeking fresh air by climbing a ladder toward the rear of the ship, where a hatch had been left open. Just a few moments of fresh air, coupled with cold salt spray in the face, went a long way to making them feel almost human. Several ingenious soldiers distracted M.P.'s, in order to slip outside where they could climb to protected higher decks escaping the carnage below. Sergeant Steve Kenrude along with his good friend Sergeant Harry Jenson were just two of the men accomplishing the successful escape. Sucking in large volumes of fresh air, their stomachs slowly began to settle down. Both men leaned over a railing allowing the freezing salt spray to wash over their faces. After several minutes they felt totally revived. More importantly, the horrible odor from below decks had been cleansed from their nostrils. Steve watched a destroyer off the port side of the ship crashing through the heavy seas. It sends huge geysers of turquoise water skyward, after smashing through each consecutive wave. Being an airborne soldier was about as rough as it could get. However the thought of being tossed around on a ship every day was unimaginable. Worse yet, the thought of having his ship sunk hundreds of miles from land, with little chance of rescue never appealed to him.

All Steve wanted now was to get back to America, and start the long trip back to the farm in Glendale, Minnesota. He had covered a lot of miles since leaving home, becoming good friends with many great guys. Some would never experience a voyage home again, while many more would suffer from debilitating injuries the rest of their lives. But now that was all behind him. He has survived the greatest war ever fought in the history of man kind.

He had seen the horrors of war, way too many deaths, and enough devastation to last him two life times. Now all he wanted was a good farm, his girl friend Karen, several children and a quiet life back in Glendale.

Those thoughts and desires were all that kept him going for so many long difficult months. The last letter he received from Karen before leaving France was crystal clear. She still loved him very much, and was desperately awaiting his return. Still, he wondered if she would feel the same about him once they were back together. He had changed many times over since leaving home in 1943. He hoped she could accept and understand the changes that had taken place.

Indeed, being in combat changed a person. Killing another human, while watching your friends die has a dire impact on a person's psychologically, like no other experience on earth.

Harry Jenson, who was also lost deep in thought for several minutes sighed deeply, he slapped Steve on the back, "Home Stevie boy, were home. I can almost smell hot dogs on Coney Island." Steve looked at Harry shaking his head, "When the hell did you ever have a hotdog on Coney Island?" Do you even know where Coney Island is?"

"Yup, it's just kind of out there on the coast by New York City. I read about it in a magazine when I was growing up. The article said they had the best hot dogs in the world. I remember what a hot dog smells like, so I can kind of imagine. You know?" Harry replied laughingly.

"Well what would you rather have? A hot dog on Coney Island or a beer in down town St. Paul"

Steve inquired studying his best friends face.

"No contest, Stevie boy. A beer in St. Paul sounds like the best thing in the whole world right now.

Guess I will have to wait until I go on my honeymoon to try out that damn hot dog."

"You're going to New York for your honeymoon? Does Marylyn know all about your plans?" Steve inquired knowing Harry would come up with some sort of off the wall answer.

"Sure she knows. In fact she is the one who suggested it. Marylyn told me one time she will always cook my favorite meals. So we need to find out how the best hot dogs in the world are made." Harry responded dancing a little jig.

It seemed like the two men had known each other forever, when in fact they first met in basic training barely two years earlier. They attended jump school together, survived training in England, and fought through some of the most vicious combat of the entire war together. It was truly a miracle both of them had survived; after all they had been through.

"Sounds crazy, but are you hungry at all?" Steve asked his sidekick.

"No breakfast this morning, Stevie boy? Don't tell me the cuisine was not up to your expectations.

After all, it almost beats those C-rations we ate for so long. Or was it the atmosphere in the dining room that did not meet with your approval." Harry responded wiping water from his face.

Steve took a long look at Harry before replying, "Well hell I asked for room service, but they said the damn butler had the day off. Is that anyway to treat a grade A Fighting man? So I just refused to eat their fine cuisine."

"Room service, Butler, man you must have some sort of fever. You sick Stevie boy, or did all those artillery rounds finally knock something loose up in that noggin of yours?" Harry answered giving Steve a slight shove backwards.

Both men stood and laughed, as a slight glimmer of sunshine finally broke through the leaden clouds that blanketed the North Atlantic skies.

"Well let me tell you Harry. Waiting to get up that ladder for some fresh air and salt spray was better than anything they could have served for chow this morning." Steve responded.

"No, I had to eat something this morning since I couldn't last night. At least I kept it down, well at least so far. It wasn't too bad for the way things have been going on this dam tub." Harry supposed as he closed up his jacket.

"So you're feeling a bit better then?" Steve inquired turning his back toward the cold wind.

"Yeah somewhat, I just can't wait to get off this can and get back on dry ground, where I can walk to a mess hall for a good Army meal, maybe even reheated C-Rations. Sound good to you?" Harry asked rubbing his stomach.

Steve laughed as he looked down at the dark water. "No I think I'd rather go to a diner somewhere. I'd spend my own money on a big T-bone steak, baked potato, and an honest to God salad, if that's even possible. Who knows what's even available with all the shortages and rationing everyone went through back home. Oh yeah! And some good well made civilian coffee, brought to my table by a waitress wearing lip stick, with a bow in her hair, and wearing a skirt with an apron. Yeah that's the ticket for me. Maybe even chocolate cake for dessert." Steve explained licking his lips.

"Wow. You don't ask for much, Stevie boy. But that sure as hell sounds good to me too." Harry agreed.

They brushed past several other men on deck as they searched for a place along the railing. Facing the stern of the Samuel Evans, they gazed at the phosphorescent water being churned up by the huge props.

"Ever think you would see the ocean, Steve?" Harry inquired as he looked about in every direction.

"You know like the saying, water, water everywhere but not a drop to drink. Man this is something.

It's just as far as the eye can see, and for days on end. Kind of makes you feel small, kind of insignificant.

Know what I mean? And how the hell did we survive all we went through, Steve? No good reason we did. No reason at all. Man someone was looking out for us. So many guys died. So many damn good men never made it. Think of all the close calls we had, the way you were wounded. What the hell was this all about? What the hell was it worth? I mean, we beat the Nazis and the Italians. It had to be done I know.

But the cost Steve, the cost, does anyone really understand what this was all about? Everyone knows it's over now. But they'll go on until the next damn war, doing the same damn things. They'll try put it behind them like it never happened. But it did. It sure as hell did. Will we ever forget or get over everything we went through? I don't think I can, Steve. There just has been too much, too many damn good men gone. I just want to go home and pretend like it never happened. Just go pick up where I left off. But I don't think I can. I don't know if any of us can. We saw too much. We saw things no one should ever see, I mean, things that just kill your soul. I just want to forget Stevie boy. I just want to forget" Harry declared brushing tears from his cheeks.

Steve turned to face his best friend, placing his hand on Harry's back. "We'll make it, but we will never ever forget. We made it because of trust in each other, survival, just plain and simple by the grace of God. There is no rhyme or reason to everything that happened, Harry. We will always wonder why Smith or Willie and not me. We'll always question all the probabilities. But we can't change a damn thing. It is what it is and that's that. We made it for some reason. The best we can do is go home, live our lives best we can, and thank God every day that we did survive. And Harry, one more very important thing, we must not let our friendship end here on this ship. We owe it to all the guys we left behind. Together we can keep the memories of who they were, and what they did alive. They will never be forgotten. No one will ever be as close a friend as you are, Harry. Promise me we'll stay in touch.

Man we came through so much together. Remember when we first met? Damn we were just a couple of raw green recruits from the country and didn't know a bayonet from a bazooka.

Much less did we ever think of jumping out of a damn airplane?" Steve said with a chuckle.

"Hell that was your idea Stevie boy. I listened to their sales pitch but I never bought it in a wink. It was you who talked me into going airborne." Harry countered shaking his fist toward Steve. "Although it did make a big difference as time went on. I'm sure damn happy we went through this entire war together. I wouldn't have made it without you."

Steve looked at Harry for a moment before replying. "We sure as hell have a story to tell the world. Some day people may even want to hear how everything happened. It definitely is a story that needs to be told by those of us that were there and experienced it. Not by planners or politicians, but by the common every day dog face soldier who fought the enemy. They need to know what it was like to deal with the cold, rain, snow, mud, and deaths of our best friends. People need to understand the total desperation we felt at times. Yeah we have a story all right, you, me, and a million other guys. It's quite a story. But how do you explain to millions of people what we went through? What if they actually don't want to know the truth? Much less, how do you make them understand what this war truly cost? Where do we begin, Harry? Where the hell do we ever begin?"

CHAPTER 2

WELCOME TO GLENDALE

In the small farming community of Glendale in Central Minnesota, it was nearly impossible for anyone to keep a secret about much of anything. Everyone shared in the happiness of births, and the sadness of deaths. When someone was struggling, the community was always there to lend a helping hand. Glendale was very indicative of small town America during the thirties. It had always been a close knit community.

However, the depression and hard times had drawn everyone closer together.

So as news of Japans surprise attack on Pearl Harbor became known, the community of Glendale sought comfort in their church, to pray for the dead and wounded. They asked for guidance, so their president would make good decisions in the tough times to come. They also prayed for Dave Morris, son of their Mayor Hank Morris. After graduation he joined the navy, and was now stationed at a place called Ford Island inside Pearl Harbor. Dave was a star athlete in high school, with a desire to serve his country as best he could.

As bits and pieces of news arrived by radio that dreadful Sunday, most of the community feared the worst for one of their own. It seemed nearly impossible that anyone could have survived the devastating attack, delivered by Japanese forces.

The Kenrude family spent that cold Sunday at home on their small farm just west of Glendale. Steve and his father Alex decided it would be a good afternoon to haul wood into the basement and back porch of the house, for the long winter that lay ahead. Steve's younger brother Mike, Sister Christine and their mother Nancy, were listening to one of their favorite comedy shows on the radio. It was just the type of quiet Sunday afternoon Nancy appreciated, after a busy week on the farm.

Suddenly, Mike charged out the back door screaming, "Dad! Dad! Steve you need to come quick! The Japanese have attacked some place called Pearl Harbor. Come and listen. They say we're at war."

The two men ran into the house where they found Nancy, sitting near the radio crying as she held a small handkerchief up to her face. They stood quietly listening to a news reporter repeat a bulletin regarding the attack. There appeared to be few specifics, as news from Hawaii took several hours to arrive in Washington.

Alex spent the balance of the day sitting in front of the radio, listening to updated news bulletins. From time to time he would shake his head in frustration, repeating over and over, "I expected such things from Hitler and his gang of thugs in Germany, but never the Japanese." He would look at his wife and ask, "How, How did they sail so far and never get caught? How could this happen? What the hell is going on?"

Nancy attempted to console her worried husband, but was unable to come up with any appropriate answers to his agonizing questions.

In order to deal with her own frustrations and worries, she began rearranging cupboards, and refolding items in the hall closet whether they needed it or not. She felt as long as she kept her self occupied while ignoring the news, it might just somehow go away. Images of young men from Glendale marching down Main Street, heading off to fight during world war one raced through her mind. Systematically, she began listing names of men from Glendale and neighboring communities, that never returned.

She dreaded the thought of seeing the day when her two young boys might have to march off to war, silently she prayed, that somehow her family might be spared the anguish of this horrible war thrust upon their home land.

Mike, although two years younger was identical height as Steve, and nearly just as strong. The two boys were very competitive, and enjoyed playing football and baseball when time away from the farm was permitted. They both did well in school, and were able to attract attention from some of the most attractive girls in Glendale. Everyone in the community knew who the Kenrude boys were. They were every bit a carbon copy of their father.

However, today as the boys sat in the bedroom, their discussion was neither on sports or girls. But rather, the deadly attack on Pearl Harbor. Both boys were wise enough to understand, this war was going to be a long and bloody affair. It would not be won without significant loss of more American lives.

They both promised one another that when the time came, they would do their part if called upon to serve.

As thoughts of war raced through Steve's mind, he felt for sure it would be over by the time he graduated in June of forty-three. He wished desperately to speak with Karen Donnelly, his girl friend regarding everything that happened at Pearl Harbor. Unfortunately, her family had driven to Minneapolis to visit her grandmother. As evening settled over the Minnesota landscape, thoughts of war and an uncertain future made the night seem a little darker, and feel much colder than normal.

During the long night Steve made a firm decision. He was ready to take whatever the war offered, and he wanted to enlist now. Bravely, he announced his intentions to his parents over breakfast Monday morning.

Before his mother could speak, Alex waved her off, giving Steve an understanding but stern look. "Son I know how you must feel. But there is no way we're going to let you enlist before graduation. Besides, there's a lot of work that needs your attention right here on this farm. I'm sorry son, but that's a closed issue. We both love you, and want the best for you. What you do after graduation is your business, but for now the war will have to wait."

Steve knew better then to argue the issue with his parents, when his dad spoke in that tone of voice.

As schools were closed in Glendale on Monday, Steve helped with all the morning chores around the farm. When everything was finished, he walked a mile to the Donnelly farm to visit Karen.

She watched from the kitchen window as Steve ascended the long driveway to the front door.

Opening the door, Karen threw her arms around Steve's neck saying softly, "Isn't it terrible, Steve.

All those men, what is going to happen?"

Not sure how to answer at first, Steve kept quiet. As Karen removed her arms from his neck, he brushed back the hair from her face and smiled. "Somehow everything will work out. We'll be alright." Steve explained, attempting to reassure the pretty blonde standing in front of him. "But I keep thinking of Dave Morris. He was sent to Pearl Harbor some time ago. I just wonder if he's alright."

As the two entered the kitchen, Janet Donnelly was removing several pans of bread from the oven. She smiled at Steve as she placed the hot pans on a wooden shelf. "I heard you mention the Morris boy. I pray to God he's alright. With all those planes and bombs, well I just don't know what to think. His poor mother has not been doing to well of late. She just does not need anymore pain in her life right now.

My heart goes out to her. I can not imagine what she must be going through." Mrs. Donnelly declared shaking her head.

Karen looked intently at Steve for a moment, then toward her mother. "I have a feeling Steve would like to enlist. He hasn't said as much, but I can feel it. And it scares me."

"Is that true Steve? Are you going to quit school and join up?" Janet inquired.

Steve looked over at Karen who was impatiently waiting for a response. He walked over to the large window by the sink. For a brief moment he stared out at Karen's father, who was moving hay bales into a cattle barn from his old truck. Turning he faced the two women. "Yes I would like to enlist. I think it's the right thing to do. But my father absolutely insists I have to finish high school first. So I guess I will see what happens after we graduate. Who knows, the war may be over by that time."

Janet walked over to the oven to check on her remaining pans. Approaching Steve, she placed her hand on his shoulder. "Your father is a smart man, Steve. He knows what's best for you. You are young and want to do the right thing. There is nothing wrong with that. But you just need to finish growing up first. Besides, you have someone else you need to work things out with before you make any hasty decisions."

"Oh, I would never have made that decision without talking to Karen, Mrs. Donnelly. I care for her with all my heart. No I would never do that." Steve replied smiling at Karen, who was wiping a tear from her cheek.

After closing the oven Mrs. Donnelly added, "You need to remember something. With the war starting, there will be lots of important work starting up. An education will be a very important tool to locking up a good job in the future. I've always said, you need to be prepared when tough times come around."

As she finished speaking, the back door swung open. Karen's father Henry entered the kitchen followed by Alex Kenrude.

"Well goodness!" Janet exclaimed, "I can't remember ever having this much company on a Monday morning.

Alex, how are you doing?"

"I'm well. Damn this kitchen sure smells good. No wonder my boy likes coming around here so much.

But then maybe, there is more to it than that." Alex said winking at Karen.

"Do you really think Steve comes around here for more reasons than my fresh bread?" Janet responded with a smile.

"Alright that's enough." Steve exclaimed shaking his head.

"Alex, why don't you take off your coat, and join us for some coffee and fresh bread," Henry asked as he began pouring a cup.

"Well, that sounds like a great offer. But I stopped by to pick up Steve. I have some more wood I'd like to get cut up, before the snow keeps me out of the back woods. And since there is no school today, I figure with two strong boys helping, we can get it hauled up to the house before dark."

Grabbing his coat and gloves, Steve gave Karen a quick kiss on top of the head. "I'll see you tomorrow at school."

"Alright, don't work too hard." Karen replied as Steve walked out the door.

Like most Americans, the Kenrude family took time out of their busy day to listen to President Roosevelt's speech, and declaration of war on Japan. The President tried in vain to assure a shaken nation that America would in the end gain the ultimate victory. However, that was little comfort for mother's like Nancy, who feared the sacrifices their sons and husbands would be forced to make.

The skies above Glendale were suitably dark and foreboding on Saturday, as the Morris family received word their son was positively identified as killed in action.

The yellow hand delivered telegram stated plainly that, Seaman Morris died Sunday Dec. 7th, while in the service of his country. It gave no other details but added, the President was sorry for their loss.

Although the news was not totally unexpected, the telegram sent a shock wave through out the town.

The entire community questioned why such an intelligent, promising young man, had to be taken from them by such an immoral and flagrant violation of America's rights.

With a large crowd on hand, the flag outside city hall was lowered to half-staff. Most shops and stores in town were closed for the balance of the day, out of respect for the Morris family.

Everywhere people gathered in Glendale over the next few days, they spoke of what a fine young man Dave Morris had been, and hoped his death would be avenged by the American military.

Angry young men from around Kandiyohi County yearned for a chance to get even with Japan. Willing to forgo the draft, they began arriving at the Court House in Glendale to enlist.

They stood in line patiently waiting for their opportunity to sign enlistment papers with the draft board, ultimately sending them off to war. By the end of the first day, thirty men enlisted for military duty.

After passing physicals, they were scheduled to leave Glendale for basic training on Monday, January seventh, exactly one month after Japans surprise attack.

On that cold Monday morning, a ritual that would be repeated countless times for the next four years took place in front of the court house. At ten o'clock, the young men surrounded by their families and friends, filled the city square. It appeared as if the entire population of Glendale turned out to see these volunteers off to war. Even the high school postponed classes for an hour, so students could attend the send off. Mothers hugged their sons and cried, while Fathers attempting to display a reassuring face encouraged their sons to be strong.

Steve and Karen stood together during the speeches. The high School Principal spoke first, followed by the chairman of the county draft board. The last and most moving speech was given by Mayor Morris. He spoke of bravery, love of country, and always staying true to your beliefs.

He referenced the loss of his son, and the continuing pain his family felt. He wished the new recruits God's speed before stepping away from the podium.

A sense of emotion and patriotism filled the crowd when the mayor finished his speech. Reverend Martin then gave a short prayer service, reading a blessing over the men.

Karen took hold of Steve's hand during the blessing. No matter how strong she intended to be, tears began rolling down her face. She looked over at Steve, who appeared to be mesmerized by the reverends words.

"I know this will be happening to you one day and I'm...." She could not finish speaking, as she fought back the torrent of tears that was building up inside her. Steve placed his arm around her waist attempting to comfort her.

"Sweetheart, with guys joining up like this all over the country, they'll have this war won before you know it.

By the time we graduate, this war will be over. No need to worry, Karen. You won't need to see me off any time soon."

In his mind he knew better. But for now, it was best to leave the discussion where it was. At eleven fifteen the bus arrived in front of city hall. Slowly, the men boarded the bus to cheers from the assembled crowd. Nevertheless, there wasn't a dry eye in the crowd when that bus pulled away from the Court House, heading south out of Glendale toward Minneapolis. It would be the first stop on the way to a war that would claim twelve of the thirty volunteers.

Although this bus had the distinction of being the first, there would be many more buses over the next four years, taking young Glendale men to such far away places as Tarawa, Saipan, Algeria, Okinawa and Normandy.

Steve watched the bus disappear down the road. He wondered what it would feel like, being on that bus heading off to war. It was simply impossible for him to imagine how it would feel, leaving Karen and his family behind, knowing he may never see them again. It made his stomach uneasy just thinking about the possibility. Yet, he was well aware thousands of men were needed to build the military might it would take, to destroy America's enemies, and return peace to a world gone mad.

While recognizing the fear within him, he still felt a strong desire to join the army to do his part.

He would just as soon go now and get it over with, than have to dwell on it for the next year.

As always, the long Minnesota winter finally came to an end. Spring brought warmer days, brilliant wild flowers, and plentiful rain.

Life in Glendale had not changed drastically since that dreadful Sunday in December; accept for shortages of gas, and empty shelves in stores, brought on by government rationing. Most noticeable, was the absence of young men and women. As men left for military duty, many of Glendale's young women moved to Minneapolis. They sought out good paying jobs in manufacturing plants, which turned out much needed war materials. Jobs that had been so scarce during the depression were now plentiful. They paid well, and offered young people a chance to get out on their own, while experiencing life in a big city.

However, continual disasters appeared to be on every war front for the United States. Corregidor fell to the Japanese in the Philippine Islands. Germany was winning countless battles in North Africa, as their submarines threatened to cut vital supply lines keeping England a float. It became evident to most people; this was going to be anything but a short war.

As spring planting started all across the country, shortages began to show up in items such as fuel, rubber, and fertilizers. But Alex had always been a resourceful man, so he made do with what he had, and made the best of it. Being such a busy time on the farm, Steve did not get to see Karen as much as he would have liked. When school ended in June he was able to see her quite a bit more, when he was caught up with chores on the farm. They did the usual things young people in love do while dating. They went swimming at the nearby lake, created fun picnics in the Donnelly's lower meadow, and attended Saturday night dances in the town hall. But dances became less frequent now, as many young men and women left town to help with the war effort.

As all summers do, this one also came to an end. Along with school work and crop harvesting, the first list of young men from Glendale killed, wounded, or missing in action arrived.

It was also a sad time for Karen's family. One cool September evening, Janet Donnelly found her husband lying in the barn when he did not show up for dinner. He died of a massive heart attack.

Nancy helped Janet with house work and cooking, while Alex and many neighbors completed field work, and storing all the crops.

The two boys found plenty of time to help around the Donnelly farm with winter preparations.

Janet grew quite fond of the boys, as they always appeared to be just one step ahead of her, no matter what they were doing.

Steve continued putting in long hours on the Donnelly farm, refusing to take pay or special gifts.

He was just more than happy to help out where ever he could. Consequently, he was desperately missed at home, where work on the farm was falling behind.

After a rather rough day, the subject of Steve's absence came up between his parents

"Steve is beginning to spend a tremendous amount of time on the Donnelly farm, instead of helping out around here where he's needed." Alex confided in his wife.

"Yes, I noticed that myself, Alex. But he isn't just visiting you know. I've seen him come home some nights pretty worn out, from some terribly hard work. He bathes, eats a little, and then falls asleep trying to do his studies. Personally, I wonder how much more that boy can take, before he just plain collapses."

Nancy responded, as she wiped down the counter top in the kitchen.

"That's just it, honey." Alex replied in a frustrated voice. "I'm damn proud of Steve and the work load he is carrying. By God he has the strength of three men some times. But, there is so much work to be done here before the snow falls. Mike and I simply will never get it all finished. And Steve will never get everything finished over there either. What's the answer? We need to figure something out?"

With that, Steve opened the back door entering the kitchen. He looked at his parents while removing his coat. "Looks like I just walked into the middle of something from the look on your face, Mother. I take it you were talking about me, since you both stopped talking when I entered."

"Yes we were, son." His father responded, as he walked toward the stove to pour him self a cup of coffee, "Would you like a cup, son? It's pretty cold out there."

Steve shook his head no as he sat down by the kitchen table.

"We kind of miss your working around here. Remember, everyone has to pull their part of the load, or the entire system falls apart." Alex stated boldly watching his son's reaction.

After several moments Steve took a deep breath. "I realize that Dad, but what about the Donnelly's?

They have nobody to do the chores. Without me the entire place will fall apart. And I can only do so much. Besides, trying to help you, plus my school work, there just aren't enough hours in the day. What am I supposed to do? Just walk away from the family of the girl I love? I plan to marry Karen after graduation.

So I might as well attempt to keep things in good shape over there best I can.

Nancy sat down at the large oak table looking intently at her son. "Have you discussed any of this with Karen or her Mother yet?"

"No, not yet, but I intend to. Just as soon as I feel the time is right. I know Karen feels the same way I do." Steve replied looking respectfully at his parents.

"Look son, there's a war going on, and it's not going to be over by the time you graduate. You best think of that too, before you start talking marriage and making big plans." Alex exclaimed in a stern tone.

After several moments of silence Steve stood up. He began pacing the kitchen floor stopping by his Mother. Placing his hands on her shoulders he looked down at her, then over at his Father.

"I know full well about the war, and responsibility, and work on the farm. I try to sort through all of that every day, but the Donnelly's need help too, who's going to do the work if I don't? They can't afford to hire someone; you realize that the same as I do; besides it's not interfering with my grades at school."

Nancy placed her hands over Steve's. Looking up at her husband she calmly responded. "Our son has grown up, Alex. He has become a man way before his time. I think it's only fair we consider his situation. Alex, whether we want to admit it or not, we both knew Steve and Karen were bound to be married. What we did not count on was Henry passing away so suddenly. We both thought there was plenty of time to figure this all out. But God had different plans I guess. I think we will just have to work things out, and make do with what we get finished. Steve's right about one thing. The Donnelly's desperately need help right now. What do you say, Alex?"

After pouring two cups of coffee, Alex handed one to Steve. Slowly he walked over to the back door, gazing outside for a moment. Then he turned back toward Steve and his wife. "Well, alright. We'll work it out. Your mother figures we can make things work, so I guess we can give it a try. I understand and appreciate your feelings toward Karen, and your desire to help them through this dilemma. If you can handle things and keep your grades up, I can go along with it. Son, you know your mother and I will always be here to back you up, whenever you need help. There isn't a thing we wouldn't do for you. I just don't want to see you take on to much responsibility, and run yourself into the ground. Do you understand?"

Steve felt totally relieved after listening to his Father. With a slight quiver in his voice he replied, "Thank you. I appreciate your understanding. You know with winter setting in, I won't have to much more work to do around the Donnelly's. Janet sold off all the livestock now, so that's a big responsibility

I won't need to deal with any more. So shortly, I should be able to help you with our livestock and repairs that need to be completed before spring.

Everyone was quiet for a few moments. Than with a smile Alex nodded his head. "Alright son, we can work it all out. Just talk to us if things get to tough." Looking up at the clock above the sink he added. Well, it's almost ten thirty, and six o'clock gets here mighty early. So I think its best we call it a day."

"I agree!" Nancy responded as she stood up, placing the chair back under the table. She gave Steve a hug and kiss on the cheek. "Good night Son. Sleep well."

Alex and Nancy walked off to their bedroom, leaving Steve alone to finish his coffee, while pondering the conversation they just finished.

War reports during the summer, allowed folks in Glendale to believe the allies had turned things around, and were now on the offensive. The battle of Midway was a huge success for the United States Navy. Besides destroying most Japanese naval airpower, it stopped their expansion across the Pacific. They had been masterfully defeated, sailing home with their tails tucked solidly between their legs. Late October, reports announced the

British Eighth Army under Field Marshall Montgomery defeated Rommel's vaunted Africa Corp, at the battle of El Alamein. The Germans were finally in full retreat across all of North Africa.

The November news was the most exciting of all. One hundred and seventy thousand American soldiers landed in North Africa. This was the first all American operation in the European Theater.

Next came the landing of U.S. Marines on an island named Guadalcanal. No one knew where this strange sounding island was located, or why it was invaded. However, reporters explained this island located in the Solomon Islands, was a strategic point in America's fight to regain control of the Pacific. Guadalcanal would almost become a house hold word, as radio commentators described exceptional bravery by young marines, fighting off fanatical Japanese attacks. These sensational news stories excited Steve, making him more anxious for school to end. He desperately wanted to be part of this world wide struggle that was taking place in so many countries, oceans and tiny islands around the world.

In January nineteen forty three, word came Rommel completed a fourteen hundred-mile withdrawal into the hills of Tunisia, where it was predicted he was regrouping. British forces were closing on them from the east, while still untested American forces were rushing to hold the line in the western desert, near Algeria and Morocco. Along with this news, came a sad report that Jeff Andrews, a young man from Glendale, was lost at sea when his destroyer was sunk during an engagement with Japanese ships near Guadalcanal.

People in Glendale never get use to the fact that their brave young men needed to die in so many battles, in so many far away places. A temporary monument was placed near the flag pole in the town cemetery, listing names of Glendale men killed in this war. Each time another man died, his name was added to the list. City officials planned to create a permanent memorial once the war ended.

An early spring seemed to be upon Minnesota in the first week of March, but cold shivers were felt, as news arrived from North Africa. Rommel had driven green American forces into a head long retreat, through the Kasserine Pass in Tunisia. Losses of men and material were extremely heavy. Questions abounded as to how long it would take to regroup the demoralized American Forces.

Within a couple of days, news reports stated a new General named Patton, had been placed in command of America's faltering forces. Encouragingly, on the twenty-second of February it was reported a poorly armed, and ill equipped American army, stopped the western drive of Rommel's forces.

They were now in the process of driving German forces back through Kasserine pass.

It was clear to everyone in Glendale, this General Patton they heard so much about, was going to turn around the war in North Africa, bringing victory to American forces.

Great spring-type weather continued across Minnesota. Soon, local farmers began field preparations for planting.

It also became evident to Janet Donnelly, there was no way she could operate the farm without her husband.

Paying someone to do the work was just not feasible. The decision was made to sell the farm to a neighbor.

Janet and Karen moved into a small house in Glendale.

At first Steve felt hurt, as his dream was to someday incorporate it with his Fathers farm. Quickly he realized, managing a farm while attending school, and helping out at home, was totally impossible. Along with field work, many buildings needed major repair, along with several new roofs. He was also keenly aware, before he could consider purchasing the Donnelly farm, the possibility of going to war was a reality. It was evident now; the war would last long after they graduated. There was no doubt in his mind; he surely would be called up through the draft.

As the last of their belongings were moved out of the farm house, Karen and Steve took one last walk through every room.

"It's kind of a grand house, Steve." Karen spoke standing in the hallway by her bedroom. "I am going to miss it very much. So many memories here of Mother and Father, holiday smells, and Christmas decorations. Fun times we had here, and yes, sad times too."

Steve placed his arm around Karen, as they walked slowly down the stairway to the kitchen.

"Oh Steve, someday I want a house like this, filled with laughter, lots of children, and good memories. I want fancy curtains on the windows, and well, mainly love and warmth."

She looked out the large kitchen window one last time. "I'm happy the people who purchased the farm have little children. They'll make their own new happy memories here."

Feeling the time was right, Steve walked over to Karen. Taking her gently by the arm he turned her so they were facing one another.

"Karen, I've known you a long time, and I know how you feel. I want the same things too. And there is one more thing I want. I want to share all those happy things with you. I want to marry you Karen.

After graduation we could get things organized, and I know we could live with my family for a while. I can get a part time job in town to make some extra money, and I'll work with my dad until we can afford a place of our own."

Before Steve could say anymore, Karen raised her hand, placing it over his lips. "No Steve.

Please stop. It just can't be that way. We both know it. Yes, I want to share my life with you too. But we have to think about the war."

She stopped speaking as she gazed about the kitchen. Taking a deep breath, she turned toward the back door. Stopping before leaving the house, she looked intently at Steve, "The war! I know you want to go.

You've wanted to enlist since the horrible thing started. I will not be able to stop you, and neither would our marriage. Don't misunderstand me Steve. I love you with all my heart, and have for a long time. But I'm afraid.

Afraid that if you go you might not come back. Afraid that I could end up married without a husband, and a broken heart that would never heal. Do you understand?"

Steve looked down at the floor for a moment then back at Karen, "But if I do enlist. What about us?"

Karen attempted hard to smile as tears whelmed up in her eyes. "I promise to wait for you as long as it takes.

There is no body that will ever interest me. You are the one Steve! You've always been the one for me.

I'll get a job in town and live with my mother. I can help her with expenses, and still save some money for our future when you return."

"It could take a couple of years, Karen. What about all the guys that think you'll be free to date?"

Steve nervously inquired, peering deep into Karen's eyes.

"I don't want those other guys Steve, only you. That's what I'm trying to tell you. No matter how long it takes, no matter what happens. I will be here when you come back. I promise with all my heart and soul." Karen added before placing her arms around Steve's neck and kissing him. "I'll be here for you.

Just come home in one piece please." She pleaded softly.

As he prepared to talk, Karen shook her head, "And one more thing. Just imagine if we were married, and I became pregnant before you left. Then I find out you were killed or missing in action, and never came home. The baby, our baby, would never know its father. I could not handle that, Steve. I can't risk that, and neither can you. There is so much at stake here. I promise I'll happily marry you when you return. But we have to wait."

Steve nodded in agreement. "You're right, Karen. I do understand. I just don't ever want to lose you."

"And you won't. Just come back to me." She repeated, as Steve wiped tears from her cheek.

"Let's go. I don't want to be in here anymore." Karen stated, as she turned to walk out the door.

Locking the door Steve followed Karen to the truck. They both sat in the truck for a moment, as Karen took one last look around. "Well, I guess that's the end of one era of time, and the beginning of another.

Get me out of here." Karen said boldly, as Steve slipped the truck into gear.

Field work went well on the Kenrude farm. Alex and his sons, worked late into the evening many days.

Lengthening days, warm sun, coupled with timely rains, turned the Minnesota landscape into a lush green carpet. As Steve counted down the last days of school, he felt the pains to break the bonds of Glendale grow inside him. He wanted to prove he was a man. Going to war, testing his bravery in combat, seemed like the ultimate challenge for any young man. He was ready to do his part for the country.

Things were looking up on all fronts. However the entire world knew, there was much fighting and dying left to be done before this war would end.

Steve saw somewhat less of Karen since she lived in town. Helping with work on the farm took the bulk of his time. However, he saw Janet Donnelly on a regular basis, as she now had a job at the dairy in Glendale.

On a quiet Sunday evening in May, Alex and Nancy sat on the front porch, enjoying the fresh spring air. Alex discussed the field work they completed that day, and what his plans were for Monday. All of a sudden there was a loud yelp from the living room, and such a commotion it actually startled them. The two boys came bounding out onto the porch yelling.

"The Germans, they surrendered in Africa. The war in the dessert is over. It's on the radio, dad. They're finished. We beat the dessert rats! We beat Rommel!" Steve yelled out frantically.

Alex quickly stood up, following his sons back into the house. He sat down in his favorite chair, where he listened to the news reporter fill in all the details his sons left out.

"On thirteen May nineteen forty three, the commander in chief of the British Expeditionary Forces in North Africa, notified Prime Minister Winston Churchill in London, all hostile actions have ceased. Remaining German and Italian forces have surrendered." The three men gave a yell. They immediately stopped, as the announcer continued. "In London Prime Minister Churchill addressed a quickly called session of the parliament informing them of the news. I am now quoting from the Prime Ministers speech he added. "Nay this is not the end. It is not even the beginning of the end. But it is perhaps the end of the beginning."

The reporter explained President Roosevelt had not offered any comments at this time, until after he conferred with his leadership in North Africa.

By this time Nancy and Christine had entered the living room, and were also listening. When the radio announcer returned to music, Steve shook hands with Mike. "It was just a matter of time. We had Rommel surrounded at Tobrok. There was no way he could hold out against British and American forces."

Nancy listened to her son, observing how happy he was. She smiled while reciting a short prayer,

"Thank you dear God, and bless those brave boys who have fought and died to bring forth this great victory."

Alex and the children somewhat stunned by Nancy's impromptu prayer all responded Amen.

As Nancy walked into her daughter's bedroom to kiss her good night, she found her sitting up in bed waiting for her. "Why aren't you under those covers young lady ready to head off to sleep?"

"Mom we need to talk. I'm scared about Steve, when he graduates next month he's going to join the army. What happens if he gets killed?" Christine inquired as tears rolled down her soft cheeks.

"Oh my, this war is making all my babies grow up too fast." Nancy said as she sat down on the bed, holding her youngest child. "Sweetheart this war has to be fought. And the sad thing is, men like your brothers are called upon to do the fighting. That's just the way it is. All we can do is pray real hard that God watches over Steve, and brings him back to us safe and sound. And we need to pray even harder, that the war ends before Mike would ever have to go. Do you understand, Honey." She asked brushing hair out of Christine's face.

"I kind of do, mom. But I'm still scared. What can I do to get over it?" She inquired of her strong mother.

"Honey I'm scared to. And it gets worse every day as school is coming to an end. We just have to pray every day, and hope God will hear our prayers, and allow Steve to return to us safe and sound. That's all we can do, Sweetheart." Nancy lovingly told her daughter as she held her tight. "Now slide under those covers and get some sleep."

Leaving Christine's bedroom, Nancy finally became aware of the fear that was growing stronger within her, how could she ever handle so much heart break?

The first week of June school ended for the year in Glendale. Alex and Nancy were having their first child graduate from high school. However, like so many families across the country, this usual happy time was overshadowed by fear and apprehension, concerning the future of these fine young men. Feelings were no different in Glendale. The graduating class of 1943 consisted of forty nine students, twenty-five girls and twenty-four boys. The ceremony took place on a warm Friday evening, followed by a small party in the school gymnasium.

After the party Steve walked Karen and her mother back home. Their new home was just four blocks from the school. Arriving at the home, Janet excused herself and retired to the house, knowing Karen and Steve wanted to be alone.

Before Steve could say a word, Karen faced him, "So when are you enlisting in the army?"

He took Karen into his arms, spending a few moments to study her beautiful face.

"Actually, I signed up this afternoon after picking up Dad's order at the grain elevator. I was going to tell you earlier this evening, but I just decided to wait until we were alone."

Karen backed away from him, she folded her arms across her chest, then walked out toward the street.

Steve followed a few feet behind her, wondering what was going on in her mind. This was the first time she had ever pulled herself free of his arms, before walking away. He felt very uneasy, but knew it was best to allow her to speak first.

Gazing at the twinkling stars in the dark night sky Karen asked, "I wonder if it's clear in Africa or England tonight. I wonder if the German's are killing people in London because the sky is so clear. Do you think that's happening tonight? Are people dying?"

Steve attempted to take hold or her arm. However Karen pulled away, walking farther down the street. After taking a deep breath, she turned to face Steve. "I love you. But I don't know what to do with this fear inside me. I know you. I know you'll never do your job half way. You'll put yourself in danger if that's what it takes. That's what scares me more than anything. When do you leave?"

"I go to Minneapolis for my physical and induction next week on Thursday. If I pass the physical, I'll leave for basic training the next day. To be honest Karen, I asked the recruiter to leave as soon as possible. I knew the longer I waited to leave, the tougher it would be to say good bye to you. And since I enlisted, I have a better chance of getting into something I would like to do, rather than just being assigned by the army. Do you understand?" He explained nervously, not knowing what Karen's reaction might be.

Karen was quiet for a few moments, as she slowly walked back toward her yard.

She stopped as she faced the small white house her mother purchased. "You know, it's not such a bad house when you get down to it. There are a lot of differences from the farm house of course. But it serves our purpose well. I think mother and I have done a good job of decorating it rather nicely. It's a comfortable place now."

Suddenly Karen turned, throwing herself into Steve's arms. "I have been trying to prepare myself for this day all year. I'll make the best of it while you're gone. I'll write you every day I promise. I just want you back so we can buy a house just like this one, and fill it with children and happiness."

She cried harder than Steve had ever seen before. Feeling much relieved after hearing what Karen had to say, he just held her, trying to sooth all her fears.

After several minutes, Steve wiped tears from her face and kissed her. "I love you so much, Karen. I'll write you too, as often as I can. Sometimes it may take a while to write, but I will when I can. And I'll be thinking of you every minute of every day. I promise you that."

Karen smiled the best she was able to under these heart breaking conditions. "You are so brave volunteering to go off to war. I'm very proud of you. Somehow I feel we will both survive, and live happily ever after. You know, just like the story books." Karen kissed Steve intently holding him tight in her arms.

As they arrived at the front door, he kissed her once more. "I am the luckiest guy in the world." he whispered in her ear.

Turning the door knob slowly Karen stopped. She kissed Steve on the cheek, "Good night my love. I'll always love you. And I'll always be here for you. Never forget that."

Steve watched her disappear into the house. Gradually he walked back toward the school, where he had parked the truck. He sat in the cab for a moment, reliving what had just happened. He took a deep breath and smiled before starting the truck.

The week went by all too fast for Steve. He did a lot of work around the farm, to help his father get ahead on some projects. The high light of the week was Tuesday evening. His mother invited Karen and her mother over for dinner. It was a very enjoyable evening for everyone.

Wednesday after morning chores, Steve walked down to Eagle Lake to fish, but mostly be by himself. Sitting on the rocky shore line, he began thinking about the war. He wondered how a war so far away, could be impacting everyone in Glendale. More importantly, it was changing every plan he had made for the last three years. He wondered what his chances were of coming home alive. There were no guarantees of any sort. He remembered Karen talking about what it would be like if he went missing in action or was killed. It was unbearable to think about. Nevertheless, now he certainly was involved, like it or not. A feeling of fear gripped his stomach. He looked around the lake toward the dainty wild flowers growing near the large rocks. Karen always enjoyed weaving them into crowns every time they visited this spot. Could this be the last time he would ever visit this special place?

Placing his fishing rod down on top of the rocks, he looked up toward the sky. He watched the white puffy clouds slide across the azure blue sky. After a moment he cried out, "Oh God if you can hear me please let me come home alive. I want to spend the rest of my life right here with Karen. You allowed me to meet her, now don't take her from me. I'm not being selfish, dear God. I just want to experience life. I haven't had a chance yet." Not feeling like fishing, Steve wound the line back on his pole. Looking back toward the sky he yelled. "Can you hear me, I need to know! I need an answer from you!" After several moments of silence he once again called out. "Answer me. Why won't you answer me?" Shaking his head, he grabbed his fishing rod from the rocks. Before walking back to the farm, he picked one of the fragrant wild flowers. Holding it up to his nose he drew in the wonderful aroma. He looked back toward the sky one more time as he muttered, "Why can't you just give me an answer." Slowly Steve walked back toward the farm, taking in all the beauty of his dad's lower meadow.

He spent his last night at home with his family and Karen. After dinner, Karen and Steve took a walk around the farm. They refused to talk about the war. Instead, they discussed their plans and ideas for when he returned. Around ten o'clock he drove Karen home. When they reached the front door Steve took her in his arms. "I'll write as soon as I know my address, promise!"

Karen smiled slightly, "I'm sure they'll keep you busy at first. But I'll be waiting to hear from you.

Steve nodded his head and smiled. "Yeah, I'm sure they'll have us chasing our tails like a dog for a while." Not sure what else to say, Steve took a long breath. "Well, I better get going so I can get some sleep. Tomorrow will be a long day. Will you be at the bus station tomorrow morning?" He inquired.

"Now what kind of a silly question is that Mr. Kenrude? Mother and I will both be there. How could we not." They both laughed for a moment.

After kissing Karen good night, he drove back to the farm. It seemed like the longest drive he had ever taken back home. There was so much on his mind tonight. Nevertheless, he was extremely happy the way he and Karen parted tonight. He knew everything was right in their relationship. In many ways, he could not be happier. If he just knew how this would all turn out.

Steve was up early Thursday morning, so he could help Alex and Mike with chores one last time.

After taking a last walk around the barn, he headed for the house. After checking over the small travel bag he packed the night before, he headed down to the kitchen. Everyone was waiting for him as he descended the stairs.

"Ready?" Alex inquired.

"Yeah, I guess so. Let's go, I need some fresh air." Steve responded exiting the house

Before entering the car, he took one last look around the farm. He knew all too well, this could be the last time he would ever see his home.

Compared to his drive home the night before, this drive into town went way to fast. Once again, Steve felt scared, and was feeling very sick. He hoped no one could sense what was going on inside him. Alex drove up to the drug store moments before the big blue and white bus came lumbering down Main Street.

As men departing for the war became all too common, there were no crowds, bands or speeches, to see Steve off on his way. Besides his family, the only other people from Glendale to see him off were Karen and her mother, the army recruiter, and Mayor Morris.

The recruiter handed Steve some final papers to take with, while wishing him the best of luck. The Mayor shook hands with Steve wishing him the best. He reminded Steve he had seen every man from Glendale off, so he would be there to welcome him back. He patted Steve on the back before stepping aside.

Next, Mrs. Donnelly with tears running down her face kissed Steve on the cheek. "Steve, come back safely, please. I want you to be my son-in-law and give me lots of grand babies. We all love you, and will be praying for you every day. God bless you, sweetheart."

Next Steve shook hands with Mike. "Well, little brother, take care and give the folks all the help you can.

Keep yourself out of trouble, and keep our fishing hole active."

Mike nodded his head. With his bottom lip quivering he replied "Give them hell, Steve. But be careful and come back home.

Christine was next in line. Steve hugged her tightly, kissing her forehead. Taking a long look at his little sister he said, "You're getting to be a beautiful young lady. Take care and mind the folks. See Karen whenever you have time. She really likes you."

Forcing her best smile possible, Christine looked at her oldest brother saying softly, "Alright Steve, don't worry about me. And I like spending time with Karen, so I'll see her whenever I can. Please take care of yourself. I love you and want you back."

He smiled while wiping a tear from his eye. Patting Christine on the head, he turned to face his mother.

Nancy grabbed him and hugged him as hard as humanly possible, "My God! My first baby off to war, it's not supposed to be this way. You haven't had a chance to experience life yet. This just isn't fair." After kissing him on the cheek she added. "Please be careful, sweetheart. Our prayers will be with you everyday."

Alex slowly stepped up to his oldest son. "Well Steve. I never thought a day like this would ever come. The last thing I ever wanted to do was see you off to war. But you are a man now. Do your best, and don't take any unnecessary chances. Remember your family, son. We'll be praying for you like your mother said. Please come home to us." He gave Steve a huge bear hug, then backed away wiping tears from his face.

Finally Karen stepped forward, "The best for last." She spoke softly placing her arms around Steve.

They exchanged a long kiss as it would have to last them a while.

Steve looked intently at his beautiful girlfriend. "I love you, Karen. Always have, always will.

Keep a light burning in the window."

Nodding her head she replied, "Remember no matter what. You are my guy. Come home to me, Steve. We have an entire life to live yet, house, kids, everything. Write when you can."

"I intend to make those dreams come true, sweetheart." He replied, kissing her again.

"All aboard, please. We have a schedule to keep young man. We have to get moving." The bus driver called out as he patted Steve on the back.

Slowly Steve let go of Karen. He took one last look at her before turning toward the bus. As he walked up the steps Karen called out, "The end of one era in time and the beginning of another."

Remembering the phrase from the last day at the Donnelly house Steve smiled. He smiled, but was at a loss for words. He simply waved as he finished boarding the bus.

Before the bus began moving, Steve peered out the window toward his loved ones. Karen placed her hand on the window calling out. "I love you Steven Kenrude."

Steve placed his hand on the glass opposite hers and smiled.

The old bus pulled away from the curb turning left on Fourth Street. Settling back into the seat, his heart was beating rapidly as he fought back tears that were whelming up inside him. He watched Glendale fade from sight, as the bus turned onto the main highway, heading south toward Minneapolis.

He wondered again what would ever become of him. He thought if worse came to worse, he would rather be listed as officially killed, then missing in action. At least that way, his family and Karen would have some closure. But missing, and always wondering, would be the cruelest thing that could happen. He closed his eyes willing himself to sleep. He did not want to think of the war, or what his fate might be.

CHAPTER 3

UNCLE SAM WANTS YOU

The sudden blast of a train whistle jolted Steve awake, as the bus rumbled into Minneapolis. In the past, Steve always enjoyed a trip to the big city, but not so much this time. He felt very much alone in a strange new world, a world at war that chose no favorites.

The bus arrived at the Minneapolis Depot about two hours after departing Glendale. Steve stepped off, asking the driver where he might find the bus to Fort Snelling.

The driver pointed to a brown Army bus parked across the street, slowly filling with young men. "Right there you go sonny. Just walk over there and show the driver your orders."

"Thanks for your help." Steve replied as he walked toward the driver in military uniform.

The bus was nearly full when Steve climbed aboard. He took a seat on the left side by a window.

Upon arrival at Fort Snelling, the men were organized in alphabetical order outside the bus. They were taken on a short walk to a registration building. Steve was impressed with the number of young men rushing around from building to building. He had to smile, when they came upon a small group of men marching to cadence, being called out by a stiff looking Sergeant. Some of the men appeared quite tired. He was told by the recruiter not to expect much sleep. Processing most often went around the clock, so the army could move the men out quickly for basic training.

Arriving at the registration building, they formed into lines by two doors marked, "A to M and N to Z". It was evident the army had perfected this process since the war began; the clerks were efficient, almost machine like, as they handled each mans documents. After completing registration, the new recruits were taken to barracks where they were assigned a bunk with a foot locker.

As it was close to midday, the men were marched to a mess hall where they sampled their first army meal. It may not have had the flavor of home cooking, but it filled their empty stomachs.

After finishing their meal, they were led to an infirmary where doctors and medical staff prepared to conduct their physicals. Medics drew blood, checked their vision, and looked up their noses, down their throats, and in their ears. The last stop in the production line was to supply a urine sample.

Throughout the process, Steve heard several men state they wanted to fail the physical, so they did not have to go off to war. All the volunteers figured they were draftees who hoped to avoid the war. They became the point of ridicule the rest of their stay at Fort Snelling.

Some men called them traitors threatening them with bodily harm. Steve could not understand how anyone would not want to serve their country at such a desperate time. But he thought it best to stay out of the discussion. He did not want to start his military life being branded a trouble maker.

Stepping into the next room, medics checked blood pressure completed a quick questionnaire then lined up the men for chest x-rays.

Around ten o'clock that evening, Steve's group was marched back to the barracks. They were told they would see a doctor in the morning, after he had results from their chest x-rays.

He was totally exhausted from the day's activities. It seemed like an eternity since he had boarded the bus in Glendale. Being extremely tired, he hoped it was possible to get a good night's sleep.

The following morning after breakfast, they made their way through a dental clinic. They were checked for any major problems. At the same time a comprehensive dental chart was prepared for each man. They were essential at times for post battle identification purposes.

After completing the dental clinic, they waited in line one more time to see a doctor. They would now find out whether or not they passed their physicals.

Steve had always been very healthy, so he was extremely confident he would pass. While waiting in line, he met a man from a small farm just outside of Clearview, Iowa by the name of Harry Jensen. It was amazing to Steve how much they had in common. It did not take long for the two men to form a bond that would last through the worst of times.

Entering the small office Steve handed his file to the waiting doctor. He flipped through the pages stopping here and there to read notations. "Well, Mr. Kenrude, I can't see anything in your file that would keep you out of military service. I am classifying you 1-A, fit for service. Do you have any questions?"

"No sir." Steve replied feeling strangely confident, and happy with the results.

"Alright then," The doctor responded, tossing Steve's chart on a large pile next to his desk.

"You can go line up in the hall and get your shots. Next!" The doctor barked out as Steve left the office.

The men lined up single file. They then walked between two rows of medics, who gave them shots in both arms at the same time. There appeared to be an awful lot of shots. The men were told each one of them was important, especially if they wound up in the Pacific.

With all medical work completed, the men were finally ready for their official military haircuts. Every man left the barbershop with their heads nearly shaved. The rest of the day was spent collecting their military clothing, packing their civilian clothes to be mailed home, and taking army aptitude tests. The Sergeant monitoring the tests stated the tests would assist in placing them in jobs they were well qualified for, once they completed basic training.

Steve found the tests to be rather easy, and actually somewhat amusing. It was evident the army had written the tests very simply, to accommodate men who did not have much of an education. He found it incredible, to watch so many men struggle with the easy tests. Many men complained they were simply a big joke. After all, the Army was going to need every man they could, to fill the ranks of infantry companies. They did the brunt of the fighting, taking the highest rate of casualties. So it was just natural that's where most of the openings would occur.

Friday evening Steve, Harry, and several other men from their barracks, were sent to the kitchen for K.P. duty. Their assignment was to clean pots and pans. It was a thankless job, but every soldier knew he would be doing much more of that before his army days were over.

After finishing work in the kitchen, they joined the rest of the men from the barracks for a quick shopping trip to a small PX. They were only allowed to purchase essential hygiene items and writing materials.

Upon returning to the barracks, a Sergeant followed the last man through the door. "Alright listen up men!" The Sergeant called out. When the men were silent he stepped into the middle of the barracks. "You men are finished here and ready to move on. Breakfast will be at 0530. Have all your gear packed, and ready to go before you head out for chow. The bus leaves for the train station at 0700 sharp, and every one of you will be on it. I do not expect to begin a search party to round up any of your sorry asses. Do I make myself clear?"

"Yes sergeant!" They replied in unison.

"Are there any questions?" The sergeant inquired as he gazed over the new recruits.

"Where are we headed to?" One of the men inquired.

"That private is a military secret. You will go where the army sends you and that's that, any more stupid questions?" No one dared utter a word. "Great, that's the way I like it.

Lights out in fifteen, hit the rack gentlemen, it will be a short night." The Sergeant called out in a loud gruff voice.

After the lights were turned off someone asked, where do you think they're sending us?

Another man replied, "Fort Leonard Wood, Missouri. All the guys from the northern part of the country go there."

A third man called out, "No, I heard they're full down there. We're going to Fort Polk

Louisiana. Man it is tough down there. They got snakes and rats as big as dogs. It's down right dangerous down there. And that damned humidity is going to kick our asses. Man, I've been there, I know what it's like."

Still a fourth man chimed in, "Naw that's not true. I heard from one of the barbers, scuttlebutt has it we're all being shipped to Fort Campbell in Kentucky. Yup, blue ridge mountains for all of us yanks."

Steve had to laugh at all the rumors. He found out early what the recruiter had told him about scuttlebutt.

"Don't believe anything until you see it for yourself. The army runs on rumors, and there will be a million a day. And you'll find out quick no one knows a damn thing!"

After all the predictions and scuttlebutt ended, Steve rolled over onto his side. He had been away from home three day now, and was beginning to feel a bit homesick. During the day with Harry clowning around, he did not think much about home. Harry was a real God send. He already felt like he could talk with him about anything. But when the lights went down at night and everything was quiet, memories of home raced through his head.

In a way, it was kind of crazy. So often he complained about having to get out of bed so early in the morning to feed animals before getting ready for school. But now, he really missed the smell of country air, fresh alfalfa, picking eggs and watching the sun come up, as he fed livestock. It was always funny to watch Blaze, their black lab chase chickens around the yard first thing in the morning. It would create such a racket, waking up anyone else who was asleep in the house. At breakfast time, Christine would always accuse Steve of riling everything up so they couldn't sleep. Sometimes there actually was a little truth to that allegation. However, ninety percent of the time Blaze was simply to blame. But it was home, and now he missed the little things he always took for granted. Of course what he missed most of all was Karen. And tomorrow he would be going still farther away from her.

At 0500 the lights came on in the barracks. "Move it gentlemen, move it. Get your asses out of bed

The mess hall is waiting, and so is your bus. You damn well better be on that damn bus at 0700, or your sorry ass will be mine and you sure as hell don't want that!"

A very fit looking Sergeant called out as he slammed a garbage can cover against the bunks, as he walked through the barracks.

Every man was moving at top speed within seconds. No one wanted to be the last man boarding the bus.

Steve and Harry dropped down in their seats directly behind the driver at 0650. "Good shape." Harry yelled out jabbing Steve in the ribs. "I told you we would make it with time to spare."

Leaning forward he asked the driver. "So where are we headed to today?"

The driver looked up in the mirror replying, "The train station!"

"We know that." Harry acknowledged, "But where is the train taking us. Everyone is betting, on it so it would be nice to have the inside scoop. Can you help me out?"

The driver once again looked up at the mirror staring right at Harry. "You writing a book, or are you just trying to make a buck?"

Frustrated Harry replied, "Look, we just would like to have some idea where we're going."

Once again the driver looked at Harry, "Now, if I knew all of that, do you think I would be just driving this damn bus. Why don't you ask someone like that Sergeant over there? I'm sure he has some idea as to where you're going. Or, you could just sit back and enjoy the ride. Either way you're not going to get anywhere any quicker, soldier."

Harry sat back. Looking at Steve he shook his head. "Man, everyone in this man's army seems to have nothing but poor attitudes, and smart ass answers. Do you think the entire army operates this way?

Steve laughed watching Harry roll his eyes. "Hmm, it looks like that attitude is starting to rub off on you right now Harry, maybe its best to ask fewer questions, and just go along with the flow."

"Oh yeah alright, I give up. I'll just sit back in my seat, close my mouth and enjoy the ride. Who cares where we're going anyway." Harry remarked in a cocky voice.

"You know, that tone of voice will get you in a heap of trouble if you keep it up." The driver called out to Harry. "You might just want to listen to your buddy there, sounds like he has all the right answers."

"What the hell! Who asked him? Damn, is nothing private in this army?" Harry inquired.

Several men in adjacent seats over hearing the conversation were now laughing, taking another bite out of Harry's already injured pride.

After several moments of silence, Harry began laughing while poking Steve in the ribs again.

"Well I might get my shit jumped into from time to time, but I'll tell you what. You just stick with me, and I'll keep you out of trouble, and get you through this army business in fine shape. I tell you Stevie boy I got it aced."

"Really, and who's going to get you through it?" Steve inquired. You seem to be off to a questionable beginning right now Private Jensen. I hope it doesn't get any worse."

"Damn Kenrude, will you just give me a break." Laughing Harry continued. "But let me tell you what. That Sergeant this morning scared the hell out of me. I sure as hell did not want to be late, or the last man boarding this bus." Harry explained as he looked out the window to see how many men were still running from the mess hall and barracks.

Precisely at 0700 the Sergeant boarded the bus. He looked up and down the aisle for a moment before completing a roll call. "Well I'll be. Every one of you sons a bitches made it." He walked half way down the aisle then stopped. "Are there any questions before I leave you?"

No one said a word.

After taking another good look at the recruits he walked back toward the front of the bus. After whispering something to the driver he stepped out calling back. "Shut the damn door. You don't want any of these clowns falling out."

The driver laughed heartily as he pulled the door closed. He slipped the bus into gear, slowly driving away from the barracks.

"Well Stevie boy, take a good look around. We can say good bye to Fort Snelling and Minnesota for quite some time to come." Harry stated as he watched the driver pull out of the Fort, heading toward the train station.

Within a half hour the bus slowed to a stop near a waiting train. The men exited the bus, grabbed their duffle bags prior to shuffling aboard the empty passenger cars. After another roll call was completed, all the doors to the cars were sealed. Ever so slowly, the smoke belching locomotive began pulling out of the station. Watching out the window, it was evident they were heading in a southerly direction.

"It appears Leonard Wood or Fort Polk might be where were headed." Harry informed Steve as they watched the Twin Cities disappear from sight.

After several minutes of silence, Harry looked profoundly at Steve. "What do you think our chances are for staying together? I really have enjoyed getting to know you. It sure would be great if we could train together."

"I haven't got a clue, Harry. As much as I would like to stay with you, I really doubt our odds are very good. With hundreds of men arriving at these bases daily, odds are we're going to get split up. But if that happens, let's try and stay in touch. What do you say?" Steve inquired of his new best friend.

"Deal, we'll figure it out, Stevie boy. We'll figure it out." Harry replied confidently.

For the most part, their train car was alive with laughter, loud talk and silly pranks. There were some exceptions, as men became engrossed in serious conversations regarding their futures.

All the while, two Sergeants patrolled the car keeping watch over their new recruits.

Steve was feeling good about his first train ride. Although he wished it had been under different circumstances, like maybe a honeymoon with Karen. Still, it was something he had never experienced before, so he was determined to make the best of it.

"Have you ever been to any other states besides Minnesota?" Steve inquired.

"Oh sure many times, Clearview is rather close to the Minnesota boarder, and kind of close to South Dakota. My mother's folks live in Sioux Falls, so we would go there to visit them quite often. Mom liked shopping in Sioux Falls when we could afford it. Clearview doesn't have much for shopping. But we haven't been there for quite some time. We'd also go over to Omaha for the livestock auctions from time to time. That was always a lot of fun. I've been in Minnesota plenty of times. I have an aunt who lives near St. Paul. We would visit her maybe every year or so. Was always fun seeing the big buildings down town. Man what a place. But that's the extent of my travels, how about you?"

Steve squirmed a bit, attempting to find a more comfortable sitting position. "No this is my first trip out of Minnesota. I would dream of traveling when I was younger. But my parent just couldn't afford to take us anywhere. So I guess army or not, this is my big chance to travel, and see some of our big old world." Steve explained with a big smile.

Overhearing their conversation, the two soldiers seated across the aisle began to laugh. The man nearest the aisle leaned toward Harry. "See the world? There ain't going to be nothing left to see. Heck, all we're going to see is a whole lot of blown up places and lots of dead krauts. And besides that, there ain't any of us coming back alive. We ain't anything but cannon fodder for the kraut 88's. Believe me. We ain't seeing anything!" Irritated by the man's bad attitude, Harry shook his head then leaned toward him. "Man, I sure hope I don't have to put up with your shit every day. You're nothing but bad luck and depressing.

But you know, Stevie boy, he just might know more about what's happening than you. And besides, by the time the army gets done training us, this whole damn war could be over."

"Could be, yep it could be over. But then we will just have to wait and see, now won't we. Shit, I'm telling you we is all as good as dead right now. You best believe it." The man added before leaning back in his seat.

Steve and Harry ignored everything the man had told them. They continued their conversation discussing everything from farming, girl friends and best places to fish.

The trip to St. Louis took nearly two full days with several stops along the way. By the end of the trip, boredom had over taken most of the men. There were far fewer conversations taking place. Just about everyone used sleep to pass the time.

Around eleven-thirty Monday morning the train rolled into the large depot in St. Louis.

"Well Harry, it looks like we have come to the end of the line. We're getting real close to home now. A couple more hours from now, we'll get to know what army life is really all about. This is getting more interesting all the time." Steve stated as he rose from his seat, stretched, then peered out the window toward the bustling platform.

Harry stood up slowly giving Steve a light punch in the abdomen. "I don't know about you any more, Kenrude. You seem entirely too eager to get at this army way of life. You know they're going to hand us our butts when we start basic. It is going to be damn rough."

Steve laughed while punching Harry back. "Well maybe I am ready to get at this. You know the sooner we get going, the sooner we can get back home. And from where I'm standing right now, home already sounds damn good."

"Now you listen to me, Steve. Don't be too anxious where you start volunteering for extra duty. I here tell they take these gung ho types and just rip them apart, just to see what they're made of. So be damn careful before you get into something you might just regret. Now, that is not a rumor either. I was told that by the recruiter who signed me up." Harry replied, actually sounding concerned for Steve's welfare.

Both the front and back doors of the car flew open, as drill sergeant climbed aboard the cars. One of them yelled at the top of his lungs, "Get off this car, grab your duffle bags, and fall in on the platform. Do it now gentlemen! Uncle Sam ain't got all damn day!"

Harry followed Steve down the aisle toward the front door. A drill instructor nearly ripped his arm out of the socket pulling him down from the car.

"What the hell!" Harry yelled, as he continued following Steve toward the pile of duffle bags, which were being unloaded from the baggage car.

Grabbing their bags, they turned toward the platform where men were beginning to assemble. However, Steve turned right into the hands of two waiting drill instructors. One pushed Steve, telling him to line up along the yellow line over by the other men. A second instructor told Harry to drop and give him twenty push ups for being slow.

Minutes later a corporal approached the yellow line. Alright listen up. From that poll, I want the first forty men to count off. Grab your bags, throw them on the truck marked 22, then get on the first bus, now!"

The men began counting off. Steve was thirty-three, Harry was number forty. Everyone ran as fast as possible, tossing his bag up onto the truck and charging head long toward the open door on the bus. Harry was the last men to board. He looked like he was in a daze as he dropped into a seat near the rear of the bus.

About two hours later, the bus approached the entrance to Fort Leonard Wood. Everyone attempted to get a good look at the huge arch over the road, announcing they were entering the fort.

A strange new world caught their attention, as the excited men looked in every direction. All the buildings were the same style, same color, and in neat orderly rows. Strange looking vehicles all painted olive drab, navigated incredibly clean streets. Everywhere were large formations of men marching in perfect unison, as drill instructors called cadence. Some of the formations were dressed out in full combat gear including weapons.

This was a real eye opener for the men. A precursor of what was to come in the next few days.

Finally the bus jerked to a stop at the reception station. As the driver pulled the door open a large drill instructor jumped on board. "Get off this bus, let's go you sons a bitches, get off this bus now!" He yelled at the new recruits, while pulling the first man by the door from his seat.

The rest of the men emptied the bus in seconds. As they hit the concrete, sergeants directed them to assemble in several different spots. Steve's heart was racing at an incredible rate. Suddenly he realized, he was not at all prepared for what military life was actually all about.

When all the buses were empty, four sergeants took a head count. After making several notations on a clip board, one of the sergeants ordered Steve's column to find their duffle bags, and reassemble in two rows on the street. Once everyone assembled, the sergeant told them to keep their mouths shut and follow him.

One by one, groups of men were led away in several different directions. Steve's group walked about a half mile past rows of two story wooden buildings.

They made a left turn walking up a driveway between two buildings, which led into a large courtyard where they came to a stop. The sergeant told them to drop their duffle bags then stand at ease. He turned quickly before walking toward a smaller building at the edge of the courtyard. Steve finally had a chance to look for Harry. He had not seen him since getting on the bus back in St. Louis. With a sigh of relief, he spotted Harry in the row behind him, about ten men away. Both men made quick eye contact and smiled, as the sergeant came walking back.

All the while they had been waiting, other groups of men continued filing past, toward the rear of the large courtyard. They were assembling around a building that appeared to be the main focal point in this particular area of the fort.

Once the sergeant stood in front of them, he ordered them to pick up their bags and follow him. He led them up behind a group of men that just finished moving through the busy building.

Once again the sergeant told them to drop their bags, that he would be right back. He ran up the stairs passing through a door marked, "Enter here."

As they waited, Steve observed men coming out of the building holding onto a small white card. They would grab their duffle bags; then show the card to a sergeant. He pointed to different areas of the courtyard where groups of men were forming.

Steve figured the men were being split up into their basic training companies. He prayed quietly, that somehow he and Harry would remain together.

Moments later the sergeant returned, directing his men toward the entrance door. In the middle of the building, stood six large wooden desks manned by corporals. They were assisting recruits entering from three sides of the building. Above each desk was a sign that read,

"Have your paper work ready. Keep quiet. Wait you turn! Speak only if Spoken to!" The corporals would take each man's paper work before checking their dog tags. He then flipped through the files, consulted several lists on his desk, made a few notations, then hand each man the small piece of paper Steve observed each man carrying. Most often not a word was exchanged.

Approaching the desk, Steve placed his file in the corporals out stretched hand, while removing his dog tags from under his shirt. The corporal looked at the dog tags for a second then spoke, "Kenrude? Is that correct?"

"Yes it is." Steve responded.

The corporal finished making notations, then handed Steve his piece of paper. Smiling up at Steve the corporal laughed. "Looks like you're combat infantry, Kenrude. Hit the road and good luck."

For a second Steve wanted to pop the arrogant son of a bitch in the nose. But there was no doubt in Steve's mind, being combat infantry contributed much more toward the war effort, than an arrogant paper shuffling no mind ass hole, regardless of his rank.

After retrieving his duffle bag, Steve walked over to the nearest sergeant holding out his piece of paper.

"Baker Company private, it's assembling on the other side of the building to your left. Get moving, we ain't got all damn year to train you guys. Damn it, get moving!" The sergeant barked in a deep southern accent.

Steve was taken back at the sudden out burst, but figured he better get used to it. Without saying a word, he rushed off following the sergeant's directions.

On the back side of the building, there was a similar courtyard where other groups of men were forming. Approaching a young looking lieutenant standing near the corner of building, Steve held out his slip of paper.

Taking a quick glance, the Lieutenant pointed over his shoulder "fall in with that group in front of the mess hall. That will be Baker Company private."

Steve was almost surprised to hear how calmly the lieutenant had spoken to him. He was expecting another loud verbal assault. Turning toward the mess hall, Steve thanked the officer before walking over toward the assemblage that would become B-Company.

Steve cringed as a drill sergeant of overwhelming proportions approached him. He took the piece of paper away from him before asking, "Name."

"Kenrude, Steven A." He responded loudly.

"Alright, son," The sergeant replied quietly. "Ah let me see. Fall in with the first rank. You're now in Baker Company, first platoon, first squad. I'm Sgt. King your platoon sergeant. We'll get to know each other very soon, any questions, Kenrude?"

"No sergeant. Not a one." He replied.

"Well than what the hell are you standing around for? Do you think we're going to have coffee or tea? Get your ass over there and fall in. Or do you need me to hold your damn hand all the way over there?"

Without a word Steve ran toward the first squad. Placing his bag on the ground he took a deep breath. He suspected he had seen the last of Harry. After a few moments, he looked desperately around the platoon, seeing only one man he remembered from Fort Snelling. Feeling rather forlorn, he hung his head. He understood chances had been slim to begin with. But it sure would have made basic training much more tolerable having Harry around.

Suddenly there was a commotion in front of the platoon, as the sergeant began screaming at a new recruit. Somehow Steve knew, only Harry could create that type of a commotion in such a short amount of time.

Looking up he observed the sergeant screaming at Harry. For a moment he felt like crying he was so happy. But laughter got the best of him in short order. Leaning toward the man on his right Steve said, "That gall damn Jensen. He's one crazy son of a bitch." He could not understand the entire conversation, but he heard the sergeant tell Harry fourth squad second platoon. Steve felt some reassurance, knowing at least the two would be in the same company.

After several additional men arrived, Baker Company was complete. Sergeant King marched them out of the courtyard back onto the street.

They walked several blocks before turning into another courtyard similar to the one they just left, just a bit smaller.

Sergeant King pointed out two barracks the men were going to occupy. First and second platoon were assigned to the same building, first platoon on the main floor, second platoon on the upper. Steve was happy with this set up. Having Harry right upstairs was not too bad of a deal.

Although it had been an extremely long day, there was little doubt it would not end any time soon. The men were directed into their barracks, where their sergeants assigned bunks.

Every bunk had two sheets, two blankets, a pillow case and a pillow on top of them. The men were given exacting directions, on how a proper military bunk was to be made at all times. After every one's bunk passed inspection, they moved on to their lockers.

Once again, their sergeants gave explicit instructions as to how a locker should look every day for barracks inspection. After each man had his area squared away, Sgt. King told first platoon to assemble outside in the courtyard.

"Gentlemen, I'm going to take you over to the mess hall for a meal. You'll have about twenty-five minutes to eat. When you have finished eating, I want you all assembled right back here. We'll have a little introduction ceremony.

When everyone returned to the barracks, Sgt. King strolled over from the orderly room.

Steve loved his deep southern drawl and cocky walk. He thought Sgt. King was the most perfect specimen of a man he had ever seen. Sergeant King stood about six foot five, probably weighing in at 260 pounds. There did not appear to be an ounce of fat anywhere on his superior frame.

Approaching the platoon he called out, "Get your sorry asses to Attention!"

Slowly he paced back and forth in front of the platoon, giving the men a good look over. Returning to the middle of the first squad, he kicked a rock on the asphalt, as if the inanimate object had really made him angry. Shaking his head in disgust, he called out in a loud voice. "For those of you who haven't figured it out already, my name is Sgt.

King. Now, I don't know what you think of me right now, and I actually don't give a damn. But, I can tell you men are the most disgusting, out of shape, disorganized, worthless looking recruits Uncle Sam has ever sent me.

I thought my last training group was bad, but you're even worse. You are by far the worst looking sad sacks this fort has ever had the pleasure of training. Where the hell did you all come from? Well let me tell you, if I had my way, I would start making men out of you right this very damn minute. However, because it sure as hell is going to take time, the lieutenant and Uncle Sam see things differently, and by God they're in charge around here. For some damn reason, they seem to think you should all get some rest, write letters home to your families, and get mentally prepared for the morning. But mark my word; come 0500 tomorrow morning, your sorry asses become my property. Lights out will be at 2100. You're all confined to the barracks and your floor tonight. And you damn well better stay there. Believe me; we keep a real close eye on you new guys. We find out real fast who the screw ups are, and who wants to play games with us. Now fall out."

The men turned immediately, running straight for the barracks door. After preparing their uniforms for the following day, every man jumped in their bunks, hoping to get a good night sleep. They all knew hell would be upon them at 0500.

CHAPTER 4

BASIC TRAINING BLUES

A light fog drifted in and out of the dense forests of Missouri, as the first day of basic training arrived for the new recruits. Sgt. King, along with his assistant Corporal Deeds, woke the men up promptly at 0500. Immediately they went for a spirited run about a mile long, followed by several sets of sit ups, push ups and parallel bars. They finally ended up near the mess hall for a hearty army breakfast. Although Sgt. King was chomping at the bit to begin training, the army required some additional paper work. Then there was the task of picking up all the field gear a U.S. soldier is required to complete his training.

After storing their new equipment, they fell back out onto the tarmac in front of the barracks. Once assembled, Sgt. King took a leisurely stroll around his new platoon. After completing his second walk around the nervous men, he came to a stop directly in front of them.

After several moments of what appeared to be deep thought, Sergeant King took a deep breath. "Let me repeat something I told you last night in case you forgot. My name is Sgt. King. I'm your platoon sergeant. I am your lord and master for the next eight weeks of your life. Every one of you may end up hating my guts by the time we're finished training. Because every time you screw up, I'm going to be there to set you straight. Every time you screw up I'm going to make you wish you hadn't, because I'm going to kick your sorry asses till they hurt. I want you to make all your mistakes right here in front of me, so I can keep you from getting killed over there. Believe me, the Krauts and the Japs are not going to give you a break if you mess up. They'll just take your sorry life right on the spot. So if you plan to goof up, you best do it right here, instead of getting a belly full of lead from them. I intend to turn each and every one of you into Kraut hating, Jap killing sons-a-bitches."

Sergeant King stopped talking for a moment, as he walked over to a bulletin board just outside the barracks door. After looking at it for a second he explained, "This is also your lord and master while you're in first platoon, it's our company daily duty roster. You'll check it every day so you're aware of what your daily responsibilities are. Heaven help the man who says he did not know what detail he had. There is one more important item we need to cover. While you are in basic training, you'll be allowed to visit the PX once every two weeks. You'll be given a fifteen minute time limit. Make sure you grab any necessities while you're there. And damn it that includes writing materials.

I don't want to get any letters from your mama asking about her little Johnnie, wondering why she hasn't heard from him. If I get just one of those letters, you all will be one batch of sorry ass son-of-a-bitches. Do you all understand me?"

Every man in first platoon yelled, "Yes Sergeant."

"Alright, then we have an understanding." Sgt. King exclaimed almost civilly, as he walked back toward the men. "In fact that is our next order of business. Once we return from the PX and you have stored your purchases, we will begin the damn training in earnest."

After a long day of drill and ceremony, running, and what felt like nonstop calisthenics, the men returned to the barracks. After a quick shower, Steve laid down on his bunk to write a few letters back home. Once he began writing, he realized there was not a tremendous amount to tell them about. So he described his arrival in St. Louis, and the trip to the fort. He told them a little about what Fort Leonard Wood looked like, and the food. He especially told them about Sgt. King. His letter to Karen was much more personal, as he spoke about his love for her, and how much he missed her. After dropping his letters in the mail box by the door, he returned to his bunk, closed his eyes drifting quickly off to sleep.

The training was much tougher than Steve had imagined it would be. However, regardless the challenge, he threw himself into it whole heartedly. Shortly Steve discovered, he was able to adjust to the rigors placed on them by the training staff with little effort.

As each day passed, Steve became more impressed with the quality of the men he was working with. They not only supported one another, but were always willing to lend a hand if needed.

Surprisingly, there was little grumbling or complaining among the men, as he had heard back at Fort Snelling.

They learned in short order that Sgt. King was a stickler for barracks inspections. He just loved to find fault with dirty floors, improper beds and lockers. The platoon worked hard policing themselves, hoping to avoid all the extra duty they received for screwing up an inspection.

The rifle range was Steve's favorite part of training. He always loved hunting in the fall with Mike and his father. Alex taught him well how to handle a rifle, so he expected to do well. His thoughts proved accurate with every trip to the range.

The battalion bivouac came during the fourth week of training. It would give the men a good idea of what life in the field would be like, once they entered the war. After consuming a hearty breakfast, the best they had eaten since arriving in basic, they lined up in front of the barracks.

After conducting a roll call, the men picked up their full combat packs, slinging them on to their backs. Each man was carrying about forty pounds of equipment, not including their weapons. At 0700 the battalion began moving out of the courtyard in columns of two. Within twenty minutes, they entered a narrow dirt road that led deep into the lush green Missouri hill country. The drill sergeants kept the men moving at a rather brisk pace.

The cool gray morning sky finally gave way to a bright sun, with scattered light clouds. It did not take long for the men to work up a sweat as temperatures began to rise.

They received their first break, when two planes flying nearly at tree top level dove down on them out of the north. All the drill sergeants yelled for the men to take cover. Both aircraft dropped bags full of powder on the road, as men scattered in every direction. The planes pulled up turning toward the west. They banked slightly, before diving back down toward the road, dropping several more bags of the white powder. After completing their run, the pilots turned toward the east, disappearing from sight.

Once the roar of the engines subsided, the men were called back out onto the road. Sgt. King stood on a large tree stump, waving his hand in the air as he called out, "First platoon assemble on me."

When the platoon surrounded the tree stump Sgt. King called out. "Let me see a show of hands as to how many of you are dead?" Needless to say, no one raised their hands. "Well let me tell you, most of you piss ants are just that. Just plain dead! When you're told to take cover, you take cover. You do not stand and look at the damn airplanes, or look around to see where your buddy is going. You get your asses down, and I mean now! What damn good are you to the American Army, if you get your ass blown away on your first mission? Those damn krauts aren't going to give you a break. They're going to give you a belly full of lead. They're going to blow your sorry asses to kingdom come. You best be watching the sky, the woods, and every other damn place the krauts could come from. You think your soldiers? Well you're not. You're not soldiers until we tell you that you are. And that gentleman, sure as hell ain't going to be any time soon.

Now fall back onto the road. We ain't got all damn day." An angry Sgt. King added jumping down from the stump.

The battalion moved on down the road, taking just a few short water breaks until around midday, when they were marched into a grassy field. A truck with several cooks stood just inside the field. As each men past by, they were handed boxes of C-rations.

After collecting his meal, Steve went looking for second platoon to see how Harry was doing. He found him sitting under a huge shade tree, just on the edge of the tree line. He removed his boots, and was preparing to open his meal.

Sitting alongside him was a tall lanky Texan named Wade Rollins, who had also kicked off his boots. Steve already came to appreciate Wade's humor very much. He was quite the character, always telling tall Texas tales, which for the most part could never be true. At least, that's what everyone figured. "Hey Stevie boy come on and join us!" Harry called out as Steve approached with his meal. "Just don't let the odor of those terrible stinky Texas feet make you sick." Harry added slapping Wade on top of his helmet.

"Man I'm starved. I don't think the smell of Wade's wet socks could keep me from eating. It has been one long ass morning." Steve replied, as he dug into his food.

As the men ate, Steve listened to all the grumbling going on around him. Complaints ranged from bad food, hot sun, to long of a hike, and not enough breaks. He figured this was about normal from what the recruiter told him.

When the men finished eating, Wade looked over at Steve. "Well Stevie boy, ya'll have blisters on those cute little feet of yours?

"No Wade my feet are fine. A bit tired, but otherwise they're just fine." Steve responded laughing at Wade

"You know this ain't really anything. Back home in Texas…"

Harry cut him off before he could finish. "Rollins, if I have to hear one more time about how tough you had it back home, and how tough you southern boys think you are, I swear to God I'm going to just plain puke."

"Come on Harry, those southern boys need to have something to brag about. After all, we kicked their sorry behinds in another war sometime back if I recall correctly." Steve interjected.

"Oh now hang on just a second there, Kenrude. Those could be fighting words. And let me tell you, Missouri was kind of on both sides of the fence in that war. In fact, there may be some good old confederate boys still hanging around these old woods, listening to your insults right now."

Wade commented, staring over his shoulder at the dark woods. "And if I can't get any help from them, I'll just start that war all over again. That is after I finish this little scuffle with Adolph"

"After you finish the war, what are you going to do? Drive to Berlin and call Hitler out on the street for a Texas style gun dual?" Harry asked his friend.

"Well you know, I ain't never rightly thought about that. Wouldn't that just be the way to end this war? Me and Hitler, having a shoot out to see who wins the whole damn crap game. Sure would save a lot of pain and suffering. I'd show him a southern style ass whooping, mark my words." Wade suggested, as he blew smoke away from an imaginary pistol he pretended to hold.

The men laughed at Wade's antics as Steve stood up. Picking up his gear, he looked back at his two friends. "Well, see you guys later. Enjoy the rest of the hike."

The battalion reached the bivouac sight around four in the afternoon. The men went to work setting up their tents exactly as Sgt.

King instructed them the day before. Dark clouds began drifting in from the west, as men hurriedly finished their bivouac sights. Before the rain began to fall, Sgt. King went among the narrow row of tents, handing out the evening guard rotation and work details. As rain began pouring from thick black clouds, the wind began to howl. Any tents not properly anchored, were soon collapsing. Things in the camp site went from bad to worse as the night went on. Large tree limbs snapped, either collapsing, or puncturing rain soaked tents. Several men sustained minor injuries from tree limbs or flying debris. The hot meal promised was cancelled, leaving the men to enjoy another meal of cold C-rations they carried in their packs.

It was a very miserable start to the week, but it prepared them for what they could expect, once they entered the war. After completing repairs the following morning, the men began their training. The week was filled with exercises in field tactics, small war games, and survival skills.

The men were learning to do things they would have never thought possible just a few short weeks ago.

Arriving back at the barracks after a week in the field was a welcome relief. There was an enormous amount of work to do before a hot shower, or a nice warm bed would be allowed.

Every weapon had to be thoroughly cleaned, damp sleeping bags and tents were hung out to dry. Muddy field gear was cleaned, and dried before it could be repacked.

Mail call that evening was great for Steve. He received a letter from Christine, his folks, and Karen. He read Christine's letter first. He laughed heartily at the funny comments, and silly questions she asked about army life. As he read the letter, it appeared to be written by someone much older than he remembered her. Was it possible she had grown up right in front of him, and he hadn't noticed? Had he been too busy with his own life, to realize his little sister was becoming a young woman? Was it possible she had needed him and he ignored her? He felt a sharp pain in the pit of his stomach. What if it was too late now to rectify all his mistakes? After thinking about the situation for several minutes he made himself a promise.

If he made it back from the war, he would slow down, and make more time for his family, and those he loved. He never wanted to feel this way again.

The second letter from home was in two parts. The first was written by his father. He wrote about shortages because of the war, the new milk cow he purchased from the neighbor, and problems with the old tractor. The second part was written in his mother's beautiful script. She wrote about the adventures of Mike and Christine, Red Cross meetings in town, and church functions. She wished him well, as she explained how proud she was of him.

He intentionally saved Karen's letter for last. Although her letter was rather short he did not mind, as she had been writing him several letters a week.

As always, she wrote about her love for him, and how much she missed him. That never got old. He loved hearing those words. She also told him about several jobs in town that opened up which interested her. She wanted to put away a sizable amount of money for their dream house, once the war was over.

He could not remember when Karen had not been in his life. From the first time he laid eyes on her back in grade school, he knew she was special. What a waste this war was he thought. It was keeping two people apart, who were very much in love. He longed to be home for a second, but then quickly changed his thought process. He did not want to get home sick and lose his edge in training. This war had to be dealt with first, before he could allow himself to think about home so deeply.

"Hey, Kenrude!" a voice called from the distance. He looked up from Karen's letter, to see Wade poking his head through the barracks door.

"What's up Wade?" He called back.

"We have a good card game going on. Harry wants to know if you're interested."

After several seconds of thought Steve responded. "No not tonight' Wade."

"Alright suit yourself." Wade replied, disappearing back behind the door.

After assembling the gear he would need for the next day's training, Steve secured his locker. Preparing for bed, he couldn't wait to crawl between those warm sheets, and use a comfortable pillow. Within minutes of lying down, he drifted off into a well deserved deep sleep.

The battalion had three dangerous, but highly important segments of training to complete yet. The first was bayonet training. No matter how much Steve thought about it, he could not imagine himself ever stabbing anyone to death with a knife. It seemed so cruel and personal. But again, this was war. You never know what might happen when you're in combat. He began to realize, war demanded strange and terrible things from a man.

Sgt. Burns from Second platoon told them, "You think you can't stab a man to death. You think you can't run a man through with this weapon. Well let me tell you, when it comes down to life and death, you will do whatever is necessary to stay alive. Mark my words men. You will."

The training was strenuous. Men were required to run a course with an uncovered bayonet on the end of their rifles. They jumped over water filled trenches, weaved around large wooden barricades, while jabbing large bags filled with saw dust, or stabbing wooden targets.

Part two was hand grenade and demolition training. Grenade training was not as strenuous, but required huge amounts of concentration. One slip, one stupid mistake, could cost the life of you, or someone else. Each man was taken by an instructor to a concrete reinforced bunker. There he was taught how to hold, arm, then toss a live grenade. They were given instructions how to use a grenade to disable an enemy tank, along with the proper way to toss a hot grenade through a window, without blowing yourself up. Each man was able to pitch several inert practice models, before moving on to the demolition pit.

When the trainer felt each man was ready, he handed them a live grenade. He stood back giving the soldier ample room to throw, while keeping a keen eye on the live grenade. The sight, sound, and concussion of an exploding grenade, made a lasting impression on Steve.

The confidence course was the most dangerous of the three. The program was designed by the army, to see how a soldier would react under severe pressure. The dirt course each man was required to low crawl through, was nearly eighty yards long. It contained semi buried logs, with barbed and concertina wire strong overhead. There were pits filled with explosives, which detonated without warning as men crawled past. All of this had to be dealt with in the dark, while machine guns fired live ammunition just feet above their heads.

Everyone was allowed to crawl through several practice runs during day light hours, without machine guns or exploding pits. All the while, sergeants and training staff walked among them, calling out encouragement, while untangling the unlucky men who became wound up in the wire.

As evening settled in, a heavy rain began to fall. After having a meal of C-rations, the men were assembled near a tin shelter. Lt. Carson who commanded the course spoke to them. "Gentlemen, what you experienced, and what you saw out there this afternoon, is changing as I speak. That dirt is changing to mud. Everything will become wet, slippery and slimy. Everything you thought you knew or learned this afternoon, is changing by the minute. And that's just fine. Because, you never know what you might run into, once you get your asses sent over to Germany or Japan. They just don't fight wars in good weather. This will be a great test to see what the hell you're made of. Tonight in the darkness and rain, you're going to be tested to the max. This is no game, and those guns are not firing blanks. If you get caught up in the wire and cannot escape, lay still. If for some reason you get injured out there, do not stand up to seek help. If you run across a snake, lay still until it slithers on by. Do not stand up. Once everyone has cleared the field, we'll cease fire, turn on the lights, and rescue anyone in trouble. Are there any questions?" Looking around the battalion and seeing no hands, he directed the officers to line up their men. Baker Company won the coin toss to go first.

As first platoon made their way into the starting pit, not a word was spoken by anyone. Each man was totally alone with his own thoughts. The only sound Steve could hear was the rain on his helmet, and shuffling of boots on the rock path.

After first platoon was in the pit, Sgt. King walked man to man checking helmets, to assure they were securely fastened. After checking his helmet, Sgt. King looked hard and cold at Steve's face. "Well, Kenrude can you do this, or are you chicken shit? Are you going to cross the field, or are you going to crap out on me? Come on Kenrude; let me know if you got the guts to make it. Naw, I think you ain't got what it takes. You'll crap out on me tonight, big brave farm kid like you, just ain't got what it takes. You're damn scared"

Steve was fighting mad regarding Sgt. King's remarks, "That's bullshit sergeant, I can crawl that course with the best of them. Scared? Sure I'm scared; there ain't a man out here that's not scared. After all, it isn't natural to crawl under live machine gun fire in a driving rain. I have confidence in myself!"

"Confidence," Sgt. King yelled, as he rammed his helmet into Steve's. "They pass that shit out at the PX these days? Where did you get confidence from, Kenrude?"

At first, Steve was not sure how to answer Sgt. King. But it was evident he was waiting for an answer. "From deep within Sergeant, My folks taught me how to be confident, and to always try your damndest at anything you do." Steve responded, shivering from the cold, damp night air.

"Hmm. Confidence you say. Well Kenrude, just maybe you got what it takes. Tell you what.

If you don't get your sorry ass blown away out there, or if you can stand up on the finish line without blood pouring out of holes in your body, you come find me. We need to talk.

You got that, Kenrude." Sgt. King mumbled as he turned to walk away.

Steve did not answer. He just stood there trying to work through the anger

Sgt. King built up in him. He knew well, if he started the course in the wrong frame of mind, he would make serious mistakes. Leaning his head back, he allowed the rain to wash over his face. It soothed him as he prepared to enter the course. Off to the west, he could see small lightening streaks against the huge thunderheads that were beginning to form.

A tremendous roar brought Steve back to reality. The dark sky above him was filled with narrow ribbons of yellow tracer rounds, which swept back and forth as the machine gunners swung their weapons from side to side. Steve drew in a deep breath just as the loud speaker gave them orders to go.

Without a moment's thought, Steve threw himself over the log wall. The sound of screaming death filled his ears, as thousands of live bullets flew over head. He desperately attempted to keep his rifle out of the mud, as he approached the first obstacle. It was a half buried log, with two single strands of wire overhead. Cautiously, he rolled on to his back, using his rifle to push the wire up, so he could slide over the log. He was happy he had negotiated the first wire so perfectly.

Approaching the next obstacle, he could see another soldier hopelessly tangled in the concertina wire.

"Lay still!" Steve yelled out, as he began to untangle the soldier. Soon, another man crawled up to assist in untangling the uncooperative soldier. "Go! You're free!" Steve called out as he prepared to cross the double log emplacement himself.

Again, using his rifle to manipulate the wire, he worked his way over the logs. He was nearly clear when his pant let caught a strand of barbed wire. No matter how hard he pulled, he could not break loose. Quickly attaching the bayonet to his rifle, he shoved the sharp point into his pants near the barb. With a mighty yank, he could feel the fabric rip as he pulled free.

Placing his bayonet back into its scabbard, a demolition pit exploded several feet away, showering him with mud and water. Surprisingly, Steve found himself laughing. No one would ever believe this night, no matter how he tried to explain it. He rolled over, continuing down the muddy field. Making his way through the last obstacle, he could see the finish line about ten yards farther down. However, there was a huge puddle separating him from that much desired line.

"Oh what the hell," he yelled out, as he began crawling right through the middle of the puddle toward a splendid finish.

After shaking off some of the water, he walked away looking for Sgt. King. He found him under a tin shelter, standing near a fire blazing away in one of several fifty-five gallon drums.

"You wanted to talk with me Sgt. King?" Steve inquired, watching his sergeant puff away on a rather fat cigar.

"Well, master Kenrude you survived. You look like shit, but what the hell you made it, except for that pair of pants. Good for you. I'll cut the crap. Headquarters is looking for good men who would like to volunteer for airborne school. You know, jumping out of planes. I think you're the man for the job. I think you could do well, Kenrude. What do you think" Sgt. King inquired while giving Steve a long look.

"I don't know what to say. When would I go, and where will this training take place?" Steve asked nervously.

"Well, Kenrude, you ain't going anywhere until I'm through with you." Sgt. King replied with a laugh. "But then you go to Camp Toccoa in Georgia. Don't know much about the place, other than its one tough S.O.B. Only the best and toughest come out of there wearing wings I hear tell.

But I have faith in you, Kenrude. Besides you get an extra fifty bucks a month."

After several moments of thought Steve asked, "When do you need to know?"

"That's the tough part, Kenrude. The army is busting their butts trying to get airborne units built up quick. They need men fast. Sorry you don't have much time to think it over. I really need to know tomorrow." Sgt. King replied pulling Steve nearer that warm fire.

Steve nodded his head understanding the sergeant's dilemma. "Tell you what. Let me sleep on it tonight, and I'll give you my answer in the morning."

"Sounds like a good plan to me. Well, I best check on the rest of my ducklings so we can get out of here, and get you boys warmed up." Sgt. King stated, giving Steve a pat on the shoulder before walking away.

By eleven o'clock the men returned to the barracks. However, warm beds were not the first order of business. Everyone began cleaning weapons, rinsing mud out of field gear and clothing, while attempting to get their chance at a hot shower.

After his weapon passed inspection, Steve dashed up stairs to have a quick talk with Harry. Entering second platoon territory Wade yelled out, "Hey, Stevie boy. Ya'll enjoy the fireworks tonight. Whew, I ain't ever seen anything like that in all my born days. Man that was something."

"Yeah that was quite the attraction to say the least." Steve responded watching Harry slide an oily rag over his rifle. "I need to talk to you guys about something. It's kind of important, and I really would like your input."

Harry stood up smiling as he walked toward his locker. "If you're asking us to go A.W.O.L. with you, the answer is no. I deeply fell in love with the army tonight, and I just ain't leaving."

"Actually that was not my question. But I did give that idea some thought earlier tonight." Steve replied with a smile.

Laughing, Harry leaned against the wall. "What's up, Steve. I can tell it's something serious."

"Yeah it is. Sgt. King approached me tonight, asking me to join the airborne army. It sounds interesting. Plus, you get fifty dollars extra a month. I could send that money home every month to Karen. It sure would make a nice little nest egg for the two of us." Steve explained, watching Harry's face to see what kind of a reaction he would get.

"Yeah buddy: I know what you're talking about. Sgt. Burns approached me and Wade tonight regarding the same issue. I think it sounds kind of interesting my self." Harry responded walking back toward his bunk.

Wade tossed his oil rag on the floor, placed his rifle on Harry's bunk, before glaring at his two friends. "I don't know what's wrong with you guys. Ain't you figured it out yet? There has to be a million things that can get you killed in this damn war? Jumping out of a plane just adds to the chances of getting killed. I ain't going, no way, no how. And I figured you two were smart enough to say no, just like me. What's wrong with you? I kind of figured we all would get together down at Fairfield, for one huge Texas style BBQ when this damn war is over. But if you're going to jump out of planes, hell you just make the odds greater we ain't ever going to see each other again." Wade exclaimed in a very angry tone of voice.

Harry looked over at Steve for a moment then walked toward Wade. "First off Wade, there ain't any way I'm going to turn down an invitation like that to a BBQ. You can count Stevie boy and me in on that. Secondly, you have to understand that, well Steve and I really want to do this, just like you want to be a damn combat engineer. Messing with dynamite and shit like that, I don't know who is more crazy you or us."

Wade smiled slightly as he looked at his friends. "You got to promise me you'll be careful as all hell. I mean it, otherwise I'm still going to be mad as hell at the both of you, and I don't want to do that."

Steve smiled at Wade for a second. "We'll be just as careful as you will be running around Europe blowing everything up."

"Alright you two, I got your point. I know we all care for one another, but let me be honest. I'm a big blow hard sometimes. But you two are by far the best friends I've ever had, and I want it to last forever."

"Agreed," Harry replied giving Wade a pat on the back.

Steve looked at Harry intently, "So we tell the sergeants in the morning that we're going, right?"

"Damn straight. Damn straight." Harry agreed.

Steve left second squad feeling rather bad for Wade. He had no idea Wade was as sentimental as that. But on the other hand, he felt good knowing Harry had the same option, and was up for the challenge.

After their customary two mile morning run, Steve approached Sgt. King. "Well, Sarg. You can write my name on your list for airborne training."

Nodding his head Sgt King smiled at Steve. "Mark my words Kenrude, you won't be sorry. I'm glad as hell you're taking the job. By the way, I was told by Sgt. Burns your buddy Jensen decided to go airborne also. You two will go places. I'm proud of both of you."

After breakfast, the men started their last segment of training. It was called the infiltration course. The men had to find their way through dense forest, using compasses along with dead reckoning.

They crossed ravines on swinging ropes or slimy wet logs, while avoiding mock enemy forces. It was tough strenuous work. But after eight weeks of training, the men were up to whatever the mission required.

Finally the most hated part of army life came to an end. With basic training behind them, the men could now move on to their specialty training. Some men were able to get a few days leave to go home. Unfortunately, anyone volunteering for airborne school would not get that privilege. They were needed down at Camp Toccoa right away.

Steve spent his final evening in the barracks writing letters home. He had already told them about his decision to join the airborne army. It was extremely evident from their letters, they did not agree with his plans. But he knew everyone would support him no matter what. Karen appeared somewhat angry over his decision. He felt she would have liked them to discuss the situation before giving his answer. However, that luxury just was not an option in this case.

He reiterated to them tonight how much he was looking forward to jump school, and his trip down to Georgia. He again told Karen to have faith in him, that he was doing what was best.

The following morning after breakfast, Steve walked up to second platoon barracks. He found Harry talking to Wade, as he finished packing his gear.

"Hey Steve, Sgt. Burns handed me my orders this morning. I got combat engineers just like I wanted." Wade reported waving his documents in the air. "In fact, I stay right here at Leonard Wood. I don't get that leave but that's alright with me. My new home is just a short half mile hike down the road. I have to be there by 0800, so I guess this is good bye." Wade handed his friends slips of paper with his new Fort Leonard Wood address, and his Fairfield, Texas address. "Now, there is no reason we can't communicate."

As the men shook hands, Harry let out a laugh. "Damn, Rollins with dynamite. I thought hand grenades were bad, but this is downright scary."

They all had one last good laugh as they walked toward the barracks door.

At 0700 Steve and Harry walked over to the mess hall, where they were directed to meet a truck for a ride to the airfield.

They introduced themselves to the other men waiting for the truck. Several men were from third and fourth platoon, and two were from Able Company.

The drive from the mess hall to the airfield took about fifteen minutes. The driver pulled up beside two C-47 Dakotas, the military equivalent of a DC-3 used by many commercial airlines.

A lieutenant checked their names of a list, and directed them toward the second aircraft. Once both planes were loaded, the pilots turned over their big Pratt and Whitney engines. Smoke rolled from the exhaust tubes, as the engines sputtered a few times before starting. Reaching proper operating temperature, the pilots released the brakes. Slowly, the aircraft rolled down the taxi way. As with most of the men, this would be Steve and Harry's first flight. For sure, it would be the most uneventful flight for all of them, for quite some time.

Steve peered out the window watching the first plane speed down the runway gaining speed, until it became airborne. Seconds later their plane followed, rumbling down the runway at full throttle until it too lifted off, reaching for the sky above Fort Leonard Wood.

As the pilot banked the aircraft, Steve had a panoramic view of the base they were leaving behind. It was much bigger than he ever imagined. It was becoming evident to him all the more that nothing about the army should ever surprise him.

It was one massive operation, striving to turn out the best fighting men in the world. These two aircraft carried volunteer's one step closer toward D-Day, and the dangerous hedgerow country of Normandy.

CHAPTER 5

AIRBORNE ALL THE WAY

Steve's plane touched down at Camp Toccoa approximately forty minutes after the first C-47 arrived. They made a quick stop over to pick up an Airborne Captain, on his way back to Toccoa after a short leave. Steve thought he looked damn impressive with all his medals and silver jump wings.

As their C-47 left the runway, it rolled over to a small hanger where several trucks were parked.

The Airborne Captain stood up in the aisle looking over the men. "Good luck guys. You are sure as hell going to need it. No one gets a free ride down here. This is where they separate the men from the boys. Some of you just won't cut the mustard." With that, he left the aircraft disappearing into an open door on the hanger.

Without being told the men disembarked. They were directed to line up by the trucks. It was hot, very hot, near ninety degrees, without as much as a wisp of wind. The humidity had to be close to nearly one hundred percent.

Sweat rolled off the men as they stood at attention in the blazing afternoon sun. Steve took a quick glance around as he awaited roll call. He was impressed with the number of C-47-s lined up near the edge of the field. He had never seen this many planes in all his life.

Moments later a Sergeant walked up to the men. "Alright fall into two even ranks." After looking over the new recruits he completed roll call. "Well I'll be damned. Leonard Wood says they're shipping me fifty recruits, and I got me fifty. Guess no one decided to jump out of this plane prematurely. Now then my name is Lieutenant Winslow. Some of you will be in my jump class; the rest of you will be turned over to Captain Smith. I know some of you attended basic training together, so we're doing our best to split you up. We don't want you relying on anyone else to get you through this hell hole. You either do it on your own, or you're out. Period!

Alright, the following men climb into the first truck, Anderson, Billings, Crawford, Kenrude, Wilkins, Traslow, Davenport, Jensen and McDonald. The rest of you climb into the other trucks, we'll drop you off along the way."

Steve was finding it hard to control his emotions, knowing he and Harry stayed together one more time. They happily shook hands while waiting to climb aboard the waiting truck. Lt. Winslow walked up to the tail gate. "This will be a short ride. About ten minutes. Just sit tight. Shortly you'll have wished you never climbed off that damn C-47."

As the truck drove off, the nine men sat quietly looking at each other without saying a word.

Steve watched out the back of the truck as it slowly rolled along the rough road. All the buildings on the base were exactly the same as Fort Leonard Wood. There seemed to be little difference, except for the way buildings were arranged, size of the base, and the large airstrip.

The nine men were the last volunteers needed to fill out Charlie Company and third platoon. Although nervous about what they had gotten themselves into, Steve and Harry were nearly ecstatic knowing they made it this far together.

Dropping their duffle bags in the barracks, the men were marched over to pick up new field gear. This would be the equipment they would use at Toccoa and overseas.

After being checked over by several doctors and completing several new forms, the men were marched back to the barracks.

Lt. Winslow stood in front of his new recruits. "Well gentlemen, this is the end of your easy life.

Tomorrow at 0500 your new world is going to meet you head on. Get your areas squared away, get some sleep, and I'll see you in the morning. Heaven help your sorry asses."

Charlie Company thought the world was collapsing around them as Lt. Winslow stormed into the barracks at 0500, running down the middle of the barracks slamming a baseball bat into a garbage can cover. "Get up, get up you airborne wanna bees. This is the first day of the rest of your life and time is wasting." Dropping the bat and cover, he walked down the aisle slapping soldiers in the head that were still lying in their bunks. Reaching the door he yelled. "You have twenty minutes to haul your sorry asses outside. You best move."

In less than fifteen minutes, all of Charlie Company was assembled on the tarmac. None of them had any inkling of what to expect next. Confidently, they considered themselves ready for anything Lieutenant Winslow could dish out. Regrettably, they promptly learned how wrong they were.

"This morning you're going to find out what makes Toccoa special. You are going to find out why Toccoa men are the toughest, best trained and fittest men, in all the damn airborne army. As you flew in, you probably saw the mountain to our backs. You probably thought how scenic it appeared. Well today you are going to meet Currahee personally. We 're going to run the three miles up, and three miles back down. And you son of a bitches will make it. You may lose what's in your belly on the way up, but those are the breaks of the game.

But every damn one of you will make it. If one man craps out, every one of you will suffer the consequences."

That being said, Lt. Winslow gave orders to move out. It took about ten minutes of running to reach the base of Currahee. The old logging road was rough and severely gullied, by torrents of rain that washed down the mountain over the years. The men struggled and fought their way toward the summit through lose gravel and rock, swarms of mosquitoes, heavy humidity, and the ever present voice of Lt. Winslow continually screaming and threatening the slower men.

Reaching the summit, every man assumed they would get a short break. That was not in Lt. Winslow's game plan. No sooner had the first men begun to arrive, when the Lieutenant came charging up the road. "What the hell are you standing around for? Get you asses back down." He began shoving several men back toward the road as additional men arrived. Steve and Harry were in the middle of the pack when they made the summit. Hearing Lt. Winslow screaming, Harry made a quick about face starting back toward the road.

"You alright Steve," Harry inquired as he gasped for air. He slowed his pace nearly to a walk to catch his breath.

Nodding his head while struggling to suck in fresh air, Steve replied, "Yeah, Yeah, how about you?"

"Fine, let's get the hell out of here before Lt. Winslow gets on our ass." Harry answered with extreme difficulty.

With a slight smile on his face Steve again nodded in agreement, following Harry back down the mountain.

Reaching the bottom, the men were utterly exhausted from their nearly two hour ordeal. This was their first experience with Currahee, but it would certainly not be their last. Running the mountain road, was a very normal punishment at Toccoa for screwing up.

After a well deserved breakfast, for those who were able to eat, Lt. Winslow assembled the men in front of the barracks for his version of a welcome aboard talk.

"You will be awakened at 0500 every damn morning, seven days a week rain or shine as long as you're here. You will train until I decide we are done for the day. And I could care less if we go all night.

You will eat good food and lots of it to maintain your weight, and stamina. However, some of you will not make it. Some of you will choose to quit, others will be washed out of the program because you're not fit to be an airborne soldier. This training is tough, demanding, and at times dangerous. It will require every ounce of guts you've got to finish. So if any of you want to drop out to avoid being embarrassed later, step forward right now." Lt. Winslow took a step back, waiting several minutes to see if anybody took up his challenge. Not one man moved.

"Alright, you all think you're superman. Well that's just fine with me. We'll start each day with a three mile run just to get you loosened up. We may run up Currahee, and maybe not. You'll then have earned a good army breakfast. After that, it will be off to some type of airborne training. Our midday meal will be served where ever we happen to be. Most often that means C-Rations. That goes for the evening meal also. Every day you'll fall out with full field gear, whether we're going to use it or not. That includes a set of dry clothing, any questions?"

Not expecting anything the Lieutenant smiled slyly. "Well than, it's time for us to settle that breakfast you just ate. Let's go for a nice run." By the time they completed a mile; several men were on the side of the road throwing up their breakfast.

Lt. Winslow called it quits for the day around six-thirty that evening. After chow, Steve took a hot shower before sitting down to write letters, giving everyone his new address. The letter to Karen was extremely long. He tried to explain to her all he had been through since leaving Missouri.

Finishing his letters he glanced over toward Hurry's bunk. He was sound asleep. Quietly Steve walked across the barracks, so as not to wake the many men who were sleeping. Dropping his letters in the box, he observed a man he recognized from Fort Leonard Wood sitting on his bunk writing a letter. Walking over toward the man, he desperately wanted to talk with someone. "Its Davenport, isn't it?"

The man smiled while standing up, "Yeah, Archie Davenport to be exact. And you are Kenrude if I recall."

"Yeah, Steve Kenrude," He responded as the two men shook hands. "I kind of was looking for someone to talk to, but most of the guys are asleep. Then I saw you sitting there and thought

I would come over. Ever have that feeling?"

"Oh yeah lots of time since I left home, come on let's go for a walk. I really could use some fresh air. We can walk down toward the airfield to see what's going on." Archie replied turning toward the door.

The two men walked silently at first, watching a C-47 circle as the pilot prepared for his landing.

"Are you married, Steve?" Archie inquired "No not yet. But I'm going to be after the war. I've got a nice gal named Karen back home."

Steve responded removing a photo of Karen from his wallet.

"Wow, she's really a knock out. I don't have anything steady going back home right now. But there are a couple of gals I'm really interested in. I just am not ready to be locked down to one woman right now. You know what I mean? Archie asked handing the photo back to Steve.

"In a way I do," Steve said, "but I've been in love with Karen so long I can't imagine looking at another woman, but your day will come when Miss right walks up and taps you on the shoulder."

Both men laughed as they watched a transport plane taxi near the hanger.

"Man I never thought I would fly on a plane, much less think about jumping out of one. I can't imagine what it's going to be like floating in midair watching the ground coming up to meet you." Archie exclaimed as he wheeled around comically, acting like he was about to vomit.

Steve laughed slapping Archie on the back. "Well, I hope to keep what's inside of me right where it belongs, at least until I hit the ground."

After watching a couple more transports take off, they turned back toward their barracks.

"So what kind of work do you plan to do when this war is over?" Steve inquired of Archie. "I'm really looking forward to getting home just as soon as I can. I intend to buy into my father's business. I work with him in a small car dealership back in good old Cleveland. Someday we'll be one of the largest dealers in Ohio. I know we can make it, because we've got the knowhow, and we sell good products with great service. I'm excited to see what we can do. What do you do in civilian life?" Archie asked Steve "My dad owns a farm near Glendale, Minnesota. When I get home we're going to expand. I would like to purchase the farm next to my folk's place. It belonged to Karen's family before her father passed away. That would give us a lot of acreage to farm. "Steve responded, suddenly feeling very home sick. It was a feeling he thought he had overcome up to this point.

Steve observed Harry sitting on the front step of the barracks when they returned. Harry also remembered Archie from several field exercises back in Fort Leonard Wood. The three men went inside, continuing their discussions the balance of the evening.

The training that would make each man an airborne soldier began the next day. They trained in hand to hand combat, the fine points of knife fighting, setting explosives, disarming land mines, while making countless trips to the firing range, to qualify with multiple weapons.

As the days continued, they began taking classes in parachute packing, examining them for damage, and how to make emergency repairs if absolutely necessary.

The men took turns jumping off a six foot high platform, performing acrobatic rolls in a huge sawdust pit below them. This was essential, to prevent major injuries when they struck the ground during an actual drop. When platoon leaders felt confident their men were ready, they advanced to jump simulator towers. Each man wore a complete jump harness. He was hooked to a mechanical parachute, before being hoisted by cable to the top of a tower about a hundred feet up. They would stand in a makeshift airplane door, and dive out when instructed to do so. The cable system prepared them for the shock of a real chute opening, when they left a flying aircraft. They repeated these exercises over and over, as more scenarios were added to the training. Steve found the simulator to be somewhat enjoyable. Kind of like a nasty carnival ride. Conversely Archie and Harry did not care for it at all. They swore the sudden jerks and swinging motions were going to tear them in half, before they ever had a chance to jump from a real plane.

A very important part of this training was how to cut away their main chute, if they acquired a major malfunction they could not overcome. Switching to their reserve chute thus became their only chance of saving their lives. However, the canopy was much smaller, ensuring them of a quicker decent, and a much rougher landing. Hence, learning how to hit and roll became essential, to keep them from shattering their legs on impact.

After completing another afternoon at the simulator, Lt. Winslow called Charlie Company together under some shade trees.

"Have a seat, gentlemen. Our Company commander Captain Fontaine would like to have a word with you. So just sit tight he'll be here in a minute.

The men began to stand when Captain Fontaine arrived. "No, no, stay seated men. You have earned a break." The Captain began as he jumped up on the tail gate of a truck, giving his men the once over.

"Well today is Friday. But then I guess you're all aware of that." Every one chuckled as Captain Fontaine removed his hat, running his fingers through his short dark hair while rolling his eyes humorously.

"Today also means you have two solid weeks of training behind you. I also want you to know, Charlie Company has the highest score in the battalion for every aspect of training so far. Even more amazingly, every man that started with the company is still here, simply amazing!"

The men roared out a cheer clapping their hands.

"Next week you'll make your first actual jump. This will separate the men who have what it takes, from those that do not. After the fourth week of training, I'll pick permanent squad leaders. Who gets those positions, will depend on how well you perform during the next two weeks. Believe me; we'll be watching individual performances, and how well you work with your team members. In combat, leaders will make or break the fighting spirit of a unit. They'll have a definite impact on the completion of a mission. These jobs are no small matter to me. We're going to give everyone of you, an ample opportunity to show us what you're all about. However, the most important thing to keep in mind at all times is safety. Work hard, train hard, and the best of luck to all of you, may you all have safe landings."

As the Captain jumped back down from the truck, the men rose to their feet, applauding their commander as he walked among them shaking hands.

Toccoa airfield was a busy place Monday morning, as aircrews and mechanics conducted preflight inspections, while doing light maintenance work. While Charlie Company waited to load, Lt. Winslow informed them of the kinds of problems they would encounter, when loading with full combat jump packs. He told them, they would need to rely on ground crews for assistance as they attempted to board.

After all safety checks were completed, Charlie Company was permitted to board their aircraft.

Once everyone was loaded, pilots warmed their engines before rolling down to the end of the runway. The C-47 Steve was on, took off effortlessly before banking into a rather tight turn. He was a bit nervous however, he knew this would be nothing compared to stepping out that door.

Every man in the plane had their eyes glued on the jump master, who was sitting in front of the plane talking with the co-pilot. When the aircraft leveled off he stood up, cautiously making his way toward the door.

"Alright, men listen up, and pay attention to what I have to say. Tomorrow we'll be jumping, so you best know what's happening if you want to stay alive."

He stopped talking for a moment as he looked around the plane, giving each man a stern look, as if they had done something wrong. "Now that I have your attention we're ready to continue. When the word is given to stand up and hook up tomorrow, this is exactly what you're going to do. You will stand facing the rear of the plane. Take the static line from your chute, and hook it on the cable running along the ceiling. Then you'll check the equipment on the man in front of you, to make sure it's secure. You will then call out from the front of the plane. Man one Ok, man two OK and so on, until we get to the last man standing by me."

As he finished talking, the red light above the door went out, as a green one came on. "If this were the real thing, the man closest to me would already be standing in the door. When the green light comes on

I'll yell go. At that point everyman moves forward, grabs the edge of the door and jumps. Look out the windows right now. You'll see panels on the ground creating a big letter

"X". That will be your target tomorrow. As you drop, use your risers to adjust your speed and direction. If you operate as you have been told in training, you should hit the field with little problem.

Now the most important part, if you should freeze in the door, we do not throw you out as some people think. We'll push you aside so the rest of the men can get out. You will be washed out of the program, no exceptions. You are through, there are no second chances.

Always remember the jump master is the boss. You do what he says, and every jump will have a safe start. However, we don't have any control over the krauts or japs, or what they might throw up at you as you're floating down. Try and get down as quick as possible. No fancy tacking or breaking your chute to see the sights. First off, it could cause your chute to collapse. Secondly, you'll make a pretty nice target just gently floating around up there in the sky."

The sergeant picked up a headset aside the door speaking into the microphone. In a minute the plane was again turning sharply, but this time at a higher rate of speed as they flew back toward the airfield.

That night Steve received mail from Karen and his brother Mike. His little brother s letter was incredibly long. He wrote about school starting up again. He was now a junior at Glendale High. Steve stopped reading for a moment thanking God Mike still had two more years of school. Surely the war would be over by June of forty-five when he graduated.

His letter went on about farm work, and a girl named Margie Becker, who just moved into Glendale. He had to smile imaging Mike out on a date. It was hard to believe his little brother was growing up as quickly as Christine was.

The letter from Karen was neat as a pin, and superbly composed. She had her own form of letter writing that was most impressive. Her main topic was about getting a job at the hospital. She told him all about her schedule, job related duties and pay. Comically, she told him how Mike reacted when she came across him and Margie, walking together down by the river. He nearly tripped over a park bench when he saw her.

Inside Karen's envelope was a small note from her mother wishing Steve continued good luck.

Finishing the letters Harry and Archie walked into the barracks.

"Hey Stevie boy," Harry called out." Let's go over to the enlisted men's club. We need a little excitement. I hear Frank Sinatra is appearing tonight," pretending to dance with an unseen partner.

"Sounds like a plan to me. I could use a little change of scenery. Let's go." Steve replied pulling his boots back on.

Tuesday was a beautiful mid- September day, as the fully loaded C-47 roared down the hot tarmac runway, heading for their jump zone. It was nearly impossible to sit comfortably with all their gear strapped to their bodies. As the plane climbed steadily into the crystal blue sky, Steve looked over at Harry.

"Knock that smiling shit off your face, Stevie boy. This is the real thing you idiot. And you know what? Suddenly this doesn't sound like a good idea anymore." Harry yelled over the throbbing engines shaking his head.

"Are you suffering from a case of buyer's remorse Private Jensen?" Steve inquired of his good friend.

"Hell yeah you smart ass. You just wait. You'll lose breakfast when that damn chute opens. I'm scared as hell." Harry replied, actually looking somewhat nervous.

"You'll do fine, Harry. Just follow my ass out the door." Steve yelled back with a slight grin.

"Follow your ass? Hell, I think I'll kick it when we hit the ground. You're enjoying this way to damn much," Harry called back winking at Steve.

Archie, sitting across the aisle leaned forward to talk to Steve. "I think I missed my connection. I was supposed to be on a plane for Miami Beach. Can you talk to the pilot for me?"

Before Steve could answer, the jump master was standing by Archie. "You're too late Davenport. I guess you'll just have to walk once you hit the ground." Everyone in the middle of the plane broke out in laughter, as the jump master slapped Archie on the helmet before continuing on down the aisle.

Moments later the jump master yelled out, "Stand up! Hook Up!"

Steve flashed thumbs up to Harry and Archie, as he struggled to stand up facing the rear of the aircraft. Sweat rolled down his face as he attached his static line to the steel cable. He gave it a good tug for safety sake, before checking his chin strap, to ensure it was also ready to go. He now could see the rear door of the plane had been removed.

Every man counted off as they were instructed. The jump master nodded his approval, pulling the first man over toward the door opening, as the red light began to flash.

In a second the green light came on. The first man baled out of the plane followed by the second, as the jump Master continued yelling, "Go, Go."

As Steve approached the door, the noise level increased ten fold inside the plane. His legs felt like lead as he grabbed the edge of the door. Taking in a large gulp of air, he threw himself out the door, securely folding his arms across his chest. He tumbled somewhat in the wake of the prop blast, as his chute ripped open. The shock was incredible. A pain tore through his left shoulder, as he reached up for his risers. Looking down, he could see the large "Red X" slightly off to his right. He began making small adjustments to his decent, in order to land in the large grass field.

All around him, he could see other men making adjustments to their chutes, as they drifted down over the Georgia country side.

Within seconds, Steve's feet made contact with the ground, his legs collapsing beneath him. After making a double roll he came to a stop. His first jump was over, more importantly; he had made a safe landing. He lay on the ground for a moment, watching the pure white chutes descending from the azure blue sky. It was quite a sight. Something he would never forget.

Somewhere not to far away a voice was calling: "Let's go, pick'em up, let's go men."

Steve jumped to his feet, disconnected his chute, and wound the cables around the silk parachute.

Harry walked past Steve, "Piece of cake, Stevie boy, piece of cake, scared the ever loving shit out of me."

Steve busted out laughing. "Well, you made it what are you complaining about?"

Shaking his head Harry looked at Steve, as they followed men toward a waiting group of trucks. "May be Wade had the right idea, blowing things up doesn't sound so bad after all." "You'll get over it Harry." Steve replied laughing all the more.

After loading their chutes into the proper vehicles, they jumped aboard one of the open trucks, waiting to take them back to base. "You know everything happened so fast, I couldn't even enjoy my first jump." Steve said poking Harry in the ribs.

"Yeah, Yeah, Stevie boy, some day we may look back at this and realize it really was a walk in the park."

Steve nodded his head as the truck drove off down the dusty road. He was all too sure Harry was right.

Arriving back at the airfield all the chutes were unloaded into a specially designed hanger for stowing, inspecting, and proper packing of the delicate equipment.

Any man experiencing a medical problem from the jump was allowed to see a doctor. Steve walked over to the infirmary along with several other men.

The doctor ordered several x-rays after completing a thorough examination. Once the x-rays were ready, he called Steve into his office.

"I just looked over the x-rays Private Kenrude. Everything looks fine. I think you just strained your shoulder somewhat, when the shock of the opening chute yanked you backwards. You'll be just fine."

"Great. That's what I wanted to hear." Steve replied jumping off the exam table. "Let me ask you a question Doc. I see by the wings on your uniform you are jump qualified. Do you ever really get use to it?"

The doctor laughed a little. "Well, yes and no. Things can be somewhat different every time you jump. You just have to be ready for whatever happens when you leave the plane. Keep a clear head, keep your mind on what you're doing, and in most cases you'll come out of it just fine.

Practice makes perfect, Kenrude."

"I'll keep that in mind next time I jump. Thanks for the check-up and the information." Steve replied before leaving the examination room.

The afternoon was spent in a classroom, where Lt. Winslow, along with several jump masters critiqued their jumps. There was plenty of constructive criticism handed out by each of the experts. Charlie Company was informed just four men in the battalion failed to jump. They were from Able and Dog companies.

Charlie Company made one jump a day the remainder of the week. Every jump was less horrifying than the first. The men learned quickly as they began operating as true paratroopers.

However, the strenuous training was beginning to wear on everybody. Tempers began to get short, as arguments became more prevalent in the barracks at night. There were some actual pushing matches that took place. Each time an altercation occurred, men from the barracks pulled the perpetrators apart, so there wouldn't be any charges filed on them by Lt. Winslow.

Regardless, Lt. Winslow and Capt. Fontaine did not let up on training. It was essential for each of the men to learn how to handle stress, along with their emotions prior to finding themselves in combat.

On Monday, the men were trucked across the base to several large fenced in Quonset huts. Lt. Winslow directed Charlie Company toward the bleachers across the street. After every one was seated he walked up in front of them.

"Alright let me have your attention. As you know from your training, an airborne soldier must be versatile. He needs to operate from the seat of his pants at times. And he must be able to operate many different types of weapons. An airborne unit needs to be versatile. It must bring into combat many different types of weaponry, to deal quickly and effectively with a well armed enemy.

Sure the M-1 Garand you've all been using is a good weapon. But we need a few more weapons, which will give us the punch we desperately require. So by platoons, you'll file into the buildings across the street with your M-1s. You will hand it to the man behind the counter as you give him your name. He may hand it back to you after giving it a good inspection. Or, he may send you down the line to draw a different type of weapon. When we leave Toccoa we need to be an effective combat unit. So we have assigned you the weapons that will give us the edge in the field."

When he was finished speaking, he directed Charlie Company across the street by platoon.

Entering the building, Steve handed over his rifle to a corporal behind the counter before calling out, "Kenrude, Steven A." The corporal checked his list before telling Steve to move on down the line. The next man handed him a Thompson sub machine gun, and several ammo pouches.

Walking back toward the bleachers, he observed Harry also carrying a Thompson.

"Can you believe this shit? Thompsons! Go figure." Harry said laughingly. "I figured maybe a new M-1 carbine, but not this beautiful piece. I love it."

Steve agreed, giving his new weapon a good once over. "I can't wait to get this thing on the range. Man this is going to be something."

Archie came walking back with a new M-1 Garand. "Well I didn't win out like you guys, but I got me a brand spanking new, just out of the crate top of the line rifle. And hell, I don't have to figure out how to use it like you guys. Just sight this baby in, and I'm ready to kill anything that gets in my way."

Steve looked around the company. He noticed several more men with Thompsons, a bunch with the newer carbines; and several men were carrying Browning Automatic Rifles, simply called BARS. Men assigned to heavy weapons platoons were carrying light weight mortar tubes, while still others were totting large caliber machine guns.

Steve was impressed with the amount of fire power they would bring into a battle.

The next few days were spent on firing ranges. It was essential every man learned how to operate, clean, and care for their new weapons. Steve and Harry had a ball firing their weapons on full automatic. However, they learned quick, short bursts of five to six rounds were more effective, than just holding the trigger down while emptying the magazine. The Thompson was hard to hold in place at full automatic, spraying bullets all over, instead of hitting the intended target.

Archie had his rifle zeroed in quickly. He spent his time wisely cracking off one shot at a time, before checking his target for accuracy. He was considered the best shot in the platoon.

The jumps became more realistic now, as the men were carrying their actual combat gear they would be using in battle. Each man carried between eighty and a hundred pounds, depending on their weapon and ammunition.

Getting use to the extra equipment was important, as the parachute handled differently with each added pound.

Simulated combat jumps became a big part of their training. They would jump into a war game that was underway, with a defined mission they were required to complete. They were never dropped close to their intended target intentionally. This provided them the opportunity to search out their targets, while evading enemy forces.

Every war game was tough, lasting several hours. Steve observed huge changes taking place within himself, and the other men in Charlie Company. They were no longer novice jumpers. They were tough, hard working airborne soldiers.

An important segment of their training was a highly important night jump. Their mission was to jump into a small field. Organize into an effective fighting unit, then move two miles to their target, and destroy it. All the while, they would need to evade, or over power enemy forces in order to complete their mission.

As the men sat waiting to take off, Harry leaned over toward Steve. "Man this gives me the willies. I'm not so sure about this night jumping thing. It gives me a bad feeling."

Steve shook his head in agreement, "Yeah, I know, I've got a knot in my stomach big as a softball. I don't like it either. But I guess in combat we can't choose our missions."

"Yeah, that's a fact Stevie boy. That's a fact." Harry responded.

Archie peered out the window as the C-47 lifted off, climbing into the cloudy dark night sky. Blue flames coming from the engines exhaust tubes, created an eerie sight.

Archie turned back, looking across the aisle toward his two buddies. "Hey Steve!" Archie yelled over the roar of the throbbing engines.

"Yeah, what's up Arch?" Steve inquired, smiling at his good friend.

"I've got this feeling. It's like nothing I've ever experienced before. It's like the cold hand of death on my shoulder."

"Knock that shit off Davenport. We're all a little scared tonight. Just suck it up." Harry responded angrily.

"Naw, I'm not really scared, Harry. Something keeps telling me this is a rehearsal for the night I'm going to die. Man it just won't go away." Archie replied, attempting to rearrange his helmet with his shaking hand.

Both men were stunned by Archie's prediction. At first neither man knew what to say.

Steve reached across the aisle to grab Archie's free hand. "Look buddy, at times like this our minds play games with us. It's just one of those crazy things. Don't worry about it, Arch. You'll be just fine. You know there isn't a man up here that's not scared out of his wits right now, including me. So just take a deep breath, close you eyes and relax a bit."

Minutes later the steady red light above the door began to flash. "Stand up. Hook up." The jump master called out.

Everyone completed their checks, and stood ready in the dark plane. About thirty seconds later the green light popped on. "Go, go, go," The jump master yelled as the first men were already departing the plane.

Steve nearly threw himself out the door without a second thought, when it came his turn. He squeezed his eyes tightly closed, anticipating the sudden shock of his chute opening. Bam! The chute opened, giving Steve a tremendous jolt. He methodically reached up for his risers. The sky was black, the ground was dark. No where was a light visible. Steve glanced off to his right, still able to see the faint blue exhaust light from a transport plane turning south. The dark night sky was cool and calm. He knew there were men all around him just as blind, floating down under their huge canopies. He prayed no one would slam into him or worse, come down on top of him collapsing his chute. That would mean certain death. It would be impossible to get out of his main harness, and deploy his reserve. Everything would become entangled as he fell to his death. He desperately wanted to get his feet on solid ground. Somewhere below was supposed to be a grassy field. He continually scanned the darkness below him, for any land marks that would help figure out how high he was. The last thing he ever wanted was to land in a tree. He had seen the damage hard wooden branches could do to man several jumps ago.

Once more Steve glanced downward. There it was. An open grassy field was just below him. Mere seconds later, his feet touched down in a perfect pin point landing. He gathered up his chute, slid out of the harness then knelt down on one knee. He just started unstrapping his weapon when he heard a sudden rush of air. Before he could move, another paratrooper came down on him from above, knocking them both to the ground.

"Damn it." Steve could hear the man cursing. "I didn't see you until the last second. There was nothing I could do. Are you alright?"

"Yeah, I'm fine. How about you," Steve inquired as he helped the man out of his twisted rigging.

"Just injured pride, but yeah I'm alright." The man replied pulling his weapon lose from his pack.

"Is that you Kenrude? The man asked

"Sure is. Steve's my first name. But I'm sorry I don't recognize your voice." Steve responded.

"That's probably because my balls are still stuck up in my throat, Anderson, Mike Anderson fourth squad. Damn that jump scared the shit out of me. Sorry for hitting you" He apologized once more.

After shaking hands, they both took a long look around the field, trying to get their bearings.

In a small clump of trees to their left, they heard the clanging of equipment.

"Let's head over there." Steve whispered.

They approached the small wooded area cautiously, staying low in the tall grass to help conceal their silhouettes. They both drew a sigh of relief, as they heard Lt. Winslow's voice emanating from the far side of the woods. The two men quickly made their way between the trees, to check in with the lieutenant. About five minutes later Lt. Winslow ordered the men to move out. They were nearly three miles from their objective. He split the company into two attack groups. One group moved on the target from the east, while the other attacked from the north.

About two in the morning, Charlie Company over powered an enemy force securing their objective.

There was only one injury in Charlie Company. Private Marks from Alpha Company broke an ankle during his landing, when he encountered a jagged tree stump. Otherwise everything went according to plan. Charlie Company received well deserved praise from their battalion commander.

The next day Captain Fontaine had the men fall into formation near the barracks. "Men, I called you together today for several reasons, first, to congratulate you on a superb mission last night. You can be proud of the way you handled your selves, job well done."

The company gave out a roar, as men clapped their hands in approval.

Smiling at his company Captain Fontaine continued." Today I'm going to appoint squad leaders. Now I know I told you it would be last week. However, when I found out when the night jump was going to be, I decided to wait. I wanted to find out how well you operated on that difficult mission. Every one of you deserves these positions.

Unfortunately, that's just not possible. So first platoon squad leaders will be: Kenrude, first squad, Jensen second squad, Smith third squad, and Cummings fourth squad." Captain Fontaine congratulated the four men, as he handed out their corporal stripes. He then moved on to the rest of the company.

Steve was nearly breathless at his good fortune. He really hoped to do well when he enlisted. Now his dream was coming true.

Harry was also stunned by the announcement. He could not believe he was made squad leader. Looking around the platoon, Harry observed other men he felt deserved the promotion. But now, he would do his best, to show the Captain and his men he was worthy of the job.

When the formation was dismissed, Lt. Winslow shook hands with each man. He instructed them to get their corporal stripes sewn on as soon as possible, so they looked the part.

Archie shook hands with Steve, telling him how happy he was to be in his squad. Steve was just as happy to have Archie, as he was a good all around soldier. However, Archie's comment the night before still weighed heavily on his mind. He felt it was best to ignore it for now, as fear can motivate men to say crazy things. But the statement was so matter of fact. He was concerned Archie might dwell on it, causing him to make serious or dangerous mistakes, killing or injuring him self or others.

Steve could not wait to write home that night, as he had so much to tell everyone. He knew his parents would be very proud of him, when they saw him doing so well.

And Karen, he knew she would be very excited over his promotion. Although he knew she loved him very much, he continually tried proving he was worth her love. Maybe it was foolish, but yet he knew it couldn't hurt to show her he was a leader, capable of making difficult decisions.

There was one more night jump to be made. Each of the night jumps began preparing the men for a mission, allied command was still preparing for the invasion of Europe. Every scrap of information from these jumps was seriously analyzed by war planners in Washington. The last night jump was scheduled for the Friday after Thanksgiving. It was a jump every man would remember forever.

Friday dawned cloudy with intermittent showers. Most of the day light hours were spent in briefings. Sand tables had been prepared, so the men could examine the mission well in advance of their jump.

By four in the afternoon, the light showers had turned into a heavy rain. Battalion leadership decided the jump was to go rain or shine. No one has ever been able to pick or chose their weather during a war.

Around nine o'clock the rain subsided a little, improving the men's morale somewhat. However the wind continued blowing nearing twenty miles an hour. It would be tough controlling their chutes with that type of wind.

At ten thirty, Charlie Company began loading onto the waiting aircraft. Rain began falling heavier, soaking the men as they waited in line to board.

As Steve's C-47 sped down the runway, he was amazed how wet asphalt made the tires sound so differently. He was concerned about the gusty winds affecting their take off. However, the pilot skillfully pulled the aircraft up from the runway into the heavily overcast night sky.

They were airborne about fifteen minutes when the plane shook violently. A loud crunching sound reverberated through the cabin. Even with all their gear, the men were tossed about like rag dolls. Steve felt cold water running down his face as he laid half way on the floor. Looking up, he observed a seriously large hole in the roof of the aircraft.

The co-pilot came out of the cockpit yelling, "Jump, get off, you need to go now!" We hit another plane. God help us I don't think we're going to make it."

The men helped each other struggle to their feet, as they quickly snapped their static lines to what was left of the cable. Steve hoped the line would hold to the pressure, as each man dove from the aircraft. Since the door had already been opened, men were baling off the plane in record time. Entering the door, it was obvious to Steve the aircraft was in serious trouble. A slimy mixture of black oil, mixed with rain was streaming across the side of the aircraft. A shower of sparks sprayed from the engine, as the prop appeared to be bent.

Steve hurled himself out the door as oil covered his face. Thankfully the static line held up, opening his chute properly. After spinning around twice, he attempted to get a look at the damaged aircraft. The sparks turned into a raging fire illuminating the left side of the plane, as it began losing altitude. Although the bright light was ruining his night vision, he could not take his eyes of the stricken aircraft. He wondered if the crew had bailed out. Amazingly the darkness was shattered by a blinding light, accompanied by a tremendous roar, as the aircraft exploded in a massive fire ball. A shock wave from the immense explosion tossed Steve violently, as he hung in midair.

He watched what remained of the burning fuselage spin wildly, as it fell toward the earth. It struck the ground throwing hot metal and parts in every direction. Just as suddenly, everything was quiet and nearly totally black again. During the explosion, Steve had seen other parachutes in the sky around him. He was confident no one was close by to cause him any problems.

His thoughts quickly turned to Archie. Could this have been what he was referring to during that first night jump? He tried to figure out if Archie had been in front of him when he left the crippled aircraft. Steve's lack of concentration during the last few minutes of his decent, were nearly fatal. He looked down spotting electrical wires coming up toward him.

He pulled on his risers, attempting to maneuver himself away from the wires and power pole he could now make out. If he hit the pole, odds were he would be tossed into the wires being electrocuted instantly. Before he could make any real adjustments, the gusting wind slammed him into the side of the power pole. He came to a sudden stop three feet from the wires, as his chute draped over the top of the pole. He gave a sigh of relief, but his problems were not over yet. The chute began to tear as the wind caught it, throwing him closer and closer to the dangerous wires. A moment later, he fell about ten feet before being jolted to a stop, as the chute was now stuck solidly on the pole. He took a deep breath as he gazed up at the high tension wires above him. His head was pounding, but his arms and legs felt lifeless. Not sure what to do, he hung there motionless for several minutes, listening to the hum of the electrical current.

Slowly feeling began to return to his arms and legs. He figured the hard slap against the pole, must have stunned his nervous system. Taking in several breaths to clear his vision, he looked down toward the ground.

He estimated there was still a good twelve feet to go. Carefully loosening his harness, Steve figured he could use the risers that were hanging nearby, to lower him self at least a good six feet. However, he had to be careful not to pull to hard on the chute. Otherwise it could rip, dropping him the full twelve feet. Sliding out of the harness, he grasped the risers nearby. Taking a deep breath he left go of the harness. He slid down the risers about six feet before coming to a stop. The parachute continued holding fine. With only about five feet to go, he left go off the risers landing awkwardly on his feet on the muddy earth. He could not believe how good it felt to once again have solid ground underneath his shaking feet.

Cautiously he made his way through the wooded landscape, searching for any signs of life.

The first person he came across was Lt. Winslow. He had taken the place of the jump master on his plane tonight. The lieutenant gave him a long look then asked, "You alright Kenrude?"

"Yeah I'm fine. But my chute has had it. It's pretty tore up hanging form a power pole." Steve responded feeling good about seeing his platoon leader.

Lt. Winslow nodded his head. "I don't give a damn about those chutes right now, Kenrude. All I want to do is find my men and make sure everyone is alright. We can replace those damn chutes. Come on follow me."

"Have you found any of the guys so far? Steve inquired of his angry lieutenant.

"Well, now that I've found you, we need just five more men to account for everyone that was on our plane. I don't have a clue regarding the crew, its doubtful they made it. Come on, I have the rest of the guys on the far side of this grove. I'm happy to report everyone so far is in good shape. A bit shaken up, battered and bruised, but no major injuries." Lt. Winslow reported as he looked around the clearing for anymore stragglers.

"How about Jensen and Davenport," Steve inquired.

"Yeah got both of them already, Jensen was a bit shaken up on the landing but he's alright. He bounced off a dead tree on the way down before falling into a rock pile. That kid must have one hard head." Lt. Winslow replied walking farther out into the field. "Come on Kenrude, let's search over here." He added pointing toward the south.

Steve's mind was at ease knowing his two best friends were safe. It took about another half hour to find the last five men.

Returning to the two squads, Steve walked up to Harry. "How you doing, I hear you had a rough landing?"

"Well Stevie boy you know what they say. Any landing you can walk away from is a good one. But I do not wish to try that again any time soon, how about you?"

"I hit a power pole, but was able to miss the wires. I had about a five foot drop after I slid down the risers." Steve responded.

"Well gentlemen, no one back at the airfield will have a clue whether we went down with that miserable plane, of were dropped early. So we might as well start hiking back. I have a pretty good idea where we're at. This road should take us to the main north-south road, leading back to the airfield."

Slowly the rain soaked men began hiking down the muddy road. About a half hour into their journey, they came across the wreckage of a C-47. Debris covered a wide area of the Georgian country side. There were still a few small fires burning, but the steady rain was beginning to extinguish them.

Lt. Winslow looked over the situation for a moment. "This must be the C-47 that collided with my plane. It's doubtful anyone could have survived this disaster, but we better check. Take a look around. Check the bodies see if there are any survivors."

Steve had never touched a dead body. He was somewhat squeamish about this entire affair, although he knew it had to be done.

As he and Harry moved off the road, they could see bodies lying in contorted positions all over the ground. There wasn't any evidence of a deployed parachute among the dead. It was evident the plane must have spun out of control immediately. That eliminated the possibility for the men to jump from the stricken aircraft.

Steve came upon a body, partially covered by his reserve chute, which had ripped open most likely, when the man was thrown from the plane. He pulled the chute off the man and jumped back gasping. The soldier was dead. There was no doubt about it. However, one of the wall supports from the plane was sticking up through the man's abdomen. It had cut him wide open, allowing his intestines and other internal organs to protrude from the wound. He placed the chute back over the man, continuing on with Harry. About ten yards from the main crash sight they found another body leaning up against a tree. Both men stopped cold in their tracks as they approached him.

Both eyes were wide open staring up at them. His mouth was curled into an almost hideous grin. He was missing one arm and a foot. Steve had seen dead people before at the Glendale Funeral home, but nothing ever like this. He turned away from the gruesome sight feeling very sick; in a minute he was totally nauseous. He ran behind a near by tree vomiting heavily.

Harry walked up behind him placing his arm on Steve's shoulder. "Hey I know how you feel, Steve. The poor bastards never had a chance."

Finding no one alive, they walked back toward Lt. Winslow reporting what they found.

As the men began to reassemble on the road, head lights appeared in the distance. A small convoy of vehicles came slogging down the muddy road. Several officers climbed out of the lead Jeep. They spoke in hushed tones with Lt. Winslow for several minutes, before approaching what remained of the fuselage. A group of men dismounted from the trucks. They began erecting large portable light stands around the crash sight, hooking their cables into a generator trailer behind one of the trucks.

Lt. Winslow returned to the road. He directed them to load up on the last two trucks in the convoy. They were back in the company area around two-thirty in the morning.

The exact cause of the crash was never determined. Both pilots were killed, along with the co-pilot from the aircraft that struck Steve's plane. The young co-pilot who warned every one to jump from their C-47 survived. However, he had been struck in the head during the explosion, causing massive head trauma. He was never able to speak, walk, or perform any other functions ever again. Although he was a hero to everyone in the plane, he was left like a lump of clay the rest of his life.

The accident had taken the lives of fifty-six men from Bravo Company. It left deep emotional scars on the men from first platoon who witnessed the crash site.

With one full week left before jump school ended, training needed to continue as scheduled regardless of the accident. There were three more jumps, along with several necessary exercises the men were required to complete.

One evening Steve sat in the barracks, reading a letter from Karen, when Capt. Fontaine entered. "Attention!" Some one at the far end of the barracks called out.

"No, no as you were gentlemen." Capt. Fontaine ordered, as he walked down the center of the building right up to Steve's bunk.

"Kenrude, I would like to speak to you and the other squad leaders. Do you know where they are?"

"Well, Jensen is taking a shower, the other guys just left for the PX about five minutes ago." Steve explained looking nervously at the Captain.

"Alright, I can speak with you, and you can relate the message to the others. As you know, our training is over December eighteenth. The men have done an excellent job in every respect. We have watched you men train with a lot of interest these past few months. Washington needs well trained good quality paratroopers, and a lot of them to win this war. Now, they have sent us a list of exercises we need to complete, so we can fill their requests for well-experienced men. That's why I'm here talking to you. All the squad leaders of this company are going to be separated from their platoons for eighteen days. You will be attached to an airborne glider group.

We need to have men well versed in these joint operations. However, we do not want to lose you men completely, as you are an integral part of this company. So the rest of the company will relocate to the north side of the base. They are being assigned as permanent troops, while you men are in training. When your training is complete, you will rejoin Charlie Company. Do you have any questions for me at this time?"

"No sir. Everything you told me is quite clear. I'll let the others know." Steve replied, feeling relieved that the Captain had not been there to chew him out for making some sort of a mistake.

"Good. Your orders will be in my office sometime in the morning. Check in around midday, they should be ready by then. That's all I have for now Kenrude. See you in the morning." Capt. Fontaine added as he hurriedly left the barracks.

Steve explained everything to Harry and the other squad leaders when they retuned.

Harry did not seem too high on the idea, but by now was willing to try anything. "Gliders hell, I still have problems riding in planes with motors. Now we have to ride in planes without motors? You do know those damn things are made out of plywood and canvas. Don't you? Who the hell has all these bright ideas anyway?" Harry complained shaking his head.

As the last day of training arrived, Charlie Company loaded their gear on to several trucks, before shaking hands with their squad leaders. After talking for several minutes, the four men jumped onto a truck sent from the glider school to pick them up.

Large Waco Gliders stood side by side on a grassy field near the far end of the airfield.

The men in glider training were also airborne troops like the men of Charlie Company. They finished jump school several months ago, and were now undergoing indoctrination and training on the use of gliders in combat situations.

Their mission was to be towed by another plane to a drop site then released. Upon landing, they would fan out, and link up with regular airborne units, giving them a much needed punch.

The gliders could handle Jeeps small anti-tank guns, along with squads of specialized infantry.

The main problem was the shortage of gliders for the men to train with. Most gliders being built were packed up, and shipped directly to England. The training unit had two severely damaged gliders sitting in a field behind the barracks. The men used these to practice loading and unloading their cargo.

There were a half dozen usable gliders sitting near the runway.

Landings were always completed on a grassy field, to avoid damaging the delicate aircraft. Many of the gliders had been patched several times. That was to be expected with all the heavy use they were getting.

The squad leaders from Charlie Company were spread out among different groups, to maximize experiences in varied situations.

Steve's first and only glider flight took place on December twenty-second. To him it was an unbelievable experience, although it was fraught with danger. There was no doubt; he would keep his mind totally focused on every aspect of their mission.

It was about nine in the morning as thirty men approached a glider, sitting on the tarmac. A C-47 Dakota sat in front of the glider with its engines warming. The ground crew of the transport was getting impatient with the airborne soldiers, who took their time loading. The crew did not want the big engines to build up excessive heat, before rolling down the runway pulling the glider.

There was no added equipment on this run, just thirty fully equipped paratroopers. As Steve walked a board the glider, it made him wonder if the damn thing would hold together when it was towed behind that powerful transport. There just did not appear to be enough structural material holding it together to suit him.

It was obvious the other men were completely used to this flimsy aircraft by now. They were calm and very matter of fact about their jobs as they climbed aboard.

The door to the glider was barely closed, before the mighty C-47 began creeping forward, taking slack out of the tow rope attached to the gliders nose.

Inside the plywood box, noise from the powerful engines, creaking wood, and flapping canvas made for a very loud take off.

After what seemed like an eternity, the glider took to the air continuing to climb, as the tow plane gathered speed and altitude.

The pilot of the glider did not appear to be very experienced, as far as Steve was concerned. He worked tremendously hard trying to keep the bouncing glider in the C-47's slipstream.

The ride was incredibly rough, and possibly dangerous. If the glider began to excessively pitch and yaw beyond the pilots capabilities, he would need to drop the cable from the tow plane to avoid a serious accident. In a combat situation, one glider not making the proper drop zone could spell disaster for an entire mission.

After a few nervous minutes, the pilot gained control of his clumsy aircraft. The flight became rather smooth, except in turns when the pilot had to fight turbulence created by the tow plane. There were instances the glider bounced and shook so hard, Steve felt for sure it would break apart in midair. However, looking around the cabin no one else appeared to get excited.

As the C-47 reached three thousand feet, the pilot radioed the glider he was heading for the drop zone. About five minute later the pilot called again, notifying them to cut lose and good luck.

The young pilot pulled the lever releasing the tow cable, then immediately pulled back on the control stick, riding the C-47's wake, in order to raise the gliders nose to prevent it from descending prematurely.

The engine noise from the C-47 could no longer be heard inside the fragile glider. Only the sounds of rushing wind, and creaking plywood were evident. It all left Steve with a very nervous stomach. He had never been air sick in all his flights but now he felt like he was going to be very, very sick.

As minutes passed Steve became very concerned. He certainly was not an expert on gliders. However as a trained paratrooper, he instinctively knew they were coming in way to fast. He glanced around toward the other men, finally noticing a look of concern on their faces. Several men peered out the plastic windows shaking their heads. He began to hear murmuring from the men, as they looked up toward the flight crew.

Everyone observed the pilot struggling with his controls, attempting to slow the glider without much success. When they were about a hundred feet off the ground, the pilot picked a terribly bad time to pull back on the stick. He raised the nose in an alarming angle. The heavy unresponsive aircraft lost its momentum, nosing over toward the ground. There was nothing left the pilot could do. They were indeed going to crash.

"Lift your feet hold on to one another." Corporal Ellison yelled out frantically.

Instantly the men lifted their feet off the floor, in case it was torn away on impact. They interlocked arms for support, as they waited out the last few seconds of their flight.

The glider slammed down in a brushy area, filled with tree stumps and wooden fence posts. The glider shook violently, followed by a massive crushing sound, as the left wing was ripped from the fuselage by a fence post.

The stricken glider spun violently toward a stand of trees tossing the men around like a bunch of rag dolls. Time stood still as the glider twisted, bounced and ground itself into pieces. Then there was total silence. The glider had come to rest against several trees.

Steve was dazed, his eye sight blurry as he gasped for air. His head throbbed horribly as he tried to move among the tangled bodies. Placing weight on his left ankle, a sharp pain ran up his leg. Only an occasional groan was heard, as men began moving, attempting to extricate themselves from the torn wreckage.

Steve could see the co-pilot attempting to talk, while shaking the pilot who must have been killed upon impact. The glider had come to rest against a large tree, directly in front of the glass window on the pilot's side of the cockpit.

Steve made his way back onto what was left of the seat, allowing others around him to exit the plane first. Finally Steve attempted to stand up. Although his ankle hurt badly, he was able to bear weight on it. He followed two other men out of a huge hole that had been ripped in the side, as the left wing had torn loose.

Corporal Ellison grabbed anyone appearing fine, to help remove injured men from the glider. Despite his injuries, Steve stood outside the glider helping to maneuver the injured out of the fuselage. However, the more he moved, the more his head hurt. He felt like he was in a daze, his eye sight came and went. He thought he heard sirens in the distance, meaning help was on the way just as he collapsed.

The emergency room at the hospital was swarming with nurses and doctors, triaging the patients as they arrived in ambulances and trucks.

As Steve came around he felt someone holding on to his arm. He rolled his head over to see a doctor preparing to take his blood pressure.

"Take it easy, corporal. Don't move around to much. You have one heck of a bump on your head. Right now I'm thinking you are suffering from a concussion. You should be alright with some bed rest. You will need to stay here for a week until we know you are back in good health."

"My ankle, what about my left ankle?" Steve inquired of the doctor.

The doctor nodded. While you were out we x-rayed your ankle as it is very swollen. Nothing is broke. You just twisted it badly. By the end of the week it will be much better. You may not run on it for another week or so, but it will get better." The doctor explained finishing up the blood pressure check.

Steve drifted in and out of consciousness the first day after the accident. About eleven o'clock on the morning of December 24th Steve awoke. For the first time since the accident he felt totally normal. His head hurt just a little, but not much more than a typical head ache. He gazed around the ward trying hard to remember everything that happened, after he realized they were going to crash. But nothing seemed to come to him. In fact, he could not remember what day or month it was. The ward was extremely quiet, as there appeared to be only five other bunks occupied by sleeping men.

Steve was just about to close his eyes, when he observed movement near the far end of the ward.

A nurse came walking down the aisle right toward his bed.

"Well good morning, Corporal, nice of you to join us. I was looking through the window when I saw you moving." She gave Steve a big smile as she checked his pulse.

"I have a few questions I need to ask you." Do you know you know what your name is?" "Kenrude, Steven A." He responded instantly.

"Good. Do you know where you are?"

"Camp Toccoa in Georgia," He stated without having to think.

"Alright one more," The pretty nurse said making notes in a chart. "What day and month is it?"

"I do not have a clue." Steve responded. I've been trying to figure that out since I woke up.

I can't remember anything since the accident."

"That is called short term memory lose. That's not unusual with moderate to severe concussion patients. You may begin to remember things little by little over the next few days. Some things you may not. But it would appear your long term memory is in good shape." The nurse instructed Steve looking very serious.

"Well as for the month and date it's Christmas Eve, Corporal. We are really glad you came around, so you could join in the festivities."

"Before I even think about that, I need to know how the rest of the guys from the glider are doing." Steve inquired of the nurse.

"I'm sorry to say the pilot was killed. However, twenty were injured, nine seriously. The nine have been shipped to Fort Benning. They should all recover from their injuries." "That's good to hear. I expected more serious injuries the way we crashed. Actually I remember the co-pilot trying to communicate with the pilot after the crash, but he wasn't responding. I figured he was dead. So how long do you think I'm going to be laid up here?" Steve inquired as he slowly sat up in bed.

"I would think you should be out of here on or about New Years Day. You had a pretty bad concussion. We want to know that you're ready to resume your duties before releasing you. I will notify your friends they can visit you tomorrow. Your friend Corporal Jensen, although a charming guy, has been a pest." The nurse answered as Steve laughed about Harry. The nurse gave him a wink, as she turned walking back toward the door.

Christmas morning Steve was awake, reading a copy of Yank when a loud commotion broke out in the hospital just beyond the ward door. Out of the blue, Harry, Archie, Bill Smith and Dave Cummings, the other squad leaders burst into the ward singing Jingle Bells. Archie wore a very bad white beard, Harry Had tinsel draped around his neck, no doubt stolen from the hospital Christmas tree. Dave handed out small wrapped gifts to the other five men in the ward.

After they all assembled by Steve's bunk they yelled out, "Merry Christmas Stevie boy."

Choking back tears Steve smiled, "Hey you guys are a sight for sore eyes, Merry Christmas!" "Man it is good to see you Stevie boy. You had me damn concerned. I couldn't lose two friends in one damn week." Harry said as a tear rolled down his face.

Steve swung his feet over the side of the bed looking up at Harry. What happened? And who?" Steve inquired.

"I received a letter from Texas, Steve. From Mrs. Walter Rollins, Wade was killed in Italy second day there. Luftwaffe bomber attacked the port facility where they were unloading their equipment. Apparently Wade was killed in the first few minutes of the attack." Harry explained fighting back his emotions.

Steve looked up at his grief stricken friend, as tears ran down his face. "Why Harry? Why did this war have to be fought? Why all the death and suffering? It just makes me so damn mad. Damn! Why Wade?" Steve said wiping tears from his cheek.

"When did any of this make sense, Steve?" Archie replied hanging his head.

"I know, Arch. Maybe I'm just feeling sorry for myself. I don't know. I guess we just have to lock up our feelings for now, and get on with the business of war. All we can do is just hope and pray we all come back alive." Steve answered while looking toward Archie, wondering what was really going on inside his head.

The ward was quiet for a few minutes. Then Harry took a small package out of his jacket pocket handing it to Steve.

"Merry Christmas Steve, This is from the guys in the first platoon. We all want you back as soon as possible."

Steve opened it slowly, watching Archie and Harry as he did so. Inside was a St. Christopher medal on a standard G.I. issue dog tag chain.

Steve busted out laughing as did the rest of the men. Wiping his eyes Steve asked, "Did anyone go broke chipping in for this unexpected, extravagant piece of holiday cheer?" "No we got a good deal on six of them for all the guys in the ward." Archie responded, taking the gift away from Steve, and sliding it down over his head.

"Oh and before I forgot, here are a couple of letters from home. I took the liberty to send a quick note to your folks and Karen, explaining best I could about what happened to you, since you could not write for a few days. I hope that was fine with you." Harry inquired handing Steve the letters.

"Hey that was great of you, Harry. I really appreciate that. You know, even being stuck in this bed a long ways from home, you guys made this a very special Christmas. I will remember this for the rest of my life. Good friends like you are too hard to come by." Steve said shaking hands with all of them.

The nurses brought in several baskets of snacks that were donated by Red Cross volunteers. They moved beds and chairs, until they had everyone situated in a circle in the middle of the ward. The men heartily enjoyed the snacks, as they swapped childhood Christmas stories, told jokes, and sang carols. When the festivities were over and the guys left, Steve laid quietly for some time, reflecting on Wade's death, it bothered him tremendously. He wondered how many other great guys he had met would meet the same end. Wanting to concentrate on more pleasant things, he began a letter to Karen.

After a long week in the hospital, Steve was very happy to hear he was ready to be discharged. He could not wait to see the guys from first platoon.

The Jeep delivering Steve back home, rolled to a stop in front of Charlie Companies head quarters at ten o'clock in the morning. He jumped out, grabbing his belongings he walked into the orderly room. Seeing Steve enter, Lt. Winslow walked over to shake hands with him. "Damn Kenrude, it's good to see you back on your feet again. I don't know if we should allow you back in a plane anymore. Your luck is going to run out one of these times." Both men laughed for a moment. "How the hell are you feeling, Kenrude, Ready to get back to work?"

"I feel fine, sir. No headache no nausea, I'm fit as a fiddle and ready to get back at it with my guys." Noticing the orderly room was a beehive of activity he continued, "What's going on in here sir, looks awful damn busy."

"We have orders to pack up and move out, Kenrude. The war department wants us ready to move out within a week. The glider company wanted you back to do some more training, but the old man nixed the plan. We wanted you back here to help your squad prepare."

Lt. Winslow responded, watching men around him pack boxes and foot lockers.

"Any idea where we'll be off to," Steve inquired.

"You tell me and we'll both know, another base, Europe, The Pacific who knows. Scuttlebutt is running rampant as you can imagine. Don't believe anything you here until we give you the word. Hell, we don't even have orders yet. But they can come at any time. Also, there are no leaves or passes into town. All letters are being censored. They will be held until after we ship out. That's about it. Head over to your barracks, get your gear packed as best you can." Lt. Winslow explained.

Travel orders for the battalion arrived on January sixth, five months to the day when they would drop into Normandy on D-Day.

The men could never have imagined as they packed, that the Supreme Command was working on the plans for their jump as this very moment.

On the morning of the eighth, more military cargo trucks than Steve and Harry had ever seen began rolling into the camp. They filled streets, courtyards and parking lots around Charlie Company. Additional trucks were arriving, to load up the balance of the battalion. There definitely was something big in the wind, as nearly every trained unit on this side of the base was preparing to move out.

When everything was loaded, convoy after convoy rolled out across Toccoa travelling toward the railroad station. It was a very impressive sight.

Steve could not believe the rumors. One guy told him they were heading for Washington to guard the President. Another guy told him they were being taken to a secret base, where they would train to jump into Berlin to capture Hitler. Another man told him they were going to Alaska. Once there, they would jump into Russia to help Stalin's forces. Some men were even placing bets on the rumors. Steve was ready to bet everyone was wrong. Arriving at the train depot a very systematic roll call was completed, as men moved from trucks onto the waiting passenger coaches.

As the train departed the station turning onto the main line, it was clear they were headed northeast up the coast. They continued their long ordeal, arriving in New York midmorning the eleventh day. The men sat transfixed, totally awestruck by the massive buildings and bridges rolling past their window. They could not believe the sheer size of this city.

The train slowed nearly to a crawl, rolling out on to a huge pier, stopping directly aside a troop transport ship. Departing the train, everyone was directed to follow the rope lines leading toward the ships gang plank. The companies were assembled in different areas of the ship. After everyone was again accounted for, they were taken below to their berthing stations.

The ship was built to hold thousands of men along with their equipment, for the long slow voyage to England. The ship sat tied up to the pier for two more days, before preparing to sail. Train after train arrived, discharging hundreds of troops and equipment from bases all over the United States.

As the weather was extremely bad, most men stayed inside the ship. They slept, read books, or played cards, anything to pass the time. Snow and rain fell as temperatures dropped into the teens. The weather reminded Steve and Harry of a typical Minnesota-Iowa January.

On the sixteenth of January, the transport slipped from its berth in New York Harbor, sailing up the east river past the Statue of Liberty heading for the Atlantic Ocean. Their ship was scheduled to join an already forming convoy for the trip to England.

Steve, Harry and Archie joined hundreds of men on the decks, watching New York, along with the rest of America, slip slowly behind them. The transport was still building a good head of steam, as the sky line of New York became distorted by clouds of thick whirling snow.

Although the temperature was near ten degrees, it did not seem to bother any man. Everyone was keenly aware, that many of them would never return to see their home land again. This was all too evident to Steve and Harry, as they spoke about Wade. No one knew how the fortunes of war were going to treat them.

CHAPTER 6

CONVOY TO EUROPE

The transport joined a huge convoy late afternoon, sailing northeast into the vast cold Atlantic. Temperatures moderated slightly, as they sailed farther from New York. It was obvious temperatures would again drop, the farther they sailed into the north Atlantic. Steve was able to count thirty ships, although he knew there were many more hidden by the ever present mist and fog.

Destroyers dashed up and down the flanks of the convoy, guarding against German U-boat activity. They appeared to be continually blinking out messages with their signal lamps to other vessels. As the seas were extremely heavy, battle ready destroyers bobbed like a child's toy ship in a bath tub. Now he understood why navy men always referred to destroyers as tin cans.

Steve was happy he was not on board such a small ship. The transport did enough rolling, to keep half the men on board sick.

The following day dawned cold and terribly windy, making life inside the ship nearly unbearable. Not many men attempted to go out on deck. Splashing sea water, combined with cold air, covered every deck with layers of slippery ice.

As days rolled on, the convoy sailed completely free of any U-boat sightings. The seas remained rough, as cold temperatures continued keeping the troops bottled up inside the lumbering vessels. Tempers flared among some of the men, as boredom, sea sickness, bad food, cramped quarters, along with lack of sleep wore on every one regardless of rank.

Officers attempted to fill some of the dead time, with classes on proper etiquette to be used around the British people. The need to inform men on these types of problems was most important. There already were bad feelings, along with numerous complaints regarding American soldiers. Some British citizenry and military leaders felt the American GI were a brash, boisterous, unruly lot, roaming about England. The standard comment toward American service people was that they were over paid, over sexed and over here.

Capt. Fontaine made it clear to the men of Charlie Company, he wanted no major complaints brought to him from either civilian, or military authorities regarding conduct unbecoming.

There were also sessions held on proper security protocol, to be used when out and around the English population. Especially in public places such as pubs or restaurants, where German spies could be listening in on conversations.

"Gentlemen, the allies are totally aware there are Nazi agents working all over England. They may be in every town or village where they can quietly fit in. These agents by now are aware of our troops arriving by the ship load. What we do in training or what we see is no ones business but ours. We don't need to tip off the krauts to anything we are doing, or what our plans may be. You never know who you are talking with, or what their allegiances might be. We can not take any chances. Every one of us is going to play some sort of roll in opening up the second front. One wrong word to the wrong person could possibly mean death to you, and thousands of our allied soldiers. If you're going to drink, don't over do it! You may start blabbing like an imbecile, endangering the very operations we're being sent there to perform. What our mission is now, or what it is going to be, nobody on this ship yet knows. The only people that have any inkling of what we're here for are in Supreme Headquarters, and they're not talking." Capt. Fontaine warned his men before arriving in England.

The eleventh day of the convoy became the most exciting, if not the most dangerous for everyone on the transport. About one-thirty in the afternoon, general quarters was sounded through out the entire convoy. A destroyer sighted a periscope. They immediately began engaging the enemy vessel. Before the sub began to dive, its skipper fired a spread of four torpedoes straight into the convoy. Every ship began taking evasive maneuvers by creating a zigzag course, making it tougher for torpedoes to strike them. Since all the ships were now zigzagging, the unified convoy began to fall apart. A tremendous explosion roared through the convoy, as an ammunition ship was struck amidships by two torpedoes. A second explosion rocked the stricken vessel, as a third torpedo ripped the bow completely off.

Thick black smoke belched from cargo holds, as sailors desperately fought to control the raging inferno. The transport began listing hard to port, as sea water rushed through gapping holes in her side. Against impossible odds, remnants of the ships crew worked savagely, trying to seal off damaged sections of the ship, attempting to keep her afloat. Several more explosions shook the vessel, as ammunition deep in her holds detonated from the searing heat. Fire fighters now contend with new fires, ignited by the latest explosions.

As the afternoon wore on, smoke and flames began to subside. It appeared the battered ship just might beat the odds, although down to a reduced speed.

As the battle raged to save the damaged cargo ship, two American destroyers played cat and mouse with the elusive German U-boat. The ships made several passes over a large area, dropping depth charges every few seconds. There would be a slight delay from the time a can hit the water, until it exploded at its assigned depth. Huge geysers of water burst into the air after each detonation. The ocean surface appeared as if it were a cauldron of boiling thick green foamy soup.

A British ship arrived to join the attack. All three vessels pummeled the U-boat for nearly twenty minutes, with a devastating amount of explosives. Amazingly, the conning tower of a U-boat appeared about a hundred yards in front of the British destroyer. A huge oil slick trailed the sub, as it moved sluggishly in the water. Several men dropped from the conning tower, running straight toward the undamaged deck gun. It took mere seconds for the British Captain to turn his five inch guns toward the damaged sub. Before the German sailors were able to uncover their weapon, the five inch gun on the forward deck of the destroyer fired.

The projectile detonated short of the sub, creating a huge geyser of water sweeping the German sailors from their feet.

Swiftly, the British gunnery officer made adjustments. All three five inch guns on the destroyer fired a corrected salvo. They were right on target. One struck the conning tower near its base. A second round struck the hull, throwing several German sailors into the water. Two more German sailors ran from the conning tower to assist with the deck gun. However, they were not going to make a difference, as an American destroyer sailed to assist the British vessel. Nearly simultaneously, both vessels fired a broadside sending six five inch rounds toward the damaged boat. The sub shuddered as five out of six rounds made contact. The deck gun exploded violently, ripping the attending sailors apart. Fire and debris flew nearly a hundred feet into the air, as thick acrid smoke billowed from the conning tower. Sailors that survived the devastating depth charge attack and murderous shelling now fought for their lives, attempting to escape their dying boat. As it began settling by the stern, a massive explosion ripped the hull apart near mid ship, throwing chunks of steel and sailors into the air. The rear half of the sub with fires still raging, hissed and groaned like an angry prehistoric monster as it slid beneath the waves, what remained of the hull rotated awkwardly in the water, before pointing its bow skyward, sliding away into the depths of the dark Atlantic. It joined thousands of tons of allied shipping already resting there, sunk during hundreds of engagements such as this.

Both destroyers turned abruptly, making their way back toward the damaged freighter. No search for survivors was conducted by the allied vessels.

By nineteen forty-four many rules of the sea regarding survivors in sea battles had long been overlooked by both sides in this conflict.

When all clear was sounded, ships quickly reassembled into formation continuing their easterly journey. With fires extinguished, crew members of the damaged freighter miraculously restored power to one engine. However, they were only able to make about five knots, as eight feet of her bow was now missing.

Convoy rules were quite clear to all hands. If your vessel was damaged and unable to keep pace with the convoy, you would have to slug it out on your own regardless the risk. In full knowledge of the perils involved, the crew refused to abandon their ship and transfer to a British Destroyer. They insisted they would bring what remained of their load to England.

After several attempts to persuade the crew their chances of success were not good, the destroyers sailed back toward the convoy. About a half hour later the freighter crew sent out a mayday. They lost power, and were going down by the bow. They were now in need of rescue.

The British Captain in charge of this convoy radioed back, informing the crew they were on their own. No escort ship could leave the convoy to assist a vessel so far away. He wished them the best of luck.

Every life boat on the freighter was either destroyed or damaged by explosions and fire. As the ship began her death dive, all the remaining crew could do, was swim away from their ship. Each man knew their decision rejecting rescue had become a fatal one. All they could do now was cling to water soaked flotsam, while they drifted in the frigid water, waiting for either death from shark attack, or hypothermia to overtake them.

Soldiers on most transports moved top side during the attack, so they wouldn't get trapped below in case their ship was also torpedoed. Everyone was interested in seeing the action, welcoming them into the war. Witnessing the full fury and finality of combat, many men retreated back inside their ship, seriously contemplating what their fates might be. The day before arriving in England, there were several more U-boat sightings. One sub Captain did fire a torpedo quickly, attempting to avoid a charging destroyer. The long silver missile must have been defective, as it slammed into the side of an oil tanker without exploding.

Approaching England on the fourteenth day, two German reconnaissance planes shadowed the convoy for some time. The pilots played a hide and seek game with the escort vessels. They would swoop down over the convoy taking photos, then climb back into the heavy overcast sky, before accurate anti-aircraft fire could be directed on them. This dangerous game played on every one's nerves. There could be little doubt, both pilots radioed the convoy's position to subs and long range bombers. Unexpectedly, three British Spitfires came screaming over the convoy. They split apart, searching desperately for the marauding reconnaissance planes. Apparently, the German pilots observing three spitfires in full combat mode, high tailed it back toward the coast choosing to fight another day. By mid day, ships began breaking from the convoy, sailing safely toward their assigned ports. Two of the troop transports including Steve's, sailed into Liverpool.

It was a welcome relief for everyone to be off the high seas, safe and sound in England. Several trains stood ready on the pier. Every other available space on the pier was occupied by countless American and British cargo trucks. It was New York all over again. However this time, the trains and trucks were waiting to be loaded, rather than unloaded.

Capt. Fontaine organized Charlie Company in their berthing stations before assembling them on the aft deck. Although they were supposed to remain in formation, everyone attempted to get some sort of look at the gritty English sea port.

Finally word came for Charlie Company to disembark. They clambered down the gang ways, loading their packs into baggage cars, before boarding rail coaches. Once the train was loaded, their engineer gave a blast of his loud whistle. Men jumped in their seats, not being accustomed to hearing the shrill whistle of a British locomotive. It was just one of many new sights and sounds each man would become accustomed to, during their stay in England.

The train rolled out of Liverpool picking up speed, as it turned in a southerly direction. It was any ones guess where they were going. Even the scuttlebutt factory appeared to be closed down for the time being.

Right now men were jovial, and full of crazy antics, as their train rumbled across the English country side. Today, it was impossible for these young adventurous Americans to have any inkling as to what horrors the German high command was planning for them across the channel, in a scenic section of France called Normandy.

CHAPTER 7

A TROUBLING ENGLAND

Segments of the 101st and 82nd airborne divisions were already stationed in England. Both divisions were in dire need of new replacements to bring them up to full combat strength. The battalion Charlie Company belonged to, was assigned to the 101st airborne division, based near the town of Newbury, about an hour east of London.
Upon arrival at Newbury, they were assigned to the 502nd parachute infantry regiment. There was no doubt something big was in the making. This camp was huge, and still growing, as combat engineers were in the process of building more half wood, half tent style structures. The tops were canvas like ordinary tents, stretched over wooden frame work, down to a four foot wooden wall. The canvas could re rolled up on the long sides, allowing air to flow through on warm days. Both narrow ends of the structure contained a screen door. Each structure was built to house a squad of thirteen men. All the hastily constructed camps were built on grass fields, adjacent to air strips from which they would operate.

As the camps were set up in fields, every time it rained, paths and roadways turned into muddy affairs. Although tents were dry, every one soon found out, the English dampness permeated everything. Keeping equipment and clothing dry was an on going difficulty. The first order of business was a lay out inspection, assuring each man had all the gear he was required to own. The second order of business was more lengthy lectures by division officers, regarding their proper associations with

British people and the always present Tommies. February first, Charlie Company received their first real leave in a long time. Three-day passes were available, along with stern reminders regarding penalties for bad behavior.

The tents were alive with loud talk, laughter, and good humored horseplay, as each man laid out his plan of attack for the weekend.

Archie could not wait to hit London. Actually, right about now any town with a bar and women would do.

As he checked over his uniform one more time he looked over at Steve.

"Hey, Stevie boy, you just wait until I get to London. I'm going to down some good English booze, find a sweet gal for each arm, get me a nice quiet hotel and spend the next three days in heaven."

Steve looked toward Harry who just entered the tent. "I think Archie needs a chaperone once the army cuts him loose."

Harry laughed, using Steve's polishing cloth one more time on his boots.

"Hey now, come on, guys. You don't mean to tell me you're going to spend three days in London sight seeing? Come on, this is Merry Old England, remember?" Archie reminded the men pretending to be dancing.

"Yeah Archie we know where we are. But I've got Karen back home. I sure as hell don't need to mess up a good thing like that." Steve replied.

Harry placed his hand on Archie's shoulder then squeezed his neck. "Hey Bud, you know I'm in the same boat as Steve. I have Marylyn back home. She wants to marry me the minute I set foot back on American soil. She's pretty damn special; no doubt the best thing that ever happened to me."

Archie spun around pushing Harry's hand from his neck. "What, you guys think there's somebody over here checking up on you, then reporting back home about your behavior. Come on, you've got to live a little."

After a moment of silence Archie shook his head. "But then if you guys feel like sight seeing is a good way to pass the time, go for it. What the heck." Archie looked at his best friends for a minute then continued. "Hey, I'm sorry for coming off on you. I've never had a serious relationship like you guys. Guess I never was ready for that. I can understand where you're coming from. If I had something like that back home, I wouldn't want to wreck it either. Sorry guys."

"No problem, Arch. Look, you have a good time any way you want. Who knows, we may run into each other over the course of the weekend. If not, we'll see you back here in three days.

But if we stand here jacking our jaws to much longer, we're not going to make the train for London. Let's get out of here and enjoy ourselves." Steve responded readjusting his uniform cap.

The train bound for London was crowded with men from the hundred and first, all headed out on passes to one place or another.

Arriving in London, Steve and Harry made their way to a U.S.O. club a few blocks from the rail station. They were in search of a good tour map of the city, along with information on lodging. Inside the club they found a large smoke filled room, filled with soldiers playing pool, writing letters, talking with British service girls, while some just stretched out on wooden benches sleeping the day away. Homesickness appeared to be the general rule for most of the men inside the club.

Harry pointed toward a desk over in the corner with a sign above it stating, "General Information."

Behind the desk was a very attractive woman in a British Service Uniform. As the two men approached the desk, a very drunk American soldier grabbed the woman from behind, attempting to kiss her. She tried desperately to struggle free from his powerful grip without success. The soldier attempted to pull her from behind the desk.

"Why don't you let go of the young lady, Mack. She doesn't seem to be very interested in having anything to do with you." Harry yelled at the inebriated soldier.

"Why don't you mind your own business pal, and step aside. She's mine unless you think you can take her away from me. And I don't think you have much chance of doing that." The drunken man yelled back attempting to push Harry to the side with his free hand.

Harry pushed his arm aside, stepping squarely in front of him. "Now if I were you, I would think real hard. There are two of us, and only one of you. Personally, I think we end up kicking your sorry ass. Now I'm not telling you again. Let go off the young lady, get the hell out of here, and everything will be just fine."

The soldier became increasingly hostile toward Harry. He pushed the young woman aside as he cranked up to swing his huge fist in Harry's direction.

Steve grabbed the man's arm before he could make contact. "Look, Mack, you're drunk. You've had enough fun for one day. Let's say you leave the lady alone, go sleep it off somewhere and try things again tomorrow."

"Let go you son of a bitch, or I'll kill you both." The man growled at Steve.

"No I don't think that's going to happen. You don't even have enough guts to even try that stunt." Harry told the soldier, as his patience with the drunk was growing short.

With that, the man pulled loose from Steve, attempting to grab Harry. Before he could do anything, Harry landed a solid blow hard into his abdomen. Steve took hold once more of the man's arm, twisting it securely behind his back, while kicking his feet out from under him. The man fell to the floor flat on his knees.

Two American Military Police Officers charged into the building, pulling night sticks from their belts.

"All right, what the hell is going on here?" A rough voiced corporal asked, eyeing the three men.

"This misguided young man was messing with that young lady. We tried to talk him out of it, but all he wanted to do was fight. He's pretty drunk as you can tell." Harry responded, hoping his answer would keep them out of the brig.

"Is that the way it happened, Miss?" The corporal inquired.

"Yes, yes, that's about it, officer." She replied quietly, still shaken by the whole affair.

"Well alright then." The M.P. responded removing hand cuffs from his belt. "All right pal, it looks like your night of partying is over. We have a nice warm place you can sleep this off. So you might as well come along peacefully." The corporal instructed the drunken soldier as he locked his cuffs on the man's huge wrists. Pulling the man to his feet, they escorted him out to their Jeep.

The woman glared at Steve and Harry not saying a word. As Steve stepped toward her, she held out her hand shaking her head.

"Miss I just want to know if you're alright. But look, all we want is a tour map of London if you have one, and then we'll be on our way."

Steve explained, watching the very petite woman adjust her uniform before sitting back behind her desk.

"All you Yank's are the same. No manners. You're crude and rather repulsive if you ask me. You come here to our home, and disrupt the entire country with your drinking, and brawling, and woman chasing. The whole lot of you should be sent directly to the continent if you want to fight so much. You Yanks and Herr Hitler should get along quite splendidly I would think." She chastised the two men with a steely glare.

"Well yes Maam, I can understand why you would feel that way after what you just went through. But believe me not all Americans are like that. I would like to apologize for the man's behavior." Steve answered politely.

"Oh really, Yank? I've yet to meet any of you so called boys, with so much of a tad of common decency or respect for the British." She retorted angrily.

Harry took Steve by the arm, pulling him a short distance from the desk, before whispering into his ear.

The young woman watched intently as the two men spoke. "If you tough Yanks have something to say to me, get it out. You don't have to stand there whispering about it." Returning to the desk Harry took a deep breath. "Look, Miss. We are really sorry for what happened. We would like to assure you, not all of us Yanks are crude and ill mannered. So if you could just give us a tour map of London before our three day pass runs out, we'll be on our way. If you could recommend a hotel for us, we would appreciate that also.

Clearing her throat and feeling her face turning somewhat red, she reached into her desk removing a tour book of London.

"Here you go, Yank." She said quietly handing the book to Steve. "As far as a hotel goes, I would recommend the one directly across the street. They also have a nice dining room if you are interested. You must understand there are food shortages. Still, they do put on a good meal.

So you should have all you need then. Have a good time, and please stay out of trouble. There will be enough fighting for you to do once you cross the channel and meet the Boche. Now be off." She said with a slight smile.

"Miss, what's your name?' Steve inquired.

Not sure whether to answer at first, she gave both men a good look over. "Why it's Marjory. Marjory Alexander. Why do you ask, Yank?"

"Well, I'm Steve Kenrude this is Harry Jensen. We would like to buy you dinner tonight, kind of a way to make up for American bad manners. We would really be honored if you would join us."

"Oh, well. I don't. Ah you see." After taking a deep breath she looked up toward the ceiling for a moment. "You see, I normally do not make a habit of going out with yanks. But then, you did come to my rescue. And it's just dinner. Correct?"

"Yes Maam, just a nice casual dinner amongst friends." Steve replied.

"Hmm. Friends you say. Well alright, I suppose I could do that." Marjory answered.

"Great. I'm glad to hear that. You say the hotel has a good dining room?" Steve inquired.

"Oh yes, but I'm afraid not very cheap, and you must remember, there are shortages. They do not always have a good selection. You know I can't say for sure about that to much. I have not been out to eat for quite some time."

"That's fine, Marjory. What time can you meet us there?" Harry asked.

"Well I get relieved around seven. So shall we say seven-thirty? She inquired interestingly. "Sounds like a plan "Steve replied smiling at Marjory.

Standing up from her desk she shook hands with her rescuers.

The two men walked across the street toward the hotel. They registered for a room, before making arrangements in the dining room for that evening.

It was the middle of the afternoon before they headed out sight seeing. They walked about the Streets of London, amazed by the sand bags on many buildings, to protect them from flying debris during air raids. They observed many bombed our buildings along the way. Some were being repaired or rebuilt, while others stood in ruins, a testament to the destructive powers of Nazi air assaults.

Arriving back at the hotel around six o'clock, they cleaned up for their dinner date with Marjory. Entering the lobby from the stair case, they observed Marjory sitting in an over stuffed chair near the registration desk. After exchanging a few words they escorted her to the dining room, where they found a table waiting for them. There was only a choice of three items on the menu tonight, as rationing dictated what restaurants could serve on a daily basis.

Marjory attempted to apologize for the limited selection. The men assured her they understood quite well.

They had a pleasant meal, along with a bottle of wine. They shared plenty of good conversation regarding hobbies, family, and what was happening in the war.

When the topic focused on families, Marjory did not share much. She heartily encouraged both men to share stories about their families, and what it was like to live in America. The subject of farming was most interesting to her, asking many questions regarding livestock, and raising crops.

About ten o'clock Marjory sighed deeply. "Well, Yanks it's getting late. It has been a most enjoyable and interesting evening. I really don't remember when I enjoyed myself so much, thanks to both of you for putting up with my tirade this afternoon."

Everyone laughed thinking back to her out burst toward them earlier in the day. "Well I should be going. It takes a while to get home with the black out." She stated as she stood up from the table.

"Thank you for joining us tonight. It made for a most memorable evening." Steve stated as they walked toward the lobby.

Marjory stopped by the information desk. "Tell you what, Yanks. If you want a real tour of London, let me be your tour guide. I have the day off tomorrow. I think I know where I can get my hands on a car. Would you be interested?" She inquired hoping they would say yes.

"Hey that would be great" Harry replied. "What time?"

"Well, how about I meet you outside this door at nine-thirty." She stated with a broad smile.

"Nine-thirty it is." Steve replied. "Is there any place we can escort you to tonight?" He asked. "Oh no, all I have to do is walk back to the U.S.O. office. Your Military Police will give us girls a safe ride home."

The men walked Marjory across the street to several MP's driving a weapons carrier, already loaded with two other women. After saying good night, the men went back to the hotel for a good nights sleep.

The morning dawned damp and cool with a typical English fog. That did not dampen the spirits of the men, as they prepared for their outing with Marjory. They waited just a few minutes before Marjory drove up with a British Staff car.

"Well that's what I call service, a military staff car to go sight seeing." Steve stated as he and Harry jumped inside.

"Actually I have it for the day. The air raid warden it belongs to left by train for Southampton this morning for meetings. You know, you just can't see the real sights of London without a car.

Well if you're ready, let's be off." Marjory pulled the black sedan into traffic heading south away from the hotel.

As she drove through London, she pointed out many buildings, explaining their significance, and historical background. She took them too many of London's famed monuments and cultural centers. They walked in several or London's fine old parks. For lunch they ate at a quiet little café, before attempting to catch a glimpse of Winston Churchill at 10 Downing Street. Marjory stopped the car near Buckingham Palace explaining the bomb damage they'd received from a recent air raid. Both men asked her questions regarding the German blitz, and as to where much of the damage occurred. She told them she would show them exactly what the bombing has done to the average British citizen.

About half an hour later, the staff car rolled down a quiet street lined with very nice small brick homes. Every yard was clean, the homes appeared well kept. As Marjory rounded a curve, the entire landscape suddenly changed dramatically. Both sides of the street were piled with rubble. Large bomb craters occupied lots where houses once stood. All that was left of many homes were chimneys, and small brick walls that stood about three foot high. The road was extremely rough, where bomb damage had been filled in but never totally repaired.

Marjory was quiet now, as she drove slowly through the demolished neighborhood. She pulled the car over to the side and came to a stop. Slowly she opened the door, stepping clear of the car. She began walking toward a house that was nearly totally destroyed. The two men followed closely behind her. Cold winds blowing through skeletal remains of buildings and twisted trees, created an eerie, almost haunting whine.

Marjory stopped walking. Turning toward the men she said nothing at first. Then she began to tremble, as tears streamed down her face. Steve took her into his arms as she sobbed. He led her back to the staff car, allowing her to sit down on the back seat.

After a few minutes of crying, she regained her composure, staring at what remained of the house directly in front of the staff car.

"Funny isn't it? Every time I come here I expect to see the house as it was. White curtains on the kitchen windows, the smell of baking biscuits, my Mother standing at the door waiting for me. Then there would be Father, sitting in the library in his favorite leather chair, smoking away on his pipe. My little brother David making lots of noise playing around the house, and little Danny." She continued crying again for a moment. "Gone now, everyone gone, Lord I miss them so. You see, I wasn't home the night of the raid. I went with some friends to the school that night for a dance. My father begged me not to go, because there was no real good air raid shelter in that particular school. Well, I went anyway. Mother was so angry with me. About ten o'clock the sirens began to wail. Some of us ignored them, because the bombs never fell in this neighborhood before. Why would the Boche want to bomb it tonight? Suddenly, there was a loud explosion. The school shook like it was going to fall down. We went running from the building every which way. There were bombs falling every where. Planes filled the sky with a terrible roar. I ran down the street as fast as I could, screaming for my mother.

There was a bright flash not far ahead of me. The concussion from the explosion knocked me over. Several houses in that block were instantly engulfed in flames. I realized the Germans were dropping those dreaded incendiary bombs, terrible bombs, the absolute worst. There were more bright flashes all around me. I stood back up continuing toward my home. By this time, there were huge walls of flame all around the neighborhood. The heat was intense. Everything seemed to be burning. The air was filled with flying debris from explosions.

Bricks, chunks of dirt, everything was either burning or being thrown about. A man came running from a house pulling his wife by the arm. Their house was burning from an incendiary bomb. There was screaming coming from inside, but there was no way the man could get back into the blazing structure. There was another close explosion that threw me back down to the pavement. I stood back up, looking over to where the couple had been standing. They were just plain gone. Gone for good I supposed, nothing but a bomb crater where they stood. I screamed and screamed, then started running down the street again toward my home. I made it to just about here. I was just in time to see the bomb explode inside the house. The neighborhood was as bright as day with fires burning all around me. Bombs continued going off toward the west, starting new fires as the planes moved on with their attack. You could here screams coming from everywhere. It was bloody awful. I took a deep breath making an attempt to enter the house, but the flames were so intense. I could here my mother screaming inside. I kept calling mother, mother. I was crying so hard.

That is the last thing I remember until the following morning. I was hit on the head by a piece of flying debris. It knocked me out cold. The neighbors that survived, along with the police, helped dig my families' remains out of the rubble a few days later. They never found little Danny. He was only a year old. He kind of came along as a real surprise to my folks. Lord, why didn't I stay home that night? I have such a guilty feeling because of the way I treated my Mother before I left the house. That was back in nineteen forty, almost four years ago. Four years of pain, four years of grief, four years of emptiness."

Marjory looked at the debris, then a round the neighborhood for several moments. "Please drive me back to the U.S. O. I really want to go home. I can't do any more touring today." She pleaded softly.

The drive back to the U.S.O. was very quiet. The two Americans were really not sure how to react to all that Marjory told them.

Parking in front of the U.S.O Marjory shook hands with the men before going inside. Steve and Harry went back to their hotel. Neither of them was much in the mood to do anything that evening, after listening to Marjory's sad story.

The last day of their three-day pass went by quickly, since the men slept late. By early evening they were packed, ready to travel back to Newbury. Steve checked the U.S.O. several times during the day, to say good bye to Marjory. She had not shown up for work. No one had seen or heard from her all day.

Checking out of the hotel, the clerk behind the desk reached into a small slot removing an envelope.

"Which one of you is Mr. Kenrude?" He inquired.

"That would be me. What do you need? Steve asked him.

"A young woman stopped by and left this for you." The man explained handing over the envelope.

Steve opened it right away, finding a note from Marjory. He read the note quietly to himself.

"Dear Yank." The note started. "I went to see my Grandmother in Essex. Sorry I could not see you off. Please forgive me, will you please drop me a line when you can. My address is on the back of this note." It was signed, "Thanks for everything. Margie."

Steve handed the note to Harry. After reading the message he handed the envelope back to Steve. "Poor thing, this damn war has been tough on her."

The trip back to Newbury seemed much quicker than the original trip to London three days ago.

Most of the men in the rail cars were rather quiet. Many of them slept as they had little time for sleep while they were in London. Steve and Harry enjoyed a quiet conversation on the way back to camp.

Archie was lying on his bunk when his two friends came walking into the tent.

"Hey troops, how was the sight seeing in merry old London?" Archie yelled out.

"Not bad, Arch. What the hell are you doing here lying around? Where are all the pretty young things you went looking for? Couldn't find any?" Harry asked.

"Well gentlemen, a better three day pass you have never experienced. Man I met the best looking, sexiest young thing you've ever seen. Ah yes, you should meet Diane. What a lady. What a great time we had. To bad it had to come to an end so fast." Archie responded to Harry's taunt, sitting up on his bunk stretching.

"So where did you meet this fair maiden, Archie?" Steve inquired as he unpacked his travel bag, placing its contents back into his footlocker.

"Let me tell you, Stevie boy, they just find me, you know? They know class when hey see it." Archie responded with a laugh.

"I suppose you aren't going to tell us about it anyway, Arch. Actually I don't think we really care, right Steve?" Harry replied poking him in the ribs.

"No not really, Harry. I'm sure Archie would tell us if she were worth telling us about. She probably has three legs and a horn." Steve joked winking at Archie.

"Alright you smart asses, just sit down and let old Archie boy tell you how it is to meet an angel."

"Angel? Good grief." Harry said in a disgusting tone of voice.

"Right Jensen, an angel, a real walking talking angel. Well you see I didn't go to London like everyone else. I took a train to Southampton, less soldiers, less competition to deal with. Anyway I get to town, and decide to go for a healthy walk. So I get down the road a ways, and there stands this gorgeous woman aside of a car with a flat tire. So I offer to change the tire for her. When I'm finished, she offers me a lift to where ever it is I'm going. I told her I wasn't headed in any special direction, so she takes me home and introduces me to her father. Get this now guys, her old man is an R.A.F. Officer. In fact, he's General William Evans of British Transport Command.

"General Evans? A General's daughter, are you totally crazy, Archie?" Harry yelled out as he stood up from Steve's bunk.

"That's right, Jensen. And no way will I mess this up. Who knows where this could get me? After all, the old man and I hit it off real well for a first visit." Archie replied.

"Where is it going to get you? A damn court martial, or the brig, or maybe shot if you really mess things up. That's where you're going to end up, Archie." Harry responded shaking Archie by the front of his uniform.

"Not a chance, Harry. I'm going to play this to the best all the way. You never know where this could end. I might even be considered for royalty when the war is over, even adopted by the King." Archie said with a big grin on his face.

Having enough of Archie's rambling, Harry picked up his bag. "I think I'll go see how the commoners live over in my tent. I think I hear my squad calling for their leader." Harry stated waving good bye to Steve.

The tent was slowly filling as men returned from leave. No one in Steve's squad failed to make it back. After listening to all their stories, Steve was sure there couldn't be a drop of liquor left in London, or a woman not chased, in all of England at least once.

He lay back on his bunk laughing at the thought, so much for Merry Old England as an Allie. The following morning started a very intense training mission that would last for a month. There were certain areas of England, which easily pass for the French countryside. These areas would be used by paratroopers to train for the expected second front they continued hearing so much about. Every soldier knew he would be part of it, but when and where it would take place was still a major secret. Of course scuttlebutt always had the latest and best news on the war. But some how, none of the predictions ever came true.

As the men were trucked to and from training, they were amazed by the huge parking lots full of trucks, tanks, artillery and engineering equipment. New aircraft of every possible type continued arriving at newly established airfields all around Newbury.

This time the invasion of so called Fortress Europe would be for real, and deadly serious. The raid on Dieppe in August of nineteen forty two, taught the allies a lesson they did not care to forget.

With the intense training all hours of the day, men had little time to do much more than eat and sleep. When they did get an evening pass to town, the pubs were packed to capacity, as hundreds of new paratroopers continued to arrive.

Pubs and social clubs were unbearable with noise and fights. American versus British, Infantry against airborne, it was nonstop.

Steve found going for walks on base, and writing letters helped more than the evening passes into town. He wrote home every chance he could. The mail was highly censored now, so it was nearly impossible to explain what kind of training they were going through, what they were seeing, or where they were going.

Censors had the power to remove anything from a letter they felt might affect security. Now Steve had one more letter to write. He continued writing to Marjory, and enjoyed hearing back from her. The letters he received from Karen were the ones he cherished most. He often wondered if he would ever see her again. By now, he was well aware this was not going to be a short war.

As the month of February drew to a close, a new training phase began, using both American and British airborne units. Supreme headquarters knew all to well, that anything and everything could go wrong during a major operation. They also knew form North Africa, it was essential to have British and American forces acquainted with each other. It just made good sense to understand how each army operated under combat conditions. Planners at Supreme Headquarters were extremely aware anything could go wrong during a massive drop of airborne units. It was entirely possible for them to get mixed up in a landing zone. Consequently, it was decided training between allied paratroopers must be mandatory.

Many British soldiers were not happy about training with Americans. They felt American forces were not up to par with British standards. There were also problems between Yanks and Tommies over girls, booze, and general attitudes. Although, British soldiers involved, were much happier eating America rations than there own.

Rather quickly, men learned to forget their differences, and cooperate with one another. Rapidly operations began to take on an entirely new look. Many friendships were made, as tough training brought the men closer together.

Early one morning Steve led his squad toward a C-47 standing on the airfield preparing to take off. The rest of the men on board were British airborne. The Sergeant in charge of the mission, was a no nonsense battle veteran. He had been one of the thousands rescued at Dunkirk, and then fought Rommel in North Africa. He stood by the door impatiently waiting for the Americans to arrive. He reached out to shake hands with Steve. "Bloody good show, Corporal. Right on time, I like seeing you Yanks be on time for a change. However you will notice, my boys are already loaded and somewhat disturbed by tardiness. It appears they are growing a bit impatient about now I might add."

"Look Sergeant, we are not on time, we are fifteen minutes early. I don't really care if you camped on this damn plane all last night so you could be first. Now, if you'll get out of the door, we will get on board so we can get going.

"Steve responded indignantly, tired of the British constant complaining, or their practice of one-up-man-ship.

A moment of silence passed as the two men glared at each other with out blinking.

Then the Sergeant busted out in a loud belly laugh. "Spoken like a true paratrooper, Yank. Let's see what you and your men are made of now. Come on aboard, Corporal come on board."

Having his feathers ruffled, Steve was still in a bad mood as he replied. "Sergeant I know what my men are capable of. They are Toccoa men. What I'm not sure about, is what those men inside are capable of!" Nodding his head the Sergeant looked again at Steve. "Fair enough, Corporal. Your men will sit near the rear of the plane. I want you to follow me up front. I would like to talk to you as we fly toward our drop zone. For the record, I'm Sgt. Wilkenson" Steve introduced himself as he directed his men to begin loading. After everyone was situated, an R.A.F. Captain came on board to address the men.

"Gentlemen, this training is most important. Not to see who can out do each other, or see who can perform their mission better or faster. No, we're all in this damn fight together. What we need to do is build a team spirit. We need to know that when Jerry pushes, we can fight together to teach the bastards a lesson they won't soon forget. Your lives may bloody well depend on it. Good luck to you all, and safe landings. Is the American squad leader ready?" "Yes sir." Steve responded from the front of the plane.

"Very well then, good hunting," The captain added as he jumped from the plane.

"Right nice of him," Archie said to a British soldier aside of him. "To bad he isn't going along with us to find out just what we can do."

"You can knock that funny shit off, mate. He's one good man. I'd follow his ass anywhere, anytime." The angry British paratrooper responded.

"Yeah, I hear what you're saying. I wasn't trying to cause problems. After all, I'm dating a British General's daughter. Far be it from me to mess things up." Archie informed the man. "Well I guess there is another reason you might just want to keep your yap shut, Yank. Some of the men might not appreciate hearing you're dating a General's daughter. I sure as hell don't. You Yanks just don't know when you're well off. Just shut the hell up and leave me alone. "The British soldier barked.

Archie swallowed hard, realizing he had made a big mistake talking about his romantic exploits. He turned his head forward looking across the plane, without saying another word to the man. The plane taxied toward the runway, taking off moments later. Winds were calm as the plane rose into the morning sky. It took less than fifteen minutes for them to reach their drop zone. As the light above the door turned green, the jump master began yelling over the deafening roar, "Go, go, move it chaps."

When the last man exited, the C-47 turned east, heading back toward Newbury. Drifting down, Steve thought it was the nicest jump he had made so far. Not a cloud could be seen as far as a man could see. The sun already was burning away ground fog that lingered in low spots, leaving the air with a refreshing ocean scent. Steve could see his men forming up as he approached the landing zone. Looking like a true leader, Steve made a perfect landing standing straight up. After gathering in his chute he took a head count. Everyone in first squad landed perfectly with all their equipment in tacked. Looking over his map, he checked to see where their rendezvous point was located. Once he figured it out, he directed his men to follow the wood line to conceal their movement. About five minute later he observed the British unit in a near by grove of trees. After scanning the area carefully, Steve directed his men toward the grove.

When Sergeant Wilkenson observed the American squad arrive completely intact, he had to smile.

Shaking his head the burly Sergeant said. "Well Yank, you have one on me already. I'm missing six of my men. Can't understand where they could have gone to. They're very good troopers."

Steve told his men to have a seat under the trees, while the British searched desperately for their missing men.

After several failed attempts at finding them, Sgt. Wilkenson walked up to Steve. "Well, Corporal we have a schedule to keep. We best get moving. If they don't find us, it will be a damn long walk back to Newbury for the bunch."

"A loss of six men could affect the out come of our mission. I sure hope they can catch up." Steve told Sgt. Wilkenson as he adjusted his back pack.

"Quite right, quite right, corporal, you know, in a real jump they all could be bloody dead, not just plain lost. But we can't wait for them any longer."

Pulling a neatly folded map from his pack, Sgt. Wilkenson placed a compass on top of it. "Alright Kenrude, here is my plan. Form up your men following the tree line like you were before finding me. Stay undercover as much as possible. One of my squads will follow behind you. The other will parallel you along the stone fence aside the road. We will move on a northerly direction until we hit this stone church." He instructed while pointing to a mark on his map. "We'll figure out our next move after that."

Steve nodded in agreement, watching Sgt. Wilkenson adjusting the strap on his enfield rifle. Both teams moved out as prescribed by the Sergeant, carefully scanning the countryside as they went. About fifteen minutes into their movement, the sound of an aircraft engine could be heard in the distance.

Every one stopped for a second to listen, as the aircraft closed on their position, everyone dashed for cover. The pilot made a quick pass at nearly tree top level before pulling up, and rolling off to the East. After gaining altitude he came back in a quick dive, flying across the paratrooper's positions. The peaceful morning was rent by the shrill scream of the diving aircraft as it bore in on their position. It appeared to take forever, but it was actually seconds before the speeding Spitfire was directly on top of them. The pilot released a bag full of powder from the bomb racks underneath his fighter. It slammed into the ground half way between the fence and the tree line.

Once more the pilot turned to make another pass, as he had one more bomb to drop. This time he came down paralleling the road. He dropped his bomb right on target. It struck the stone fence where four British soldiers had taken cover. Finished with his work, the pilot climbed toward the south, disappearing from sight. Sergeant Wilkinson stood up calling for his men to reassemble.

"Let's get a move on. No more time to waste. Form up, move out."

Just as the men continued down the road, several British officers wearing blue helmets came walking out of the woods to their left.

"Umpires, damned umpires!" Sgt. Wilkenson said disgustingly watching the men approach. "You get lost out there in the woods?" The Sergeant inquired. "You can follow along with us if you would like." He added.

"Lost? No not at all. One moment Sergeant" A major called out. You just lost four of your men to bombs. They are out of this situation I'm afraid. I am Major Fredric's head of the umpire corp. for this exercise.

Those four men at the end of your patrol are dead, Sergeant." Major Fredric's explained pointing at four young soldiers covered in a white powder.

Shaking his head in agreement Sgt. Wilkenson responded. "Yes Major I can see that. In fact, I think their ghosts have already come back to haunt us.

Every one chuckled except the four men. "Well you boys have a seat. A truck will be along in a while to pick you up." Sgt. Wilkenson instructed his disgruntled soldiers.

They removed their packs mumbling some derogatory remarks concerning the bloody R.A. F. As the teams once again prepared to move out, Sgt. Wilkenson's six missing men came running down the road. After reporting in, they took up positions in their squads. Arriving at the stone church, Sgt. Wilkenson told everyone to take a five minute break. He and Steve looked over the map, discussing their options to capture a command center about a mile away in an old gravel pit. After formulating a plan, the men took up their positions heading back out on the road. Approaching a curve Steve motioned for Sgt. Wilkenson to stop. After looking around Steve dashed across the road to meet with the Sergeant, who was kneeling near a brush pile.

"Something's not right. Listen, there aren't any birds chirping. Someone is up ahead." Steve warned his leader.

"I disagree, corporal. Yes, curves are a great place for an ambush, but I would do it near the next curve, where the bridge is on a slight rise. No, we are good to go, mate. Let's move out." Sgt. Wilkenson directed Steve. After another quick dash across the road, Steve motioned for his men to move out.

Steve eyed the terrain intently. He could feel the hair on the back of his neck standing up as he walked slowly forward. What is it? Where is it? Steve wondered. Something just felt out of place.

Abruptly, two machine guns just past the curve opened up. Sgt. Wilkenson yelled out, "fall back, fall back, take cover. Steve's men jumped for cover behind trees just feet away. Several of the British men just dropped where they were, retuning fire with blanks. The others jumped over the stone fence. Immediately Steve's men joined in the fight. Sgt. Wilkenson motioned for Steve to drop back beyond the curve. Just as he told his men to start moving, the sound of an approaching tank became evident. Archie yelled out, "Kraut tank, Kraut tank!"

"Into the woods, into the woods, Steve yelled out to his men and the British squad following him.

The tank came lumbering down the road from behind their position. It was an American Sherman, flying a home made German Panzer flag from its antenna. The machine guns ceased firing, as nearly thirty American soldiers wearing fake German uniforms approached slowly from the curve. The tank commander turned his turret first toward Sgt. Wilkenson's men, then over toward the woods where Steve's men had taken cover.

It was nearly impossible for Steve to control his breathing, as he was looking directly down the muzzle of a seventy-five millimeter cannon, pointed in his direction. He felt they could surely hear his breathing over the throbbing Detroit Diesel Motor.

Steve signaled his men to crawl deeper into the woods. He desperately searched for a good escape route.

Incredibly a voice behind him called out, "Achtung! Halt! Stay where you are. You are now my prisoners."

Steve spun around to see nearly a platoon of American soldiers wearing similar fake German uniforms, but carrying real captured enemy weapons. They came out of the woods closing in on his men.

Steve stood up, slowly dropping his Thompson on the ground. His men followed suit as more enemy soldiers entered the woods from the road. Steve knew any attempt to escape was over. They were completely surrounded.

Major Fredric's walked into the woods near Steve looking over the situation.

"Alright corporal, pick up your weapons, gather your men and fall out on the road. Oh and by the way corporal. For your information these enemy soldiers were responsible for detaining the six men right from the beginning. If this had been a real mission, you probably would have all been cut to pieces when you landed."

Out on the road, Sgt. Wilkenson's men were sitting around with the tank crew and the fake German soldiers.

Major Fredric's walked over to speak with several officers sitting in a jeep that just arrived. After several minutes of conversation the Major walked back to the tank. Climbing on board, he sat down on top of the turret.

"Let me have your attention, men." The smiling Major called out.

"You people did an excellent job today. You can expect just this type of thing to happen once we meet the bastards in real combat. Corporal Kenrude, your surrender plan was a good idea. Surrender if necessary, so you can live to fight another day. You're not much good to us if you're dead. They have to tie up troops and equipment to guard P.O.W. camps, not cemeteries. Only problem is, gents, the damn krauts don't always live up to the Geneva Convention. They probably would have gunned you down right there in the woods, before you would have ever seen them. They off course were tipped off by the pilot as to your direction of travel. All they had to do was readjust their defenses in order to set up this trap. They did a damn good job of it.

If you jump behind enemy lines and are captured, the bastards are going to shoot you on the spot. Period! Corporal, I could not see any other way for you to have handled your situation. I can tell you this. There may be times when you will have to make a life and death decision on a moments notice. You keep your head. You live. You lose your concentration, you are just dead. Always look for a way out, one other thing. When you are surrounded and everyone is scurrying about, watch where you fire. You do not want to kill one of your own. In the end, your best bet is to fight as a unit, work as a team. Don't cooperate with Jerry unless you have no choices. But above all, do as much damage to Hitler's finest as possible. Bloody awful way to look at things I suspect. But the truth of the mater stinks, that's what you'll be up against from the very start. That's all. Have a good day men."

The tank crew climbed aboard their Sherman. Rolling over the huge Detroit engine they drove off with Major Fredric's standing behind the turret.

The paratroopers laid around about an hour until a convoy of trucks arrived to pick them up.

Arriving back at the tent, Steve was instructed to report to Capt. Fontaine's office immediately.

As he entered the orderly room, Lt. Winslow was also waiting to see the Captain. "Well Kenrude, how did things go today?" Lt. Winslow asked puffing on a big cigar.

"Not bad, sir, It was an interesting exercise. It kind of brought reality home." Steve responded.

The door to Capt. Fontaine's office opened. The men in the orderly snapped to attention.

"As you were men," The Captain directed, as he walked from his office over to one of his clerks.

Four squad leaders from third and fourth platoons walked into the orderly room. They walked over to Steve and Lt. Winslow, as they were also told to report to the Captain.

After several minutes Capt. Fontaine walked over.

"Well good evening men. It looks like everyone made it back all right. All of you spent time today with our British counter parts in one way or the other. I just finished talking with General Evans. He gave me a glowing account of your cooperation, and good comments on today's exercises. Some of the missions were set up to fail on purpose. God knows we'll not complete every mission we go on, or win every battle we're involved in. So we need to be prepared mentally, as best we can for every possible scenario. Today gave some of you an idea of what can go wrong. As we approach the war, we'll continue with training sessions just like we did today. We will try to get as many of our men involved as we possibly can. Your cooperation today was excellent. I am damn proud of you. Each of you now must go back to your squads, your platoons, and pass on what you learned today.

Now I know we have been working every one pretty damn hard. But we need to be ready when the time comes. Tomorrow is Friday. I know everyone was hoping for a three day pass. I know everyone could use one right about now. However, that's not going to be possible. Saturday morning we'll be going on a full field march. All the equipment we have goes with us. We'll march the entire distance. Their will be no jumps involved, as far as I know right now.

We will be out for a week going through war games, and training sessions on how to operate behind enemy lines. So get your men ready. We move out at 0700 hours. Breakfast will be at 0600. That's all I have, dismissed!"

Saturday dawned rather cool, but with a clear sky that promised plenty of sunshine, to warm the men as they moved out for the march.

Charlie Company took their position in the battalion line up. The shear numbers of men and equipment preparing to move out looked rather impressive to Archie.

"Just look at this, Steve, the might of America, getting ready to spring upon those Nazi bastards." Archie said glowingly, as Steve was checking the equipment of each man in their squad.

"Don't feel too confident, Archie." Harry stated as he walked behind him. "Remember, all along the Atlantic wall, Hitler has his best Panzer troops just waiting for us. All battle hardened veterans." Harry added as he took up his position at the front of his squad.

Lt. Winslow had been listening to the men of his platoon. He walked up to the squad leaders, checking with each man to make sure their squads were ready. After checking with Steve he looked over toward Archie asking, "Well, Davenport, you think this force looks impressive?"

"Yes, Lieutenant, I do. I think we have the power to take those krauts right out of the picture."

"Well I'm not questioning our determination, or will to win this war you understand. Because as sure as I'm standing here, the day we hit the continent, it will be a jump into hell. Count on that Davenport. The devil himself will be there, guiding those kraut sons-a-bitches, trying to throw us back into the channel. And believe me; he'll see a lot of blood shed that day. He'll see strong men cry, and weak men rise to the occasion. When we get home, every one of you will be able to say we walked through the fires of hell. Keep that in mind, Davenport." Lt. Winslow explained coldly staring into Archie's frightened eyes.

Shortly the battalion moved out of the cantonment area into the countryside. It was slow gong at first, with all the vehicles getting bunched up on the narrow dirt road. But it was good to see the huge force that was mustering and perfecting their trade, in order to bring total defeat to the Wehrmacht.

The week went by rapidly, as everyone was kept incredibly busy. Training was difficult and repetitious. But honing the skills of each man was required, if they were going to survive in combat. By now squads operated as efficient combat teams, capable of holding their ground, or clearing buildings with efficiency.

Every man was tired and dirty the following Sunday, when they arrived back in the cantonment area. Each paratrooper felt he had learned things he could take into combat, making him a more complete soldier. And maybe, just maybe, improve his chances to survive the up coming battle.

After the battalion commander dismissed the men, they went back to their respective companies. Capt. Fontaine called Charlie Company together in front of the orderly tent. He walked by each platoon looking over his men. Returning to the front of his company he smiled. "A dirtier more disgusting looking bunch of paratroopers I have never seen."

The men hooped and howled at their Captains sense of humor.

"But not a better bunch of paratroopers in all of England let me tell you! Job well done men, you are getting sharper all the time. It's incredible to see how far you have come since Toccoa. Let's get this next week under our belts, then come Friday three day passes for everyone."

A cheer went up from Charlie Company after hearing the great news.

The following week was not an easy one. Lt. Winslow drove the men late into the evenings working on specialized night tactics. When Friday finally rolled around, the men were itching for a nice leave. After morning roll call, Lt. Winslow handed out their passes. The company area was nearly deserted in the next hour, as men left for predetermined destinations all over England. The train bound for London was crowded, and extremely loud, as soldiers began blowing off steam before arriving at the rail station.

Harry accompanied Steve to London again, although he knew Steve would probably want to see Marjory, leaving him on his own for a while. They checked into the same hotel, as it had been comfortable and very inexpensive.

After getting settled, Steve was ready to see Marjory at the U.S.O. club. Harry went along for the walk to say hello to their friend. They found her sitting behind her desk reading a newspaper.

"Hello Marjory." Steve said excitedly.

"Steven, how nice to see you, how are you doing? And Harry, so nice to see you again, this is absolutely wonderful of you Yanks to stop by. I didn't know you were coming to London. You should have written, letting me know when you were arriving." Marjory declared as she stood up from her desk to shake hands with both men.

"Hey Steve, I'm going to check out those pool tables a while so I'll see you later. Let's see if I still have the touch. Maybe I can win a few extra bucks." Harry said with a big smile on his face.

"Nice to have seen you, Harry, have a good time and win big. You can take us all out to dinner then." Marjory stated as she winked at him.

Steve waited for Harry to walk away before he again spoke to Marjory. "Can you get away from the desk for a while? I would like to go for a walk with you."

She walked into an office for a moment. She returned with another young woman to take her place. "Steve this is my best friend Sylvia. We have been friends since, well goodness I don't remember how long." Marjory explained removing her purse from a desk drawer.

"Nice to meet you, Sylvia, I appreciate you covering for Marjory so we can go off and talk a while. If that soldier by the wall with the cue stick wins to much money, just lock it up until I return." Steve instructed Sylvia pointing toward Harry.

Smiling, Sylvia assured Steve it was not a problem covering the desk.

"Shall we be off then, Steve?" Marjory asked taking Steve by the hand.

They walked down the busy London Street not saying much the first couple of blocks. Then Marjory turned to Steve inquiring, "Do you have a young lady waiting for you back in the states?"

Steve hesitated before answering. "Yes I do, Marjory, to be totally honest with you. Her name is Karen. I've known her for a long time, almost my entire life."

"That's nice, Steven. I'm happy you have someone waiting for you. I know this may sound frightfully silly of me to ask. But do you love her, Steven?" She inquired studying Steve's face.

Steve turned toward Marjory taking a deep breath. "Yes I do. In fact, we plan to Marry if and when I ever get home again."

"That's lovely, Steven. I'm so happy for you. I really am. You see, I had to ask you that question. I had to know because I don't want you thinking about getting involved with me at all. Yes, I like you Steven, but not in that way now, or maybe ever. I just don't know. I just can't have any personal relationships as long as this damndable war goes on. I couldn't stand the hurt of having another loved one taken away from me. And I have been thinking Steven, that we should just be good friends. Plus, after the war I don't know what I will be doing or where I might go. I have been thinking about that a lot lately. Can you understand what I'm saying?"

Nodding his head Steve replied, "Yes Marjory I understand. I do. None of us know what will happen tomorrow, or even when this war will be over. Come on; let's step inside this café for something warm to drink."

When they were seated and served hot tea, Steve studied Marjory's face for a few minutes. He could not think of anything to say at first. She looked so sad again today.

"It must be terrible for you to lose your family in just one short moment like that. I can see the pain in your eyes. I don't know how I would handle something like that. Does anything help?"

"No Steven, nothing helps. I have such terrible nightmares that scare me silly. Even with you and Harry. The night after we were together, I had nightmares of you both being killed. That was one reason I went to my Grandmothers, instead of seeing you both off. It almost scares me to see you two again. I want to escape from it, but it's always there. I question myself. What should I do? How do I put it all to rest and find peace?" Marjory said sadly hanging her head.

"I'm so sorry, Marjory. I just don't have any answers for you. I wish I did. But you need to remember, what happened was not your fault. There was no way you could have seen the attack coming, or stopped it once it began. The important thing is for you to live on for them. Keep their memory alive. Live up to the dreams and hopes they had for you. That's what they would have wanted you to do." Steve replied, knowing he wasn't really getting through to her.

Marjory finished her tea, gently placing her cup on the saucer with out saying much. The rest of their conversation was short, practically tense at times. Steve began questioning his feelings toward Marjory.

"I'm sorry, Steven. But I must get back to work now. Will you walk me back to the U.S. O.? She inquired smiling.

"Yes of course I'll walk you back. But first answer one question for me. Will you have dinner with us again tonight or maybe tomorrow evening?" Steve asked hoping she would say yes.

"No I'm sorry, Steven. I'm going to be incredibly busy the next couple of evenings I'm afraid. But maybe next time you're here we can enjoy a meal together again." She replied, as she looked down toward the floor wringing her hands.

Steve could tell she was very upset as they left the small café. Slowly, they walked back toward the U.S.O. hand in hand, with out speaking another word. As they entered the smoky building, Marjory turned to Steve. "Have a nice leave now, Yank and be careful." She stared deep into Steve's eye for a moment, before giving him a big hug and a soft kiss on the cheek.

"Be careful always, Steven." She whispered in his ear. As she slowly backed away she added, "Good bye, Yank."

Before Steve could say another word, Marjory quickly turned and walked into the office, closing the door behind her. He wanted to call out for her to wait so he could tell her good bye. But the door slammed behind her, some how it felt final.

Steve felt rather depressed about Marjory's state of mind. He knew there was nothing he could do for her. That thought just made his heart ache worse. A sinking feeling came over him, knowing he was never going to see her again. He agonized over his feelings for several minutes. All the while, images of Karen rolled through his head like a slide show. He remembered his promises to her, and how many times she had openly professed her love for him. Maybe the best thing he could do for Marjory and him self, was to never see her again. No matter how hard he tried to convince himself otherwise, he knew he had feelings for Marjory.

But yet, he knew he loved Karen very much. This was the toughest dilemma he had ever faced concerning his inner feelings.

Harry walked up to him, "Anything going on, or are we heading somewhere. I won twenty bucks so dinner is on me, good buddy. Will Marjory be joining us?"

"Hey that's great, Harry. No nothing is going on. She won't have dinner with us tonight for some reason. Come on, let's get out of here and enjoy the rest of the day." Steve replied giving Harry a reassuring smile.

"Sounds great Stevie boy, let's you and me go have some fun. He replied as they walked out toward the street. Strolling along the Thames River, they watched tug boats carefully push newly arriving cargo ships against wharfs for unloading. In a park near by, they watched several artists paint portraits of young lovers or nature scenes. They enjoyed talking with many of the older London citizens they met in the park.

After a good meal in the hotel dining room, Harry suggested a movie that was playing at a theater about two blocks a way. Steve liked the idea of a movie. He felt it just might take his mind of off Marjory for a while.

Arriving back at the hotel after the movie both men were very tired, it had been a long week with little sleep. A warm comfortable bed in a quiet hotel seemed like the proper prescription.

About seven in the morning, they were awakened by someone at the door. Steve rolled back the covers from his bed beginning to get up.

Who ever was at the door was very impatient. They continued pounding on the door harder than before.

"Hold your damn horses before you knock the damn door down." Steve called out, struggling to pull up his pants.

Harry was sitting up in his bed, rubbing his eyes as Steve approached the door.

They were both totally surprised as the door swung open. The hotel manager stepped aside, allowing two uniformed police officers plus, a man in a dark suit to step past him.

"If you would have waited one more damn minute I was about to open the door." Steve said angrily as he tightened his belt.

"Sorry for the intrusion and using the pass key gentlemen, but this is very important." One of the uniform officers commented as he looked around the room.

"I'll bet you're sorry. This had better be damn good." Harry blurted out as he glared at the police officer.

"Is either of you Corporal Kenrude?" The older man in the dark suit inquired.

"Well now one of us might be, then maybe we aren't. Why don't we start out by knowing who you are? You're asking like a damn Gestapo agent for God's sake." Harry called out as he began getting dressed.

"Well maybe we should deal with this down at the station. Shall we go?" The man suggested. Before Steve could say a word, Harry pushed a night stand out of his way, walking toward the man appearing to be in charge. "We're not going anywhere with you. Not until you tell us who you are and what you want. You're not railroading us for anything just because we happen to be

American Soldiers and you think you can get away with it," Harry barked out taking a threatening stance.

Looking at Steve the man in the black suit asked. "Is your friend here always so rude and belligerent?"

"Yeah, he is pretty much like that most the time. I don't need an attack dog when I've got Harry around. Now listen. I have done nothing wrong. If you want any type of cooperation from either of us you best come clean on what you're after. Or get an American M.P. we can deal with." Steve told the man with a sly smile on his face.

"Well alright. We don't need problems with the U.S. Army or this young man. My name is Detective Smith form the homicide office. Let me explain to you what is going on, as I am not a Gestapo agent as your friend chose to call me." The detective said staring at Harry, who was enjoying the detective's uneasiness.

"We were in a hurry to find you. We did not want you to leave London on the early train. It would have made this situation all the messier."

"What situation?" Harry inquired stepping closer to the detective.

One of the police officers walked over, standing between Harry and Detective Smith.

Harry stared the officer down causing him to back away.

Shaking his head regarding Harry's belligerency, Detective Smith inquired. "Do either of you know a young woman named Marjory Alexander"

"What happened to her?" Steve asked.

"So you do know her I presume." Detective Smith stated looking at Steve.

"Yes I do, but not real well. What's going on here?" Steve asked again.

"And you. You know her also?" Detective Smith inquired of Harry.

"Well now I might, and I might not. Tell us what the hell is going on if you expect cooperation. Get my point, Detective." Harry yelled out.

"Slow down Yank, we aren't the enemy here. Save your anger and rage for the Nazi's." Detective Smith stated boldly removing a small note book form his pocket. "Let me see here. Oh alright. The fire brigade was called to Miss Alexander's apartment about three this morning regarding a gas leak. When they entered, they found Miss Alexander on the floor. All valves on the stove were turned on as well as the oven. The oven door was open; she was just feet away from it. She was already dead; they did not attempt to revive her. A definite suicide it would appear. We found an envelope with the Name Steven Kenrude on it with this Hotels name. Can you shed any light on the matter?" Detective Smith asked starting to get impatient.

The men were shaken by the news of Marjory's suicide. Steve sat down on the edge of the bed looking over at Harry, then back to the Detective. "This whole thing is a surprise to us. We'll do everything we can to help you out." After taking a deep breath Steve continued. "Last we saw her was about three-thirty yesterday afternoon at the U.S.O. club. I had gone for a walk with her. We had tea and talked for a while. I can almost guess suicide would be correct. She was really down yesterday. The war had taken a toll on her, and she was very distraught. She said good bye to me several times. I never imagined she was going to take her life. Did you think someone killed her? Who would have done that to someone as sweet as Marjory?" Steve responded to the detective as tears rolled down his face.

"No corporal, we didn't think anyone wanted to hurt Miss Alexander. We have a suicide note from her. It is confirmed to be her hand writing. We also have the envelope with your name on it, and the name of the hotel. The letter has not been opened. We would like you to come with us to identify the body. We understand she has no immediate family left in London. We need an actual

Identification for the records, your envelope is at the morgue with her belongings." Detective Smith stated matter of factly.

"All right, all right, I will go with you. Just give me a minute to finish getting dressed. Steve replied picking up his shirt from a chair near the bed.

"I'll go with you, Steve. This isn't going to be easy for you or anyone." Harry explained looking over at Steve. His face totally reflected the amount of grief he was feeling.

"So, you can also identify Miss Alexander?" The detective inquired of Harry.

"Yeah, yeah I can. I knew her also. She does have a grandmother in Essex. "Harry replied. "Yes we are aware of that. But she is old and not in good shape to travel. So we thought this would be an easier way to handle her identification." Detective Smith informed the men. "So if we are ready, let's go." Detective Smith said leading the way out the door.

The drive to the morgue was very quick. It was just two miles from the hotel. Arriving, the two officers led the two men to a room in the basement, above the door hung a sign, "NEW DELIVERIES."

"You need to understand, this place can be very busy at times with all the bombings." Detective Smith explained. Inside the brightly lit cold room were two young men sitting in a small office playing cards. There were seven large bench type fixtures in the middle of the room. Each bench contained a body covered by a sheet. Detective Smith walked over to the office. After exchanging a few words with the two men he turned toward the police officers. "Last one on the left."

The police officer walked ahead of them, stopping by the bench.

"Go ahead." Detective Smith instructed him.

The office pulled back the cover just enough for Steve and Harry to make identification. Both men stood motionless as they looked down at Marjory's discolored face.

"Is that her? The detective inquired.

"Yes, that's Miss Alexander, she looks so terrible, the color of her skin." Steve answered staring at her lifeless figure.

"That happens to a person asphyxiated by gas." One of the morgue attendants explained, as he walked up behind them.

"How about you, corporal, can you identify the woman?" Detective Smith asked Harry.

"Yeah that's Marjory. I can't believe she's gone just like that. She had no family left, except for her grandmother in Essex. That's all the family we are aware of. What happens to her now?" Harry responded wiping a tear from his cheek.

"Actually, she is being buried this afternoon I'm afraid. With the bombing and all, we can't hang on to bodies long, or we'll be backed up very fast. Since she has no family to make arrangements, we just feel it's best to bury her right away. All we would need is a break out of some disease, and things could get out of control. We have had problems finding bodies after raids you can imagine. So far we have been extremely lucky. The police can give you directions to the cemetery if you wish to attend the service."

The morgue attendant looked at Harry. "We'll bury her around two this afternoon. It will give you plenty of time to catch the late train back to your base." He then respectfully placed the sheet back over Marjory's face.

Everyone walked back into the hallway where detective Smith asked if there were any questions. Both men stated they were satisfied. Harry apologized for his actions in the hotel.

"Son, just keep that attitude when you meet the Hun. You can single handedly end the war six months early." Every one had to laugh a little at the Detective's comment.

He then handed Steve the envelop he told them about. The writing on the outside was very neat. Steve recognized Marjory's handwriting instantly. It read, "Corporal Steven Kenrude, King Arthur Hotel."

He tore open the sealed envelope removing the letter. The writing in the letter was a beautiful long script he came to know from her letters. The note was short, coming right to the point of what was on her mind before committing suicide.

"Dear Steven,

Thank you for such a nice time during your last visit. Your letters were super. They always raised my spirits. I'm happy you have a young lady back home that you love. We all need some one special in our lives. I loved my family so much. I can't wait to be with them again. I miss them so very much. Stay well always, and please never forget me. Please keep my memory alive so that I can find peace and rest. This is the only way, Steven.

So, please be careful when you go to war. Always be cautious, and take care of your best friend Harry. He is a lovely man. I cherish both of you. Good bye.

Marjory"

Steve handed the letter to Harry. They stood quietly as Harry read the simple good by note. "It's so final. Lord, the mental pain she must have gone through these past few years. But she is at peace now. God have mercy on her soul." Harry said quietly passing the letter to Detective Smith.

After reading the letter he handed it back to Steve. "I am one hundred percent convinced, Miss Alexander's passing was a suicide. Thanks to both of you for helping us out in this matter. I know it could not have been easy for either of you. My officer will give you a ride back to the hotel if you are ready."

"Yeah I guess we're ready. Nothing more we can do here." Steve said turning toward the sand bagged staircase.

No one said a word while driving back to the hotel. Steve thought if he had just not told Marjory about his feeling toward Karen, she might still be alive. But what did that say regarding his love for Karen? What about all the plans they made for the future? Steve's feelings were totally confused over so many important issues.

When the car stopped at the hotel, the officer handed Harry a map to the cemetery, he drew out on the back of a traffic citation.

Steve spent the best part of the day sitting around the hotel room. Harry knew Steve wanted to be by himself. So he went for a walk in a small park down near the river, where he too could be alone with his thoughts and feelings.

About one o'clock the two men took a taxi to the cemetery. The only other people there were six employees from the U.S.O, including Sylvia, Marjory's best friend, and Detective Smith. Steve thought the service was rather quick and impersonal for some one special like Marjory. Sure people in London had become accustomed to death, but every one at the funeral appeared to be cold and stoic. It made Steve hurt all the worse.

As mourners left the grave sight, Steve knelt down beside the wooden coffin containing Marjory's worldly remains. He bowed his head saying a few prayers, before placing his hands on the wood speaking quietly.

"Marjory you will never be forgotten. I promise. I will remember you as long as I live. Maybe when I meet you again in a better place and time, you can take me on a tour of heaven. I'd like that."

Harry walked up to Steve placing his had on Steve's shoulder. "Are you alright, Steve?" Looking up at his best friend he answered, "Yeah I'm fine. Let's go"

The two men walked a short distance when Steve suddenly stopped. "Wait a minute, I'll be right back."

Steve walked quickly back to the coffin. "Marjory, I came back for one more thing. Please pray for me, Harry and my men when we go into battle. I know you'll be closer to the big man than I will be. When I left home we were not on a good talking basis. So do what you can for us. Thanks Marjory."

He walked back to Harry. After looking at each other for a moment he said, "Okay, buddy let's go now."

Harry drew in a deep breath. "You know there is nothing you could have done, Steve. It's not your fault. She was really in a bad way about her family. For some reason she just couldn't get passed that night."

A light mist began to fall as the men walked toward the taxi stand. Steve leaned his head back, letting the cool mist fall on his face. Wiping his face he looked toward Harry. "I don't know, Harry. I just don't know. Maybe I never will. I do know that my feelings got all messed up over her. I deeply love Karen but there was something special about Marjory."

"Yeah, she was special alright. There is no doubt about that. I had feelings for her too good buddy. But, I knew she really liked you a lot. In the long run Steve, what really matters is you stayed faithful to Karen. From the beginning you knew where your heart was at. You could never have cheated on Karen, like I could never cheat on Marylyn. And that's a fact." Harry replied feeling very empty inside.

Arriving back at the hotel they packed their bags, and walked to the train station. For Steve it was a very long ride back to Newbury. He felt like he could sleep for a year. The emotional drain of the last few days left him feeling empty and some what depressed.

Archie arrived back from Southampton about nine o'clock Sunday night in a British Staff car. The girl driving the large sedan was a very attractive blonde. Archie jumped out of the car hustling over toward the tents.

"Hey Steve, Hey Harry, got someone out here I want you both to meet. Come on outside. Hurry it up fellas she can't wait out here forever.

Harry stood up following Archie out the door. Steve exited the tent a bit behind Harry joining the others by the staff car.

"Took you long enough, Stevie boy, well anyway men, I want to introduce you to Miss Diane Evans. Diane this is Harry Jensen and the slower one is Steve Kenrude."

"So nice to meet both you boys, Archie's told me so much about the both of you. I feel like I already know you very well." She declared shaking hands.

"It's nice meeting you, Diane." Harry responded looking over the very attractive young blonde.

"Yes, Archie has talked about you a lot lately. It's nice to meet a real legend." Steve replied smiling at Diane.

"A legend, Archie what have you been telling these friends of yours?" She inquired of Archie, whose' face was now bright red.

"Nothing really, Steve just used a bad choice of words. You know how ignorant farm boys can be." Archie replied as they all laughed.

"Really nice to have met you, Diane, I'll see you around. Good night for now." Steve smiled as he walked back toward the tents.

"Hey what's bugging Stevie boy tonight? That ain't like him at all." Archie inquired of Harry.

Harry explained to Archie and Diane what happened during their three-day pass to London. He explained to them how hard Steve was taking Marjory's death, and how he felt he should have been able to stop her.

About ten-thirty Diane drove off. Harry and Archie walked back toward the tents. Slapping Archie on the back, Harry said good night as he strolled over toward second squad's tent.

Archie walked into first squad's tent. He noticed Steve was sound asleep already. Not wanting to wake him, Archie quietly went to his bunk and turned in.

Charlie Company was eating breakfast at 0600 Monday morning when the air reverberated with the sounds of many approaching aircraft. The roar became louder and louder. The mess tent began vibrating from the thunderous sound waves. Everyone bailed out of the mess tent excited to see what was going on. Overhead, they observed a large number of C-47 Dakotas circling like a swarm of angry hornets. One by one they made their approach to the airfield before settling down on the runway.

Archie yelled out to be heard above the noise. "There must be a hundred of them damn things."

Harry yelled back, "Oh yeah. Well who counted them for you?"

Archie gave Harry a shove as the entire platoon broke out laughing at their antics.

During morning formation Captain Fontaine filled in the men on what they observed during breakfast.

"I know all of you observed our little parade of aircraft this morning. We now have our own transport unit assigned to this regiment. Each aircraft comes with its own maintenance crew, who will occupy the new tents by the airstrip. We will begin training with their flight crews today. These are the planes that will take us into combat when the time comes. This is not a sign of anything imminent for us. It is merely the next step in preparation for our eventual move onto the continent. These aircraft are American as you could tell. But they are under orders of transport command, which is currently run by the British. The commanding General is William Evans. I know he may be a British General, but we will cooperate with him fully. You will get your chance this morning. We will be making a jump at ten hundred hours with full combat gear. So go get ready. The trucks should be here shortly to pick us up. Good jumping men."

The men started toward the tents to gather up their equipment. Harry intentionally bumped into Archie as they were walking. Grabbing Archie around the neck, Harry yelled out for everyone to hear, "Hey Arch, nothing like keeping it all in the family, General William Evans in charge. Soon to be General William Evans and Son, Royal Air Force at your disposal. So why didn't you tell us daddy was moving into the neighborhood. We could have planned one hell of a house warming for him and the Mrs."

"Hey come off it, Harry. I didn't know he was moving one of his flight groups up here. Honest I didn't." Archie pleaded rubbing his sore neck.

Lt. Winslow was walking directly behind Harry and Archie. Over hearing the conversation he had to smile. But business was business. As he had many things to accomplish before the men could jump, he avoided getting involved with their conversation. Nevertheless, he decided a good verbal ass chewing was in order, just to keep them on their toes.

"Alright let's knock off the bullshit. Get your sorry asses in gear. You heard the Captain; we have a jump to prepare for. I don't want to be the only company that keeps the general waiting. So get moving."

The two men took off like a rocket when they heard the Lieutenants voice. As they entered their tents, Lt. Winslow couldn't help but laugh.

About ten minutes later trucks began to arrive outside company headquarters. Carrying packs weighing nearly a hundred pounds, the men assembled in the loading zone, beginning the arduous task of climbing aboard the trucks.

Steve and Harry checked over their squads. They made sure each man carried the equipment they were assigned. Learning from all their exercises, the men became very proficient preparing for a jump. Their packs were set up exactly as they should be for a combat operation. Their load consisted of a primary and reserve parachute, their individual combat weapon, plus a forty-five automatic pistol, with ammunition for each weapon. They also carried a canteen, first aid kit, a three day supply of rations, gas mask, compass, pocket knife, smoke grenades, flash light, mess kit, entrenching tool, change of clothing with several pairs of dry socks, candy bars, cigarettes and any other small items they felt necessary for long periods of time in combat. Since part of their mission would be to jump behind enemy lines where resupply could take days, they also carried half a dozen hand grenades, an anti-tank mine and a gammon bomb made from plastic explosives. Some men carried small saws and TNT for dropping power poles or other demolition work. Some men carried additional mortar rounds for their mortar crew.

On board the trucks, everyone found it extremely difficult to move around. Luckily the trip to the airfield lasted only about five minutes.

Arriving at the airfield, Steve was impressed with the amount of activity taking place. Transport planes continually took off, while others were returning. Maintenance crews worked diligently on their respective aircraft, making sure everything was up to par. Fueling crews topped off large thirsty tanks.

All around the field trucks and Jeeps darted back and forth, loaded with cargo and men. Charlie Company was definitely not the only company jumping today. There were hundreds of paratroopers loaded with the same equipment, waiting to board their planes. It was all very impressive. Steve was positive this was a rehearsal for something bigger coming their way in the near future. Every where you looked, officers with clip boards took notes, while others poured over diagrams encased in plastic.

Charlie Company made their way toward their transports planes, already warming their engines. Swiftly the men took their places on the canvas seats inside the aircraft, once they were shoved through the door.

Lt. Winslow and Capt. Fontaine kept a close eye on the boarding process of each aircraft. When ever they observed a problem, it was immediately addressed. Notations were then written down on a clip board by a company clerk. After Charlie Company was loaded, the two officers climbed into the last transport with fourth platoon.

As soon as the aircraft were secured, the pilots taxied toward the runway. Receiving a signal to take off, each pilot threw the throttles wide open, sending their planes down the runway.

When they were airborne, Archie turned toward Steve studying the intense look gripping his face.

"I was sorry to hear about Marjory. I couldn't believe the news when Harry told us. You must feel terrible."

Steve really did not feel like talking about Marjory at this point in time. However, he understood Archie was being completely sympathetic.

Drawing in a deep breath Steve responded, "Thanks Arch. I still can't believe it my self. I just can't accept it for some reason; it just doesn't make any sense no matter how I look at it."

Archie looked about the plane for a few seconds. Then back toward Steve. "Just hang in there Stevie boy. Don't let this get you down so you start making foolish mistakes. The squad depends on your leadership."

"No Archie, that won't happen. She's alive in my memories and always will be. I mean she was a good friend. There was nothing more to it. She could never have taken Karen's place. She was just some one very special. You know, Arch we're going to win this damn war for her, for all the innocent people that have suffered for so long because of this insanity." Steve explained trying to reassure Archie.

Inside Steve knew she was more then a friend. He felt guilty for the feelings he had for her. Nothing like this was supposed to happen, ever. He loved Karen with all his heart, and wanted no one but her. He felt miserable, almost ashamed that he had let himself get so involved with another woman. He wondered if Karen could ever understand if he told her the entire story.

"What a mess." Steve said softly.

"What was that, Stevie?" Archie asked. "I didn't hear you with all this damn noise."

"Nothing Archie nothing at all, just thinking out loud," Steve replied adjusting the straps to his helmet.

"O.K. Stevie boy talk it all out, get your head back in the game. We got a mission to go on. Archie replied elbowing Steve in the side.

That was about enough. Archie's attitude was now upsetting him. He wanted to tell Archie to shut up. There was enough to be concerned about without Archie playing psychiatrist with him.

The plane continued on for about another twenty minutes before they reached their jump zone. The jump master stood up calling out, "Stand up. Hook up."

Instantly every man stood up, hooking their static lines to the cable before checking the man in front of them as they had been trained.

Like robots thought Steve. Like a bunch of robots. However robots don't bleed and die. They don't leave families behind like some of these guys are going to do some day.

Steve stood motionless wishing the jump were over. He wished he had never joined the Army. Suddenly life's meaning was all mixed up. He had never felt this way before. Back in Glendale everything made sense. Every aspect of life had a reason. It was all so easy. Graduate from high

School, marry Karen, buy a farm, have kids, then live happily ever after. This damn war had turned everything upside down. Nothing made sense anymore. He wondered if he would ever get his emotions back where they belonged. What if he couldn't? What if his state of mind got himself or one of his men killed. Maybe he should give up his job as squad leader. That would take a lot of pressure off of him. Right now Steve felt trapped, closed in. He wanted off that plane. He needed fresh air fast. Steve's breathing was off the charts. His head felt like it was spinning, he actually felt dizzy. Sweat poured down his face. What the hell was happening to him?

The green light went on above the door. Harry led second squad out the door as the jump master began yelling "Go, Go, Go."

The line in front of Steve thinned as each man exited the plane. When Steve arrived at the door, he threw himself out with all his might. First squad followed right behind him.

Steve gulped in fresh air as he hung below his swaying canopy. The cool air not only dried the sweat from his face, it made his head quit hurting. As the dizziness disappeared, he began to focus. Steve felt amazed. He had been so agitated when he left the plane, he didn't remember his chute snapping open.

Although his head was back in the game, his hands still shook as he reached up for his risers, looking down he picked out a prime place to land. As he angled for that position, Steve thought maybe he should even quit the paratroopers.

What good would he be with this state of mind?

Seconds later, his feet contacted the ground with a perfect landing. After dropping his chute, he rounded up his squad. They walked to the assembly point about a half mile away. Capt. Fontaine was already there writing in a notebook. Once Charlie Company was assembled, he placed the book into his pack.

"Men we have completed a lot of jumps and you have done well. But don't let this fool you for a minute. Things will be totally different when we jump into combat. Many of you may die as soon as you hit the ground. It won't be simple. Keep that in mind today and always. Hit the ground, be ready to fight. Everything will be against you. The enemy will be ruthless." The Captain explained studying the faces of his men.

The Captain barely finished speaking as trucks arrived to transport them back to camp. The balance of the day was spent packing chutes and cleaning weapons. As they worked, each man began wondering when they would be called upon to make their first combat jump.

Capt. Fontaine continued working their tails off day and night. He attempted to give them every possible opportunity to stay alive, when they made their first jump. The regiment was becoming a tightly wound spring, ready to be unleashed against the enemy. There seemed to be more American's in London than English residents these days. Every place offering any type of entertainment was over crowded and extremely loud. Although the British people understood why American troops were there, clashes broke out between them. It was inevitable with rationing and over crowding. But as each new day dawned, the business of war took center stage. As the month of May drew to a close, every man knew something big was up. Something huge was about to happen. No mater how Supreme Allied Headquarters attempted to down play scuttlebutt, rumors of a second front starting soon flowed like water.

Many infantry units around Newbury began to pack up. One by one they disappeared from their camps. Vehicles that were stored in massive parking lots around England began disappearing. Large convoys clogged narrow British roads night after night. Every road leading toward the coast were jammed with convoys stretching for miles. Trains no longer made as many passenger runs to

London. Now locomotives pulled flat cars loaded with tanks, artillery, bulldozers and bridging equipment.

Passes into towns now became extinct. Guards were doubled on the huge bases containing airborne soldiers. The army did its best supplying them with movies, and other forms of entertainment at night to help pass the time.

Each airborne soldier was supplied with his newest piece of equipment. A simple child's toy called a cricket. When the metal tab on the back was pushed inward it made a clicking sound.

They were to be used for identifying friend from foe in the dark of night. One click of the toy was to be answered by two for proper identification.

The pace of activity intensified as June first rolled around. Many of the men placed bets on the jump off date for the invasion.

Every day that past, Steve began to find a sense of peace over Marjory's death. Although he still wondered, if admitting his love for Karen had anything to do with her despondence. It was possible he may ponder that question the rest of his life. He was sure of one thing. Karen was the only woman he had ever loved, and she always would be the only recipient of his affections. Steve knew he dared not write Karen about the incident. But someday, he would have to talk to her about it when the time was right.

"Steve was sitting on his bunk writing a letter when Archie flew through the door. "Well buddy boy do you want to place any bets on invasion date or drop date? The pot is growing huge. Every one is getting in on it."

"Knock it off with the bets will you, Arch. This is stupid because if you're right, you may be moving out before you collect your winnings.

And, if you plan on waiting until we get back. Well, hell, who knows if any of us will ever get back?" Harry explained in a disgusted tone of voice.

"Thanks for the information Harry, but I was asking Steve if you don't recall." Archie snapped back.

Steve turned to look at Archie. "Harry's right you know. That betting thing is kind of stupid. No I don't want to bet Archie, not on something like this. Tell me Archie, when do you think we're going?"

"That's easy, Stevie boy. June 5th." Archie replied as he began walking toward his bunk.

"Why the fifth," Harry had to ask.

"Simple. The fifth is a Monday. I figure the brass will want to start the week off with a bang." Archie replied with a big smile.

"That's it! You base your wager on some dumb idea like that? Man, how did you ever get to hang around with guys like us? We are way to smart for you Arch." Harry replied tossing a magazine in Archie's direction.

Steve thought for a moment about Archie's idea. "You know, Harry that may not sound so dumb at all. It just about adds up and makes some sense. And if Archie is starting to make sense, then we're in a real world of hurt, and I'm worried."

Everyone in the ten laughed as Steve lay down, placed his hands over his belly, and began moaning as if in pain.

"Well go ahead and laugh. But I'm telling you we go Monday. Let's see who laughs then," Archie said angrily throwing the ragged magazine back toward Harry.

Sunday June 4th was a very wet day. It rained on and off, with gusty winds nearly tearing the canvas off several tents. But out in the English Channel things were far worse. Gale warnings were up for the beach areas around Normandy, where the invasion was to hurtle its might against fortified German positions. The Supreme Allied Command, planned to send airborne units in during the dark of night, followed by the full invasion at the crack of dawn on Monday. Planners kept a close eye on the weather, knowing they would have to make a decision before any planes were in the air.

Around eight o'clock Sunday evening plans for the invasion were still on. Paratroopers were instructed to gather their equipment and prepare for their first combat jump.

Archie was whistling up a tune as he packed his gear. "I told you the fifth. But no one listens to Archie. Yeah we go on the fifth. I'm telling you guys, you heard it from me first. Yes sir, Archie knows the score alright."

"Oh be quiet, Arch! We all know what you said. Now knock it off and get ready." Steve demanded, peering out the door into the dark sky, as rain came down is sheets. "I hope the weather is better over the channel. Otherwise, this will be one spooky jump tonight."

Lt. Winslow walked into the tent stepping past Steve. "Gentlemen listen up. Remember to blacken your face and hands before we go. Also double and triple check each other, to ensure we have all the equipment we are supposed to have.

Let's not leave anything to chance tonight." He took one more look around the tent before moving on down the line, giving the same talk to everyone in Charlie Company.

At ten o'clock, word came for the paratroopers to board the trucks. The jump was on. They were now just hours away from war. Men strained under their heavy loads, as they trudged through thick, sucking mud, toward their waiting convoy.

When every man was aboard, and all their extra equipment was loaded, the lead escort vehicle pulled out heading toward the airstrip.

At assembly points beside the airstrip, C-47 Dakotas were being readied for flight. Nothing could be taken for granted now. Every plane would be holding paratroopers with a designated job that must be fulfilled, if the invasion were to be a success. It was imperative each plane arrived at their prescribed drop zone on time.

Steve assembled first squad aside of Harry's second squad. After exchanging a few words, Harry led the men toward the transport Lt. Winslow assigned them.

A Jeep with flashing lights barreled down the runway at a high rate of speed. The driver skidded to a stop near Capt. Fontaine's Jeep. A lieutenant jumped out running over to the Captain. It was clear to Steve; something had changed in the plans. After exchanging a few more words, the Lieutenant jumped back into his Jeep signaling the driver to head out. The driver drove off down the line toward the next assembly points.

Captain Fontaine spoke quickly with Lt. Winslow, directing him toward transports on their left.

The Captain walked up to Steve. "It's off, Corporal. We aren't going anywhere tonight. Get your men back on the trucks."

"Yes, sir," Steve responded saluting his commander.

Returning to their quarters, the area was awash in mud. Rain continued pouring down, as they labored to unload all the equipment they had packed about two hours earlier.

Lt. Winslow walked into first squad's tent, taking a look around at the men. He then looked down toward the muddy mess on the floor. He could not help but smile. "What a way to get you guys finally to take a shower," everyone in the squad busted out laughing. "Finish getting your gear cleaned, and then get yourselves some sleep. We'll see what tomorrow brings." Placing his helmet back on his head, he walked back out into the pouring rain.

"I can't believe this. I can't believe this is happening to me." Archie yelled as he continued removing his wet gear. "I had it all sewed up. I just went down the tubes on this damn bet. We were so close, so damn close. I think I'll write a letter to Roosevelt himself about this. What a damn shame."

The men laughed and harassed Archie, not giving him one ounce of sympathy.

Steve threw a wet glove at Archie. "Well I think you'll survive, Arch. Maybe a little less rich, but you will survive."

"Oh yeah, you're so damn comforting, sir squad leader. Ever think of becoming a psychologist?" Archie responded throwing the wet glove back at Steve. "Yup it's only money, and you can't take it with you anyway, right Corporal?" Archie added angrily. "Yeah that's right Archie. You can't take it with you no matter how hard you try." Steve explained wishing the conversation would end. After thinking about what he had just said to Archie, he was a little uncomfortable. He thought back to the day in training, when Archie made the comment referring to his own death before a jump. A strange sensation came over Steve, as he observed Archie stowing his gear. No matter how hard he tried, during the night he could not shake the feeling he had about Archie. About four in the morning Steve awoke shaking, soaked with sweat. Fear seemed to grip every part of his body. Today is the day. Today is the day kept rolling over and over in his mind. Today is the day we get to meet the best of the German Wehrmacht. Steve looked over toward Archie's bunk. He was sound asleep.

That strange sensation came over him again, as he observed Archie. If only there was a way to keep him here, and not let him jump. That was wishful thinking, but totally impossible. Steve knew in his heart, Archie would be dead by this time tomorrow. He tried hard to shake the feeling but could not, no matter how hard he struggled with it. Now, he felt sick with fear, wishing he were any where in the world but here.

The rain stopped around six o'clock. Sounds of movement could be heard outside the tent. Steve rose from his bunk dressing quickly. There were several officers walking through the rows of tents, talking about trucks and convoys. There were sounds of aircraft engines warming up coming from the airfield. Fighters, Steve supposed, preparing for morning patrol. He stared up at the sky as dawn crept over the rain soaked camp. He let his mind drift back to Glendale. It seemed like an eternity since he boarded that bus taking him off to the Army. Once again he felt home sick, wanting to see Karen in the worst way.

He wondered if they would ever marry, if he would ever see her again. Suddenly he was distracted as two Military Police Officers approached the tent.

Steve smiled at the two men walking patrol. One of them stopped for a moment. "Good luck, Mack. Give those damn krauts a good kick in the ass. Let them know Uncle Sam is here."

"Thanks. We will. You can count on it." Steve responded.

The men walked off continuing their patrol of the cantonment area. Steve went back to thinking about Karen. He wondered what she would do if he never returned. It was obvious, eventually she would move on with her life. What else could she do? Certainly she would not spend the rest of her life pining over him. All though he had no control over that matter, it bothered him greatly.

For a moment he thought about all the plans they made before he left. But that was the future if he made it home. Right now he wanted to go home and see Karen. He was tired of war, tired of England, tired of preparing for combat and angry with everything that kept him here. A deep anxiety came over him as he looked toward the bright morning sky. So many thoughts ran through his head, Wade's death the plane crash during jump school, Archie's continual comments regarding death, the fighting still to come and its uncertainty. Life was not supposed to be this way. Glendale seemed like a distant dream, almost a cruel dream at times. Everything had order, and everything that happened was explicable. Now there was Normandy. It was hard to believe a section of France he had never heard of before, would decide his destiny, maybe even his vary life. The only thing certain to Steve right now, was that many good men were going to die, fighting to liberate this place called Normandy.

He hoped all the angles were worked out, allowing them at least a slim chance to not only win the battle, but survive it.

He stepped out of the tent, walking a short distance away. He looked up into the morning sky as he prayed. "Oh God I don't want to die today. Please give me the strength to do my job to the best of my ability. Let me lead my squad as bravely as possible. Please watch over us. Give us the strength in battle to defeat the enemy. Please bring as many of us home alive as possible. I know that is a tall request, Lord. I know right now you're hearing from a lot of men. Do your best for all of us."

A familiar voice made Steve turn suddenly. It was the voice of Father O'Healy, the Catholic Priest assigned to the camp.

"I'm sorry sir; I didn't hear what you were saying." Steve apologized.

"I asked if you were alright. You were standing there looking just a bit lost. Is everything alright?" The Padre inquired.

"Actually no I'm not alright, Father. I'm scared. I'm so scared and I don't know what to do about it. I lead a squad of men. I don't know if I'm up to leading them into combat. I might get them all killed. I was just standing here praying. Father, I don't even know if I was praying the right thing." Steve responded walking nearer the priest.

Father O'Healy chuckled a bit. "Well I think God can figure out what you wanted to say. I'm sure he has heard this type of prayer you were saying many times in the past. War is a strange thing, son. All you can do is what you were trained to do. Leave everything else for God to figure out.

Steve nodded his head agreeing with what Father O'Healy told him. He looked down at the muddy ground for a second. "I have never known fear like this, Father. There is a guy in my squad that has talked of death on several occasions. And a friend of mine was killed in Italy and…." Father O'Healy stopped Steve in midsentence. "There is much to be scared of, Corporal. I won't lie to you about that. But don't let fear cripple you. Men will depend on you for direction that could decide the outcome of a battle. Pray for guidance, be strong. But also remember, each man's fate in battle will be decided by some one more powerful then any man that has planned this war. Yes Corporal, some will die. Perhaps even you or me. Each man on that beach will need a friend, a comrade, and a good leader. Try to do your best, Corporal. That is all any of us can do. It is never easy to tell someone this. But today before you join the battle make peace with your God.

Then you will have nothing to fear."

Steve took in a long breath of the damp morning air. "I understand Father, but I kind of left home after having a long argument with God. In fact, I even yelled at him. Maybe he doesn't want to hear from me anymore."

Father O'Healy laughed. Corporal, God has been yelled at many times. He knows our weaknesses and out human frailties. Remember though, he created us, and walked among us. He always knows what's in out hearts, Son."

Steve nodded his head again. "Thanks for the talk. It has helped a lot."

"Well I needed to go for a walk myself this morning. I know today I will need to minister to many young men, Some Catholic, some Methodist, maybe a Jewish boy, and others that maybe don't even believe in our God. Some may be dying; others will be injured for life, men with lost arms and legs, some that will have lost their way and despaired. I pray that I can find the words for them all. Some will have died alone, not knowing the comfort of God. Yes, Corporal, I too carry a heavy load into battle today, very much similar to the one that will be strapped to your back. So when you pray today. Please say a prayer for me too, that I may do God's work and comfort all those in need of it" Father O'Healy explained smiling at Steve.

The two military police men came walking back from the far end of the compound. "Good morning Padre. Out for your morning walk?" The same M.P. that had spoken with Steve earlier called out.

"Yes, Sergeant, The tent was closing in on me. Some fresh air sounded very good." The smiling chaplain called back.

The sound of morning reveille echoed through the camp, as the company bugler blew out those long familiar notes.

Steve turned toward the tent then stopped. "Thank you Father. This talk really did help."

Father O'Healy stepped up to Steve, making the sign of the cross on his forehead. "May God be with you today and guide you on your journey into war, bless you my son."

"Thank you Father and May God bless you in your work today." Steve responded.

Both men turned, walking off in different directions.

The men in first squad were getting ready for morning formation as Steve walked up to the tent.

"Where the hell have you been, Steve?" Harry inquired walking over from Second squad tent.

"Just out for a walk, I needed some air." Steve responded, watching his squad exit the tent, as they ran over to the assembly area near the Company HQ tent.

Lt. Winslow held morning formation, just as he had every other morning since arriving in England. However, today he spoke with a sense of urgency. "Men yesterday we had a dry run.

Things went well in most cases. We knew right from the start the weather did not look good, and the operation could be scrubbed. But today our weather is improving for the most part. We need to stay close by the tents. Be ready to go at a moments notice. If I were a betting man, I would say today is the day. I don't know what the weather is like in France, or over the channel only the top brass does.

But if this is any indication, things are looking up. After chow, assemble your gear and stand by."

Word quickly worked its way down the chain of command, that General Eisenhower made the decision to go. There would be a short break in the bad weather, giving allied forces enough time to launch their invasion. Every drop zone could expect marginal visibility, which was considered acceptable by the planners. For sure, the invasion was on for June the 6th 1944. That meant every airborne unit would jump tonight. Now, all the months of planning and practice would be put to the test. The airfield was busy, as the large C-47 transports were once again rolled into their staging areas. Another full inspection of each aircraft was conducted, as fueling crews once again topped off every fuel tank.

Gliders were assembled on the runways behind their tow aircraft. Jeeps, light artillery, medical equipment, extra ammunition and food were crammed into the gliders, as officers checked off each item. Every piece of equipment was essential for sustained combat behind enemy lines.

The day warmed slightly, as the sun broke through heavy clouds drifting off toward the northeast.

Each platoon spent time pouring over their maps, reeducating themselves with their missions.

Every unit had a separate, but no less important task they were required to perform if time permitted.

All the missions were interwoven into a larger plan, known only to planners of the Allied Expeditionary Force.

A hearty meal was served to the airborne soldiers around one o'clock. Some of the men cracked jokes about being served their last meal, before being sent off to their executions. But for the most part, men were quiet, contemplating what was to come. Around four o'clock Capt. Fontaine called Charlie Company together giving them a small pep talk. The men were mostly in good spirits, appearing to be ready for what ever awaited them

Steve finished writing home around six o'clock. Dropping his letters into the mail box, he was confident everything that needed to be said was taken care of. He felt comfortable about everything that had happened while they were in England. He loved Karen pure and simple.

Everything seemed to be as it should be, or at least as best it ever could be prior to going into combat. No one could be certain as to how the invasion might end. It was like a bomb being dropped from a plane. Everyone knew it was there. It just hadn't hit the ground yet. If they were thrown back into the channel, thousands of men would die.

Such a crushing defeat would leave America's two airborne divisions, along with two British and one Canadian division trapped behind enemy lines, with no way out. They would be hunted down and massacred by overwhelming Wehrmacht forces. It would be a blood bath of epic proportions. That was a scenario Steve did not want to think about.

It was as if the entire world was holding its combined breath.

Harry strolled up to Steve, shoving several letters into the packed mail box. "Well, Steve did you write that you loved them all and hope to see them again?"

Steve took a deep breath looking at his best friend. "Well not in those exact word. But, yeah

I guess I covered the same message. Say have you seen Archie?" Steve inquired looking around the compound.

"Yeah, about a half hour ago, I saw him drop a couple letters in the box as I was coming from the orderly room. He and Mike Anderson from fourth squad walked off down the road. I didn't see where they were headed, anything happening, Steve?" Harry inquired.

"No, I didn't see him most of the day. I was just wondering what he was up to. Let's go back to the tent. There are a few things I need to take care of yet." Steve replied giving Harry a good shove.

"Save it for the krauts, Kenrude." Harry responded returning the shove.

There was a lot of chatter going on in the tents and around the company area.

Steve thought it strange all the men were so boisterous and full of energy. Maybe it was their way of handling stress. Maybe it was a good thing as morale appeared high. Most of the men appeared to be rather calm, despite what they knew was waiting for them later tonight.

Steve just wanted to talk through his thoughts these last hours of peace with Harry. The two of them were always able to work well together. Harry always seemed to know the right thing to say. He was the best friend to have around at a time like this.

Archie arrived back in the tent about five. He appeared to be acting normal, not telling anyone what he had been up to all day. Steve was glad to see him.

Trucks started lining up on the road around eight o'clock, for the drive to the airstrip later that evening.

Small charcoal fires were lit, so men could use soot to blacken their faces and hands before their jump. Once again Jeeps and trucks maneuvered about, as officers called out orders as to where they wanted them parked. There were groups of officers holding last minute meetings, going over maps, and details just one more time. No one wanted to make a mistake.

Steve looked around at the activity, wondering how anything this big could all come together, with out any serious over sights or problems.

What appeared to be mass confusion a few hours earlier, suddenly came together around ten o'clock. As the night before, individual units were called together for their final briefings.

Capt. Fontaine called Charlie Company into a gathering by one of the waiting trucks.

"Alright men listen up." He looked over a note book for several seconds then continued.

Unfortunately the krauts have a few surprises lined up for us. They have damned up some rivers and streams behind the beach head, flooding some low lands. It also appears they have set more posts in the ground. From recon photos, it looks like the posts are systematically connected by wires. Some of the wires appear to have mines hooked to them. If you get tangled up in these wires when you land, be cautious.

Some of these posts are in areas where gliders are scheduled to land. They could tear the hell out of the gliders.

This is not going to be a picnic by any stretch of the imagination. Get down, get organized, head to your objectives, and kill as many German as possible. If we give them a chance to get organized, they will capitalize on it. If that happens, pure and simple the game is over for us. I wish each and every one of you the best luck possible. You all know your missions. Try to accomplish them best you can."

Capt. Fontaine looked over his assembled company one last time. He knew very well the next time he would call them together, many of the bright happy faces he came to love would be missing. Others would be seriously wounded and some would never be heard from again.

Capt. Fontaine moved through the company shaking hands with each of his beloved men.

The order was finally given for Charlie Company to load up on their assigned trucks.

The anxious, the scared and the brave, all took their place in line to board the aircraft. There was no time for changing plans, or second-guessing weather. You were either ready mentally, or you were not. There could be no turning back now. It was all business now as Fortress Europe awaited them, on Hitler's term.

As always, every man needed assistance from ground crews, or the man behind them, to make the climb into the aircraft. As ground crews helped each man aboard, they wished them the best of luck.

Steve tried to get as comfortable as possible for the long ride. That was not an easy task with all the bulky equipment they were wearing. He watched the rest of his squad settle in. Some men sat with their eyes closed; some stared straight ahead showing little emotion, others appeared apprehensive, as their looks darted around the plane. For some reason, mental photos of Wade flashed through his head. Steve thought about his death in Italy. How sudden it was without warning. He figured that was the way death came to most men in war. Death was not a word that had ever seemed particularly familiar to Steve. Now it was becoming a routine conversation, it was almost considered a way of life. He wondered how many of his men would perish in the darkness over France, in the next couple hours. Would he even survive to see another sunrise?

Silently he prayed for himself, and the men he would lead into combat. He knew, many other men loaded in C-47s, and those flimsy gliders were all saying their own prayers right about now.

Steve was still praying as pilots turned over their big Pratt and Whitney engines. As always, they smoked and sputtered a few times before roaring to life. The aircraft vibrated, as their pilot ran the engines at a high rate of speed in order to bring them up to operating temperature. Through the small window across the aisle, Steve could see the familiar blue flames emerge from the huge exhaust ports on the side of the engines. On every training flight, he always found the flames roaring from the tubes to be somewhat fascinating. However tonight, they looked ghostly and forbidding.

The engines were now throttled back to a steady idle. Steve new the engines were now ready for take off. Just that quick, the plane shuddered as it began rolling forward across the grass parking area. As they reached the taxiway surface, the pilot began adding power to his engines.

This was it. They were on their way. Victory depended on the actions of each man in this plane. A line of transport planes stretched down the tarmac already, as their C-47 took up its position.

Steve took a look around his squad, with his eyes coming to stop on Archie. In the shadows of the dim red lights inside the fuselage, he could see Archie was very nervous and restless. Harry sat motionless, with his head slightly down. Probably praying, just like everyone else on this aircraft. Finally the plane moved forward turning onto the runway, as the aircraft in front roared down the asphalt. The engines roared to a crescendo for several seconds before the brake was released.

Steve's transport now sped down the dark runway, gaining speed before lifting off into the dark British sky. Looking up and down the plane he observed several men making the sign of the cross, while others just sat motionless.

Each pilot jockeyed his aircraft into a pre-planned position in the huge armada taking shape over central England. The formation made one more small turn toward the east before beginning its run to the French Coast.

After long arduous months of training, and non-stop preparations they were actually on their way to liberate Europe. Who would survive the night? How many would be alive when the sun came up in the morning? Would anyone on this aircraft ever come home again? Steve knew these were questions that could not be answered by anyone here tonight.

Glendale almost seemed like a dream. It was so far away, so far removed from what was happening here. Steve didn't feel like he even belonged to that world or those people any more. He had become a member of a new family. All his brothers sat around him prepared to die this night for their country.

Funny how his mother used to tell him, "Watch what you wish for, you just might get it."

He remembered how much he wanted join the army after Pearl Harbor. How he dreamed about quitting school so he could enlist. It would be such a grand adventure. Now here he was. All his dreams and wishes had come true, along with his Mother's dire warning. But this was no grand adventure. Shortly, as this aircraft approached the coast of Normandy, his men, his brothers were going to die. How could he have ever wished to be part of something like this?

On the ground in France, Steve knew there were men ready to repulse this attack. German men, the enemy, but still, just the same men like him, men with the same dreams for life, and fears of dying in combat. Steve felt both sides had been caught up in an unstoppable chain of events.

No one was able to stop this run away train. Some of them will die, some will also live. Both sides demand victory from their armies. But only one side would be victorious. Surely, Steve felt, the cause of the allied armies were just. They were going to Europe to free a suffering people.

God had to be on their side. He couldn't allow Germany to continue destroying a continent, a world.

Leaning his head back against the wall of the plane, Steve attempted to clear his mind for a few moments. The formation finally began crossing the English Channel. The coast of France, the German army, and a war their president vowed they would never get involved in, were just a few miles away.

CHAPTER 8

FRUSTRATIONS ON THE HOME FRONT

Thunder reverberated across the parched fields of central Minnesota, offering farmers a prospect of much needed rain. After a winter with extremely light snow, the scarcity of moisture continued through out spring into the summer of 1944. To many folks on the Great Plains, it was a fearful reminder of how the dust bowl days of the thirties began.

Alex Kenrude stood on the porch drinking a cup of coffee, as dark storm clouds rolled in from the west.

"Do you think we're going to get anything out of those clouds?" Nancy asked joining her husband on the porch.

"Honey, if I could answer that question we wouldn't be just poor dirt farmers." Alex responded placing an arm around his wife "Oh pooh! Who ever said we're poor dirt farmers? Alex Kenrude I ought to boot you in the butt for talking that way. You can be proud of what you have done with this place. We always have food on the table, feed for the live stock, crops to sell, and a little money in the bank. We're not rich, but we're comfortable. Don't you think?" She inquired looking up at her strong husband.

"I agree we have done alright. Things could always be better, but they could be worse. No, Honey I'm satisfied with our farm, our lives, and our great kids. We've done just fine." Alex responded as the first large drops of rain began to fall.

"Fantastic, just what we need." Nancy exclaimed as rain began to pour from the darkening sky. Can I get you more coffee before you head out to work?"

"No, I'm good." Alex replied setting his cup on a nearby table.

Is there something else bothering you, Alex," Nancy asked studying her husband's sunburned face.

Alex took in a deep breath before turning to face his wife. Yeah, I've been doing a lot of thinking lately. Steve and I had big plans for this place before he went off to the army. We knew the day would come when I would not be able to handle things any more. He figured by that time, he and Karen would be well settled, so it wouldn't be a problem for him to run things with me as a back up. But what if he doesn't return? Where the hell is he now? Those last few letters gave me a bad feeling. Hell, we don't even know if he's alive right now." "Don't you think things like that Mr. Kenrude, no, don't you ever think that. Our boy is some where doing what the army needs him to do. We may not know where he's at or what he's up to, but we need to keep faith he's alive.

We have to pray the Lord will bring him back to us. You know I keep waking up at night hearing him call out for me. Like when he was so sick, when he was three. I still can't believe my baby is off over there fighting this awful war." Nancy replied wiping a tear from her eyes.

Christine walked onto the porch attempting to place her hair in a ponytail. "I miss my big brother too you know. I wish he were here every day."

Nancy turned smiling at her daughter. "Need some help, Hon?" Christine nodded, handing her mother a blue bow.

"What time is Karen coming to pick you up?" Alex inquired as he slipped his well worn mud rubbers over his shoes.

"In about fifteen minutes. Mrs. Donnelly says there's a lot of work to do for the summer festival. But, it doesn't seem right to be doing things to have fun, when Steve and so many other boys are off fighting a war." Christine added looking toward her father.

"Well sweetheart, the money we raise will go to the Red Cross to help Steve and other GI's. So what you do helps out in a very special way. It's good we all try doing our part for our fighting men." Alex responded kissing the top of his daughters head.

He then kissed his wife, before opening the screen door and dashing through the rain toward the barn.

A few minute later Karen drove up to the house in her mother's car. "Good morning Mrs. Kenrude she called out through a half open window.

"Good morning to you." Nancy called back as she waved at her future daughter-in-law. "What time will you have Christine back home?"

"Probably around three, is that alright?" Karen called back.

Nancy nodded her head, as Christine threw the door open racing toward the car, attempting to avoid puddles.

As Karen turned the car around in the yard, Christine waved to her mother. Nancy smiled waving back.

Hearing noise in the kitchen, she walked back into the house. Mike was standing by the cupboard; eating cold oatmeal from the kettle she had left standing on the stove.

"Honey, do you want me to make you something warm? It's plenty chilly out there this morning." She inquired of her youngest son.

"No this is fine. I wasn't really hungry anyway." Mike responded setting the empty kettle in the sink. "I'm just glad today is the first day of summer vacation. I couldn't handle another day of old Mrs. Waldorf. She was driving me crazy." He added.

Nancy laughed at her son's comment. "Well Honey, I've known Abigail for nearly all my life. She's a wonderful teacher. She does mean well. Although I agree she is a bit odd at times. So what are your plans for this day?" She inquired.

Before answering her question, Mike walked onto the porch to watch it rain. Nancy followed him, curious as to why he didn't answer her.

"Mom, now that I completed my junior year, I want to enlist in the army. I want to go do my part for the country. You have to convince Dad to let me go." Mike stated firmly.

Nancy took a deep breath before responding. "Son, we've had this talk before. You know how your Dad and I feel about that. Neither of us is going to sign papers allowing you to go off to war until after you graduate. That's final. There'll be no more discussion about it."

"What about Dan Bradforth's parents? They signed for him?" Mike insisted.

"I'm sorry Honey, but Dan's parents were wrong in doing so. He's just a young boy like you. Neither of you have any business going off to fight a war. Your father needs you here on the farm. You know he's not been doing so well since the accident in the barn last fall. Besides, you can do more good here growing crops to feed out men, than shooting a gun. You'll finish high school and that's that. I don't want to hear one more word about this. Having one son fighting is bad enough. I'll not have two!" Nancy responded feeling as if her heart was going to pound right out of her chest.

"The news says we're going to open a second front any day now. We're going to need thousands more men once we get a shore. Steve will be there. You know he will, Mom." Mike continued.

"Stop, just stop, Nancy demanded. If they need more men, Mr. Roosevelt will figure out a way to take care of the problem. Sending boys into battle is not the answer, Michael. Please, let's drop this subject right now. Please I beg you. I love you very much, Son. I could not handle it if anything were to happen to you. Don't you understand that?" Nancy asked gently.

Mike spun around pushing open the screen door. He left the house running full speed toward the side door of the barn.

Frustrated and concerned over her son's insistency on joining the army, she sat down at the table. Her eyes caught the newspaper from the day before. She remembered a news story regarding the death of another Glendale boy killed in action. He had been killed on an island in the pacific with a very strange name. She reached for the paper searching to find the name of that island. Opening the front page, she hurled it to the floor. She didn't want to know the name of the island. What difference did it make anyway? Now there was another Gold Star mother. Another one of those dreaded gold stars hanging in a window of a house. The young man was dead, another family was suffering. It really didn't matter where he died. Slowly, she began counting how many had been killed from Glendale. She came up with eight names. What a shame these young men had to die. No matter what, she was determined her second son would not go to war if she could help it.

Slowly she drew in a deep breath. She could not believe how much alike her two sons had become. They were both tall and handsome. Physically they could pass for twins. But on the down side they both had the very same head strong, stubborn mentality that was very much a Kenrude trait.

Karen and Christine met several other young girls along with committee members at the church. Mrs. Rockfort was the chair for the festival. After everyone arrived, she walked toward the front of the church. "Alright ladies, I guess the outside work will not happen today. But there's plenty we can do inside. Group leaders grab some of the help and let's get it done."

Mrs. Rockfort took several women along with Karen and Christine on her way into the kitchen. "We need to get his place cleaned up and organized, for all the cooking we'll be doing this weekend. So start tidying up, move tables and racks where we need them, and don't forget to wash all the roasters. I'll be back and forth if anyone has any questions.

Karen and Christine began wiping down counter tops and tables. After a few minutes Mrs. Albertson walked over to Karen. "So what do you hear from your guy, any news?" Karen kept working on the shelves near the stove as she replied, "No nothing new lately. He doesn't say much about what's happening over there. I guess a lot of things are secret. His letters get pretty chopped up by the censors sometimes. In a way, I'm glad I don't know what's happening. I really don't want to hear what kind of danger he might be in."

"Oh, keep your chin up Honey" Mrs. Albertson said patting Karen on the back. "You know my son Albert is in the Marines. I do miss him so."

Karen turned smiling. "I heard he went into the Marines. He was always so much fun in school.

Where is he now?"

"Last we heard he was going on some troop ship to some God forsaken island, some where in the middle of the pacific to kick butt on the Japs." Mrs. Albertson responded slamming her hand down on top of a table. "I worry about Albert, but I know he can handle himself, especially against those little Japanese fellas."

She began laughing along with Mrs. Turner and several other women, who had entered the kitchen to get some coffee.

"Oh hell Olivia, that war in the Pacific should be over by now. I can't believe those little yellow guys can give our men such a tough time. You would think once they got a good look at our big

American boys, they would run head long back to Tojo in Japan and quit this damn war. After all,

I hear one of our men is equal to ten of those damn japs. Karen believe me, this entire war will be over by Christmas." Mrs. Turner exclaimed.

Karen looked intensely at the women for a moment. "Home in forty three. Wasn't that what we all said last year? And this war isn't much closer to being over than it was then."

Mrs. Turner took another sip of coffee, before looking around the room. Everyone had stopped working by now. They were all paying close attention to the conversation between her and Karen. "Sweetie don't get so upset, no one knows when this damndable war will be over. But they are right about one thing. Our boys are twice the men that our enemies are. After all, Honey they all wear those thick glasses and probably can't shoot straight either." All the women in the kitchen laughed agreeing with Mrs. Turner.

Christine threw her cleaning rag down. "I was just eleven when they attacked Pearl Harbor. It seems to me, they could see well enough to sail half way across the Pacific and find Hawaii. I may be young, but I read the newspapers and listen to the radio with my brother. I think we still have a long war ahead of us yet. Sadly, I think a lot of our boys are going to end up dying before this is all over. I don't think the Japs and the Germans are anything to laugh about. You might look at what they accomplished before we came into the war."

"Oh hush up, child." Mrs. Turner demanded. "Who are you to tell us what this world is about?

We went through world war one before the two of you were even born. Both of you are still wet behind the ears, and don't know anything.

And you Miss Donnelly, hell you don't even know what love is. You just think you are some sort of martyr. You know full well Steve is off gallivanting around England with all those cute little

British girls, since all their men are away doing all the fighting. Face it honey, he's having a great time while you sit here pining over him."

The room was quiet. Everyone looked toward Karen to see what she was going to say. "I'm sorry, but I don't agree with you. I know two things for sure. There's a second front coming soon that will require all our men. Secondly, Steve is a good man. I trust him. He wouldn't do that to me."

Mrs. Turner looked angrily at Karen. "Grow up, darling. Your Steve has probably had more girls over in England than you can count."

Karen began crying as Mrs. Turner laughed at her.

Removing her apron Karen threw it on the floor. She walked out the back door of the kitchen into the falling rain.

"Honey come back in here," Mrs. Albertson called out. "You'll catch your death out in that cold rain; don't let all this stupid talk get to you," she added glaring over at her friend Jean Turner.

Before any more could be said, Karen took off running down Walnut Street. The cold rain pelting against her face felt soothing, as she dodged pools of water collecting along the street. The more she tried to stop crying, the more she wept. After running for several more minutes, her heart was pounding, and her lungs burned as she gasped for air. Slowly she brought her pace down to a walk.

Her clothes were completely soaked. She shivered as a light breeze blew down the street. For a moment she stopped, looking back toward the church, but really did not want to go back there. Not sure where to go, she stood under a large oak tree. She was frightened at the prospect of never seeing Steve again. She missed him terribly. How would she ever go on if something happened to him? When they met for the first time in fifth grade, she knew he was the guy for her. There was something wonderful about him. Then she wondered. What if he went missing in action, and she never found out what happened to him? What if he died and was never found. "No, no, no."

She screamed, before running across the road toward the cemetery where her father was buried. Walking along the back row of stones, she decided to visit her father's grave. On the way there she passed several Veterans' stones.

Several read World War One, one read Spanish American War. Stopping by the newest grave, she brushed mud from the stone. It read, "William H. Garding, born August six eighteen ninety, died May first nineteen forty-four, Veteran World War One.

She remembered what a gentleman Mr. Garding had been, and what a charming person his wife Anna was. Continuing through the cemetery, Karen stopped at her Father's grave. Kneeling down, she pulled out a few long weeds that had grown around the stone.

"Hi Dad," Karen spoke softly choking back tears. "I sure miss our talks. Mom and I are doing alright for the most part." She looked up toward the sky allowing the gentle rain to fall on her face. After running her hand across the granite stone she stood up. "I have some one I need to talk to, Dad. But I'll be back. Bye for now." Karen explained as she kissed her hand, before placing it on top of the stone.

Leaving the cemetery she walked back toward the center of town. About a block from the church, she turned onto Second Avenue walking toward Anna Garding's house. For a moment she looked back toward the church grounds, giving thought to going back to get Christine and the car.

Instead, Karen continued walking down the avenue. Arriving at the Garding house, she walked up on the porch. A small light was evident in the living room. As she was about to knock, the door suddenly opened.

"Child, what on earth has happened to you? Come in and get out of the rain and cold." Anna Garding stated taking Karen by the arm, leading her into the warm living room.

The warmth of the house felt wonderful. Anna grabbed a blanket off a chair, gently placing it around Karen's shoulders.

"Let me get you a towel so you can dry off a little, Honey. You are so wet. "Anna said, walking briskly into the bathroom. Returning, she handed Karen a towel. As she began wiping her face and hair Karen walked over to the fire place, examining the neatly arranged photos. Picking up the Garding's wedding photo she smiled. "You were a very lovely couple. The two of you had a good life together. Any regrets?" Karen inquired.

"Oh dear no, our marriage was everything I dreamed about when I was a young girl. William was a very special man. I miss him very much. He has been gone just about a month now." Anna replied looking at the photo over Karen's shoulder.

"Yes I remember. Mother and I were at the funeral. Actually, I just visited your husband's grave a bit ago, when I went to see my father."

Placing the photo back on the mantel Karen turned toward Anna. "Did you know William during the war?"

"Oh my yes, that was such a tough time for me." Anna replied picking up a photo of her late husband in uniform. "This was taken just before the battle of the Meuse-Argonne in 1918. Two days latter he was wounded. He took some shrapnel in the leg and shoulder." Although not bad enough to get him sent home. Two weeks later he was back in action. Now let me think. We started seeing each other in nineteen sixteen. Back when Glendale celebrated what they called harvest days. It was so much fun."

Karen smiled looking at the slightly water damaged photo. How did you deal with him being off to war? I have such a hard time with Steven being gone."

"Yes it was terribly hard for me also. Wondering where Bill was. If he was alright, was he dead.

You know, we did not have the news and radio back then like we do today. Some times, we didn't hear about a battle for nearly two weeks after it was over. I always thought the war would never end. But like all wars it did. Bill came home a proud soldier. We married just shortly there after. He built this fabulous house for us." Anna stopped talking as she walked across the living room, removing a photo from the wall. "This is my favorite photo of Bill and me. It was taken at our daughters wedding back in 1938. That was such a grand day." After replacing the photo Anna turned toward Karen, "Memories child, all beautiful memories now. But Bill isn't really dead, you know. He lives on in my heart every day. So he'll never die as long as I'm here."

Karen took Anna by the hand squeezing it gently. "Thank you so much for sharing all that with me."

"Honey it's always special to have a visit from some one like you. But you are so wet. What are we going to do about that? And tell me, how did you end up out in the rain in the first place?"

Anna inquired.

Karen smiled rolling her eyes. "It is a long story. And I promise I will tell you about it. But not today, I think I should just head back over to the church, get the car, and go home to get dry clothes. I'll stop back Thursday after work to tell you the entire story. Talking with you has been nice. Thank you for the towel and blanket."

"Oh that was no problem, Karen. I look forward to seeing you Thursday. You know I'll be here for you any time."

Anna added as she turned toward the window. "Look the rain has stopped for now. This might be a good time to get your car."

Karen left the Garding house walking back toward the church. Carefully peering in the back door of the kitchen, she observed Christine working by her self near the ovens. "Christine!" Karen called out.

"Where have you been, what happened to you? You're soaked get in here." Christine demanded, seeing how wet Karen was. "Are you alright? I went looking for you but you were no where in sight. Then I came back in here and gave Mrs. Turner a good piece of my mind. After I was finished, every one left the kitchen. I'm sure mother will here about my language." Both girls laughed as they hugged one another.

"I'm fine, just real wet and cold. Come on, I have to go home and get changed. Let's get out of here. We can go to our place, make some hot coffee and talk about it."

Christine nodded grabbing her purse, then ducking out the back door with Karen.

During the first week of June, news from Europe was limited basically to Italy, as the allies closed in on Rome. There was little to be heard else where, due to news blackouts and security measures, because of the coming invasion. Around Glendale as in every other city in America, most conversations were about the latest war dispatches. There were always rumors and wild accounts of battles, some that were never even fought. However in the first week of June, rumors abounded furiously regarding a second front in Europe, but no one knew anything for sure. As always, Mike listened to the news intently. His parents knew he longed to join the fight. However, they longed to keep their youngest son safe at home.

Tuesday morning Mike accompanied Alex to the feed mill in Glendale. Alex Parked his truck near the loading dock. Opening his door, he looked over at Mike. "Are you alright son? You haven't said a word since we left home. Are you going inside with me?"

"Yeah, I'm fine, Dad. Guess I was just day dreaming a bit." Mike replied as he stepped out of the truck. Walking around the back of the truck, he caught up with his father. "How long will this take?" Mike inquired looking up the street.

"Well, son not just to long. But there are a few other things I could check on since we're here.

That would save me another trip back to town, and help save ration coupons this month. If you have something you want to do, I guess we could spare about an hour." Alex replied, examining a list he removed from his overalls.

"That would be great, Dad." Mike responded.

"Remember no more then an hour. We have a long list of things we need to get accomplished today. And your mother wants your help in the garden today for a while." He reminded his son.

Mike nodded in agreement. "Not a problem."

As Alex walked into the feed mill, Mike walked up Grove Street toward the center of town. In minutes he was standing in front of the Army Recruiting Station. The words his mother had spoken to him the other day, still rang loud and clear as he entered the Station. The small office was decorated with flags, patriotic posters, and Uncle Sam, pointing toward the door saying, "I want you."

The recruiting Sergeant was on the phone, as Mike picked up a brochure on Army enlistments. He smiled at Mike saying, "Be right with you, son. Take a look around."

Mike nervously smiled as he looked over several brochures.

Hanging up the phone, the sergeant scribbled a note on a yellow piece of paper. Standing up he held out his hand toward Mike. In a deep booming voice he introduced himself. "Staff Sergeant Lester's my name. Interested in signing up today, son?"

Mike shook hands with Sgt. Lester. With as much confidence as possible he replied, "My name is Mike. I guess I am just not sure yet. I'm still checking things out."

Sergeant Lester laughed. "Those navy guys down in the Court House haven't got you hooked yet, do they?"

"No I haven't been there. I was strictly thinking about the army." Mike responded even more nervously.

"How old are you, Mike? Sergeant Lester inquired studying Mike's young face.

"I guess old enough to know what I want to do with my life, and for my country." Mike responded, trying to look Sergeant Lester straight in the eye.

Walking back to his desk Sergeant Lester picked up his coffee cup. After taking a large swallow, he placed it back on his desk and sat down. "Why don't you come sit down so we can have a talk about things, I have some papers in the desk you might like to look at. But first we need to get something straight, Mike.

This is Glendale, Minnesota not Minneapolis. Every one knows every one's business in a town this size. So if you're trying to lie about your age, it just won't work. Not here. Not with me. Not here in Glendale. So Mike, what did you want to talk about?" Sergeant Lester inquired leaning back in his huge wooden desk chair.

Feeling somewhat deflated by the sergeants last comment, Mike hung his head. "I'm too young to enlist, sir. I really want to do my part for the war effort. My brother is in an airborne unit, and I'm afraid the war will be over before I get out of school."

Sergeant Lester leaned forward giving Mike a long hard look. "Come over here, have a seat, Mike."

Sitting down across from the sergeant Mike listened intently to what he had to say. "I appreciate your willingness to enlist, your patriotism and love of country. Its boys like you and your brother that are winning this war for us. I fought in North Africa and Sicily with hundreds of good men just like you. Hero's! Every damn one of them! I hope to hell this war is over before you get a chance to enlist. Mike there is nothing good about it. Believe me, there is no glory in war, no matter what the big newspaper reporters want to make you believe."

Mike was quiet for a moment before responding. "But, Sergeant I want to go so bad to fight along side my brother. But my parents won't sign for me. They insist I finish High School first. I know they want to protect me, but I can take care of myself. My brother, Steve learned enough to be a paratrooper. So can I."

Sergeant Lester could not help smiling at the young man in front of him, "Mike whether you believe me or not or even agree with me, your parents know what's best for you. Finishing high school is very important. To be honest, some day you'll thank your parents for being so responsible. Your brother is lucky to have you willing to risk your life, to keep him safe. But Mike, we'll need strong men like you to rebuild this world when the fighting ends. I think that will end up being a much tougher job than most people imagine. Son, don't be in such a hurry to grow up. Some of our boys will never get the chance you have right now. Some of them are not coming home ever again. They will never get the chance to love, raise a family, or enjoy what this country has to offer. You are a patriot for being here today offering your services, offering to put your life on the line during this time of war. Tell you what. After you've graduated, if you're still interested in the Army come see me, I'll work out a good program for you. The army will always need good men, Mike."

With that, Sergeant Lester stood up extending his hand.

After shaking hands Mike smiled slightly. "Thanks for talking with me. Sorry for taking so much of your time."

Sergeant Lester gave out one of his big belly laughs "Apology accepted Mike. You stop back in and talk to me any time you want. I'll always be willing to listen."

Mike walked back down Grove Street toward the feed mill, feeling good about his conversation with Sergeant Lester. Nevertheless, he was still somewhat upset. There appeared no easy way for him to enlist.

Approaching the truck, he observed his father walking from the hardware store with a small bag in his hand. Alex tossed the bag at Mike, "Here are the bolts you'll need to fix the plow when we get home."

Looking in the bag, Mike removed one bolt examining it for a moment. "Yup, I guess those are the one's we need alright."

"Did you take care of all your business while we were here? Alex inquired looking over his list one more time.

"Yeah I guess so. Guess I'm ready to go home, Dad. "Mike responded as he gazed back up Grove Street.

"Everything alright son, you look a bit down. So what's her name?" His father inquired, giving his son a light nudge.

"What's her name? Come on, Dad I wasn't seeing a girl." Mike replied climbing into the truck.

Alex laughed as he slid in behind the wheel. "I'm not so sure. I can think of only two things that will make a guy look forlorn like you do. It's either getting caught with your hand in the cookie jar, or a young lady. And frankly, I don't see any cookie jars around."

Mike smiled, "Well Dad, you wouldn't know her. She's kind of new to the area. Besides, I don't think she's my type anyway. A man has to know when to walk away I guess." Alex chuckled as he turned the truck around, heading out of the parking lot toward home.

Mike was quiet as they drove down the country road past Miller's pond. Usually this time of year the pond was full of water, and ringed with colorful wild flowers. But this year the pond was half empty. The flowers had dried in the harsh sun, as did most of the aquatic plants near the pond. Mike felt the same way. He felt empty and alone, as the entire world was turned upside down, leaving him standing on the outside looking in.

There just had to be away to make things work.

That evening after chores, Mike grabbed his fish pole, and walked down to the lake.

He had only been fishing about twenty minutes when he heard Christine say, “Catching anything or just hiding out?

Mike turned to see his sister leaning against a big oak tree about ten yards behind him.

“Checking up on me? Did mom send you after me? “He inquired.

“No, why should she? You’re grown up enough to walk down here by yourself. It seems you’ve grown up enough to learn how to alienate yourself from every body that cares about you too.

What’s going on Michael? Christen questioned as she pulled a small flower from the base of the tree.

Mike began pulling in his line. “You know some times fish like to follow the bait before they strike. Steve taught me that. He was always a better fisherman than I am.” He responded, trying to change the subject.

“Fine, Michael be that way. I know when I’m not wanted. Enjoy your self.” Christine replied indignantly as she turned to walk away.

Mike felt angry with himself for treating his sister that way. He knew she always looked up to her two big brothers.

“Christine, wait! Don’t go. Please!” He called out, as he stood up preparing to go after her.

After a few more steps Christine stopped. She turned around slowly holding the tiny flower up near her nose. They both stared at each other for a moment.

“Come sit with me.” Mike pleaded, placing his fishing pole down on the rocks.

Half smiling, Christine made her way over the lose rocks near the big boulder Mike was sitting on, at the edge of the water.

Sitting down she smiled at her brother. “You haven’t been yourself lately, Michael. Tell me what’s wrong.”

“Oh you know, Sis. I want to join the army but mom and dad won’t sign for me. That’s all. I just want to go join Steve.”

Christine nodded her head. “I pretty much figured as much. I over heard you talking with mom and dad one night before school let out. I know they won’t sign for you. But be honest. Do you think it’s a picnic for Steve?

Don’t you think he has plenty to be worried about? I’m sure he even gets scared at times, although he would never admit it. Mike, I don’t want you to get in the war right now either. I need a big brother to talk to and, well, help me with my homework."

They both laughed as she placed her head on Mike's shoulder. After some silence Christine slid off the rock, holding out her hand. "Come on let's walk home before it starts getting dark."

After picking up his fishing pole Mike helped his sister across the lose rocks.

"You do know I'm just as proud of you as I am Steven? I love you both, and don't want anything to happen to either of you." Christine informed Mike placing her arm around his waist.

"I know that, Sis. And I love you too, always have always will." Mike's responded, feeling good about spending time with his sister. She seemed to be growing up so fast. He took the little flower from Christine's hand, and placed it in her hair.

They both laughed. "Come on let's check on the new calves before we get to the house."

Christine requested, pulling her brother in the direction of their barn.

Mike felt his heart break, as he knew Christine would be crushed if he followed through with his plans. He really did not want to hurt his sweet vulnerable sister, but the war was not going to wait for him. Some day she would come to understand, and forgive him. Like it or not, he was willing to take that risk.

During the night, lightening streaked across the dark Minnesota sky, as claps of thunder shook the windows in Mike's room. Startled by the tremendously loud thunder, Mike sat up in bed gasping for air.

He walked over to the window peering out at the raging storm. His head felt like he was in a vacuum. "Steve" he thought. "Where are you big brother? What are you up to tonight?"

As he watched, another bolt of lightening struck the ground not to far away, the hair stood up on the back of his neck. He stared into the raging storm. "Steve, Steve, What the hell are you doing tonight? Oh dear God protect Steve where ever he is." He whispered

CHAPTER 9

A JOURNEY INTO WAR

Another storm brewing over the English Channel, was about to unleash its fury across the continent of Europe. This storm would be a lethal mixture of fire and steel. This storm would be an ultimate battle of good versus evil. This storm would test the vary souls of men brought together in a maelstrom of such violence, no man had ever witnessed before. Hundreds of C-47s flew through the dark night, carrying their cargos of men, munitions and fear.

Steve glared out the window across the aisle. He watched the eerie blue exhaust flames dance along side the massive engine. Over the wing, he could see an occasional glint of lightening from a thunder storm over the western coast of France. He watched a lightening bolt slice across the heavens and then fade away. He couldn't hear the thunder. All he could hear in the darkened fuselage was the steady pulse of those Pratt and Whitney's rotating in perfect synchronization.

He remembered how he and Mike would sit by the window watching lightening displays when they were youngsters. No matter how hard they tried to avoid it, they would always jump when the crashing thunder shook their home.

Steve smiled for a minute imaging them standing by the window, shivering in their pajamas.

Abruptly Steve was jolted back to reality, when the plane bounced harshly several times. He took in a deep breath then closed his eyes. He began to pray, but some how, the fear inside him made it entirely impossible to concentrate. He had known fear before, but nothing like this. Right now he would give anything to be back home where it was safe and warm, where everything made sense.

If only he could play with Mike and Christine one more time in the cool grass in the back yard, as their mother hung laundry on the clothes line. Those were the days. They seemed so long ago.

What happened? Why did the world grow up to be so terrible?

Steve thought about all the work that was needed around the farm during a summer. He felt bad about all the times he complained about it in the past. How he tried to get out of work, placing the entire load on his father. How selfish he had been. If only right now he could make things different. A host of thoughts whirled through his head. The amazing aromas coming from his mother's kitchen, her angelic singing voice would fill the yard as she worked in her garden.

His heart felt so heavy. He would give anything if he could hear her sing right now.

He opened his eyes as the C-47 bounced heavily again. Was it turbulence, or German anti-aircraft fire rocking their plane? He glared out the window across the aisle, looking for any trace of a tell tale sky burst. However, the sky appeared to be black. The only sound he could still hear was still the giant engines throbbing away outside. After a few seconds, He decided it must simply have been turbulence.

When was the flack going to start? When would men begin to die? If only he could sleep, but that wasn't about to happen. He was sure, not one man on his plane, or any other transport was sleeping tonight.

Minutes later, the first group of transports and gliders crossed the French Coast line. Instantly flack began to burst around the vulnerable planes. That one was high; the next one appeared to be low. When were they going to get the range?

The aircraft bounced around, as more deadly anti-aircraft rounds exploded in the night sky. He closed his eyes, trying to block out the sounds of airbursts, which now bracketed their plane. An image of Marjory came into his mind. She was dressed all in white, with small flowers in her hair. She was attempting to say something to him. "What? Speak louder! I can't hear you."

Steve wanted to scream. Now Wade Rollins came into focus, standing beside Marjory. He was wearing his dress uniform, looking very proper. He appeared to be holding out his hand to him.

The C-47 shook violently, tilting toward the left. Steve jumped in his seat, realizing he had actually drifted off to sleep for a moment. He brought his left arm up to his face to check his watch. It was just passed midnight. The jump was mere minutes away. They were to be on the ground by 0015hrs.

Unexpectedly, some one tapped him on the shoulder. He turned to the right facing Archie. "Almost time, Arch, we'll be on the ground in no time now." Archie nodded forcing a slight smile. "I'm scared Steve, real scared. I can't even pray. I don't want to die out there tonight."

Placing his hand on Archie's leg, Steve tried to give him a reassuring smile, "Me too, Archie. I've been trying to pray too, but can't come up with the words."

Archie looked down then away from Steve for a quick moment. Turning back toward his squad Leader he continued. "I'm going to die tonight, Steve. I know it. I've had dreams for months about this."

Steve looked intently at Archie for a second before replying. "Don't talk stupid, Archie. We've all had dreams. It's just normal at a time like this. You'll be fine, Arch. We'll all go home together, you me and Jensen."

"No, Steve, this is for real. Tell Diane I died a brave man. Because I will be brave, Steve! You got to tell her for me."

"Alright, Archie knock it off. Nothing is going to happen to you tonight. That kind of talk is just plain crazy. You stay by me when we get down. Do you hear me? You stay by me! Steve yelled above the roar that reverberated through the fuselage.

Archie nodded his head as tears rolled down his face, "Yeah, Steve. Okay."

Observing how desperate Archie was becoming, Steve attempted to reassure him over and over that everything would be alright. Regrettably, it didn't appear to help.

Steve quit speaking when a sharp explosion rocked their C-47. Through the window he could see the flaming wreckage of another C-47, tumbling down to the French coastlands.

Anti-aircraft batteries now had the range. Heavy flack filled the night sky. Large explosions pierced the dark sky, as several more transports blew apart before falling to earth.

Their plane bounced and shook nonstop, with every round that detonated around them. Shrapnel could be heard striking the sides and floor in rapid succession. Several small holes were torn in the thin skin of the plane, but so far no one had been injured.

He knew everyone on board was scared and nervous, just as he and Archie.

Thunderous flak along with brilliant explosions nearly illuminated the entire night sky. This was real. This is what war felt like. Another plane directly in front of their transport was torn apart. Steve wondered if any of the lumbering transports would arrive in tact over the drop zones. He closed his eyes thinking of all the men in those planes. They never had a chance. What a horrible death. What a terrible way to die. But was there any good way to die in war? He tried hard to pray they could get through the flak field, making it to their drop zone. He preferred taking his chances on the ground, rather than falling to earth in a ball of flaming wreckage.

By this time, the pilot ignored his orders to stay on his assigned flight path, regardless of the flak. He was twisting and turning violently, as if he could predict where the next flak burst was going to be. White tracer rounds from heavy German machine guns joined the artillery, in an attempt to bring down the invaders.

Tongues of flame lit up the sky outside each time a round exploded. The flak appeared to be getting heavier if that was possible. The noise inside the fuselage was deafening. A constant roar filled Steve's ears, as fear gripped his very soul.

Several men became sick and were vomiting. The smell in the tight confined area did not help matters one bit.

Archie grabbed Steve's arm leaning toward him. "Promise, Steve. Promise you'll tell Diane I died as a man."

Steve's mind was running wild as he answered Archie. "Yeah, Okay, I'll tell her, Arch. I'll tell her."

The next blast threw every one on Steve's side of the plane off their seats. Steve landed on the man across the aisle. "Sorry about that." He said, attempting to slide himself back onto his seat. The man sat silent not responding in anyway. Steve's hand felt sticky. He brought it up toward his face. It was covered in blood. He leaned forward to check on the man, but there was nothing he could do. A huge piece of shrapnel came through the roof of the aircraft, lodging in the second squad mans throat. Blood was running onto the floor, making it extremely slippery.

Steve wiped the blood onto his reserve chute cover, trying not to let Archie see what he was doing.

The plane jerked incredibly violently from the next explosion. A large hole appeared in the roof of the C-47 near the front of the aircraft. Wind whistled through the fuselage, as pieces of the aircrafts frame fell to the floor. A man near the cockpit, most likely from his squad screamed, he had been hit. It was impossible to recognize the man's voice amongst all the noise and chaos.

He began screaming for a medic. The only medic on board was seated near the rear of the plane. Instinctively the medic fought his way forward to assist the injured paratrooper.

Everyone on board was now active in their seats. They all become completely unnerved by the latest incident.

German anti-aircraft fire was taking a tremendous toll on the transports near by. There were more loud secondary explosions, alerting each man onboard to the death of another transport.

Every one knew that was another load of paratroopers falling to their deaths.

The jump master stood up by the door. Steve observed him attempting to talk with the cockpit through his headset without success.

He pulled the headset off, throwing it to the floor as he pulled the door open. The green light came on immediately. "Every one stand up, hook up. We're going now! You need to get off." The jump master continued yelling in a frantic voice.

Everyone stood up hooking their static lines to the cable, as they had done in all their training flights. Just as they began counting off, a shell exploded right outside the open door. The jump master spun around, screaming as blood gushed from his face. He twisted around once more, than disappeared out the door before anyone could grab him.

Russ Abbott from second squad was nearest the jump master before the explosion. He was the only man who had been able to make an attempt to save him. He watched the jump master fall for a second before looking up at the green light. He began to yell, "Go let's go."

Abbott dove out the door followed by the next men in line. As Steve moved toward the door, he noticed the floor was extremely slippery from blood and vomit. He reminded the men behind him to watch their step.

Steve was finally at the door. Flak shells were bursting all around as machine gun tracers flowed in winding ribbons from every possible direction. He grabbed the side of the door, pushing him self into the dangerous sky with out hesitation. His chute deployed instantly, as the static line came to its end. Routinely Steve rearranged his Thompson, so he could use it on the way down if necessary, before slipping the safety lever to the fire position. As he hung below his big white canopy, he felt alone and very much a target, as if in a carnival side show. "Yes sir step right up. Take three shots at the parachutist for just five cents." Normally Steve might have laughed at that thought, but not tonight.

Some where below him in all the chaos was Archie, the rest of his squad was coming down behind him. He thought about the severely wounded man on board that could not jump. Was he lucky or not? If the plane was able to turn around, they would have to fly through that flak field one more time before heading out over the channel. If the plane took to many more hits, they would end up going down God knows where. If they went down in the channel, the man was going to die for sure. As he thought earlier back in the plane, no matter how things go tonight, there will not be any good way to die.

Steve peered toward the west. The column of aircraft continued coming from England. Deadly flak and machine gun bullets continued climbing up to meet each new transport. He watched two more transports explode in mid air, spewing deadly shrapnel right toward the oncoming aircraft.

Wings, partial fuselages and bodies all tumbled to the earth, all those men that had trained so long and so hard, now gone in an instant. It made him feel like vomiting, but this was not the time to get sick, the ground was closing in fast.

Steve could see muzzle flashes from small arms fire directly below him. Paratroopers were already engaged in combat with the vaunted German Wehrmacht.

Several small fires burned around the landing zone. Nearing the ground, he could make out the silhouette of a C-47 tail section crumbled up against a tree. Small fires helped Steve gauge his relationship with the ground. But it also created strange shadows, making it hard to identify tree branches or wires. A whining sound zipped past his left ear. He knew some where in the darkness below, a German soldier was taking aim at him. He watched for another muzzle flash as he swung his Thompson out in front of him. A second shot flew past his right ear, but he still could not see any signs of the enemy soldier.

Steve came crashing down through tree branches landing with a thud. He lay perfectly still for several seconds, waiting to see if anyone appeared. When no one approached, he slid out of his harness, before diving for cover by the tree he just dropped through. He gazed carefully in every direction. He knew some one was out there, he could feel it. Cautiously he slid closer to the ground. A muzzle flash to his left told Steve exactly where the enemy was. For the first time he fired his machine gun in anger. He let go a short burst followed by a second. Two more shots rang out from the trees to his left, striking the tree directly above his head. Then a short burst of machine gun fire sprayed the area around him. Chips of bark hit him in the face. Now he knew there were two Germans to deal with. Sliding all the way to the ground

He crawled to the opposite side of the tree aiming his Thompson in the direction of the two Germans. As soon as another shot was fired, Steve's sprayed the area with every round left in his magazine. Hearing a man scream, he quickly slammed another magazine into his weapon. The second German let go a long blast from his machine gun. Above the din, Steve could hear two men arguing in German. One sounded frantic. That had to be the injured man.

Holding his breath, Steve waited to see what was going to happen next. Another blast from the machine gun kicked up dirt around the base of the tree. Then he could hear the sound of some one running. However, it appeared the man was leaving the area. The sound of his foot steps faded into the distance.

Steve's pulse raced, as sweat poured down over his forehead burning his eyes. Carefully he wiped the sweat from his eyes, as he gazed into the darkness. There didn't appear to be any movement from the dark shadowy trees. Placing his weapon down, Steve quickly released his emergency chute. After rearranging his pack, he took a good look around. He was still some what worried the second man would circle around, to come up on him from behind. He was going to have to act quickly, to avoid getting trapped or worse. He crawled back to the other side of the tree. Slowly standing up, he used the tree for cover. With every ounce of energy Steve could muster, he spun back around the tree, firing toward the enemy position. He ran head long toward them.

Crashing through the scrub brush, he looked for any sign of enemy activity. There was a body lying on the ground several feet in front of him. Cautiously walking toward the man, he did not see any one else in the area. The German soldier was definitely dead. One of his rounds hit him just below the left eye. Cautiously Steve knelt down looking at the soldiers insignias.

He had been a corporal in the Waffen SS. During all their training and instruction, there had never been any mention of SS troops operating in the area.

Feeling a bit more at ease, Steve knew it was time to find his men.

Small arms fire and explosions continued through out the landing zone. But it could not erase the drone of the C-47's overhead, dropping more paratroopers into the Norman invasion zone. He wondered how many men had been killed already, but even more, he wondered where the hell his company was, and the squad he was supposed to be leading. Using extreme caution Steve moved back to where he landed. Removing his compass, he laid it on the grass to get a good reading. After studying it a moment, he could figure out which would be the best way to go. He knew the invasion beaches would be to the west. But how far inland was he? He remembered the jump master saying they would have to go now. So were they off course? Did they jump in the wrong area? Where the hell was he? After taking a reading, Steve slid the compass back into his pocket. West toward the beaches just made the best sense.

Ever so slowly, he began moving from tree to tree in a westerly direction. A small battle erupted about a hundred yards in front of him. Keeping close to the trees, Steve cautiously approached the fire fight. It was impossible to know which men were Germans, and which men were Americans. He stepped behind a large tree with plenty of brush around the base for cover. In the dark, he had not been able to see what awaited him. He walked into a body dangling from a parachute caught up in the tree. Startled, Steve fell back onto the ground looking up at the motionless body. Slowly he stood up walking toward the paratrooper.

Placing his hand on the man's throat he checked for a pulse. Instead, he found the man's throat to be torn wide open, blood covering the entire body. Placing his Thompson against the tree he removed his bayonet from its scabbard. After cutting the parachute lines, he laid his dead comrade on the ground.

"My God in Heaven," Steve said in a loud voice. As the soldier fell forward, Steve got a glimpse of the face. It was Archie.

Archie's premonition came true. He was killed before making it to the ground. He not only died as a man, he died a hero in Steve's mind. Only a real man and a hero could jump from a plane into a sky filled with death.

Gently he laid Archie's body at the base of the tree, removing his watch and billfold so they could be returned to his family. He did not want Archie's belongings falling into the hands of some German souvenir hunters. Respectfully, he covered Archie's body with part of the parachute he cut with his knife. He placed his hand on Archie's head, "Bye old friend. Sleep well Arch. I'll contact Diane liked you asked me to do"

Steve wiped a tear from his eyes as he placed his bayonet back into its sheath.

The fire fight ended while he was dealing with Archie's remains. Picking up his weapon he turned his attention toward the area where the fire fight took place. But now it was deadly silent.

Taking a deep breath, he moved forward using the heavy foliage for cover. He felt confident there had to be other paratroopers close by. But he was wrong. He found cartridge cases and empty ammunition clips, but no bodies or paratroopers. He examined one of the ammunition clips. It was definitely German. Throwing the clip back to the ground, he continued moving west toward the beach, hoping to run into someone from his company, or any other Americans he could join up with.

He had not gone very far when he heard the distinctive clicking sound of the toy crickets they were all issued for identification. One click from a soldier was to be answered by two clicks. Steve reached into his pocket removing the cricket. Kneeling down on one knee with his Thompson at the ready he snapped his cricket.

Several moments passed with out any other nearby sound. Steve was breathing so hard and fast, he felt he would give himself away. Surely everyone west of Paris could hear his heart pounding. Then two clicks came from the dark, some where in front of him.

To be safe, Steve once again clicked his cricket, then waited. He wanted to get up and move, but was unsure of what was around him. The last thing he wanted was to be shot by some nervous paratrooper. It seemed as if hours passed since he had made his second click. Then slowly a figure emerged from the brush about fifteen yards in front of him. The shape of the helmet and pack assured Steve the man was an American. Nervously the soldier walked right up to Steve keeping his rifle pointed at Steve's chest.

Kenrude, is that you?" The soldier inquired.

Yeah, sure is. Willie is that you?" Steve asked relaxing a bit. "Mind pointing that thing in another direction?"

Steve asked pushing the barrel away from his chest.

"Sorry corporal. This place has given old Willie the jitters. Sure is good to see some one from our squad. Seen any one else, Steve?" "Yeah,

"Yeah, just one, I found Archie just a short ways back there. He didn't make it. Looks like shrapnel got him in the air. He was dead before he hit the ground." Steve responded shaking hands with Willie.

"What a way to visit France. You know Archie always talked about…" "Yeah, I know what Archie always talked about, Willie. You don't need to remind me." Steve responded rather sharply. "Now let's just drop it. We need to find more of our men and do what we came here to do."

Willie nodded in agreement, "Which way do you recommend we go, Corporal"

"Well I think our best bet is west toward the beach. I think the planes got all balled up with the flak, and we were dropped all over the damn place." Steve responded as he pointed off to his left.

The two men started forward moving slowly, using trees and brush for cover. They had gone about a hundred yards when they came upon a road. Steve stepped out from the brush along side the road, looking in both directions.

It appeared to be quiet, maybe too quiet. There was shooting going on in the distance. Steve stepped back off the road looking at Willie, "Seems quiet along here. Let's parallel the road to see where we come out." Willie did not say a word; he just nodded as he looked around. Steve began working his way along the wood line until it turned into a hedgerow. These earthen mounds covered with trees, brush and rocks existed through out Normandy. They would claim many American lives before the allies could break out of the coastal country.

"We'll stay behind the hedgerow and away from the road for now." Steve whispered to Willie.

They tucked in close to the thick brush of the hedgerow, making their way forward. A shot rang out from their left, narrowly missing both men. The round slammed into the hedgerow directly between them. Steve dove behind a small pile of brush for cover, as Willie just threw himself to the ground. Another shot rang out striking a tree inches from Steve's head.

This time he saw the muzzle flashes. Steve turned his machine gun in the direction of the sniper letting go a quick burst of fire. Willie rolled over while taking in a deep breath. He sprang to his feet, firing his M-1 in the same direction. Steve fired a second short burst from his Thompson as he rose to his feet. They ran toward a dry irrigation ditch that ran under the road. Willie fired several more rounds toward

the sniper, who was clearly after him now that Steve was out of sight.

Moving along the ditch Steve figured he should be able to come up behind the enemy sniper. Suddenly a second figure popped up in front of him. He heard the man yell, "Halt!" He dove for the ground firing as he dropped. The German began firing his sub machine just as Steve's rounds struck him in the chest. The soldier spun around, falling over backward with his finger still on the trigger, spraying fire all around the ditch. When Steve was positive the soldier was dead, he once again began moving down the trench. He stopped just a second to see what branch of the Wehrmacht he was from. The firing between

Willie and the sniper continued, as Steve worked his way down the ditch toward the enemy position. The sniper was lying in hole left by an uprooted tree. However, the tree was still lying along the road offering the sniper perfect cover and protection.

Steve crawled up to the tree, stopping to listen as firing had stopped. He could hear two men talk for a second, before one of them fired back toward Willie. Steve observed another man crawl out the side of the hole.

Their plan apparently was for the third man to crawl up closer, taking Willie out from the side. Steve knew he had at least three soldiers to deal with, and he would have to be quick about it. Crawling as close as he could to the hole, he unhooked a grenade from his pack. Carefully removing the pin, he prepared to throw the live grenade. Just as the snipers let go another round Steve tossed the grenade into the pit. A sharp blast shook the ground, followed by another larger explosion from inside the depression. Jumping up quickly, Steve let go a quick blast from his sub machine gun toward the soldier who was crawling from the pit. He became an easy target, as he had sprung to his feet when the grenade exploded. Both Steve and Willie had an excellent opportunity to take him out. Cautiously Steve worked his way into the pit, making sure everyone was dead. A small fire still burned on one of the back packs lying in the crater. It gave him enough light to look over the situation. There were four dead German soldiers lying in the pit torn up from the explosions. The second explosion Steve figured was caused by the large amount of spare ammunition they had, along with several boxes marked "minen."

Willie approached the tree at a run, partially bent over keeping his silhouette low.

"Kenrude you here," Willie called out softly.

"Over here Willie." Steve replied from the other side of the tree, "Looks like we got them all, five here and one in the trench."

"You killed one in the trench too?" Willie asked.

"Yeah, he got in my way, Willie. Only thing I could do with him." Steve responded nervously. "Nice work Kenrude. Lets get out of here before any of their buddies come looking for them." Willie suggested emphatically.

"Good idea, Willie. Let's go." Steve replied as he slipped a fresh magazine into his weapon.

The two men followed the irrigation ditch back toward the hedgerow. "Want to follow the same course or change directions?" Willie inquired as he leaned against the earthen mound.

"Maybe we should stay with the ditch, Willie. At least we have better cover on both sides. We were way to open in the hedgerow. Let's get moving." Steve replied leading the way back toward the ditch.

As the two men made their way forward, a large battle began to take shape in front of them. Steve came to a stop, watching muzzle flashes in the distance to get an idea of what might be taking place. With a hand gesture, he signaled Willy to continue forward slowly. Around a small bend in the ditch, Steve came to another stop. A short way down the ditch he could make out soldiers firing toward the road. He took a long look recognizing the outline of their helmets. Although there was a rather large battle raging, Steve felt somewhat at ease. There was nearly a squad of American paratroopers ahead of them involved in the fighting.

Heavy automatic weapons fire was coming from enemy vehicles on the opposite side of the hedgerow.

Steve turned toward Willie and whispered, "They're our men. I'm going to crawl up there and see who they are and what's happening. You stay here keep our backs covered. Don't let any krauts get into this damn ditch."

Willie nodded heading back toward the small curve to keep an eye out for trouble, as Steve began crawling toward the action up ahead. Bullets whistled over his head, others slammed into the bank near by, splattering him with dirt and small rocks. One of the paratroopers observing Steve crawling toward them backed down the ditch in his direction. "Welcome to the party, corporal but I think we're all a bit crazy for being here." The soldier yelled over the fighting.

"You could be right about that." Steve replied with a small grin. "Who's in charge of this mess?" Steve inquired ducking quickly as a piece of dirt flew over his head.

The Paratrooper replied, "Corporal Jensen. Over there the one with the Tommy gun. I think he's a bit crazy corporal."

Steve nodded and replied. "You've got that pegged right. He was dropped on his head as a baby. He hasn't been right since." He told the man with a smile. "Crazy or not, I'm going to crawl over there and talk to him."

The soldier followed Steve taking up his firing position back on the ditch wall. Steve crawled behind the row of paratroopers toward Harry. There were four dead men lying about the ditch that had been killed in the fire fight.

Regrettably, Steve had to crawl over their bodies. "Are you a sight for sore eyes." He called out while crawling up behind Harry.

"What the hell?" Harry yelled dropping down below the edge of the ditch. "Where in God's name did you come from? And I really don't give a shit either Steve, I'm just so glad to see you. How many men have you got?"

Harry inquired as he changed magazines on his Thompson.

Just one Willie, He's back down the ditch a ways covering our back sides so we don't get any unwanted company."

"Good, we don't need anymore Germans right now. There are ten of us left. We started out with seventeen after we landed. These bastards caught us just on the other side of this damn ditch, took out seven of us like no body's business.

You got ammo in that thing?" Harry inquired.

"Yeah sure," Steve replied.

"Let's help out here a second, Stevie boy." Harry directed, moving back up toward the top edge of the ditch as he began firing at the entrenched enemy. Steve threw himself onto the ditch wall firing into the hedgerow until his magazine was empty.

Harry slid down after Steve reloaded his weapon. "Can we get the hell out of here down this ditch?" Harry inquired wiping sweat from his forehead. "If we stay here, eventually we're all going to run out of ammo. Then they'll just pick us off one by one. We need to find a way out of this."

"Yeah, we came down along the hedgerow and had some trouble. After we shot our way out we took to the ditch.

We were fine until we ran into you." Steve replied before taking a swallow of water from his canteen. "We could Retreat back down the ditch a couple at a time. Last men out could give cover fire until we reach the bend. Then he drops and crawls like hell!"

Before Harry could answer, there was a tremendous explosion on the road behind the hedgerow. One of the German vehicles erupted in flames. There appeared to be a lot of confusion among the German troops as fire was pouring in on them from across the road. Another explosion set the second vehicle on fire, lighting up the surrounding area.

"Hold your fire, hold your fire!" Harry called out to his men. "Keep your eyes open, but hold your fire."

A ferocious battle was taking place across the hedgerow near the burning vehicles. Steve turned to Harry asking,

"Are they our guys or are they resistance?"

"Don't know pal. But I am not stupid enough right now to go and check it out either." Harry responded.

Quickly the roar of the battle died away, except for the sound of burning vehicles. Both men watched intently to see who might appear from the hedgerow. Voices could be heard near the burning wreckage.

"That's English Harry, has to be our guys. I'll go check it out" Steve whispered.

As he prepared to crawl out of the ditch Harry pulled him back down. “Everyone is nervous and jumpy, Steve.

Be damn careful out there.”

“Right,” Steve responded as he began crawling out of the ditch again.

Clearing the ditch he observed several figures coming over the top of the hedgerow behind the burning vehicles. Steve threw himself on the ground pointing his weapon at the moving figures. Even though the fires were dying out, he was able to make out the shape of American helmets. Gently Steve removed the cricket from his pocket giving it a snap.

There were four return double clicks, as several men in the hedgerow began signaling back.

Still nervous about the entire situation Steve called out, Flash!”

A voice called back, “Thunder.”

Letting out a sigh of relief, Steve was excited to hear the proper exchange code. However another nervous paratrooper out near the road repeated the password, “Flash!”

Frustrated with this situation Harry yelled out, “Thunder damn it thunder!”

A deep voice called out, “Alright buddy come on out from that ditch, but remember you’re covered.

“Let’s go men.” Harry called out. “Slowly don’t spook anyone.”

As the paratroopers climbed onto the road, a group of men approached from the shadows of the hedgerow. “I’m Lt. Daniels. Who’s in charge of you men?” The tall thin officer inquired.

“Well Sir,” Harry started, “I found these men lost like I was, and collected seventeen. The Krauts took out seven so there are ten of us left. My name is Corporal Jensen. This is Corporal Kenrude. He just stumbled onto us with one more man. That makes an even dozen, Sir.”

Willie walked up to Steve from the ditch, not really sure of what was going on. “Is everything alright Kenrude?”

“Yeah Willie were fine. Good job back there.” Steve said slapping Willie on the shoulder.

“A dozen, well that’s not bad. I’ve got about twenty left with me after that fire fight. We heard the fighting and thought we would check it out. Appeared like you men were pinned down, so we felt we could get them from the blind side. We have a bazooka, so we took out the vehicle first. Then we went after the troops since they were completely of guard." Lt. Daniels reported boldly.

"Well Sir you were a very welcome sight." Harry responded.

"You men belong to the 101" The lieutenant inquired.

"Yes Sir and proud of it, who are you?" Steve asked unable to see their uniform patches.

"You fellas are in the wrong sector. This area belongs to the 82nd. I thought I saw 101st. patches on your uniforms before the fire died out. Well as you don't have any officers with you, I'll take charge of the squad and place you under my command, any problems with that?"

Steve and Harry looked at each other for a moment, then turned toward the Lieutenant replying, "No Sir."

"Good. Here's the plan I have in mind. Our plane was supposed to drop us close to the bridge over the Merderet River on the road to Sainte-Mere-Eglise. We are to hold it or blow it, if German units try to force a crossing to the beach. By my calculations we're only a couple miles from Sainte-Mere-Eglise itself. We're going to have to work our way back down the road toward the bridge.

Any questions," Lt. Daniels inquired of his new men.

"No Sir." Steve responded.

"I do, Sir." Harry answered taking a step forward. "What German units are we working against?"

"Well corporal, the intelligence we had back in England was that the 709th infantry division occupies this sector.

But with all the commotion we've caused, who really knows right now. My guess is we have krauts running in every direction." Anything else Lieutenant Daniels inquired.

Before Harry could answer Steve jumped into the conversation. "Yes sir I have something you might want to know. When I hit the ground I came under immediate fire from two Germans. I killed one the second one disappeared. When I checked the body I noticed he was wearing Waffen SS insignias on his collar."

"Are you sure, Corporal? Waffen SS?" Lt. Daniels inquired of Steve.

"No doubt about it. When I saw the SS markings on his collar, I took a real good look at his uniform to see what we would be dealing with." Steve replied.

Shaking his head Lt. Daniels replied. "That changes the complexion of things a bit. But we still need to check out that bridge and soon."

Sliding the lever on his M-1 carbine back to the fire position, Lt. Daniels looked toward Steve. "Okay, take four men with you and take point. Jensen, you also grab four men. Cover our rear. The rest of you form up in two columns. We'll stay with the road it's much faster and easier than the fields. But stay in close to the hedgerow for cover."

Steve took Willie along with three other men. They started down the road, Willie taking point.

Lt. Daniels waited a few minutes giving Steve a chance to scout ahead before moving out with his two columns.

Harry along with his four men followed about ten yards behind.

They walked about a mile before the sounds of heavy fighting erupted to the west. Smaller skirmishes were picking up all around them. Steve had his men take cover as he ran back toward Lt. Daniels.

"Sounds like some pretty heavy fighting going on up ahead in the direction of Sainte-Mere-Eglise. There appears to be a lot of fighting all around the town. Do you want us to keep heading toward the bridge, or check out the fighting?" Steve questioned his Lieutenant.

After a moment of thought Lt. Daniels responded, "Corporal, we need to hold that bridge. That's our only objective for now. That bridge can't be to far up ahead now. Get back to your men and move out."

Without saying another word Steve returned to where he left his men.

As he arrived Willie motioned for him to get down. "Steve, there's movement in the field over to our left.

Watch over by the big hay stack. Can you make any thing out?" Willie inquired as he stared nervously into the dark field.

"Yeah I sure can, Willie. Who ever it is hasn't seen us yet. Looks like they want to head this way, but are a bit unsure. Hold your fire until we can be sure who it is."

Lt. Daniels along with his two columns caught up with Steve's scouting team. Steve motioned for them to get down pointing out the men in the field.

"What have you got, corporal?" Lt. Daniels inquired almost angrily.

By the hay bales, sir. I counted three men. We're not sure right now if they're ours or Germans.

Once the soldiers made up their minds to cross the field, Steve left them come until they were about thirty yards away. He then snapped his cricket as he prepared to shoot. Instinctively the three men dropped to the ground before responding with two clicks. Steve stood up signaling them over toward the road as he called out, "Over here, damn it over here!" The men jumped up immediately, running toward Steve. Just before they reached the road Steve called out, "Flash."

"Thunder," was the response, as the three ran with out breaking stride, "Good to see you, Corporal. Man what a sight you guys are." One of the men exclaimed as he dropped to his knees catching his breath.

Lt. Daniels stepped forward looking at the three panting men. "Just what the Doctor ordered three new men.

Where are you boys from?" He inquired.

Charlie Company, Second Battalion, 502nd Regiment. The big 101." The same man responded as he took a drink of water. "And we're so damn lost. We've been dodging krauts all over the place. We killed a couple over by the hay stack before you guys came along. Our plane was hit badly; we were zigzagging all over that damn sky.

We jumped as the plane was starting to go down. It was a bitch trying to get out that damn door. I don't think too many of our guys got out before it crashed."

Steve looked at the man who was doing all the talking. "I thought you looked familiar when you took your helmet off."

"You too, Corporal. We were in fourth platoon; you were in the second with Lt. Winslow. Glad to meet up with some of our own. He's dead by the way." The soldier said looking up at Steve.

"Who's dead? You mean Lt. Winslow?" Harry asked.

"Yeah. We were with him for about fifteen minutes right after we landed. A Kraut machine gunner nearly cut him in half. We took the machine gun nest out, but there was nothing we could do for him. Lost one more man trying to get that damn machine gun. Sorry to give you the bad news Corporal." The soldier explained.

"That's enough rest men. You three are now with us. Hang with Corporal Kenrude and be our scouts. We are on our way to hold a bridge over the Merderet River. I better take a look and figure out where we are. We have got to be damn close by now, if we're on the right damn road." Lt. Daniels said removing a map, flash light and poncho from his pack. Dropping to his knees, he covered himself with the poncho. After several seconds he stood up placing the equipment back in his pack. "Yeah, according to the map this is the only road crossing the

Merderet from this direction. We need to capture it before the krauts can get any more organized.

Kenrude, move on out."

"Yes sir." Steve replied sending Willy and one of the new men to take point.

"Okay, we sure as hell need to get something accomplished tonight." The new man responded sliding his helmet back on. Nodding toward Lt. Daniels he took off after Willie.

Slowly they began their advance down the dark road toward the bridge. The sound of the raging battle up ahead was more intense, as was the fighting across the entire landing zone. They had gone about two hundred yards when the sound of truck engines could be heard ahead of them. Willie, who was slightly ahead of the new man and ten yards in front of Steve, stopped raising his hand in the air. Steve moved up to Willie who was kneeling beside a small bend in the road.

"We need to take a look around this curve. Stay put until I give you the all clear." Willie told Steve and his men as he cautiously rounded the bend. Seconds later he returned. "The bridge Lt. Daniels wants to hold is about a hundred yards ahead. But I can't tell from here if any one is guarding it."

Steve grabbed the man that had been walking point with Willie. "Troop what's your name?"

"McGruder." The man replied.

"Alright McGruder, you go back tell the lieutenant to stay where he is. Tell him we can see the bridge but aren't sure what's happening with it. Let him know we're going to reconnoiter it before they come this far forward.

You got that?" Steve asked the nervous man.

"Yeah, sure do, Corporal." He responded before turning to run back down the road.

Steve motioned for the other two new men to move up to his position. "You men stay here; keep on your toes, but stay out of sight. Willie and I are going to move ahead to see where the engine noise is coming from, and what else we might be running into up there. If all hell breaks lose, give us cover fire, but don't come running forward. You got that!" The men nodded as they took cover in the hedgerow. Steve and Willie moved along the hedgerow slowly working their way toward the edge of the bridge. They carefully scanned the area around the bridge several times, trying to pick up any sentries that may have been guarding the approaches. Trying not to make any sound Steve tapped

Willie on the shoulder nodding his head.

Willie nodded back then whispered to Steve. "I'll lead across, Corporal. Stay a few feet behind me and keep low. Not much of a guard rail for cover." Steve shook his head in agreement patting Willie on the back.

The men set out across the bridge feeling like they were on an open stage. Arriving on the far side of the bridge Willie pointed to his right. About twenty yards back of the road was a small farm house and barn. In the yard were several vehicles. One was a staff car the other two were transport trucks. Several German soldiers were standing near one of the transports with their weapons at the ready. There were other enemy soldiers in the house and barn, coming and going.

Steve tapped Willie on the shoulder pointing back toward the bridge. "We need to check for demolitions under the bridge before we head back. Be careful going down the bank. There may be trip wires." He whispered to Willie.

Cautiously Willie began descending the bank toward the river with Steve right behind him. The water was about two feet deep, but not flowing very fast. Using their red filtered flash lights, they took a quick look under the structure. Confident the bridge was not set with explosives, they retraced their route back up to the road.

Scanning the area carefully, they took a long look toward the small farm yard. Nothing had changed. It did not appear they were in any hurry to leave.

Swiftly they reversed their course, until they were safely past the bend in the road. Lieutenant Daniels and Harry were impatiently waiting for them with the rest of men. "Sorry for not following your directive, Kenrude. But if there was going to be any action regarding that bridge I wanted to be the one making the decision." Lt. Daniels advised Steve.

"Understood sir." Steve replied.

The two men filled everyone in on what they had seen but were not able to give Lt. Daniels the one thing he wanted most, a good estimate of how many Germans were there.

Lt. Daniels knelt in thought for a few moments. "There were no sentries at all? Well, they don't expect the bridge to be a target. I don't think the farm is any kind of a headquarters either. Most likely they assembled there with all the equipment and are figuring out where to go and what to do. Probably waiting for orders to come on a radio set. They're probably just as confused as we are. Alright, here is what we're going to do. Kenrude, you take ten men and cross the bridge. Work your way down the river bank and get behind the buildings. Jensen, you take ten men and follow Kenrude across the bridge. Get yourself in position along the hedgerow near the drive way.

I'll take the rest of the men down the river bank behind Kenrude. We'll set up on the bank west of the farm.

We'll have them covered from three sides. If they don't see us and start shooting first, I'll open the attack with a bazooka round into the two ton truck Kenrude mentioned. Then we'll put another round into the barn. By that time all hell should have broken loose. Be careful when you open fire so we don't shoot one another. Alright let's do it men."

Steve took Willie along with nine more men. They moved down the road and across the bridge quickly. When they reached the far end of the bridge, Steve guided them down the east river bank. Once everyone maneuvered down the slippery river bank, he joined them under the bridge. After explaining their course of action, Willie led the squad along the bank. They went about two hundred yards before ascending the high slippery bank. They came up directly behind the farm.

Harry moved across the bridge next. They paused near a short stone wall to check the farm yard for activity.

Seeing none, Harry led them toward the driveway where he dispersed his men along the hedgerow. Lt. Daniels finally moved his men toward the bridge. Just as they were about to cross the span, two German soldiers came walking down a path toward the bridge on the east side.

Everyone froze where they were. It was totally apparent the German soldiers were on high alert as they approached the wooden bridge. They swung their weapons back and forth looking in every direction. However it was apparent, they were not aware of the paratroopers' presence. They peered over the river bank for a few moments before crossing the road. One sentry walked slowly along the road preparing to follow the stone wall. The second soldier called him back, motioning for them to cross the bridge back toward the west. As they alertly crossed the bridge, Lt. Daniels and his men were right in their path. If they finished crossing the bridge, they would be face to face with the Lieutenants point man.

Unfortunately there was no way to jump them on the open bridge without creating a disturbance. Shots would be fired, alerting everyone at the farm. Lt. Daniels pondered the situation for a moment.

Out of the blue, the scream from an incoming shell made the sentries drop for cover. The errant round landed in the field across the road from the farm. After the explosion, the two nervous sentries raced back across the bridge. Jumping over the short stone wall, they ran headlong toward the barn.

No one was exactly sure where the artillery round had come from. Regarding it as a blessing from heaven, Lt. Daniels made the most of it. He directed his men to move across the bridge at break neck speed.

Exiting the bridge, they slid down the west river bank following the path made by Steve's men. Before joining his men, the lieutenant hunkered down by the stone wall. He observed the two sentries talking rapidly with two other men near the trucks.

Several times they pointed toward the river. Seconds later a similar explosion rocked the country side just east of the bridge. Lt. Daniels chose this opportunity to join his men awaiting him under the structure, as a third round crashed into the river on the west side of the bridge seconds later. It was impossible to know whether these rounds were being fired by American pack howitzers brought in by gliders, or if they might be a German attempt to destroy the bridge before the allies rushed a shore in the morning. Either way it did not make much difference now. The explosions had alerted everyone in the farm yard.

Lt. Daniels led his men along the bank for about twenty-five yards. He then directed them to climb the bank, and take up firing positions along the stone wall.

Steve and Harry had their men in position ready to attack. All they needed now was the opening salvo from the bazooka. Both teams waited impatiently, wondering why Lt. Daniels had not begun to fire.

Unexpectedly, small weapons fire erupted along the river bank. A seven man German patrol following the river bank stumbled upon Lt. Daniels squad. The Bazooka team was killed instantly, as they prepared to fire just when the Germans spotted them. Lt. Daniels men had no cover from the rear, as the Germans raked their positions with sub-machine guns. The fight was murderous, as several more men attempted to fire the bazooka, but were also cut down in the process. Near the farm house a sergeant hastily assembled a group of about twenty men, leading them toward the river bank.

Harry knew he had to do something or Lt. Daniels men would be cut to ribbons. Having a good view of the action from atop the hedgerow he ordered his men to open fire. They cut down most of the German infantry as they were caught in the open with out cover. The remainder retreated back toward the trucks and barn.

Harry's men were now engaged in a fire fight with enemy soldiers coming from the barn, as well as those that had turned back.

From the river, came the distinctive sound of a bazooka being fired. The round slammed into largest truck in the yard causing a good sized explosion. Bodies flew through the air. Men that had crawled under the truck for cover came rolling out with their clothes on fire. Steve's squad was about to open fire when they were attacked from behind. Eight German soldiers exiting a wheat field discovered the paratroopers preparing for the attack. One soldier tossed a grenade that landed several yards in front of Steve's squad, but it never exploded. Instantly both sides opened fire. Sounds of the ever increasing battle drew more enemy soldiers from inside the house.

Apparently spooked by all the confusion in the dark of night, the eight men began running toward the farm yard. They quickly found themselves trapped in a withering cross fire. Within seconds they all lay dead.

With the patrol neutralized, Steve's squad quickly turned their attention toward the Germans exiting the house.

An MG-34 machine gun on the second floor of the house opened up, spraying hot lead in the direction of the wheat field directly behind Steve's men. Hot white tracer rounds lit up the night sky above Steve's head.

Without saying a word Willie jumped up, running toward the house.

Steve yelled out," Cover him damn it!" The rest of his men turned their attention toward the open windows forcing the machine gun crew to back away.

Several enemy soldiers that had started toward the wheat field now turned back toward the house, attempting to escape the hail of bullets being put up by Steve's squad.

Willie shot the last soldier running toward the house, as he dove to a stop under the second floor window where the machine gun was located. Pulling a grenade from his belt, he yanked out the pin. After taking a deep breath, he jumped out several feet from the wall, lobbing the grenade through the open window, before dropping to the ground. The explosion rocked the house, sending a sheet of flame roaring out the window. One of the gunners fell from the second floor narrowly missing Willy. Although the gun was silenced, Willy now had more problems. A side door on the house flew open as three German soldiers emerged just feet from where Willie was laying. One soldier spotted Willie. He stopped, spun around, while lowering his Mauser point blank toward Willie.

Yelling out, "No way you bastard." Steve jumped up with McGruder directly behind him. They ran headlong toward the three men with weapons blazing, the soldier about to shoot Willie, along with one other man were cut down instantly. The third man although wounded, dashed back into the house.

The remainder of Steve's squad still in the wheat field finished off any Germans that were attempting to escape Harry's onslaught out front.

Once the firing ended, Steve's men raced toward the house taking cover along the back wall.

Willie continued lying on the ground several feet from the house. As Steve approached, he rolled over looking up toward his corporal.

"Got'em good, boss."

Pulling Willie to his feet Steve replied, "Yeah you got'em good you crazy son of a bitch. Are you all right?"

He never responded. Instead, grabbing his weapon he took up a position near the side door.

Looking at Steve, he motioned toward the half closed wooden door.

Steve nodded in agreement. Cautiously they moved nearer the door along with two other men. Just as Willie peered into the house Steve yelled, "Grenade!"

A German potato masher flew out the door. It landed just inches from McGruder. Diving toward the ground McGruder somehow was able to grab hold of the wooden handle. He tossed it back through the door as he rolled off to the side.

It exploded just inside room sending flame and debris out into the yard. After waiting several seconds, Steve stepped carefully toward the door to get a good look around. A fire was started on a rug in the middle of the room, giving ample light to view the destruction. There were five bodies lying on the floor of the room, and one more on the staircase leading to the second floor. Flames from a fire started by Willies grenade were burning at the top of the stairwell.

Except for Willie, Steve's men had taken up a position at the corner of the house nearest the barn. After backing away from house, he and Willie joined the others. There was no movement coming from the barn or anywhere else in the yard. Harry's men had ceased firing as well. Not a sound could be heard from the river bank. Willie made a quick dash from the house to the side of the barn. Steve was concerned Harry's men might fire at anything that moved, and shoot him by mistake. Without a word, two more men made the mad dash to the barn covering Willie. Seconds later, the three paratroopers charged into the barn weapons blazing. After several anxious moments, Willie stood in the door way giving Steve the all clear.

Carefully, Steve moved along the side of the house toward the front yard. Bodies and burned vehicles littered the area directly in front of the house. He waved his hand toward the hedgerow, hoping Harry would see him. Not getting any reply, he removed the cricket from his pocket giving it a snap. Instantly, two snaps emanated from the dark hedgerow.

Several moments later, seven paratroopers led by Harry walked across the front yard.

"You alright, buddy boy." Steve inquired of Harry when they were still several feet apart.

"Yeah, fine. I lost four in the fighting. How about you?"

"We're all okay. Didn't lose a man. That was a miracle with Willie on the loose." Steve responded as he smiled at Harry while shaking his head.

As they spoke Steve was watching the river bank for any signs of life. After scanning the carnage in the yard, Harry also turned his attention toward the river bank.

"I think we better check on the lieutenant. I don't see anything happening over there at all. They had quite a battle going on over there when this mess began. Let's go take a look, see if we can help anyone." Harry explained.

At that moment several figures topped the river bank running toward the house. It was easy to see in the light of the fires they were all American paratroopers.

"Good to see you Lieutenant." Steve exclaimed as he studied the muddy face staring back toward him. "What the hell happened down there?"

"Just as we set up to launch our first bazooka round, a patrol of krauts came out of no where from the west. They opened fire on us taking out the bazooka team instantly.

Well from there the fight turned ugly. Several more men tried to fire the bazooka but they were cut down. Several more krauts came running from the west joining the battle. It got bloody. We had no cover. There we were fully exposed on that damn river bank. I ran out of ammunition. I took on the last man with my bayonet. We have one more man below the hill badly injured. I don't think he's going to make it. So we are the only three left. How many total do we have Kenrude?" Lt. Daniels inquired looking down at his watch. "Well Sir, I lost four, Harry lost four, so counting you three we have twenty-one left. Not counting your wounded man." Steve reported.

"He won't make it so you can count him out. We patched him up, but we don't have what's needed to keep him alive." Lt. Daniels explained shaking his head.

The sound of an approaching vehicle on the road caught everyone's attention. With out a word the men took cover, preparing to fire on the vehicle cautiously approaching the bridge. Coming to a stop at the bridge approach, one man stepped clear of the vehicle. Cautiously, he began walking across the wooden structure. As he cleared the east side of the bridge he waved at the driver to proceed. Once the vehicle came to a stop the men exchanged words for a moment. They both peered over the railing down toward the dark river bank. "Our man! They must hear him moaning down there. We need to take them out before they kill him." Lt. Daniels demanded as he prepared to run toward the bridge.

"Hold on!" Steve exclaimed. "I think that's an American jeep towing an anti-tank gun." Lt. Daniels was correct. Now that the fighting had stopped they could also hear their wounded man calling for help.

Desperately wanting to help his wounded man Lt. Daniels stepped out from behind one of the wrecked trucks, signaling his men to follow.

Seeing so many men coming out from the farm yard, the two men on the bridge took cover behind the stone wall.

Lt. Daniels called out, “Flash!”

“Thunder,” was the immediate reply.

The two men lowered their weapons watching the paratroopers walk toward them.

As they approached the road Lt. Daniels inquired. “Where the hell did you guys come from?”

“We dropped in on a glider. What a mess. Our Lieutenant was killed on impact. Took us nearly an hour to clear

the wreckage and bodies so we could get our rig out. Figured this would be a good place for an ambush on the Krauts.

We can knock out most anything with our 37 millimeter we’re towing. Looks like you had a hell of a battle here already, Lieutenant.” The Sergeant stated as he looked toward the burning farm house.

“Yeah, Heck of a fight, Sergeant. It cost us way to much.” Lt. Daniels responded.

Harry came up the river bank with a couple of men. “He’s dead sir. But we picked up the bazooka and a couple of rounds for it.”

“Thanks Jensen.” Lt. Daniels replied giving the entire situation a lot of thought. “Well Sergeant, my orders were to hold this damn bridge. Not to let the krauts destroy it. But if you feel you can hold it, it’s yours. We will move on to Sainte- Mere-Eglise. Maybe we can run into more of our men.”

“That’s quite a hike from here, Lieutenant. You need to remember the whole countryside is crawling with nervous Krauts, and just as nervous, lost and bewildered paratroopers, ready to shoot at anything that moves.” The Sergeant warned as he cautiously lit a cigarette. “You are welcomed to stay with us. You could patrol the area keeping us informed as to what’s coming down the road.”

“Well, I think you have what you need to hold the bridge, Sergeant. We’re heading out.” Lt. Daniels replied as he looked around at his ever shrinking force. “Corporal, did you pick up ammo and what ever else we needed from the dead.”

“Yes Sir.” Steve replied handing the lieutenant several clips of ammunition. “Not a lot of extras, but it will help I’m sure.”

“Corporal, take two men you have point again. Jensen, take two, you’ll cover our rear again. Let’s go.” Lt. Daniels directed his men.

Steve called for Willy and McGruder to join him as he began walking down the road in the direction of Sainte-Mere-Eglise. There was sporadic weapons fire coming from every direction. Heavier fighting with large explosions came from up ahead. They all knew those were out numbered paratroopers involved in a life and death struggle for Sainte-Mere-Eglise.

The men walked about an hour cautiously watching the hedgerows for any sign of movement. It was nearly impossible to make out anything for sure in the tangled mass of trees and brush growing out of the high mounds. Germans with a machine gun or small artillery could easily be waiting to pounce upon them.

Willie and McGruder had their senses working overtime as they poked and probed their way through the predawn darkness. Steve was amazed at their constant vigilance, checking every tree and rocky outcropping. They had to be just as tired as he was, but they just kept moving.

All at once, the air around Steve came alive with machine gun fire. McGruder dove into the hedgerow as did Steve.

Everyone else just dropped flat on the road. In near record time Willie came low crawling back to Steve.

"Where did that come from?" Steve asked helping to pull Willy into the hedgerow.

"Damned if I know Corporal. I didn't see a thing." Willie replied gasping for air. It's still so dark we can't make out anything. And these damn hedgerows are the best cover."

The hidden machine gun fired several more short bursts in the direction of the road. Lt. Daniels and the rest of the men worked their way up to Steve's position.

"Where the hell is that firing coming from?" Lt. Daniels yelled

"We don't know, Sir. It is hidden out there in the hedgerow." Steve replied.

"Damn it, we sure as hell can't sit here until daylight. Someone is going to have to find that gun and take it out.

I suggest we get moving on that right about now, Corporal." Lt. Daniels demanded angrily.

Just as Steve and Willie prepared to move, Harry came from behind. "Lieutenant, if Kenrude is crawling up there I'm going with him."

"Then go, damn it. Just get that gun silenced!" Lieutenant Daniels decried shaking his head. The three men made their way forward to McGruder, who was keeping watch.

"Anything McGruder?" Steve inquired.

"No corporal not a damn thing. But the muzzle flash from the last two bursts tells me it's on this side of the road.

I think they jump out and fire, then duck back in. Or, the gun is sitting right on the edge of the road covered by trees or rocks. That's my best estimate."

"Thanks. That actually helps a lot, McGruder." Steve replied as he turned toward Harry. "There was a small opening in the hedgerow about ten yards back. I think we could get on the other side of this thing. Willy and McGruder could continue drawing fire. When we are by the gun we crawl up the hedgerow and take them out. What do you guys think?"

After everyone nodded in agreement with the plan. Steve and Harry backed down the road to the small opening.

Both men slipped through the hedgerow, not sure what they might find on the other side. Warily they began moving forward, as Willy and McGruder made small moves, keeping the machine gun crew interested.

Just as they decided to climb the hedgerow they were pinned down by another machine gun firing from some where in front of them. Harry grabbed a grenade from his belt. "Let's try this."

"Well that's fine, Harry. But make sure that thing goes all the way over the hedgerow or it will bounce back down and kill both of us sure as hell!" Steve nervously warned his friend.

Smiling, Harry pulled the pin allowing the arming lever to fly. After counting to three, he pitched it up and over the hedgerow.

When it exploded, they could hear several screams followed by small weapons fire appearing to be American M-1s.

"Willie is that you?" Steve called out.

"Yeah you got'em. We finished them off. Where the hell is that other machine gun?" Willie called back from the opposite side of the hedgerow.

Looks like a large two story stone building in a grove of trees. Looks like it was an orchard." Steve replied as he visually swept the area in front of them. Send McGruder back to get Lt. Daniels. Tell him our problems aren't over with yet. We'll stay put right here unless they send someone out looking for us." Steve called back to Willie.

Moments later Lt. Daniels joined Willie. "Kenrude what can you tell us about this house?"

"Nothing much sir. It would appear there's a machine gun in a second floor window. The house is about ten yards back of the hedgerow. They have a commanding view of the road. If we try crawling over the hedgerow we'll be cut to ribbons. Only way we can get at it is through the opening you passed on the way up here. That's where Harry and I crossed. Problem is, we caught them off guard. You come through that hole and it will be plain suicide.

We can offer cover fire, but not enough to pin them down. The house is past our range." Steve replied.

Lt Daniels was silent for a moment. "We need to take it out. Suicide or not. We're heading back toward the opening. You need to get closer, Kenrude. If we can't pin them down nobody might make it through that damn hole."

Harry poked Steve in the arm. "Let's try low crawl up to those first fruit trees. If we stay near the base of the trees we might be hard to make out. Our fire may not be real accurate, but it just might help keep their heads down."

"Let's do it." Steve responded in agreement.

The two men slid to the ground, low crawling along the hedgerow. The German gunners lost sight of them in the dark, firing occasional bursts up and down the hedgerow.

Willie led the men through the hedgerow, just as Steve and Harry arrived near the edge of the orchard. Two paratroopers ran past Willie, alerting the enemy gunners to their presence. One was cut down immediately. The second man ran deeper into the orchard where he stepped on a land mine, blowing himself up.

Steve and Harry began firing toward the farm house. They knew they were in range as sparks flew from ricochets off the stone walls. The rest of the men coming through the opening learned quickly to drop for cover, then low crawl forward.

After making his way along the hedgerow, Lt. Daniels joined his two men. "Well that was costly! Two more men dead one man seriously wounded. But I have a plan. Follow me back to the hedgerow."

When all the men were assembled Lt. Daniels took a quick look around the orchard. "OK here's the plan. We'll work our way back into the orchard near the second row of trees. From there we should be able to fire a bazooka round into the window near the back, and one into the upstairs window where that gun is located. The last round we have will go into the upstairs window facing the road. That should keep everyone down for a few minutes. Kenrude, then you take half the men hit the front of the house. Jensen you take the other half with me.

We'll slip around the side of the house and cover the back. I think that's our best chance. Questions?" "What about mines, sir? McGruder inquired.

"Yeah I thought of that to. But I don't think they would mine that close to the house. Just follow the way we came out, and I think we should be alright.

Without another word they formed up into two squads. Slowly they crawled into the orchard, hoping Lt. Daniels was correct about the mines.

Private Kettle carried the bazooka. He and McGruder slid forward from the two squads. When McGruder had the round ready to fire, he tapped Kettle on the shoulder. Taking aim, Kettle fired the round. A loud explosion reverberated across the orchard as the bazooka discharged its lethal projectile. It was right on target.

McGruder quickly slid around to the rear of the tube, slamming in the second round preparing it to be fired. Once again he slapped Kettle as he dove away from the dangerous back blast. The second round flew straight through the upper story window. The explosion sent the machine gun and one man tumbling to the ground below. One more time, McGruder hastily reloaded the tube, then dove to the side as Kettle fired their last projectile.

It struck the window frame, blowing a huge chunk of stone and wood out of the wall. Immediately the men burst through the orchard firing toward the house as they ran.

Steve led Willie up to the front door. The rest of the squad lined up behind Willie. Holding up three fingers Steve nodded at Willie. Understanding, Willie nodded in return. Just loud enough for his men to hear, Steve counted, "One, two, three."

When he hit three Willie kicked the door in. Steve sprayed a burst of machine gun fire around the room. Everyone entered cautiously.

The men branched off into adjoining rooms searching for any enemy that might be left alive. At the end of the room was a long hallway and a staircase leading to the second floor. Unfortunately movement could still be heard above, as German troops scrambled about. Steve turned to Willie whispering. "I'll take two men with me upstairs. You take the rest finish the search. Check for a cellar."

Willie nodded in agreement

Taking McGruder and Kettle with him, Steve cautiously made their way to the stair case. Willie continued with his search toward the back of the large house. Steve climbed just a couple of steps when a door at the top flew open. Several dark figures rushed out onto a landing firing short bursts from their machine guns. Steve threw himself flat on the steps returning fire. Kettle screamed. Fatally wounded he fell backward onto the floor.

McGruder, hit by Kettle's body fell backwards down the stairs.

Willie and Jesop returned from the back of the house. They joined McGruder at the bottom of the stairs firing at the dark figures.

One German fell forward breaking the banister, dropping to the stairs below right next to Steve. The second man fell backwards dropping to the floor.

"Come on!" Steve yelled as he charged up the stairs firing into the hallway. Willie and Jesop reloaded as they followed Steve and McGruder to the second floor.

When they reached the top they found Steve peering down a dark hallway.

Willie pressed close to Steve. "Kettle caught it from those Krauts."

Nodding nervously, Steve started down the hall. There appeared to be three rooms to deal with. One to the right, one to left and the room at the vary end of the hall where the machine gun was located. The door to their left was partially blown apart from the bazooka explosion. The door to their right was closed and intact. Steve and Willie continued down the hall toward the room where the machine gun had been located. The room had been obliterated from the bazooka rocket. Other than two terribly mangled bodies, the room was empty.

Steve backed out into the hall with Willie, where McGruder and Jesop stood by the door on the left.

Steve and Willie turned their attention to the room with the closed door. McGruder kicked in the partial door as he and Jesop fired around the room. They quickly began searching closets for hidden enemy.

Steve stood aside the in tact door. "I'll kick the door in then give a quick burst of fire. Then you toss in a grenade"

Willie nodded removing a grenade from his belt.

As the door burst open, gun fire raked the door frame. Willie flew back against the wall screaming, "Son of a bitch."

Blood poured from his chest and upper leg.

"Damn you!" Steve yelled as he spun into the room firing a long burst from his machine gun.

"Look out Steve!" Willie yelled as he pitched the grenade he was holding. Steve jumped back out as the grenade blew in the middle of the room. The enemy machine gunner flew into the wall then crumbled to the floor. Steve peered into room carefully from the hallway. Abruptly, the closet door flew open. A large German Soldier came out of the closet carrying a rifle.

Steve swung his Thompson around pulling the trigger. Click! Was the only response he received, His magazine was empty.

The soldier fired a round wildly as Steve backed out into the hall. In the darkness Steve frantically tried to reload his weapon. However, the agile enemy soldier dashed across the room turning toward the door. Steve slammed himself against the wall trying to make him self a smaller target. Finally the magazine slid into place. But before he could cock his weapon, three shots rang from the floor. The bullets whined as they flew mere inches from his face. The angry German soldier gasped, then spun around falling backward firing one more shot into the ceiling. Steve looked over his shoulder. Willie was lying on the floor in a pool of blood aiming his M-1 toward the room. "I got the bastard, the no good son of a bitch." Slowly the rifle slid from Willies hands. He lay motionless on the floor.

Steve bent down checking his neck. There was no pulse. Willie was dead.

Taking his hand Steve closed Willie's eyes before removing one of his dog tags. "What a waste. What a waste."

Steve repeated observing Willie's lifeless body.

McGruder and Jesop stepped out of the room they had searched down the hall.

"We killed two in the other room, Corporal. Is Willie dead?" McGruder asked.

"Yeah, he's gone." Steve responded. "He was one hell of a soldier."

McGruder leaned over rubbing the top of Willie's helmet. "Damn you, Willie I told you to be careful!" When they made their way back down to the main floor the other men were waiting. "All clear Corporal. Cellar was empty. But I'm afraid Kettle's dead Corporal." A lanky private with a deep Southern drawl reported.

Steve nodded his head in affirmation as he listened to sporadic gunfire behind the house. "Yeah, so is Willie. Come on let's see how things are going out there." Steve replied angrily as he walked toward the back door of the house.

Cautiously opening the door, Steve observed Harry and a couple of men approach the house. "You all clear in there." Harry inquired wiping dirt from his forehead.

"Yeah we're clear. Cost me two damn good men. One was Willie the other was Kettle." Steve responded.

"Willie? Damn it to hell." Harry responded furiously

Leaning on McGruder Steve asked, "How did you guys do?"

"We lost five along with Lt. Daniels. That stone building over there was some sort of a radio communications center. The bastards fought hard for it. I have a couple of men going through the place looking for anything good." Harry replied as he turned to walk back toward the stone building.

Everyone followed Harry to the communications building. There was a Major, two Captains and a Sergeant lying dead in the room.

"Find anything interesting?" Steve asked as he looked at the shot up equipment.

"No, just personal things in their pockets. A lot of papers on the desk. But who knows what they are. None of us can read German." The private replied looking around the room.

Steve and Harry walked out into the yard between the two buildings. "Well there are fifteen of us left, Harry.

This has been one costly night. Let's take a quick break before we move on. The men are dog tired." Agreeing, Harry told the men to take a quick break. "Grab some chow but keep your wits about you." Removing his pack for a few minutes Harry looked over at Steve. "What time is it, Stevie boy? I lost my watch back at the river."

Looking at his watch Steve responded, "Believe it or not it's four-thirty. We've been on the ground just four hours. Seems like a life time already."

Harry took a deep breath as he chewed on a candy bar he'd taken from his pack. "What do we do next?" Harry Inquired handing Steve part of his candy bar.

Shaking his head Steve responded. "Thanks, Harry. I'm not hungry at all. My stomach is not up for anything right now. I'm thinking we should go on to Sainte-Mere-Eglise like the Lieutenant wanted. We need to link up with some of our forces and find some ammo and grenades pretty soon. Without replenishing our equipment, were going to be in a real world of hurt. First though, we need to get that map Lt. Daniels was carrying. Where is he? I'll go get it." Steve inquired.

"I picked it up right away." Harry responded pulling it out from inside his shirt.

"How far to Sainte-Mere-Eglise?" Steve asked as he began replacing his pack back.

"About two, maybe three miles best I can tell. Damn long way by foot. But there's transportation if you want to take a risk." Harry responded with a smile.

"What do you mean by that?" Steve inquired thinking any transportation would be better than walking the entire way.

"There's a kraut half-track back there in the trees, just waiting to go for a ride. Although it's a German vehicle.

Could make for problems in certain neighborhoods." Harry replied picking up his pack. Steve didn't even have to think very hard about it. "Damn it let's do it With all the confusion I've seen tonight we just might make it the last few miles. Men! Grab ammo and grenades from the dead if you haven't already. We're going to borrow that Jerry truck and get the hell out of here." Looking around he called out, "McGruder!"

"Yeah, Corporal what do you need. I'm right behind you."

"You said you used to drive truck. Think you can operate that beast?" Steve asked with a smile "Hell yeah I can drive that thing. A truck is a truck is a truck. Besides, that one is made by Mercedes.

Let's do it." McGruder responded as the men pulled the camouflage covering off the vehicle.

"By the way my given name is Joshua, Josh for short."

Laughing Steve responded, "Well alright Josh McGruder, let's go for a ride in a German half-track. You get in the cab with me and Jensen, everyone else hop in the back."

The men went to work rearranging sand bags by the tail gate and sides, offering them extra protection if they should get into a fire fight.

Pushing in the starter on the floor, the engine roared to life. A bit rough at first, but then it leveled off to a nice idle. When the men were settled Steve motioned to McGruder. Slipping the truck into gear he rolled the heavy vehicle out of the bushes, past the house onto the narrow dirt road. They had gone about a mile when the engine began sputtering and smoking.

"What's the matter, McGruder?" Harry inquired.

Looking down at the dimly lit gauges on the dash he pointed toward the temperature gauge. It was all the way into the hot zone.

By chance did anyone put a bullet through the radiator?" Steve inquired of Harry who was already shaking his head.

The engine coughed a couple more times as McGruder pushed it to its limit. Finally, it sputtered to a stop at the base of a small rise on the road. Everyone bailed out taking cover along the hedgerows. Steve walked around to the front of the truck checking out the radiator.

"Kind of what I figure, Harry. Some one ventilated the damn thing."

Looking over the small band of tired men kneeling near the road Steve took a deep breath. "We got about a mile closer anyway. Let's get moving, it will be daylight before we arrive in Sainte-Mere-Eglise. I know everyone is tired but keep your eyes open and listen for anything. There will be a thousand Germans crawling around this damn country by now."

The men lined up single file as they began walking vigilantly along the road with Steve and McGruder taking point.

About half a mile down the road the unmistakable sound of a tank was heard coming toward them. Steve took cover while ordering McGruder to run back and warn the others.

"Over the hedgerow, tank, tank, move it fast." McGruder yelled.

As tired as the men were, it did not take them long to climb through the brush and jump down to the opposite side of the hedgerow.

They all fell silent where they landed as the tank approached. Harry stayed near the top of the mound so he could watch which way the tank was going. He could make out silhouettes of at least ten men riding on top of the slow moving machine.

As the tank rolled down the road, Harry slid down from the hedgerow. He took a look around before crawling over to Steve who had now joined them.

"What did you see, Harry?" He asked quietly.

"A damn tiger tank with about ten men riding on top. They were heading toward Sainte-Mere-Eglise. I didn't see anything else following them." After taking a drink from his canteen Harry continued. "I don't know, Steve.

Every move we make we run into problems. We're not getting any where we're not meeting up with anymore troops. The fighting has died off somewhat toward Sainte-Mere-Eglise. Do you think we lost tonight and the invasion might be off?" Harry inquired removing his helmet. After rubbing his wet head a few times he continued.

"I don't know, Steve, I just don't know what to think. We're all tired, and dirty and getting pretty beat up." Steve nodded in agreement before looking over toward their men. Every one of them was in some sort of cover and fire position. "I think they'll make it, Harry. Look at them. They all know what to do with out being told."

Finally Steve called them all into a group. "As we get closer to dawn, I think there will be more traffic on that road.

The ground may be a bit uneven but I think we can make better time if we cross this field and stay off the road.

Any comments or questions," Steve inquired of his men.

"What about mines, Corporal?" One of the men asked.

"Good point. But, I'm guessing the krauts had mines near that opening in the hedgerow back there as a safety measure, to keep anybody from sneaking up on their position. But they were not expecting us to be scattered all over Normandy. I don't think this field is mined. I'll take point. Everyone follow in a single column. Try and stay in my foot prints. There is no cover of any type. If we get caught in a fire fight we'll need to drop for cover. Or, move as fast as we can toward that far tree line. Any more questions," No one said a word.

Picking up his Thompson Steve began walking across the field. In a way he knew they were sitting ducks.

But this appeared to be the safest route unless they were strafed. Light began filtering across the Norman country making Steve feel almost naked. He couldn't wait to arrive at the grove of trees at the far edge of the field.

He was confident the woods were safe. Had there been any Germans in that grove, they could cut his squad to pieces in a matter of seconds by now.

About a hundred yards from the grove, there was an explosion to Steve's left, then another to his right.

The men dropped to the ground as another explosion threw dirt and rocks into the air.

"Mortars damn it, Mortars." One of the men yelled out.

"Get down, get down. Stay down low crawl. Don't stand up." Steve called out to his men.

Steve began crawling toward the grove when McGruder called out. "Corporal we have company in the woods. I saw several men moving around."

More rounds landed near by. One of the men let out a blood curdling scream.

Steve scanned the grove but was unable to see anyone.

Several more rounds slammed into the field behind him. A second man screamed, "My leg! Oh God I'm hit."

It was evident a Germans mortar crew had this field zeroed in. Steve knew if they did not get into those trees soon they would all be cut to pieces.

A paratrooper appeared near the tree line waving his arms and yelling. "You're zeroed in! You've got to move or you're all dead."

Steve stayed where he was encouraging the men to keep moving.

McGruder was first to exit the minefield. He crawled into the trees as fast as he could. One by one the men made the grove.

That left Steve all alone in the field, scared, and angry over the loss of so many good men he decided to run the last ten yards. Knowing full well he could be committing suicide, he jumped to his feet. Running as fast as possible, he aimed toward a pile of brush near the edge of the woods. He dove the last three feet, coming to stop against a tree.

Harry and McGruder quickly grabbed hold of him, pulling him deeper into the safety of the woods.

After catching his breath he completed a head count. "We're missing two."

The paratrooper who had yelled from the woods handed Steve a pair of binoculars. Scanning the field he observed the two men who had been hit. There did not appear to be any signs of life. As he continued scanning to the west he observed four more bodies. "Who are they?"

"My Lieutenant, Sergeant, and two more paratroopers. We were leaving the grove toward the west looking for help, when the first mortars came crashing in. We need a medic bad for two of our guys. Have you seen a medic any Where?

"No. I'm sorry I can't help you with that request." Steve replied handing back the binoculars.

"You can keep them, corporal. There are two more sets in our glider." The paratrooper informed told Steve handing over the case.

Harry approached Steve while he was talking to the paratrooper. "Steve there is one more guy back here with a BAR.

We could also get plenty of ammo and grenades from their wrecked glider."

After taking one more look across the field Steve placed the binoculars in the case. "Alright, I guess they've had it. Let's find this glider"

The paratrooper led everyone back toward the second man who was standing near the remnants of a building.

The two men made quite an odd couple. The soldier that had been talking with Steve, stood was about six foot six weighing about two hundred thirty pounds, making his M-1 carbine look like a toy. The other man looked like he couldn't weigh a hundred pounds soaking wet, yet he was carrying a deadly but heavy B.A.R.

The bigger man held out his hand. "I'm Private Larry Woodward this is Francis Martin Doogan the third otherwise known as Franny. Don't let his size fool you. He'll kick the hell out of the best of them and he knows how to use that pea shooter, better than anyone else in this man's army.

Steve shook hands smiling at the comical introduction. "I'm Corporal Kenrude this is Corporal Jensen. Good to see you guys. How many men have you got?"

This is it, Corporal. We came in with our glider on the second wave. We took a lot of flak on the way in and heavy machine gun fire on the way down. I think the pilot was dead before we hit the ground. We smashed into the trees on the other side of this grove. There were eight of us alive when we came to a stop. Two were seriously wounded. We did the best we could for them. Our Lieutenant wanted to find help. That's when we started across that damn field. Mortars rained down on us like crazy. Franny and I played dead for a while. Then we took off running back toward this grove.

They lobbed a few rounds at us, but we out ran the shrapnel I guess. No one has bothered us since we have been here. We stuck it out here waiting for someone to come along. We haven't seen or heard a living soul until you guys arrived." Private Woodward explained.

"Let's take a look at your crash site. We need ammo and supplies. We can take those off your dead." Harry replied patting the lanky private on the back.

They walked through the grove to the crash site. The glider was torn wide open. Both wings were ripped from the main fuselage. Steve shook his head at the mess. It brought back painful memories from his training mission.

McGruder and Doogan began a thorough search of the glider and bodies. All the ammunition, grenades or anything else the men could use was piled up on one of the wings.

Woodard led Steve to the other side of the wrecked glider. There were two men lying on the ground under tarps.

"This one has both legs broken, and I am guessing broken ribs. This other one I don't know. He has some sort of head injuries. He went head first into a tree when we hit. He's never been conscious."

Steve knelt down by the soldier with the broken legs. "Private we can't take you with us. It's just not possible. We'll send help for you as soon as we find some. This landing has been a mess and we don't know where anyone is.

I'm afraid that's about the best I can offer you."

I understand Corporal. Just leave me with water, rations, my weapon and extra ammo so I can defend us if need be. And maybe a small shot of morphine from the medical kit. Other than that we'll be fine until help arrives."

The wounded soldier stated keeping a brave attitude. Then he added. "Good luck Corporal, Good luck Woodward, thanks for all you're doing for us. I know you'll send us help"

Steve stood up walking over to McGruder. "Give him several clips of ammo, rations a canteen of water, and a shot of morphine from that medical kit. Then we'll move out."

"We're going to find help for our guys first? Right?" Franny inquired.

"We will do what we can. There've been men dying all over France tonight. Some just like you're wounded. No medics, no supplies to treat them, no way to get them help. Some will make it, some will not, private. I never expected it to be like this. It is a shame, but that's where we're at right now." Steve responded in a stern tone.

"Yeah, I guess I understand. I just don't want the krauts to come by and slaughter them." Franny replied. "I don't either, Franny. We want them alive." Steve responded as he turned to walk away.

After picking up ammo and grenades he looked at Harry. "Well what next?"

"We keep going just like we planned. It's going to be light soon. If the invasion is still on men will be rushing ashore. We must be needed somewhere." Harry replied slipping his helmet back on his head. "Lead away Stevie boy. I got our rear."

Smiling, Steve turned toward his small group of men. "Okay, Woodward and Doogan you will be coming with us. We're headed toward Sainte-Mere-Eglise. Hopefully to link up with our unit. By now invasion boats are on the way toward the beaches. We need to secure some of this backcountry and keep the krauts pinned down. We lost two men back there in the field before we picked up you guys, so we still have fifteen men. Not many, but we can make it work. Let's get going."

Harry ran up to Steve as they approached a small streambed.

"I think we should follow the stream bed, Steve? It provides some cover now that it's light. Odds are it's not mined.

I'll take Doogan with his B.A.R. and walk point. You've been up there all night." Steve agreed before looking down at his watch. Six o'clock, Harry, They're coming a shore if the invasion is still on. I hope to God everything is going in our favor.

Massive explosions to the west continually shook the ground. Those rounds were being fired from large caliber naval guns bombarding German positions near the beaches. Now that it was day light fighting across the Norman countryside picked up considerably, with fighter aircraft adding to the tumult.

Harry and Franny took point working their way forward in the streambed. The rest of the men followed about twenty yards behind. The ground the paratroopers were walking on was firm which made for easy walking. Trees, tall grass, and brush along the stream bed provided relatively good cover.

About seven o'clock, and still a half mile from Sainte-Mere-Eglise, Harry observed a German patrol moving toward the stream bed from their left. He pointed them out to Franny who was about to point out a similar patrol on their right. Unknowingly they had walked right between two enemy patrols converging on Sainte-Mere-Eglise.

Which enemy patrol fired first was unclear, as the men dove for cover, several appeared to be hit. They were caught in a wicked crossfire.

Whining bullets, screaming men and chattering machine guns punctuated the morning air.

The tall grass Steve was lying in obscured him from the Germans, but was not good protection from bullets. As He surveyed the situation, he could hear foot steps running up behind him. The patrol on the east bank had split into two squads. One squad had jumped down into the stream bed and was now running up behind him.

Spinning around Steve raked the squad with his Thompson.

Three soldiers fell immediately. The remaining two men dropped in place returning fire. They were firing through the tall grass toward Steve but were shooting wide. After taking a quick look around making sure there were no other German forces coming toward him, Steve jumped up. He sprayed the tall grass where the Germans were kneeling with hot lead. One of the enemy soldiers yelled out in pain, as he spun around landing on his back. The other soldier jumped up running toward Steve, with a bayonet fixed on his Mauser.

Although surprised by the charge, Steve never flinched. He squeezed the trigger emptying the balance of his magazine into the onrushing soldier. The man dropped his weapon; stumbled forward, reaching out toward Steve as he fell just yards away. Immediately Steve slammed another fresh magazine into his Thompson. He turned around to see what was happening behind him. The patrol attacking from the east appeared to have been wiped out, or fled the battle after taking major losses.

The patrol attacking from the west had also broken down into several attack elements. One group had taken cover behind the brush on the bank above the stream bed. The other squad was back several yards from the bank, preparing for a separate attack. Steve ran back about ten yards before crawling up the bank, to see where the German soldiers were lining up.

Harry and Franny crawled forward in the tall grass, attempting to flank the enemy patrol. Just as they prepared to climb the bank Franny jumped up yelling, "The hell with this shit!" With the BAR at his waist Franny charged up the bank onto the dirt road, firing into the Germans preparing for a second attack.

McGruder and Harry raced up the bank covering Franny.

Caught totally unprepared for Franny's attack, enemy soldiers kneeling near the brush stood up. They were confused by the sudden outburst of gun fire behind them.

Every paratrooper still alive down in the stream bed capable of fighting stood up. They began firing at the enemy soldiers standing on the bank above them. One by one the confused enemy soldiers dropped to the ground or fell backward rolling down into the deep ditch.

When the shooting ended Harry took a quick look around. After taking a head count he asked "Anyone seen Jones or Aarons?"

"Jones is down in the tall grass. Aarons tried to follow you and Franny but he never made it up the bank. They're both dead. I checked them, Corporal." Jameson, the tall southern boy reported.

Harry looked over toward Franny, "You do that once too often one of these goons will end it for you!" Before Franny could speak Woodward cut him off. "One thing I forgot to tell you about Franny. He is certifiably nuts. When he gets mad enough, well you just saw what can happen."

Harry had to smile a little as he looked over Francis Doogan the third. "Well, Franny keep it to a minimum if you can help it. We need you alive. By the way you guys, we're glad to have you with us."

Franny nodded his head slightly, still some what upset over Harry's tongue lashing.

The thirteen survivors assembled on the west bank. Steve looked in the direction of Saint-Mere-Eglise. It appeared to be deadly quiet. Only an occasional rifle shot could be heard emanating from the town.

"Alright we're going into the town. We don't know who is in control, or if we are even holding any part of that mess. We'll approach carefully from this side. Let's stay together and no fancy work. Got that Doogan? We need everyone alive." Steve explained to the weary men.

"Just thirteen of us left. What difference do you think that will make, Corporal?" Franny asked sarcastically. "Maybe not a whole lot Doogan, then again maybe we make a difference. Anyway, those are our men in there fighting and dying. Maybe we throw ourselves into the fight, and we help secure the town. You go running in there crazy like you did before, and we'll have twelve left." Harry stated to Franny in a stern voice.

"Well Corporal, if they want to mess with Francis Martin Doogan the third I'll show them what I'm about. I ain't taking no crap from these kraut sons a bitches. Understand!"

"That's enough." Steve said to the two men. "Everyone works as a team. No hero's, no theatrics. We need everybody doing what he is supposed to do. Now let's move out. Stay in the grass, keep low and stay together.

And I mean no one goes flying into the battle before I tell them. Is that clear!" Steve barked at the squad. Every one was quiet as Steve looked around at each man. "Good, let's move."

As they closed the last half mile, Steve listened to the sounds of heavy explosions and machine gun fire coming up from the beaches. It was June sixth. D-Day, the attack on Hitler' Fortress Europe. This day would go down in history. Steve felt it hard to believe he actually was part of this monumental operation. Back home in Glendale no one would believe what had all happened to him since ten o'clock last night. He always wondered how he would react when it came time to kill his first enemy soldier. Funny thing was, everything happened so fast he never really had time to think about it. It happened exactly like they drilled it into them back at Toccoa. "Kill or be killed.

You won't have a choice. Freeze up and you're dead."

Now in just a short seven hours, he had killed more men than he could have ever imagined possible. How would he ever come to grips with all this when the war was over? Could he ever be normal again? But the war was not over yet. In all reality, it was just beginning for him.

Though the sky was dark and dreary, daylight was a welcome friend. They fought and survived the long dark nervous night.

At eight o'clock, they finally entered the embattled town of Saint-Mere-Eglise. The men were tense, expecting enemy soldiers to pop up from behind every window and open door. Not a shot was heard as the small group of men made there way toward the town square. What greeted them was beyond anything they could have ever imagined. Fires still burned in several buildings surrounding the small square. No matter where they looked, death stared them in the face. Lifeless paratroopers swayed in the morning breeze as they hung from trees or light posts.

They became easy targets for German soldiers when they landed during the night. Their parachutes swirled in the breeze like angry ghosts above the dead men who still wore them. Scattered about the ground were more parachutes and harnesses dropped by troopers before engaging the enemy.

German and American soldiers lay mixed together in macabre positions, as pools of blood surrounded them. Two horses lay bloated and bleeding near a watering trough that became the final resting place of an old man with a white beard.

There were bodies of German soldiers hanging out of windows, blood running down what use to be meticulously kept store fronts. In the far corner of the square stood a burned out German staff car. The driver hung out the door, his tunic still smoldering. His associate in the passenger seat sat fully upright but was burned beyond recognition.

His arm was partially extended as if to be giving directions even in death. It was a very ghoulish sight.

The light breeze drifting through the town square was foul with the stench of burned and decaying flesh.

"My God." Steve said quietly, gazing upon their gruesome surroundings. Can you believe this?"

"Where is everyone?" Harry asked, "Not everyone from town can be dead?"

Franny placed his BAR against the corner of the building they were standing aside of. After a moment of thought he turned to Steve. "If you plan to go out there do it with out me. Those krauts are hiding, waiting for us to step out. Before we get ten feet they'll cut us to ribbons. Look around, Corporal, this is a death factory. You can go, but I am staying put."

"Pick up your weapon, Doogan." Steve said harshly. "We're going to look for our guys and everyone goes. We need that BAR with us. We'll follow this row of buildings toward the burning building on the other side of the square. Keep your eyes open and be ready for anything." Franny shook his head before picking up his weapon.

After lining up behind Harry they slowly began making their way along the row of buildings.

They had covered about half the distance when an old man covered in blood came walking from a side street into the square. He wore a large bandage on his head. Stopping suddenly, he looked over nervously at the paratroopers who were watching him with great interest.

"Americans!" He called out.

Steve motioned for him to keep quiet.

Nevertheless he called out again, "Americans, you are Americans. Help me. Please help me." The man spoke with a deep French accent.

He signaled for them to follow, as he turned back down the side street he had come from. "What the hell, Steve?" Harry asked.

"Well if the Germans didn't know we were here, they sure as hell do now." Steve replied tensely.

"What do you think?" Harry inquired observing the strain on Steve's face. "Think it's a trap?"

"Nah. My gut tells me this is on the level. He's hurt bad and probably has more wounded he wants help with.

Could even be some of our guys that survived last night." Steve responded as he gazed around the square looking for any other signs of life. "Let's follow him see where it takes us."

"Across that courtyard? Are you nuts?" Franny interjected as he moved his heavy BAR back and forth covering the square. "That would be plane suicide, Corporal."

Steve took one slower look around the quiet square, before turning to Harry. "Cover me." Drawing in a deep breath he sprinted across the square, jumping over bodies, waiting for a hail of fire to come at any moment from well hidden German infantry.

After reaching the far side of the courtyard Steve took cover behind a large

Donkey cart. Examining the courtyard from this new angle everything still appeared to be unrealistically calm.

After waiting another moment he signaled Harry and the rest of the men to follow him. One by one they dashed across the open square following the same route, over the dead and around piles of debris, until they all stood beside Steve in the entrance to a ruined flower shop.

Taking great caution, they started down the side street where the old man had disappeared. About five buildings down, they found the old man leaning over a woman with a major chest wound.

"Sophia." The tired old man explained looking up at the paratroopers. "My wife Sofia. She is hurt bad. German shot her this morning as he ran out of town. Why? She hurt no one."

Harry knelt down by the old woman checking her neck for a pulse. Looking up he shook his head.

Looking at the old man who was sobbing and wringing his hands Steve said compassionately, "She's gone sir."

"Sophia, my Sophia. She never hurt anyone. Do something for her." The old man pleaded. "She's gone. Dead." Harry said as he stood up. "How bad are you hurt, sir?"

"No, No, my Sophia she can not be dead. We celebrate anniversary next week. Forty years. Oh Sophia why? You say we will survive this war, like the last one." He fell to his knees, laid his head on hers and wept all the harder.

Steve motioned for the men to leave the building, allowing the man to have some privacy. As they assembled on

The street Harry looked around. "What now Steve? None of our guys are around here. Everyone has moved on."

"Let's go back to the square and check out some of the buildings. See if we can find anyone that can give us some good information."

They walked cautiously back to the flower shop where they gathered after crossing the square. The main floor of the shop was torn up from the battle. Steve walked through the shop stopping at a stairway leading to a second floor. He motioned for Harry to come forward. "Franny and I will check out the top floor. You take a couple of guys check out the cellar; leave the rest for look outs."

The two men slowly made their way up to the second floor. Every window had been blown out. The walls had been pock marked by machine gun fire. The covers on the bed had been turned back and a nightgown lay neatly across the blankets.

"The people living here must have been just getting ready for bed, when all hell broke lose around them." Franny told Steve before making his way over to a window which looked out over the side street, where they left the old man. Instantly he jumped back. "Krauts! We got krauts." He whispered to Steve.

Quietly the men made their way back down to the shop where Woodward and Jameson were already watching the Germans patrol.

Harry led the squad out of the building, carefully approaching the corner of the store. Removing his helmet, he peered cautiously around the corner. "Damn. They must have ducked into a building. They're not on the street any more." He barely finished speaking when a shot rang out. "The old man!" He yelled.

The squad ran down the street to the store where they left the grieving old man. Two German soldiers stepped from the building, walking toward a small alley across the street. They spun quickly facing the onrushing paratroopers, but it was too late. Harry fired a short burst from his Thompson. One man screamed as he fell to the cobblestone. The second man uninjured raced headlong toward the alley. Edwards fired two quick rounds from his carbine striking the man in the back. He made two more staggering steps before falling forward to the street.

After checking the bodies, Harry walked into the building where they left the old couple just minutes ago. He knelt down beside the man. "They shot him in the back of the head. Those murdering son-of-a-bitches."

Several shots rang out from across the street. One round hit Jameson. He flew back against the wall before sliding to the floor. The bullet struck him in the cheek, blowing part of his face completely off. Blood tissue and bone fragments sprayed the men who were standing near by.

Another round hit the floor near Franny. "Snipers on the second floor and three guys in the alley."

"Get down, get down." Steve called out. "Harry, you take Franny, Willis and Brant. Get across the street. Take those bastards out on the second floor. We'll lay down cover fire for you. After you get across, we'll go after the bastards in the alley. After making sure everyone was set he yelled. "Fire!"

Harry and his men raced across the street as Steve's team kept up a good amount of cover fire into the windows and alley opening.

Once inside, Franny dashed up the stairs followed by Phil Brant. A grenade met Franny at the top of the stairs near the open door. Phil slid in underneath Franny pitching the explosive back into the room yelling, "Grenade."

The already damaged structure shook as the weapon exploded. Franny spun around against the door frame, firing several rounds from his weapon toward a soldier emerging from behind an over tuned night stand. The man dropped his weapon grabbing his throat with both hands. He lips moved as if trying to speak, as he fell to his knees. Slowly rolling to his side, he tumbled to the floor.

As they started back down the stairs shots rang out from the cellar. Seconds later Harry came through the cellar door followed by Willis.

"We got two more down there. They came in through a side window facing the alley. I'm guessing when Steve made his sweep they ducked inside hoping to come around from behind. There are also three dead civilians down there. They've been dead a while. Probably were killed last night." Harry explained to Franny and Brant.

Steve and his team carefully worked their way down the alley watching every window and door for signs of movement. Halfway through their sweep, Steve observed a cellar window being pulled shut from the inside. He motioned for his men to back away. They walked around the building finding an open door on the south side. There was a middle aged woman standing just inside the door. She waved her hands at them but spoke not a word.

Steve motioned for her to come out. She shook her head no. Once more he signaled her to come out. After looking over her shoulder, she took a few steps toward Steve. Woodward grabbed her arm pulling her away from the open door. She was about to scream when Steve placed his hand over her mouth.

Removing his hand, she started speaking frantically in French. He shook his head. But she kept repeating the same thing several times.

"Any of you speak French?" Steve asked his men.

They all shook their heads no.

"She wants to tell us something that's for damn sure. But what?" Steve explained to Woodward who was watching for movement in the house.

"Corporal, it looks like the door to the cellar is straight across the kitchen. Do you want me to sneak up to the door and take a listen?"

"Yeah that's an idea." Steve told McGruder to stay by the woman as he covered Woodward with his Thompson.

After listening for several seconds Woodward backed out through the door by the squad.

"I could hear kids. Sounds like a couple of them for sure."

Steve knelt down by the crying woman. "Children? Children? Is that what you're trying to tell us?"

He inquired making a motion as if he were rocking a baby.

Wiping her eyes with an apron she nodded her head yes.

"How many?" Woodward questioned as he counted on his fingers.

The woman responded by holding up two fingers.

"How many krauts? You know, Boche. How many?" Woodward asked, continuing to count on his fingers again.

She shrugged her shoulders then raised her hand counting three than counting four. She shrugged her shoulders again shaking her head.

"Alright we're dealing with four maybe five with hostages. Let's see what we can do here." Steve said as he stood up. "Woodward, McGruder come with me. Edward you watch her, stay by the door, everyone keep your eyes open."

Steve walked up to the cellar door calling out, "Achtung! We are Americans. You are surrounded so let the children go and come up here."

They waited several seconds with out a response. Again Steve called out, "Achtung. We are American paratroopers."

Before he could say another word a man called out in rather good English. "Ya, we hear you."

Steve took a long breath. "Alright come up, do not hurt the kinder."

"Ah you speak Deutsch" The man called back.

"A few words. Just come up here so we can talk and get this rectified." Steve once again requested.

"Here is the deal. You guarantee our safety out of town, and we let the children go. Otherwise we all die. I am an officer of the third Reich. I give you my solemn promise." The man yelled up to Steve.

Woodward leaned close to Steve. "Damned officer of Hitler's, and we're supposed to take his murdering word?"

Steve nodded his head in agreement but added, "We need to get them out of the cellar. Once they're up here things might be different. We need to play it for now."

Turning his attention back to the cellar Steve called back. "You need to understand, we do not control this town. We just wandered in here looking for our men. I can't guarantee you anything."

"That is too bad. Look, either you give us safe passage, or my men will kill these children. I am an officer, and they will follow my orders. Do you understand?" The desperate officer yelled back.

Shaking his head Steve thought for a moment. "Look, why don't you come up so we can talk with out all this yelling. We can work things out much better face to face."

"Alright we will come up. Stand away from the door please." The officer finally agreed. "Okay move back, but be ready for a double cross." Steve said as they backed across the kitchen.

Moments later a German Captain followed by three soldiers emerged from the cellar. A sergeant held a knife to the throat of a girl about three years old. One of the privates held his Lugar tight up against the head of a boy roughly six years old.

Seeing the American soldiers the boy called out, "Amis! Yes. No Boche!" He said before spitting on the floor.

The soldier holding him was angered. Pushing the gun tighter to the boys head he vigorously shook him.

The third soldier stepped forward holding an American grenade. The pin had been pulled, but the man held tight to the arming lever.

"You see I am not playing with you, Corporal. You hold nothing. I hold all the cards. Where are your officers?" The Captain inquired.

"Right now I honestly don't know. We were separated last night." Steve responded.

"I see. Well if we are going to negotiate, you must point that machine gun in another direction. Otherwise I do not know if this is going to work. After all we are ready to die for our Fuhrer. It is your call, Corporal." The arrogant Captain chided Steve.

Slowly lowering his weapon Steve looked at the children. "Again, Captain I do not control this town or the surrounding area. I...."

The Captain stepped forward angrily cutting Steve off. "You will guarantee our safe passage or we all die. Right here! Right now! My name is Captain Joachim Manvold. I give you my word when we are a safe distance away, we will release the children. That is a promise."

Steve couldn't help smiling. "Captain, how am I supposed to trust you? First you said you would release the children on the edge of town. Now you say when you are a safe distance away. You sure as hell will kill those children just like your men killed that old man down the street. No deal, Captain."

Straightening his tunic Captain Manvold glared at Steve. "I do not know what happened to this old man you are talking about. Maybe those men did not even belong to me. I don't care. That man's death is nothing I choose to worry about. Now, Corporal what is your decision?" Captain Manvold demanded slamming his left foot against the floor.

It was totally evident this man was a Nazi fanatic. He was willing to die no matter what the cost, as along as he could do it in the name of the Fuhrer.

Nodding his head Steve glared at the Captain. "Alright. We'll get you out of here."

Steve was very unhappy with the situation as it stood. He motioned for his men to let them walk past.

"Are you crazy, Kenrude? Edwards asked angrily. "We let them go so they can kill more of our men. I don't think so, Corporal. That doesn't sit well with me."

"Shut up, private! Steve yelled at his man. "We will do this my way. Now back outside and get that woman away from the door."

Steve turned quickly back to the Captain to gauge his reaction.

"That was good, Corporal. A man like that would never make it in the Wehrmacht. Now you know what needs to be done so let's get on with it." The Captain said boldly with a sly smile on his face.

Steve glared hard and long at the German officer before stating fearlessly. "And you can wipe that smile from your face and shut the hell up. You want this to happen you follow me and shut up. That's it. Do you understand?"

Immediately the German officer quit smiling. He realized Steve was the wrong guy to cross at this point in time. "Very well, Corporal." He replied.

Harry and his men arrived outside the house. He was curious about what was happening as Steve's men were backing away from the house into the alley. "What the heck is going on here?" Harry inquired as he watched the enemy soldiers exit the house with the children. The soldier with the grenade raised his hand into the air for everyone to see as he yelled out something threatening in German.

"We have to get them to the edge of town and let them walk away, or they will kill the kids and some of us. Hans there pulled the pin on that grenade." Woodward informed Harry as they met in the alley.

Nodding his head Harry stepped a few feet to his left, getting Steve's attention. "We will lead the way, Stevie boy."

"No, no that is not acceptable. We will walk in front. You will follow us." The Captain yelled out nearly frantically pointing his pistol at the crying woman.

"Captain, when your men walk into that square you will get blasted if there are any Americans watching.

We won't have a chance to stop them. This call is yours." Steve explained to the outraged Captain.

"Sorry Corporal. We do it my way. You just better hope your countrymen look before they shoot. Now we must go." Captain Manvold screamed motioning for his men to lead the way.

Harry signaled his men to step aside as the German Sergeant entered the street. He turned toward the square still holding his knife tightly up against the girl's throat. The private holding the struggling boy came next, followed by the rest of the strange procession.

"That's far enough." An American voice called out.

Steve hurriedly walked forward past the German Sergeant, stopping by an open door occupied by an American paratrooper wearing the rank of Staff Sergeant. Steve informed him of what was transpiring, asking him to let them pass.

"No corporal that will not happen. "They are either prisoners or they are dead. You tell them that." The Sergeant informed Steve as he turned his Carbine toward the Captain. "And tell the heinie Captain he goes first the arrogant son of a bitch."

"Corporal we are not playing games here. You tell him to step aside or we shall all die here." Captain Manvold yelled shaking his Lugar in the air.

Steve walked up to the Captain nearly nose to nose. "Something tells me this man is not alone. You might want to change your plans. You'll never make it out of here alive if you don't give up. I really don't think he gives a damn one way or the other about those kids living, as much as he wants to see you dead. You know, a P.O.W. stockade for the duration might not be just a bad idea, Captain. Think real hard before you make a decision."

Knowing things were not going well the soldier holding the grenade darted out in to the middle of the road yelling, "Nicht Schiesen, Nicht Schiesen." He was struggling to replace the pin in the live grenade.

The soldier holding the boy removed the gun from his head. He pointed it toward the American Staff Sergeant for a second, before cocking the hammer and placing it back against the boy's head.

A shot rang out from a second floor window above the flower shop. The German soldier fell backwards, firing a shot wildly before collapsing to the cobblestone. In unison two more shots rang out from windows above the street.

The German Sergeant received a round right between his eyes. The little girl screamed as she attempted to break free from the Sergeants death grip. The knife fell away from her throat, slicing her deeply across the shoulder. Bleeding profusely, she ran screaming in the direction of the soldier holding the grenade.

A fourth shot rang out striking him in the leg. Dropping to his knees he threw the pin then grabbed for the wounded girl.

McGruder fired at the soldier, striking him in the upper chest. Falling forward he pushed the girl to the road, allowing the grenade to drop free. Apparently having a quick second thought, the soldier jumped up, pushed the screaming child aside before diving on top of the grenade. His body bounced several inches into the air as it absorbed the entire force of the explosion. Willis and Brant ran to the girl attempting to control the severe bleeding.

The Staff Sergeant smiled for a second continuing to point his carbine at the German officer. "You know I sure love it when a plan works out. Sorry Mein Fuhrer." The Sergeant exclaimed sarcastically before firing two rounds into the Captain's chest.

Steve walked over to Captain Manvold who gasped deeply for breath as he lay dying on the cobblestone street.

"Sorry it had to end this way, Captain. But you knew it wasn't over between you and me yet. You should have surrendered." Steve said as he watched blood pooling around the Captains uniform.

Looking up at Steve he attempted to force a smile. "It is alright, Corporal. I knew one of us would die to day. There was no way this was going to end well for either of us. You were a worthy adversary. A warrior should die in combat." With that his head rolled to the side.

A medic came running down the street from the square. He knelt down by the girl working with Willis and Brant.

Everyone else stood where they were trying to grasp what had just transpired in the last few moments. Another small contingent of paratroopers came walking toward them from across the square, led by a rather tall man wearing Captain's bars.

"Who's in charge here?" The Captain inquired as he looked over the tired group of men. "Well, Captain I'm Corporal Kenrude, that is Corporal Jensen over there. We both have been sharing that duty." Steve replied walking away from Captain Manvold's body.

"One of my men spotted your group coming into town this morning. He sent a runner to contact me at the C.P. We've set up shop on the west end of town. I sent most of my men out on patrols this morning trying to keep the krauts out of town. Before we could get back to you, we heard all the shooting. We were pretty sure you had been taken out by this German patrol. My lookout said he saw you run down the street and all hell broke lose. So we assembled a few men and set out to cover any situation that might arise. Looks like you guys caught them with their pants down. Good job." The Captain stated shaking hands with Steve and Harry who had now joined them. By the way I'm Captain Lewis. It's good to see you men. We can use a few more men here to hold this town until the troops gets here from the beach."

"You must have had some battle here last night." Harry said to the Captain.

"You don't know the half of it, Corporal. The jump was a disaster in terms of logistics. But then you are well aware of that. We have troops scattered all over the damn place. My men ended up coming down right here in town.

The German infantry assigned to hold this place ran out into the square, side streets, roof tops, any open windows, they just poured fire into our men as they were landing. Many of our guys were dead before they hit the ground. Some of them dropped into burning buildings across the courtyard and plain blew up when their ammo hit the fire. Hand to hand fighting took place all night long. It was brutal and bloody. We finally took the upper hand around seven this morning. What ever enemy we did not kill, high tailed it out of town. Some I suppose are in basements still hiding out. Others are patrolling back to see what our strength is. I have nearly fifty men back at the C.P wounded in one fashion or another. We need medical help from the fleet bad, or some of those brave guys are going to die." Captain Lewis explained, watching the medic pick up the girl before heading toward the C.P.

"How many men have you got in fighting condition, sir?" Steve inquired as he watched several paratroopers begin cutting down the dead still hanging in the square.

"Like I said about fifty wounded, some from the fighting last night. Some wandered into town like you men and we picked them up. Well, ready to fight probably about sixty very tired men. All short on ammo, grenades and high explosives. But I think we can hold this town if we do not get shelled to death or over run by tanks. Did you see any tanks on your way here?"

"Yeah we saw a tiger tank around five this morning I would estimate. It was headed away from here. There were about ten men sitting on top of it." Harry responded.

"Good. That's good." Captain Lewis replied looking at his watch. "How many men do you have, Corporal?" The Captain inquired as he motioned them to follow him.

"Just the twelve you see right here. We lost one man in the fire fight. But we lost a lot of men over the course of the night. I feel bad, I can't even remember how many we picked up and lost." Steve replied looking over at Harry.

"Don't feel bad, Corporal. It's been a hell of a night. I lost so many good men last night and this morning that it makes me plain sick. Come along now to our C.P. You can get some rest for a while. I have men on guard duty and a few patrols watching for kraut movement. We're still actively trying to hunt down more paratroopers who are lost. I'll try rotate men best I can, so everyone gets a crack at a nap and some chow. Sergeant," Captain Lewis called out.

A thin Sergeant walking across the town square came running over. "I don't care what you were supposed to be doing. Get over there and help get those poor men cut down. We can't leave them hang there like that." Captain Lewis ordered in a stern voice.

After a few minutes walk they arrived at a building near the edge of town. "This is our C.P. It's not pretty but it's adequate for the job." The Captain informed them as he pointed to a small wood building.

"Our wounded are in the storage building behind us. You men can find some floor space next door in the stable. Take a break, get something to eat. I'll send one of my runners if I need you." The Captain added.

Franny quickly stepped forward before the Captain walked off. "Sir I have a request." Turning back toward the men Captain Lewis looked at Franny. "And what might that be?"

Franny passionately explained about the two injured paratroopers they left back at the glider.

"I'm sorry, soldier. Right now we have just three medics for this entire town. Secondly, we can't afford to send any men that far out right now to pick up your boys. When we get some help from the beach, I'll see what I can do." Captain Lewis replied giving Franny a sympathetic look.

Although the stable was old it was in good condition. It was filled with tired, dirty paratroopers and their gear. Some were trying to get sleep, while others were eating; a few just sat appearing to be deep in thought.

Harry found a good sized area over by an old feed trough. Each man removed his pack then claimed a spot on the floor to sit or stretch out. Not a word was spoken by any of them. Steve knew that like him, they were attempting to process the horrible events of the past night.

Removing his helmet, Steve ran his hands over his sweat soaked head. He thought about eating, but sleep sounded like a much better idea. He laid his head down on his pack closing his eyes. How would he ever be able to tell anyone about the experience of his first ten hours of combat? Could anyone even attempt to understand? Feeling safe for the first time since crossing the channel, he drifted off into a fitful sleep.

CHAPTER 10

FIGHTING IN THE HEDGEROWS.

Steve was awakened abruptly as a paratrooper ran through the stable yelling, "Tanks! Kraut tanks! Everyone on your feet let's move."

Men scrambled to their feet, grabbing their packs and weapons, tossing ration cans in every direction as they dashed for the door.

Captain Lewis arrived outside the stable just as the men were exiting. "Alright men listen up. We have three Panther tanks approaching from the east with about fifty infantry. Another patrol reports two more tanks, could be Panthers, about a mile south of here. No report on a number of infantry with those tanks, but a good guess would be about the same number as the first group. We don't have much to fight with, but we need to hold this town as a break out point for the beachhead.

A shrill scream filled the air as German artillery rounds began smashing into Sainte- Mere-Eglise.

Buildings crumbled as high explosive shells penetrated roofs detonating inside.

"Eighty-eights," Captain Lewis yelled out. "Everyone find some cover. Corporal Kenrude you and Jensen come with me."

Arriving at the C.P, the Captain studied a map for a few seconds as shells continued to pummel the old city. "Alright, you guys came from the south. Grab about eighteen men so you have two squads of nine. Then see what you can do about those tanks. I figure the only real way they can get here is by this main road. Sergeant Brighton will take about twenty men and go after the group to the east, Questions?"

"No sir." Both men responded as they turned to leave.

They ran back toward the stable. Most of the men were still inside ignoring the Captains directives to seek better cover. Kneeling down by their men Steve laid out the job they were given.

Franny was the first to get up, "We're with you Steve. Just get us out of here before we get blown to bits."

Nodding his approval he and Harry picked out six more men to take along so they could have a good sized squad. Several more men volunteered to go. They felt their chances were better meeting the Germans head on than being blown to bits in town.

After agreeing to take the extra men Harry called them all together. "When we leave the stable I want you to run like hell down the street directly in front of us. It will take us to the edge of town. After that we should be clear of the artillery. Let's go."

Exiting the stable the men ran past the C.P, not stopping until they were about fifty yards out of town.

Harry stopped by a small grove of trees waiting for everyone to assemble. Once everyone arrived Steve took a head count. They ended up with twenty four paratroopers, slightly more than they were ordered to take. But there was no way they were going to send the extra men back to endure the artillery barrage. What Steve and Harry appreciated most was that several men carried Thompsons. Nice equalizers in a fire fight. One private had a German Panzerfaust slung over his shoulder.

"Where in hell did you get that?" Steve questioned the smallish soldier.

"Off a dead German I found lying in a ditch last night. I was going to pitch it this morning at first light, but then figured it may come in handy." He replied with a wide grin.

"It sure as hell will. What's your name, private?" Steve inquired as he slapped the man on the shoulder.

"Sam Newton, Corporal."

"Alright Newton, you hang lose and close to me. Okay here's what we're going to do. If anyone has anything to input let me know as we go along. We're going to follow this line of trees south. It will take us to a streambed with a small dirt road. We had a battle there earlier this morning. Follow the gully toward the main road, and stay low. If we get there before the tanks, it will make a great ambush sight. We can block the road using the hedgerows. We'll worry about the second tank once we get the road blocked. If they get past before we get there, we catch up to the last tank firing that panzerfaust up its rear. Then deal with the lead tank. Any thoughts?" Steve inquired.

Harry took a quick look around at the men. "Come on let's do it. Steve, I'll take half the men and the panzerfaust. You follow up and give us all the cover you can."

With that, Harry pointed out the men he wanted with him, and took off for the streambed. The balance of the men fell in behind Steve following several yards behind Harry's team. As Harry reached the spot in the streambed where they fought the two enemy patrols he stopped. He crawled up the bank taking a good look toward the south. As the ground continued shaking from the continuous barrage on Sainte-Mere-Eglise, everyone stole a few seconds to look back on the town. It was nearly completely obscured by a dark pall of smoke and dust.

Harry motioned for his team to continue forward down the stream bed, hoping to beat the tanks to the culvert that ran under the main road. Nearing the hedgerow Harry slowed down, straining his ears as he listened for tank engines over the continuous roar of exploding shells.

Franny crawled forward stopping beside Harry. "Jensen, want me to work my way up the hedgerow to get a good look?"

"To dangerous Franny. You poke your skinny little head out at the wrong time and we haven't got a chance in hell to get them."

"And if I don't stick my skinny little head out there, we'll never know for sure where they are." Franny responded with his trade mark grin.

Harry almost had to laugh at Franny's face. He had several days' growth of beard, and was dirty beyond belief. But his teeth were so white they almost glowed when he smiled. "Alright. Take Brant with you. Get a good look but be damn careful." Harry replied as he relieved Franny of his heavy BAR, handing him a Schmeiser from one of the dead Germans lying in the ditch. He looked the weapon over smiling back at Harry. "Thanks, this will work just fine."

Cautiously Franny and Brant climbed up the backside of the hedgerow from the stream bed. Reaching the top, Franny spread the brush aside looking down the road. The lead tank was parked on the road about a quarter mile away, surrounded by about twenty German soldiers. They had guards posted on top of the hedgerows aside of each tank, watching the nearby fields for activity. No one appeared to be in a hurry.

The two men returned to the streambed where Harry and Steve awaited them.

"Looks like they're sitting back waiting for the barrage to stop before they move. Sentries posted on the hedgerows on both sides of the tanks. We try and move on them they'll cut us to ribbons before we get there." Franny informed the two Corporals. "Okay. Sounds like we wait." Harry responded looking over at his partner. "We can't take them from the front. We can't get behind them without being seen. We don't have much choice." Frustrated by the situation, Steve just stood motionless as he watched Sainte-Mere-Eglise being torn apart by very accurate artillery fire. "What a waste. Wish we could take out those eighty-eights, wherever they are. They're destroying two hundred years of culture and they just don't give a damn."

Willis crawled forward in the trench to see what was going on. After Franny informed him of the situation, he quickly crawled over to Steve. "Kenrude, you still have your Gammon bomb? I do." "I do too. So what?" Steve replied studying Willis's face. "You need to plant that thing on the tank and pull the pin to make it detonate. We can't get close enough for that."

"I know." Willis replied. "But when they come past, we use the panzerfaust on one and place a gammon bomb on the second."

"Infantry you knuckle head. They've got infantry. Probably about twenty men per tank. How do you plan to get past them to stick the bomb on the tank without getting your butt blown off?" Franny asked pretending to slap Willis on the head.

"Now listen to me. I work my way down the hedgerow and….." Willis began to say just as the barrage lifted on the town. Franny and Brant frantically crawled back to the hedgerow to get a look at what the German's were doing. After watching them for several minutes, they hustled back to the streambed.

"They're getting ready to move. Infantry in front of the first tank still appears to be about twenty strong. I'm guessing they probably have the same number around the second tank." Franny reported as he picked up his BAR, handing Harry the Schmeisser.

Steve immediately called for Newton to come forward, explaining what he wanted him to do. Harry set up the men from both squads so they would have good penetration of fire on the road.

Without being seen, Willis slid down from his position. He began crawling along the base of the hedgerow in the direction of the German tanks. He stopped and listened, as the first tank rumbled past him on the other side of the hedgerow. Cautiously he climbed back up the hedgerow peering over the top. The second tank was just about even with him. However it was followed by about ten men. Willis waited until the last man was past, then made his way through the tangled brush ending up on the road. Lowering his weapon he ran up behind the infantry opening fire. Five of the enemy soldiers fell to the road, as rounds from the carbine tore into them. The rest of the men turned in utter surprise to see what was happening. Willis ran straight toward the tank in an effort to stick his gammon bomb on the armor plate near the engine compartment.

From the position of Harry's squad, there was no way to know who was attacking or what had happened behind the last tank. The commander of the lead tank ordered his driver to stop. He continued yelling orders into his head set as the turret began turning toward the rear. As the turret from the second tank began turning around, infantry from the lead tank rushed rearward toward the fighting.

Steve, hoping Newton knew what he was doing yelled, "Fire!"

With the tank stopped Newton had a good aim. His round hit right at the base of the turret near the cannon. A sold blast rocked the tank. A fire ball roared out of the turret, nearly incinerating the commander who slumped forward in his seat.

Shrapnel flew in several directions killing infantry that were still close by. Steve's squad well protected in the hedgerow poured fire on the remaining infantry below. The second tank began backing down the road. Edwards quickly climbed to the top of the hedgerow, before jumping down on the stricken tank. A volley of fire from a machine gun on the retreating tank struck him several times. Seriously wounded, he lunged toward the open turret hatch, dropping a grenade inside. There was a muffled blast inside the huge panther tank when the grenade exploded, followed by a secondary explosion that shook the steel monster. The second tank was now well down the road, still retiring with the surviving infantry along side.

Except for the raging inferno in what use to be a powerful enemy tank, the action on the road had ceased.

Slapping Newton on the helmet Harry yelled out. "Nice shooting kid."

Newton looked up at Harry as he removed his helmet. Rubbing the top of his head he asked, "What went wrong, Corporal? Who started a second attack?"

"I don't know. What do you think, Steve?" Harry asked his partner.

Steve Just shook his head as he stood up carefully on the hedgerow, trying to see how far the second tank had retreated. "They're way down the road, Harry. And to answer your question, I haven't got a clue as to what started that entire mess."

"Come on, let's check it out." Steve replied as he crawled through the brush of the hedgerow, sliding down the other side. He lay quietly for a moment looking in the direction of the tank. Feeling confident the area was safe, he motioned for the rest of the squad to follow. Harry and Franny pulled Edwards of the tank, gently laying him aside of the road. He was covered in blood. Two rounds struck him in the chest and abdomen while a third went straight through his neck. Edwards grabbed Harry's arm as he struggled to speak.

"Save it Edwards. Save your strength." Harry told the dying man. He gasped several more times before letting go of his life. His arm slipped from Harry's shirt as peace overtook his tortured body.

Steve and several other men observantly made their way toward the spot where the shooting began, checking each body as they went.

Brant was the first to come upon the body of the dead paratrooper lying face down in the middle of the road. The retreating tank had backed over his legs turning them to mush. Brant knelt down rolling over the body. "It's Willis, Corporal. The damn fool. What the heck was he trying to do?"

Steve walked over by the dead soldier as did the rest of the men. "He was a hell of a good man." Steve commented as he knelt down on one knee beside Brant.

"He shouldn't have tried to be a hero. Look what it got him, Steve." Brant said quietly as he removed a letter from Willis's jacket pocket. "He couldn't sleep back in the stable. Said he felt uneasy. So he started this letter to his Dad. Guess I'll finish it for him if that's alright with you. Don't seem right to send home a letter unfinished. They'll never know what he was going to say. But I can tell them I liked him, and I knew what he was trying to do when he was killed. He died a hero in my book." Brant said stuffing the letter into his jacket, as he wiped tears from his eyes.

Steve nodded and stood up. He was angry as hell over the losses he was suffering as a squad leader. Removing his helmet he walked a short distance, trying to gather his thoughts. Suddenly he spun around, walking back to his men who were helping Brant move Willis's remains off to the side of the road. He took Brant by the arm, "Yeah you finish the letter. Tell them their boy was a hell of soldier, and one brave son of a bitch. You tell them its men like their son that will win this war. You tell them all of that, Brant!"

"Thanks, Kenrude." Brant replied picking up his rifle, as he followed the rest of the men back toward the drainage ditch.

Other than the loss of Edwards and Willis everyone else survived the quick battle. "Well, I'm not sure what we do now. Any ideas, Harry?" Steve inquired as he watched smoke roll out of Sainte-Mere-Eglise.

"I was thinking maybe we should send some one back to check with the Captain. See what he wants us to do? Guess most of us should stay here in case they come back." Harry responded from where he sat leaning against a shattered tree trunk.

"I'll go back." Franny volunteered as he reloaded his weapon.

"Alright. We'll wait right here for you. Unless we need to move if the krauts come back. Get back as soon as you can. Be careful, and keep your tired eyes wide open." Steve admonished him.

Franny slightly smiled as he began running down the stream bed. The rest of the team took up positions on the hedgerow in case the enemy returned.

In Sainte-Mere-Eglise, Franny found the C.P. partially damaged but still acting as the headquarters for the town. Entering, he observed Captain Lewis talking with several men as they looked over a torn map spread over a make shift table.

The Captain looked very concerned as they discussed the situation east of town.

Franny stepped forward toward the table then saluted. "Private Doogan reporting from Corporal Kenrude's patrol, Sir."

"Good timing, private. What can you tell me?" The tired Captain inquired.

"We knocked out one tank and some infantry. The other tank backed down the road undamaged. We lost two men, but we're still in good shape. Kenrude has the men scattered in the hedgerows right now, keeping the road under surveillance." Franny replied.

"Can you show me where you have your patrol set up?" Captain Lewis inquired of Franny as he pointed to the map.

Franny spent a few seconds looking over the well worn map. Finding the streambed he followed it to the road. "Right here. A large culvert goes under this road. The water is shallow so a man can walk through it if he keeps low. The destroyed tank sits almost on top of the culvert. Our men are posted along here."

Franny explained, running his fingers along the hedgerows.

"Alright that sounds fine. We did not fair so well to the east of town. But we've picked up more paratroopers in the last half hour. Report back to Kenrude and just sit tight for now. Sorry I can't give you some heavy explosives, but we're all out as you can imagine. Do what you can, but do not let any armor get through if you can help it, I'll send a runner out if I need you, or if the situation changes."

Franny saluted the Captain as he prepared to leave. Walking back out into the street, he could not believe the damage that had been done to the city by German artillery. Slowly he turned, retracing his route back to the streambed and his men.

When Franny returned, he observed Harry standing on the hedgerow near the culvert. "See anything, Jensen?" He asked.

"Naw, just a couple of dancing girls doing the hula bare ass naked in the middle of the road. Nothing you would be interested in Doogan."

Franny laughed as Harry came down back into the ditch. "No, nothing moving out there. Steve took a few men down the road apiece to see where the tank went. We planted a couple of Gammon mines in the road. We have them rigged so we can set them of if another tank shows up. As least we hope we can set them, off I should add." Harry explained with a chuckle. "So what did the Captain have to say?"

"Just sit tight. He'll send a runner if the need arises. Sounds like things did not go well east of town. I did not get specifics on what happened. Man you ought to see that place, Harry there ain't shit left of it."

Franny explained as he removed some food from his pack. "Man I'm starved."

"Kenrude's back." One of the sentries called down to Harry.

Steve joined Harry and Franny in the gulley. "They must have backed down that road a long way. Maybe all they way back to the next crossroad. We went close to a mile and didn't see any sight of them."

Franny filled in Steve as to what he heard from Captain Lewis, and what he had seen in the C.P. He also told the men about the condition of the town. After some discussion, it was decided Harry would take several men and set up a look out position about a quarter mile down the road near a small indention in the hedgerow.

Around two in the afternoon Steve noticed a large group of paratroopers coming down the gulley from town.

As they entered the area near the culvert a young second Lieutenant approached Steve.

"Are you Kenrude?"

"Yes, Sir. What can I do for you?" Steve inquired as he studied the nervous man's face. "I have a squad of fifteen men with me. We're going to take over your position. You and your men are to follow me back to the C.P. Captain Lewis has a new assignment for you. He wants you back there right away. Explain what you have going to the Sergeant. He'll be in charge." The Lieutenant informed Steve. Harry collected all the men as Steve explained about the gammon bombs, and everything else he thought was pertinent. When everyone was ready, they made the trek back toward the C.P.

They had barely entered the gloomy headquarters when Captain Lewis summoned the two corporals over to his make shift desk.

"Men we have a real problem. Omaha Beach was a disaster. The men were cut to ribbons as they hit the beach. As we understand it, some progress is being made, but it appears its tough going. Utah faired somewhat better. But things there are not moving as we had hoped either. I haven't a clue when we can expect to be relieved. However we're going to hold on to this town come hell or high water. But as I said, I have a major problem. We're running out of everything. Food, ammo, medical supplies, you name it.

If the German launch an all out offensive instead of the probing attacks, we won't be able to complete our mission. We'll fail. If we get caught up between major retreating units from the beach, and strong units in the east, we'll get over run. You men had some success fighting your way here through the hedgerows last night. So I want you to leave

Sainte-Mere-Eglise, and fight your way to the Utah beachhead here." The Captain said as he pointed to an area on the coast of France. "There are two towns they will be heading for as they break out of the beachhead. One is Saint Martin-de-Varreville, the other is Mesieres. Although Mesieres is somewhat closer, it is located on the far right of the lodgment, and may not be the town they push for the hardest. Saint Martin-de-Varreville lies smack damn in the center of the drive from the beach. Both towns were in the area to be controlled by the 101st. But who knows what's going on out there the way our drops went last night. Its possible Germans still hold those towns. If that's the case, our drive up from the beach will be even slower. Lt. Ravens, who brought you here, is organizing two squads. You will each take a squad under Raven's command and fight you're way toward the beach. Rendezvous with any American troops having equipment, and extra supplies, and get them here fast. It's understood you may run into stiff enemy resistance on your way. There's no telling if you'll even make it through. But damn it, we need to try. Any questions?" Captain Lewis inquired of the two corporals.

Harry scanned the map shaking his head, as he looked over at Steve. "Can we take the men we've been fighting with all day? We know them and they know us. I think it would be for the best."

"Absolutely, Corporal. Spread them out between the two squads. Anything else?"

Steve looked down at the map as he drank from his canteen. "Looks like this could be a tough nut to crack. We could be running into one hell of a lot of Krauts as we try breaking through to the beach, and they're attempting to retreat inland. It's a crap shoot. But we'll give it a try, Sir."

"I'm totally aware of what you just pointed out. I appreciate your willingness to give it a try. We have some ammo, a few grenades and extra rations in back of the building. Make sure you get what you need. I would like to have you move out within the hour." Captain Lewis requested as he folded up his map.

"One more thing, Sir. Steve added. "I noticed a paratrooper by the name of Mike Anderson from our fourth squad sitting outside by the fence. I would like to have him in one of our squads."

"By all means." Go ahead and take him the Captain replied as he shook hands with them. As they left the C.P. Harry stopped Steve. "I'll take Franny you take Mike with his BAR. Both men are good automatic weapons men."

"Yeah, sounds good, Harry. I like the match up." Steve agreed as they walked over to Lt. Ravens.

"Alright everyone listen up. We'll move out in about thirty minutes. Get some chow or rest, gear up on ammo. The two Corporals will get you set up in squads." The Lieutenant informed his men.

Sitting with the men Lt. Ravens had assembled was Mike Anderson. As Ravens walked off he stood up and walked over to Steve and Harry. "Man it's great to see the two of you." He said as they shook hands. "I've been all over this country today, and you're the first guys I met from our platoon."

Steve informed him about Archie and Lt. Winslow. Then he gave Anderson a quick run down on what they had been through since they landed. Harry divided up the men into two twelve man squads. Franny, Newton and Woodward went into Harry's squad, while Steve took Anderson, Brant and McGruder to fill out his squad.

About twenty minutes later Lt. Ravens walked up to the men as he finished a cigarette. "We need to get moving. Kenrude your squad will lead out. I will follow back with Jensen's squad. You can set the pace, but let's not fall into any ambushes if we can help it. No one gets killed while I'm in charge. Is that clear?"

Stunned by the Lieutenant's last comment, Steve responded he would do his best. It confirmed his suspicions that their leader was not up to this mission. He could not have seen much combat since they landed. It gave Steve a strange feeling in his gut. Looking back at Harry one more time, he told his quad to move out with McGruder and Brant taking point.

Thunderous explosions from heavy artillery rolled across the country side, as fighting on Utah Beach raged on. Smaller explosions, along with the rattle of automatic weapons fire could be heard all around them, as pockets of paratroopers continued engaging enemy forces through out the Norman coastal area.

By now danger of the hedgerows were firmly implanted in Steve's psyche. The tangled brush could hide individuals, small anti tank guns, or entire squads could be lurking in ambush for unsuspecting Americans.

In about forty minutes Steve came to a stop near a small crossroads. He signaled for Lt. Ravens to come forward.

"Sir, which way do you want us to go? The sign stuck in the hedgerow over there says Ravenoville is dead ahead, and Beuzeville would be to our right. I think we should continue forward." Steve informed the Lieutenant.

After studying the map for several minutes Lt. Ravens shook his head. "If we go straight we'll not get to the towns Captain Lewis pointed out. We should turn right toward Beuzeville." Steve looked over at the map running his finger along the route. "That is true, Lieutenant. However, this road appears to be a main route from the beach back to Sainte-Mere-Eglise. Don't you think the invasion force would try using this road for an inland assault?"

"Well they might, Corporal. But our orders are to achieve either Saint Martin-de-Varreville or Mesieres. And that's where we are headed. So we go right. Any problems with that, Corporal?" Lt. Ravens answered indignantly.

"No, Sir." Steve replied, as he motioned for McGruder and Brant to move out to their right.

The new road they were on was much narrower. Thick hedgerows still paralleled the road on both sides. After several hundred yards Steve told his men to stop, waiting for Anderson to catch up with him.

"It's way to quiet, Mike. Way to quiet." Steve explained as he knelt down on one knee. "I don't like it. We're boxed in with no where to go."

Before Mike could respond, Lt. Ravens was standing over them. "Problem, Corporal?"

"Sir this road is just a death trap. We don't know if any one is dug in up ahead, or who holds the fields on the other sides of these damn hedgerows. I think we should fall back and follow the main road toward the beach. We don't have the resources to take on a battle in this situation."

"Oh you think so, Corporal! Well I'm in command here and I make the decisions, and I also follow orders. We keep on going. Is that clear, Kenrude."

"Sir, I understand what the Captain requested. But they aren't any good if we get massacred on this road." Steve replied staring Lt. Ravens in the eye.

"Do you wish me to have Corporal Jensen take lead?" Lt. Ravens snapped angrily. "Do you wish to have a court martial for failing to follow orders? What do you wish to do, Corporal?" "I'll lead, Sir." Steve responded as he waved for Brant and McGruder to come back to him. After the Lieutenant walked back, Steve talked to his point men. "I'll keep an eye on you; you keep an eye on me. No more than five yards out front. I can't see you when you get around those curves. Understood?"

Both men nodded their heads as they retook their positions.

The road began twisting and turning nearly every quarter mile, making the route more precarious and unnerving. Steve ran up to his point men, signaling his squad to close up behind them.

As they reached a sharp curve Steve told his men to stop. Mike Anderson came running up from behind.

"Let me take point, Steve. With my BAR, I can push the bastards back if need be. I know how you want things done. I can do it."

After a moment of thought Steve agreed. "Slow, Mike. Take it real slow. Something isn't right out there."

Mike nodded in agreement as he started cautiously round the curve.

"Holy shit! Damn it no one move! We've got mines." Mike yelled, "We've got mines." He repeated.

Steve stepped up aside Mike to look around the bend. In the road were bodies of a man and woman, along with a demolished two wheel hay cart. Their belongings were scattered about the road.

As they were looking over the situation, Lt. Ravens came charging up from the rear. "What is it now Corporal, we can't keep lolly gagging around all day."

"Sir the road is mined. We're going to have to back up and follow the main road like I talked with you about earlier." Steve informed his angry lieutenant.

"What makes you think a mine did that. It could have been a mortar or an artillery shell. You don't know there are mines in that road." Lieutenant Ravens argued angrily.

"Lieutenant, that hole is too small for an artillery or mortar round. That was done by a mine." Anderson explained as Harry now joined them.

"He's right, Sir. One of those poor people stepped on a mine big enough to take out a truck or blow treads off a tank." Steve stated backing up his BAR man.

"I'll show you there are no mines out there. Follow me." Lt. Ravens stated boldly as he began walking toward the shattered cart. "See, what did I tell you, now lets get moving." "Watch your step." Steve told the men as they slowly walked up to the cart.

Inside the cart wrapped in a blanket, was a small girl. Harry checked for a pulse as Brant and McGruder checked her folks. "She's dead. Her back is all bloody. What ever hit her came up from underneath this wagon. That was a mine sir. No doubt about it." Harry informed the Lieutenant as he peered down the road.

"Everyone get down." Franny called out, picking up a rock about the size of a football. "See those small rocks in the middle of the left rut. There's a mine planted right there. Look at the dirt around it. I'm telling you sir, you better get down." Franny angrily told Lt. Ravens as he pitched the rock.

Franny was one hundred percent accurate. When the stone landed on the loose rocks the mine exploded, sending a shower of dirt, rocks and steel in every direction.

"Alright everyone retrace your steps back to the curve and follow our same path back to the crossroads. Stay on the side of the road." Steve explained calmly.

"No! Everyone stay where you are. Corporal we're not going to walk all the way back to the crossroad.

There's an opening in the hedgerow just a short way back. We'll crawl through it and take a short cut across the field on the other side." Lt. Ravens screamed.

"Sir if this road is mined you can bet your bottom dollar so is that field. That's plain suicide sir, and I'm not going to kill my men over such a dangerous plan." Steve screamed back at Lt. Ravens.

"I've had enough of you insubordination, Corporal. Consider yourself under arrest. I'll have you court marshaled when we get to the beach. Corporal Jensen you're now my team leader. Back the troops up and take us to that opening we passed. Anderson, you will assume Kenrude's roll." Lt. Ravens ordered as he glared at Steve.

"Sir, I will do as I'm told, but I agree with Kenrude. That field for all intent and purposes is mined. We should go back to the crossroad." Harry attempted to explain.

"No, Corporal we cross the field. That is an order!" The Lieutenant raged as he waved his arms toward Harry.

Nodding his head Harry walked back around the curve, leading his men toward the opening in the hedgerow.

After Franny and Anderson crawled through the hole with their BAR's, Lt. Ravens pushed Harry aside. "I'll go next. I'll lead, Corporal. It will demonstrate at Kenrude's court martial I knew what I was doing. Have the men spread out across the field so we can cross it quicker. None of this single file bullshit." Lt. Ravens directed Harry, as he began walking into the recently plowed field.

As Steve was the last man through the hole, Harry stopped him. "I don't like this, Steve." "Yeah I know, let's hope the Lieutenant was right and I was wrong, or we may lose some real good men." Steve replied as he began following McGruder's foot steps.

They were less than half way across the field, when an explosion sent the last man on the right flying through the air.

"Mines!" Harry yelled out. Stop where you are. Carefully turn around. Retrace your steps. Be careful, some of these mines may be hooked in sets. One goes off; it blows up three more with it."

Most of the men dropped to their knees, took out their bayonets and began probing the ground in front of them. "Got one Woodward called out."

"Mark it with that stick lying next to you then move on." Steve called out.

Lt. Ravens spun around. "Kenrude you keep your mouth shut. You're no longer in charge of anything."

He began walking back at a brisk pace as he continued berating Steve.

"Sir, Stop! You need to watch for mines." Harry yelled out.

Just then Lt. Ravens left foot struck a mine. The click was loud enough for most of the men to hear it.

"Shit!" Steve yelled. "Don't move sir. Let me crawl out there and see what we can do. Just don't move!" Steve knelt down pulling out his bayonet. He had probed about three feet when Lt. Ravens began to yell.

"This is ridiculous, Kenrude. If I just take a good leap, I can maybe get away with just a minor injury."

"No Sir. Don't do it." Harry warned him. "You take your foot off that mine and it goes right now. It'll blow you to shit. Even if you don't get hurt bad, you may just land on another mine. And remember, these mines could be linked together for maximum casualties. So damn it, just fucking stand still!"

Figuring everything was under control, Steve once again began to probe.

"Found another one." Newton called out. "And you're right, Corporal, this one has a wire running away from it. They are tied together."

"One more here" Brant yelled as he worked his way around it.

"Hell I can do this. Lt. Ravens yelled as he prepared to jump.

"No!" Steve screamed as he covered his head.

Attempting to jump forward, Lt. Ravens pulled his foot from the mine, It exploded, ripping his left leg totally from his body. A second explosion sent Newton flying through the air. A third mine exploded far enough away not to cause any more injuries.

"You ignorant son of a bitch! You son of a bitch!" Steve screamed at the dying Lieutenant.

"Help me, Kenrude. I, I don't want to die out here. Help….," were the last words Ravens spoke before he succumbed to his injuries.

One by one the men made it back to the hedgerow. Crawling back out to the road they all sat down to rest their nerves.

Steve took out his binoculars hoping to see some sign of life from Newton. But after seeing the body close up, it was clear he probably never felt a thing.

Harry stood aside of Steve before crawling back onto the road. "What a damn disaster. Newton was a good man."

"Yeah, yeah he was." Steve replied shaking his head.

Once they were back on the road, Harry called the men together. "Alright listen up. Ravens placed me in command when he demoted Kenrude. As most of you know, Steve and I have always worked as a team. It has worked well that way. Plus the Lieutenant wanted Kenrude court marshaled. So here's the way it is. If you want me and Mike to lead let me know. If you want Kenrude and me to continue as we were let me know."

"I'm done with replacing, Steve. I didn't want to do it in the first place. But to be honest, I knew if I said no, the S.O.B. would have court marshaled me too." Mike Anderson stated as he looked over the rest of the men.

Private Juarez, one of the men they picked up at Sainte-Mere-Eglise stood up. "I vote we forget about everything Ravens did or said. When we find a superior officer, we tell them about his death in a mine field, and leave everything else out. Kenrude I trust you and Jensen. I heard what you guys all went through this morning. I think you can get us through this alive."

Everyone instantly agreed with everything Juarez proposed.

"Yeah Steve, you and Harry have kept a lot of us alive. You need to keep working as a team." Phil Brant added, giving Steve a thumb's up sign.

After listening to the men Harry stood up. "Alright, that makes it official as far as I'm concerned. Guys, we're way behind schedule. We need to figure out a plan. I wish we had the Lieutenant's map but it's out there with him. So what do you think, Steve?"

"First off, we need to get back to the crossroads and turn west. After that, we keep going toward the beach or link up with more of or guys. That's the best we can hope for right now as I see it." He informed the men.

Everyone agreed. With out being told Brant, McGruder and Anderson took point, leading them back down the narrow road.

Arriving at the crossroad, the Corporals met at the intersection. They scanned the roads in every direction hoping to see Americans.

"Well west it is, Stevie boy." Harry said to Steve with a big grin on his face.

Juarez, Woodward and Franny took point, as they began their west ward trek. About two miles down the road, they came to another crossroad. Steve looked over the only road sign that lay in the hedgerow. It stated Beuzeville was to their left about half a kilometer.

"Do you hear that?" Juarez asked Harry. "Sounds like someone is moaning."

"I thought that was just me. Where's it coming from?" Harry responded as he strained to make out the sound.

"Over here, over here." Franny called out from the hedgerow to the west.

A paratrooper lay in the underbrush covered in blood, with most of his right hand missing.

"Where did you come from?" Harry inquired as several men tried to bandage the man's severe wounds.

"About ten of us headed south about a half hour ago. We ran into krauts. Thick as hell. Tanks, artillery everything you can think of. We thought we could fight our way down to the breach. But they murdered us. I guess lucky for me, a shell from a naval gun landed near by. Sent me flying. That's when I lost my hand, but the krauts for got about me so I crawled away. I was the only one to get out of there. Don't."

The man began to choke as blood poured from his mouth. "Don't go that …" He coughed several times before his head turned to the side.

Harry reached over closing the man's eyes. "I guess he answered that question for us. We go toward Beuzeville."

"Yeah, no doubt. Alright let's form up." Steve directed their men.

Woodward and Franny took point again, as they began walking the half kilometer toward Beuzeville. The closer they walked toward town, the more it became apparent control of the city was up for grabs. Smoke rose from burning buildings, as small arms fire and small explosions echoed through the streets. Just on the edge of town, Harry observed three paratroopers coming up out of a drainage ditch.

The Sergeant leading the men noticed Harry about the same moment. He waved at Harry wanting him to approach.

"Sergeant Shrider is my name. Glad to see you are part of the 101st. Who are you and what are you up to right now?"

"I'm Corporal Jensen this is Corporal Kenrude. We came from Sainte-Mere-Eglise. Captain Lewis sent us out to find help to hold the town. He hoped we could break through to the beach." Harry informed Sgt. Shrider.

"You aren't getting through to the beach any time soon. There are a thousand krauts between us and our guys. But we have a small battle going on right now. We hold nearly the entire town again. We threw the krauts out twice, but they keep coming back. The last attack was in force. But we took control after quite a battle. There's one group of krauts left in the church. We figure about twenty of them. Then we have one more group in that stone apartment building near the town square. We don't have any idea how many are in there. They keep running from floor to floor, window to window. We are just about ready to take the church. We have it surrounded. The apartment building will be an entirely different story. We ducked out of the battle for right now. We're headed over to the C.P. to report to Lt. Gossman. He's 82nd and in control of all the forces holding the town. You better come with us.

I'm sure the Lieutenant will be glad to see a few fresh faces. We can use all the help we can get." The Sergeant reported wiping several layers of dirt from his face.

"Sound good to you?" Harry inquired of Steve.

"Yeah this whole jump was a mess. Let's do what we have to do for now." He agreed. "Alright follow us, our C.P. is on the east side of town." Sgt. Shrider stated as he headed out.

The C.P. in Beuzeville was much better than the shanty in Sainte-Mere-Eglise. Lt. Gossman had taken over a small one story brick building near the eastern edge of town, just as the Sergeant prepared to open the door, it swung wide open. Standing in the doorway was a tall Lieutenant.

"Where the hell have you been, Sergeant and who are these men?" He asked angrily.

"We had trouble fighting our way out of town. I lost two more men; they had us boxed in pretty good.

I found these men approaching up the main road from Sainte-Mere-Eglise. I told them to come along we needed extra help." Sgt. Shrider responded.

Nodding his head Lt. Gossman said, "Fine. I have ten men up by the panther waiting for us. One way or the other, we're going to kick those sons a bitches out of this town. I don't care if we are short of ammo, or men, we'll hold this damn town. Now follow me." The Lieutenant demanded walking briskly down the street.

Approaching an intersection, Steve observed about fifteen men huddled beside a burned out panther tank parked about ten yards from a large church. Lt. Gossman spoke with a Corporal a few seconds then turned to Steve.

"I'm sorry, Corporal but I need to have your men help us out. Go along with the Sergeant. He and his men are going to attack a multi-storeyed apartment house. But they don't have enough help to do it efficiently.

Kill every one of those murdering sons-a-bitches. If they're dead, I know damn well they won't give me another problem like they have up to now. Clear it out; finish them off while we throw these bastards back out of the church again. Any questions," Lt. Gossman inquired with cold steely eyes.

Harry and Steve looked at one another before responding they were ready to go.

Sergeant Shrider led the men through several severely damaged buildings, then down a side street to the town square. Several paratroopers were using burned out vehicles for cover, as they returned fire toward the three story building. "If we charge out across that court yard we'll get our asses shot off, Steve. We need to find a better way in." Harry stated. "I got an idea. Wait here." Taking a deep breath Harry dashed out into the town square, as bullets slammed into the ground behind him. He dove for cover behind a burned out truck, where a paratrooper was reloading his rifle.

"Is there another way into that damn place? Any type of frontal charge would be suicide." Harry asked the soldier.

"Sure Mack. I can get you right up to a side entrance, over there right behind that statue. You just need to work your way around the block to get there. If you try to get there any other way, they'll pick you apart.

They have the courtyard covered. Some times they get up on the roof. Then even these wrecks don't provide much cover. Someone needs to get in there and flush the bastards out. We didn't have enough men here to keep them penned up inside, and assault at the same time. Glad you could join us." "Well our invitation to this party just arrived. Other wise we would have been here earlier." Harry responded, removing his magazine to see how much ammo was left in his Thompson.

The soldier laughed at Harry's response. "Don't let my old man hear comments like that. He's the Post Master in Cleveland."

"Okay, thanks for the tip. I won't move to Cleveland after the war." Harry replied slapping the man on top of his helmet.

Darting back to the rest of the team, he dropped down beside Sergeant Shrider. Speaking slowly, he explained the directions the man in the courtyard had given him to reach a side door.

"Alright sounds good to me. Let's go." The Sergeant answered.

Following Sergeant Shrider, the men slipped into the alley, just as a large volley of fire roared out from the windows of the occupied building. They maneuvered their way through a couple of side streets, and two burned out buildings, before coming to a stop near the side entrance of the apartment building.

"Here we are guys." The Sergeant said nervously, as he pointed to the bodies of civilians, Germans, and paratroopers lying about in the square. "It has been pure hell. We could keep a couple men across the road in that store front, covering this door so no one can escape. Maybe one of your BAR guys?"

Steve nodded. "Anderson, take two men with you into that store front. After we go in, no Germans come out."

"That's good, Corporal. When ever you're ready we'll go." Sgt. Shrider told Steve, as he looked up toward the currently unoccupied second floor windows.

As soon as the three men were set up across the street, Steve tapped Sgt. Shrider on the arm. "We're ready.

Kick the door in, toss a grenade and we go." Steve suggested preparing his Thompson for the assault.

Sgt. Shrider removed a grenade from his belt and pulled the pin. He gave the wooden door a mighty kick with his left leg, pitched the grenade, while ducking for cover to his right.

As soon as the blast subsided, Harry jumped in front of the open door, spraying fire from his Thompson.

He charged forward with his squad following in close order. Steve scrambled through the door followed by his team. They dashed up the stair well just inside the door, taking the Germans on the second floor by surprise, but they reacted quickly. At the far end of the hall they had built a barricade to keep anyone from moving from one side of the building to the other. There was an MG-34 machine gun barrel staring Steve directly in the face.

Luckily the gunner hadn't finished reloading his weapon.

"Get back, get down." Steve called out to his men as they dropped prone on the stairs." Machine gun bullets began ripping into the ceiling above them, as well as into the floor in front of them, sending sharp splinters of wood toward their faces.

"McGruder get down stairs and grab Franny if he's available."

Rolling on to his side, Steve pulled a grenade from his belt. He yanked the pin, then blindly tossed it towards the barricade. He heard it bounce of the wall about half way down the corridor before it exploded.

The gunners ducked for a few seconds, then resumed their fire as Franny charged up the stairs.

"If I stick my head up there to aim they'll take it clear off, Steve." Franny explained looking bewildered.

"Yeah I know. Can you just set it over the top stair and fire a long burst to get their heads down. During the delay I'll toss another grenade."

"Oh yeah that I can do," Franny replied, cautiously sliding his weapon on to the floor. When Steve had the grenade ready, Franny opened fire. The German gunners ducked as bullets from the BAR tore chunks out of their barricade.

Steve pitched another grenade but had too much height on this throw. It hit the ceiling, before dropping to the floor where it exploded, several feet in front of the German position. "Damn it! Steve yelled angry at himself for missing a second throw. "They won't fall for the stunt again."

Steve said shaking his head.

"Oh yeah, Send some one out to relieve Anderson. They won't be able to resist two BAR's firing." Franny said smiling.

Without being told the man nearest the bottom of the stairs ran out to get Anderson. Seconds later the big BAR man dashed up the stairs to Steve. After explaining the plan, Mike moved up toward the top of the stairs laying down aside of Franny.

Before they fired, Juarez grabbed Steve's arm. "Corporal, let me throw the grenade. I was pitching minor league ball before the war. I can toss that thing into a fish bowl if that's what you want."

I don't need it in a bowl Juarez; just get it behind that damn barricade." Steve explained as a huge section of ceiling plaster was ripped off by the German MG-34.

Smiling, Juarez took the grenade then nodded at Anderson.

"Counting down from five," Mike said holding up his hand.

Dropping his last finger both men opened fire. As Franny predicted, the gunners dropped behind the barricade.

Juarez stood up, throwing the grenade down the corridor as if pitching a fast ball toward a catcher's mitt.

It bounced off the wall directly behind the barricade exploding in midair.

Ignoring all the doors in the corridor, Franny charged the barricade firing his BAR the entire way.

One member of the MG-34 crew was dead. The second man although badly wounded, made an attempt to retake his position. A quick burst from Franny's weapon sent him tumbling to the floor.

The rest of the squad immediately dispersed among the rooms looking for any Germans still hiding on the floor.

Harry's squad charged up to the second floor ready to assist. "We own the first floor, Stevie boy. We lost two men in the effort. This place is a death trap." Harry informed the men, signaling for his team to hold up.

"Good, that's good." Steve replied taking another grenade from his pocket.

"Are you growing those damn things?" Harry asked comically.

"No. Kind of wish I could though." Steve smiled as he hooked it on his belt. Just one of the extras I took from Capt. Lewis's supply room.

With the second floor clear, Steve's squad assembled below the stairs leading to the third floor. "We killed two more. I think most of them ran upstairs when we attacked. "Anderson reported knowing the third floor assault was going to be bloody.

"What's the plan, Steve?" Franny inquired. "If we don't have a good assault plan, we're going to lose a lot of good men over this lousy building.

"First problem is, we only have one way up and they know it. Second problem it's an open staircase. We have no cover as we head up. We'll have to send them scurrying before we make an attack. Best idea I have is to toss several grenades, then you and Mike Spray the corridor as we charge up the stairs. That should give us a level playing field." Steve explained as he pulled the grenade from his belt.

"Hey I have an idea." Pulling a lighter from his pocket Franny suggested. "Let's just set the damn place on fire. We start it here on the second floor. We wait outside. As they come out to escape we shoot them like rats in a barrel."

Harry shook his head. "Sorry Franny that's not an option. I'm ready when you are Steve." "Alright let's do this." Steve said as he and Brant prepared to pull pins from the grenades they were holding.

All at once there were two thumps on the stairs behind them, "Grenades! McGruder called as he reached for one potato masher, tossing it back over the open banister.

Franny kicked the second one down the stairs toward the first floor. Everyone attempted to scatter one way or the other to clear the flying debris.

After the grenades detonated, two German soldiers wearing SS uniforms charged down to the second floor, Schmeiser's blazing. One man in Harry's squad dropped to the floor, as a second man screamed grabbing his abdomen. Anderson jumped out of the first door on the left side of the corridor. He let go a long burst from his BAR. One SS soldier stumbled before falling flat on the stairs. The second man dropped to his knees, then threw himself down the staircase toward the first floor. Hitting the landing, he jumped up running toward the door. Nevertheless, the two men Steve assigned to cover the entrance from across the street, opened fire stopping him in his tracks.

Steve signaled the men to reassemble just below the staircase. He was just about to explain his plan of attack when huge explosions began to rock Beuzeville. No one moved as dust and plaster began falling from the ceiling. Everyone looked at each other for a moment, just before the unmistakable shriek of a British Spitfire roared overhead.

"Bombs get out, get out!" Harry yelled, pushing men toward the shattered staircase.

In full panic mode, the men rushed down the splintered stairs, as more whistling bombs fell from the attacking aircraft.

Germans occupying the roof of the apartment building fired at the attacking planes with every weapon they had. The next Spitfire streaking in from the south released both of its bombs as it approached the apartment building. One crashed through the roof detonating on the third floor. The second bomb struck a balcony on the second floor exploding seconds later.

In an instant, the apartment building was turned into a massive pile of rubble. The side walls collapsed inwardly, as their supports disintegrated. It would have been impossible for anyone to survive such a horrific explosion.

Several more Spitfires raced past at near roof top level, strafing anything that moved. Franny looked up from the cobblestone street shaking his fist at one of the pilots. It was evident the British

Pilot recognized the American uniform. He backed off his machine guns, before pulling up hard and banking off toward the east. The remaining pilots immediately ceased strafing or bombing the town.

Two pilots circled once more, before making a slower pass over the devastated town, waving their wings in recognition of friendly forces.

After the last spitfire flew off toward the east, paratroopers began emerging from their hiding places.

Steve called the squads together. However, two men failed to answer.

The men split up searching through the rubble of the apartment house that now filled the streets.

One paratrooper was found lying face down, just feet from where he had exited the doomed structure. He had been struck in the back of the head and neck by machine gun bullets. The second man was lying toward the rear of the building, partially covered by debris. After uncovering his body they found a board sticking out of his chest. Steve knelt down, sliding his hand over the man's face, closing his eyes forever.

As Steve stood up, it was the first time he realized there was not a shot to be heard in Beuzeville.

After reassembling the men, he led them back toward the church where Sgt. Shrider was standing with a couple of his paratroopers.

"How many did you lose corporal?" Sgt. Shrider inquired of Steve.

"We lost four men trying to take that damn place." Harry responded angrily. "How many did you lose taking the church?"

"Three. But al least now we hold the entire town. And with air cover, we shouldn't have to worry about another counter attack. Come on, Lt. Gossman wants us to meet him at the C.P." Sgt. Shrider informed the men as he turned to walk down the street.

After taking a long look at the damaged church Steve called out. "Hey Sarg, I have some business to attend to.

I'll meet you at the C.P. in a few minutes."

"Alright don't be long, Kenrude." Shrider called back as he continued toward the C.P. Walking into the church, Steve removed his helmet. Stepping over several dead German soldiers he walked up the center aisle. Placing his helmet and machine gun in the first pew, he knelt down below a large crucifix dangling precariously by just one cable.

"Oh God," He began, "I don't know how to start this. Your teachings tell us killing another human being is wrong. But that's all any of us have been doing today. None of this makes any sense. I've seen things today that have shaken my very soul. I'm not sure if I have what it takes to finish this mission. I'm terribly tired, physically, mentally and spiritually. Give me the strength I so desperately need. My men depend on me for guidance. But I'm not sure I have anything left inside of me to give. Help me dear God."

Standing up, he observed a small metal stand with vigil candles still burning over in a corner. He walked over lighting a fresh candle in a blue glass holder. There was a small steel box for donations. He dug in his jacket pocket, pulling out a French Frank he found on the street in Saint-Mere-Eglise earlier in the day. He folded it several times before being able to slide it into the box.

"Merci." A woman's voice said softly from behind him.

Startled, Steve instinctively grabbed his knife as he spun around. A young nun stood just feet behind him. He could not understand how she had walked across all the rubble without alerting him to her presence.

"You will not need that I assure you." She said pointing at the knife.

Feeling embarrassed, he quickly slid it back into its sheath. "I'm sorry." He told the woman who was smiling up at him.

"No need to be sorry. It is your job to be wary. I should not have walked up on you like that." She apologized.

"You speak good English. Did you study in America?" Steve inquired.

"Yes, for two years at a college in New York. Is there anything I can do for you?" She asked as she studied

Steve's very tired face.

"No. I just stopped by to talk to God for a few minutes. I should be getting back to the C.P." Steve replied, as he walked over to pick up his helmet and weapon. "What is you name sister?"

"Sister Carmella. And yours?" She inquired.

"Kenrude, Corporal Steve Kenrude, From Minnesota." He replied with a smile.

"Ah, Minnesota I was there in 1938. Such a beautiful state, I visited a rather large Benedictine Monastery for women in St. Joseph, with several other sisters from New York. We spent three days there with the congregation. It was a wonderful experience. There is a Monastery for monks, along with a men's college about five miles away if I recall correctly. It's built by a huge lake with a rather strange name, surrounded by beautiful pines" She explained.

"I know a little about those places. They're maybe sixty miles or so north of my home town. I knew a girl that went to the women's

Monastery to become a Nun like you." Steve informed Sister Carmella, suddenly feeling real home sick.

"Well I need to go. I have to check in at the C.P. They are waiting for me."

"Ah, yes. Lt. Gossman. I do not particularly appreciate his attitude. Of course I just met him this morning.

So I might be mistaken. I will be most grateful when this war passes us by, so good luck Corporal Steven Kenrude. Perhaps I will get back to Minnesota some day after the war. We could visit again under better circumstances. What is the name of your home town?" The petite sister inquired.

"Glendale, Minnesota. If you ever get there, I would love to introduce you to my family and have that long talk." Steve responded as he smiled at the saintly looking woman.

Sister Carmella stepped forward, making the sign of the cross in front of Steve's face, as she recited a prayer quietly. "God be with you Steven. I shall pray for you." Steve smiled as he prepared to leave. After taking a few steps toward the door he stopped. Turning back toward Sister Carmella he said. "Sister you probably have a better connection with God than I do. When you're praying will you ask him to end this war, my younger brother wants to join the army. I don't want him involved in all of this.

I don't want him seeing all this death and destruction."

"Yes Corporal, I can ask." She replied nodding her head.

Not sure what to say, Steve smiled then walked toward the door. Replacing his helmet, he walked slowly down the aisle as the young sister began removing debris from the Alter in the front of the church.

He had not walked very far when he heard a familiar voice.

"Kenrude is that you?"

Steve turned to see Oscar Joblanski, one of his first squad men coming out off a side street with several other paratroopers.

"Hey Joblanski where the hell have you been," Steve inquired as the two men shook hands.

"Hell, Corporal I don't have a clue. I was captured by a bunch of krauts when I hit the ground. They locked me in a cellar for several hours, before a group of 82nd men took the house and killed the bastards. I yelled and kicked like hell before they realized I was down there. So I stayed with them until we got here. I've been a gopher for Gossman since then. Can you get me back on the squad? I need to get back into this war."

Joblanski explained as they walked toward the C.P.

"Consider yourself back on the squad, Oscar. Where the hell is your carbine?" Steve inquired as he observed Joblanski carrying a German sub machine gun.

"Hell I don't know. The kruats took it away from me when I was captured. I haven't seen it since. So I grabbed one of their pieces and ammo before I left the house. Figured I'm going to use this thing all the way to Berlin, and let Adolph pay for the ammo." Joblanski explained, as they turned onto the street leading to the command post.

Arriving at the C.P, everyone who knew Joblanski clapped and whistled.

Harry stood up from a pile of rubble he was sitting on. He walked over slapping the wayward paratrooper on the shoulder.

"Good to see you, Oscar." Harry said smiling at the capable soldier. "Guess what, Steve I found one of my men too. Gossman had Russ Abbot working as a clerk in the C.P. I told Gossman he was mine and that was that."

Before the two men could say any more, the Lieutenant walked out onto the street.

"How many men did you lose?" He inquired of the two Corporals.

"Four!" Harry responded angrily. "That was four to many for that damn building. We would have lost more if we would've had to assault the third floor. What a damn shame." "Look, Corporal no one really needs your attitude right now. I've lost more men than I care to think about since we landed.

You're not in this war alone. Some times we just do what we need to do, and take the good with the bad." Gossman yelled back at Harry.

"With all due respect sir, if we continue wasting lives on buildings like that, we'll run out of men long before we run out of krauts." Harry replied indignantly.

"And that will be enough, Corporal. That's an order." Lt. Gossman responded glaring at Harry. Turning to Steve he continued. "Bed your guys down for the night in the building with the red store front over there.

I will have a mission for you in the morning. Any questions?" Lieutenant Gossman asked as he prepared to walk away.

"Just one sir, I ran across Joblanski. He's in my squad. I would like to have him back." Steve requested in a very civil tone.

"Fine, take him. If you find anymore of your men here you can have them also. Just bed them down and get some rest. Tomorrow could be an equally long day. I'll have someone get you around 0500.

Any thing else," Lt. Gossman asked as he glared at the two corporals.

"No sir that will be all." Steve replied.

After Lt. Gossman walked back into the command post, Harry led the men toward the building they were assigned to. It had been a hat making shop. After some rearranging, the men set up their sleeping areas before breaking out some well deserved rations.

Steve leaned back against the wall right inside the door, as he ate slowly from a ration can. It wasn't home cooking, but it tasted damn good after the long day. No one was saying a word. The only sound inside the building was the sound of spoons clinking against the sides of cans. Steve tried to reexamine what had all transpired since he left that damn plane. It was all pretty much a jumbled mess. He thought how strange war could be. Inside the church dead Germans were lying all over the place, while a young nun was concerned with dirt on the alter. He thought about how frightened Lt. Ravens was that it blinded his good judgment, getting himself and one other man killed.

After finishing his meal, he slid down to the rug he was sitting on. He adjusted the small pillow he found in the back room before closing his eyes. It was extremely hard to relax enough for sleeping. All around Beuzeville fighting continued. Huge explosions vibrated the floor, as both side's poured artillery and mortars into the nonstop battle. D-Day had come and gone. Somehow through out it all, he had survived. To say the least, he was extremely grateful. He tried hard to pray, but somehow the word s would not come. He thought about Sister Carmella's words. "God be with you Steven. I will pray for you."

He knew she meant every word she had spoken. And for tonight that was good enough for him. Slowly he drifted off to a fitful sleep.

Around 0500 Steve awoke to a soldier shaking his arm. "Corporal, the Lieutenant wants you and your men ready to go by 0600 so you better get a move on."

"Alright." Steve responded as he slowly sat up rubbing his eyes.

"Okay guys. Wake up. Gossman wants us out at the C.P. in one hour." He called out loud enough for everyone to hear him. It was surprising. No one complained, no one grumbled. They all went about their business, getting ready to start their second day at war.

Steve and Sgt. Shrider had their men assembled in front of the command post by 0600. Lt. Gossman was looking over several pieces of paper his orderly handed him.

"Alright first off. Yesterday our men did establish beachheads on Omaha and Utah beaches. It appears a break out could happen from Utah this morning. That is what we need. So Kenrude and Jensen. You can pick any eight men you want to take with you. Work your way toward the breakout and get us some trucks, ambulances, or anything we can use to get our injured to a field hospital. Secondly, get us and your Capt. Lewis munitions, food or what ever else can be provided to strengthen our positions. The men you do not take, turn over to Sgt. Shrider. He needs them to relieve our perimeter positions. Do you have any questions?"

Both Steve and Harry were fine with their orders. They walked away from the rest of the men discussing who they were going to take. The decision was pretty simple.

Harry walked back toward the men. "Joblanski, Anderson, Brant, Woodward, McGruder, Juarez, Abbot and Doogan grab your gear. You're going with us. The rest of you see the Sergeant. Franny you and Juarez will have point. We are following the road out of town past the church. Lead off when you're ready. Brant, you and McGruder cover our rear." As they walked through the town square Steve observed Sister Carmella along with about a half dozen men removing the dead from their church.

Briskly she ran up to the squad. "Where are you headed, Corporal Kenrude?"

"We established a beachhead yesterday on Utah. We're going to get the Lieutenant some much needed help." He replied smiling at the young woman.

"Good. Get some medical help if you can. We have many wounded church members. We could use a doctor. Our doctor was killed the night you landed. We're going to try and set up a clinic in the church.

But we need supplies." Sister Carmella advised he men.

"We will get you all the help we can." Harry assured the nervous woman, as they continued on out of town.

Streams of sun light were just breaking over the eastern horizon when the sounds of aircraft engines filled the air.

"Take cover, get down!" Harry yelled out as he pointed toward two diving German ME-109s.

Bullets began kicking up dirt as everyone dove for cover either in the hedgerows to their left, or the orchard on their right. Both planes made a quick turn, then came roaring back for a second pass flying south to north.

The first pilot fired his machine guns in short spurts aiming toward the hedgerows. The second fighter screamed overhead without firing a round. After the second pass, both pilots continued on a northerly course.

When it was evident the fighters were not returning, everyone reassembled on the road. Now, they kept a closer eye on the sky, in case more Luftwaffe fighters should appear.

"What do you suppose that was about?" Mike asked Harry and Steve. "You wouldn't think they would quit so fast."

"Maybe they were empty. Maybe we weren't their first targets this morning." Harry replied as he scanned the horizon looking north.

Steve was just about to tell the men to move out, when several German vehicles came driving through the orchard directly toward them. A half-track led the procession to the edge of the orchard before stopping. A Sergeant attending an MG-42 mounted machine gun yelled out. "Halt! Stay as you are or I will shoot. Drop your weapons and packs. Put your hands in the air."

Several more German soldiers came running from a truck stopped behind the half track. They surrounded the small band of paratroopers nervously pointing their rifles at them.

Carefully the men lowered their weapons before removing their packs. One by one they raised their hands.

A black staff car drove around the other vehicles stopping on the road. Two men in black raincoats emerged from the back seat.

"Gestapo or S.S?" Harry asked Steve. "We better watch what we say. These guys don't play nice."

"Shut up!" The taller of the two men called out.

Several more men in black uniforms came walking from the orchard. They all wore insignias of the S.S.

"Who would be in charge here? Hmm, let me see. Two Corporals and no officers. Did we kill your officers? Or are you a rogue operation?" A tall arrogant looking German wearing a monocle inquired of Harry.

"Hitler was a Corporal in the last war. He did alright the way it looks." Anderson responded indignantly.

One of the S.S. men swung his rifle around, planting the stock into Mike's abdomen, causing him to fall to his knees. The soldier cocked his weapon placing the muzzle tight against Mike's head.

A shorter more rotund SS officer with a sly grin on his face looked down at the gasping man.

"Do we need to be rough, or are you going to cooperate? I do not have time for games gentlemen. You are all on German soil and behind your lines. That makes you spies or covert agents. I have the right to shoot you on sight. I can do with you as I please, as you are surely commandos."

"We are clearly not commandos." Steve replied pointing to the American flag that had been sewn on the sleeve of every American paratrooper.

Laughing, the officer removed a Lugar from his holster. "You may think that, Corporal. But here I make the decisions. Do you see anyone from the Geneva Convention around to explain all the rules of war?

No, I'm afraid not. You are here unwanted and uninvited by my country. You parachuted here and have killed German soldiers. I say you are commandos maybe even trained assassins."

"First off, we are in France not in Germany. You have no authority over this sovereign nation. And it does not matter how you personally chose to see things, we are covered by the Geneva Convention as combatants and prisoners of war." Steve said in an angry voice.

"So you must be the man in charge, or the one with the biggest mouth. Which is it?" The taller of the two men inquired. Picking up Steve's Thompson the SS Officer examined it for a moment, "nice looking, but not as accurate as our submachine guns, so back to business. You are the man in charge?" He again inquired.

"You can call me the man in charge, or what ever you wish. And that weapon works just fine. There are plenty of bodies all over Normandy that can attest to it." Steve replied smiling at the German officer.

"So you admit killing German's here in this occupied land, which you feel is not part of the Reichsland. Your attitude or bad American manners, which ever it is, does not impress me Corporal. You see, your men have been thrown back into the channel. The invasion was a disaster. The blood of your countrymen runs deep in the English Channel this morning. So you see, every one of you are now commandos and can be shot." The younger S.S Officer replied pointing the Thompson directly at Steve's chest.

"If that's the case, who's doing all the fighting we can here?" Franny asked indignantly.

"Oh well, there are some pockets of your men left to clean up. But be assured, it is of no consequence any more. By the end of the day peace will have returned to all of Normandy, and the glorious third Reich will continue its thousand year reign. Ah. Excuse my bad manners. I'm so sorry I have not introduced myself or my partner.

I am SS Lt. Dietrich and this is SS Lieutenant Bowman. It is only right you should know who your executioners will be," the tall officer announced boldly.

Lt. Bowman stepped forward muttering. "Let's be done with this foolishness. Sergeant, line these spies up along the hedgerow so we can finish and move on."

The soldier manning the MG-42 in the half track smiled as his Sergeant pushed and shoved Steve's men into line near the hedgerow

"Corporal, I condemn you and your men to death for the..." Lt. Dietrich never finished his words as the first fifty caliber rounds from a low flying P-51 Mustang tore into his lanky body.

Two American P-51 Mustangs roared into the area at tree top level firing rockets into the parked vehicles.

The half track erupted into a ball of flame throwing the gunners body a good ten feet into the air. One truck exploded in a wall of flame as the gas tank ruptured. A second truck nearly disintegrated as two rockets slammed into its side simultaneously. The driver of Lt. Dietrich's staff car threw the transmission into reverse, seeking cover in the orchard, but he never made it. Machine gun bullets riddled the vehicle from front to back. He slumped over the steering wheel as his car came to rest against an apple tree.

The German soldiers, who were guarding the paratroopers and survived the deadly strafing run, dove for cover in the hedgerow as did the ten Americans.

The fighter pilots turned a tight circle then roared back, machine guns blazing. Several more rockets slammed into the two remaining vehicles, setting them a blaze. The pilots then pulled up turning north, appearing to make a wide circle around the area. Franny was first to scramble to his feet. He grabbed his BAR, firing into the hedgerow where the Germans had taken cover. Oscar rolled across the road grasping his German submachine gun. Jumping up, he followed Franny supplying him with cover fire. The soldier, who struck Mike, ran head long into the orchard, attempting to avoid the massacre in the hedgerow. No matter how fast he ran, there was no way to out run a hail of lead delivered by a short burst from Mike's BAR. Lt. Bowman survived the attack by swiftly dropping to the road. Standing up, he still held his Lugar menacingly by his side. However, now he found himself peering down the barrel of Harry's Thompson.

"Toss your weapon away Lieutenant." Harry yelled at the short SS officer.

"Well Lieutenant, things have changed, looks to me like we're still in this ball game." Mike said angrily as he thrust the barrel of his BAR into Bowman's midsection.

"I don't scare easily, private. I have been with the Nazi movement while you were still drinking out of a bottle.

Save your intimidation games for someone else." The SS officer sarcastically explained. As Mike prepared to back hand the officer Steve yelled, "Enough Anderson.!

Respecting Steve's directive, Mike backed away.

"Now toss that Lugar, Lieutenant or I'll seriously amputate that hand with one burst from my weapon."

Harry once again instructed the officer.

After a moment of thought, Lt. Bowman handed the pistol to Juarez.

Franny, Oscar and Brant returned with one wounded soldier. "The rest are dead, Steve." Franny reported pushing the weeping soldier to the ground.

"Quit your sniveling. You are a soldier of the Third Reich. Stand up and be a man." A very red faced Lt. Bowman screamed at the wounded soldier.

The private responded saying something in German, upsetting Lt. Bowman all the more. After completing a tirade of what appeared to be German insults, the angry Lieutenant attempted to kick the young private.

Franny pulled the man away, lest the angry officers kick injure him further.

Lt. Bowman turned to Steve as he yelled, "If I were in charge right now that man would be shot. He would pay the ultimate price for his cowardice. He is not an exemplary soldier of the Third Reich."

"Well Lieutenant, it's a good thing you're not in charge. Plus your days of giving orders are over." Harry informed his SS prisoner.

As the Germans were well covered, Steve turned his attention skyward. Both Mustangs were screaming back at them from the east. He and Juarez waved vigorously at the pilots, hoping to assure them everything was under control. Correctly interpreting the hand signals, both pilots waved their wings at the paratroopers, before disappearing back toward the invasion beaches.

"Alright let's continue, Lieutenant. You will be turned over to the allied command when we link up with our men. I'm very sure they'll be glad to see you." Steve informed the arrogant officer.

"I would rather die for the Furher." Lt. Bowman replied snapping to attention.

"Yeah right, Adolph" Franny commented insultingly pushing the Lieutenant forward. Sounds of heavy fighting could be heard all around them. It was clear the landings had been a complete success, contrary to the false information Lt. Dietrich had given them. American forces were now locked in desperate combat with the retreating German army through out the hedgerow country. They desperately needed to expand their beachhead toward the main east-west highways.

After walking several hundred yards, Lt. Bowman stopped cold near a curve in the road. No matter how hard Franny pushed him, the Lieutenant refused to walk. "Steve, something's up. Adolph's got some sort of problem." Franny called out.

"What's the problem, Bowman?" Harry asked, "Mines? You guys plant mines through here?"

"Let's just find out." Woodward countered, grabbing the Lieutenant by the arm shoving him forward as hard as he could.

The injured private nervously called out, "Nein, Nein. Mein feldt, nein." Bunker gehen vorwarts."

Lt. Bowman spun around glaring at the timid private before replying. "Nein! Mines! Mines all over the place!

The fool wants to get us all killed!"

"What did the private say? Something about a bunker?" Harry apprehensively asked Steve.

"I think he said if we continue forward we'll run into a bunker." Steve replied somewhat agitated.

"Who the hell do we believe?" Brant inquired shaking his head.

"I'm not sure, but I have a hunch the private wants to live. The Lieutenant just wants a crack at escaping, so he could care less if we get our asses blown away." Steve retorted as he grabbed the private by the arm.

"Come on Harry, we need to talk with him."

Steve led the private over toward the hedgerow, as Harry followed several feet behind. Speaking slowly Steve asked. "Is there a block house around that next curve?"

Sweating profusely, the nervous private looked at Steve, then over at Harry who was visibly angry. Several times the soldier looked at Harry's face, and the deadly Thompson pointed at his chest. After taking a deep breath the private nodded his head. He replied. "Ya. Stacheldraht. Sehr viele M-42's, Mortars. Ungefahr dreisig men.

Ya Bunker, nicht meinen."

Harry looked at Steve. "How much of that did you get besides machine guns and mortars?"

"Well dreisig means thirty. So there must be about thirty men there. Viele has something to do with an amount. Because when Dad paid at the hardware store some times he would ask Wie viehle or something on that order. But Stacheldraht I haven't a clue." Steve explained totally unsure of his translation.

"Ya sehr Stacheldraht." The private said nodding his head.

"Okay that I don't get." Steve said tentatively trying to figure out a way to come up with an answer.

"Sehr Stacheldraht?" Steve said slowly shaking his head.

The private looked around for several seconds. Cautiously he stepped over to the hedgerow. Picking up a piece of telephone wire, he twisted small pieces of vine around it several inches apart, before handing it to Steve.

"Stacheldraht" He said smiling.

"Barbed wire," Harry acknowledged.

Patting Harry on the shoulder the private said, "Ja! Stacheldraht!"

"And I am guessing there would be a lot of it near a bunker." Steve added to the conversation.

The private knelt down by the side of the road. Picking up a stick, he drew a circle. "Bunker." He then drew four concentric circles around the bunker. "Stacheldraught. Ja?" Steve acknowledged nodding his head.

"Gut!" He then drew six small lines coming out of the bunker. "M-42's." Thinking for a moment, he drew squiggly lines in the dirt coming from the machine guns.

"Over lapping fields of fire?" Harry inquired nervously looking at the drawing.

The private, not sure of what Harry just said waved his arms in the air one over lapping the other.

"Ja?" He said looking at Harry.

"Ja!" Harry replied smiling at the private.

The soldier erased everything then drew a circle again. "Bunker." He then drew three smaller circles, one on each side of the main bunker, inside the second and third rows of wire. Next he drew one more circle behind the main bunker, inside the first and second rows of wire. "Mortars. Ja?"

Steve feeling somewhat confident asked. "Wie viele?"

Smiling the soldier drew a number one in each small circle.

After thinking for a moment he pointed toward the east. Taking his finger, he erased small openings in the wire.

"Eingang. Aber langsam. Nicht gut."

"What the hell!" Harry asked. "Eingang. Entrance through the wire must be on the east side? And I am guessing you would have to work your way through the wire it would be slow going" Steve said slowly.

"Ja Eingang Osten." The private replied pointing again toward the east.

Then he pointed toward the hedgerow. Standing totally erect he brought his hands up toward his eyes, as if using a set of binoculars, "Ja?"

Steve nodded his head. "They have a look out somewhere on top of the hedgerow facing the beach. We could never breach the wire without being seen. They would gun us down before we got in. We need to take out the rear mortar pit and look out position first off. Then figure out the rest."

"I don't know, Steve. Six M-42's inside that bunker. We don't have what it takes to blast that damn thing.

We need to by pass this position and get some help." Harry replied, knowing full well he was right.

"Let's see if we can get a good look before we abandon it." Steve said reassuringly to Harry.

Steve signaled McGruder to join them. "Keep him here, away from the Lieutenant." Returning to the rest of the men he pushed Lt. Bowman into the hedgerow. "You stay right there.

Joblanski, if he attempts to scratch his nose, or shout out one word, shoot him!"

"Got it, Steve!" Oscar replied aiming his submachine gun at the very nervous SS officer. Franny, Mike grab your BAR and follow us. Everyone else stays right here, keep your eyes open.

Using extreme caution, Steve made his way around the curve, tucking in as close to the hedgerow as possible.

After walking about a hundred yards, he was able to see the top of the bunker rise out of a field on his left.

All three mortar pits were clearly identifiable from the rear, as the soldier had drawn them. They were covered with camouflage netting, concealing them from allied aircraft patrolling the area. Any American forces following the road from the beach would be cut to ribbons before they knew what was happening.

They continued quietly searching for the lookout position tucked masterfully into the hedgerow.

Suddenly, all three mortar tubes began firing rounds toward the west. Several of the M-42's sprang to life firing short bursts down the beach road.

"Our guys?" Franny inquired.

"Could be. Sure as hell could be, Franny." Harry responded.

"What do we do, Stevie boy? If you don't have a plan I sure as hell have half a plan." Harry whispered to Steve.

Pulling back a few yards Steve looked intently at Harry. "What've you got?"

"All right. We get everyone up here. Then cut Bowman lose. The man's a fanatic. No matter what, he's going to warn the block house. His commotion will disrupt the operation for a few seconds. Then Franny and Mike poor fire on the block house openings keeping the gunners heads down for a few minutes. Juarez plays World Series winning pitcher again, lobbing grenades into the back pit. I take Brant and Woodward around toward the east side. We should be able to grenade the east pit from outside the wire. Then we take cover in the woods.

From there I'm not sure what we do next." Harry explained knowing the plan had way to may problems.

"I don't like it, but we have to give our guys a chance." Steve responded. "Alright, let's do it. Mike, get the others."

When the men arrived Steve had to smile. Oscar had gagged Bowman with his own necktie.

"Nice job, Joblanski." Harry said chuckling. "But now we're going to let Adolph go free. We can't hang on to him and do our job. Untie his hands, and tie the private's hands, front or back I don't care. Then redress his shoulder. He's losing too much blood." Signaling for Juarez, Harry retrieved the Lieutenant's Lugar.

Dropping the magazine and emptying the chamber, he handed Lt. Bowman his weapon. "I don't much care what happens to you, so get the hell out of here." Harry explained angrily pushing Bowman toward the bunker.

Just as Harry suspected, Bowman ran straight toward the block house yelling, "Hilfe, Hilfe, Americans.

Nicht Schiesen! Nicht Schiesen!"

Both the rear and east mortar crews stopped firing, as they watched the frantic SS officer running toward them.

Juarez took off at a dead run toward the first strand of wire, as Franny and Anderson opened up on the block house. Harry and his two men ran east, firing toward the mortar pit.

Juarez threw a perfect pitch into the pit, followed by a second grenade, just as a bullet fired from the west pit struck him. Brant and Woodward each tossed grenades, as Harry poured machine gun fire at the scrambling weapons crew. All four grenades exploded in perfect unison. Just as Steve was going to join the assault, a massive explosion threw him to the ground. Then a second, a third a fourth followed by an uncountable barrage of large caliber rounds, raining down on the area. Smoke dirt and shrapnel filled the air. The ground shook as if the very gates of hell were opening below them. Steve knew full well, these deadly missiles were indeed the product of well aimed American artillery.

As the final round crashed south of the bunker, Steve looked up to see Harry, Franny and Woodward emerging from the tree line to the east. They charged the blockhouse door that was now partially open.

After tossing a grenade inside the blockhouse, they entered, spaying fire in every direction. Surprisingly, some enemy soldiers survived the vicious artillery and grenade attack. They fought back tenaciously until the very last man.

Steve and Mike worked their way around the rear of the block house searching for Juarez. They found Lt. Bowman's body tangled in remnants of the barbed wire barrier. His abdomen had been split wide open by shrapnel. All his internal organs lay on display aside of him.

As they continued walking west, they observed what was left of the observation post the Germans constructed in the hedgerow. Both spotters lay dead among the ruins.

"Corporal! Over here." Steve heard Juarez call out.

Steve and Anderson looked around but could not see him. "Where are you?" Mike called out.

"Behind you, under the rubble." Juarez called back.

After being hit, Juarez crawled back into the hedgerow. When the observation deck was struck, several large pieces of concrete slid down in front of him, blocking his escape.

Quickly the men pulled the rubble out of the way. "How bad you hit?" Steve inquired, as he pulled debris away from the injured soldier.

"Through and through my left shoulder, Corporal. Hurts like hell but I got the bleeding stopped from the front.

Looks like I get a shot at clean sheets in a hospital." Juarez stated as he crawled out from the hedge row.

Mike began bandaging his entire shoulder, as Steve made his way over toward the bunker door.

Standing next to Harry was a Captain, along with nearly a platoon of soldiers.

The Captain smiled at Steve. "I'm Captain Washburn, Fourth Infantry Division. How are you doing Corporal?"

"Well not to bad, we have one injured man that need's medical assistance, along with a German prisoner who also requires medical aide." Steve reported to Capt. Washburn. Steve looked at Harry's bloody face. "How bad you hurt?"

"The only thing hurt is my fucking pride, Kenrude. That sorry son of a bitch in there got off the luckiest shot in the world. It busted off the stock on my Thompson. The damn thing bounced up hitting me in the face giving me a bloody nose. Do you know how hard it is to fire this thing with out a stock and a messed up receiver?"

"Oh quit your bellyaching, Jensen. Here, Merry Christmas from Himmler." Franny said jokingly as he shoved a German Submachine gun and spare clips into Harry's chest. Everyone had to laugh as Harry gave Franny a shove.

Several medics in a Jeep fixed with stretchers drove up by the blockhouse. They went right to work caring for the wounded.

"Where were you men headed when you ran across the bunker?" Capt. Washburn inquired.

"Actually we were looking for you." Harry responded using water from his canteen to wash the blood from his face. "Lt. Gossman back in Beuzeville and Capt. Lewis in Saint-Mere-Eglise were in pretty rough straights.

Many wounded not enough medical supplies, and running short on ammo. They sent us out, hoping we could connect up with you guys and bring them some help."

"Well gentlemen our mission was somewhat the same. We are an advance column. We were told to link up with paratroopers, get the lay of the land and offer any and all assistance you require. However, our main objective is to make sure we hold Saint Martin de Varreville, so our tanks can roll on through it. That is our prime objective. But we could send off a small contingent to Beuzeville to help out your Lt. Gossman. Is the road open all the way to Beuzeville, or would we have to fight all the way there?"

The Captain questioned as his platoon Sergeant handed him a map.

"It's mostly open. There are no mines. But the krauts keep trying to slow traffic when they can. This entire area is hedgerow country.

They can hide in these damn things and hit you when you least expect it. Believe me Captain these damn things will cost us a lot of good men before we can break out of this beachhead." Steve informed Captain Washburn, as all his men listened intently.

"We had been making good time this morning until we were hit by these mortars. We got a fix on the position, so we called in the 105s. They were right on target. Then we heard all the damn shooting going on up here, so we kind of hung back a bit, until we could make some sense out of everything. Once the medics are finished you can lead us to the Beuzeville, Saint Martin de Varreville road junction. We have several trucks behind us with supplies.

Once we hit the crossroads, I can dispatch men and supplies to Beuzeville." Captain Washburn stated handing the map back to his Sergeant.

One of the medics approached Steve. "We have the German and Juarez ready to travel. But Juarez is refusing to leave until he can talk to you.

Steve walked toward the jeep where Juarez was lying on a stretcher. "What can I do for you, Billy?"

"I want to come back to the unit when I get out of the hospital. I don't want to be assigned anywhere else.

Promise me you'll get me back here."

Smiling Steve nodded his head. "I promise no matter what it takes I'll get you reassigned back to Charlie Company. Just go get well and take care of that arm. The Dodgers might need your help some day."

"Got that right, Corporal. No bullet wound is going to stop Billy Juarez from pitching in the World Series."

After shaking hands with Juarez, Steve called over to the driver letting him know they were good to go.

"Not so fast!" Harry called out.

He came walking forward with McGruder. His right hand was covered in blood.

"What the hell happened to you?" Steve inquired.

"Damn piece of shrapnel got me pretty good. But I can work it out, Kenrude. Please don't send me back."

Steve looked over toward the medic who was shaking his head. "No, he needs a doctor. He can't stay out here."

"On the Jeep, McGruder! We'll see you when you get out of the hospital." Steve told the very capable young man.

Hanging his head, McGruder walked over to the Jeep sitting down aside of the driver. After the jeep drove off, Harry walked up aside of Steve. "We just lost two damn good men."

"Yeah we did. But at least they're alive. We can get them back later on." Steve responded, as he turned back toward their men.

"Ready to go, Stevie boy?" Harry inquired handing Steve the balance of his Thompson ammunition.

"Yeah, let's do it. Franny you and Brant ready to take point again?" Steve inquired hating to take advantage of his tired men "Count on it, Steve." Franny replied motioning for Brant to follow him.

As they started back toward Beuzeville Capt. Washburn assigned a Corporal carrying a Thompson to join Franny and Brant on the scout detail.

Nearing the spot where the battle had taken place with the SS unit, Franny explained to the Corporal every thing that had happened. They were just approaching the hedgerow where he and Joblanski had killed many of the Germans, when they observed someone running between the burned out vehicles.

Brant dropped to one knee on the road as Franny and the Corporal fanned out looking for the intruder.

Seeing Franny bear down on him with his BAR, the lone German soldier threw his hands in the air while calling out, "Nicht Shiessen. Bitte. Nicht Schiessen."

The corporal walked up behind the soldier pushing him to the ground before removing his Lugar.

"Kapitulate! Ja? Kapitulate!" The man called out to Franny as he looked back toward the east. "Kapitualte."

Franny pulled him back to his feet, shoving him toward the road where Brant was still at the ready.

Capt. Washburn and the others arrived as Franny and the Corporal arrived back near the hedgerow.

Before the Captain could say anything, the soldier nervously repeated. "Kapitulate. Bitte!" Brant who was still keeping his eye on the road called out. "We got company. Not Krauts, I'm not sure who they are."

Captain Washburn along with Steve and Harry walked forward aside of Brant. From the rear of the orchard came a group of what appeared to be civilians, carrying German and French weapons.

Not quite sure what to make of the situation Captain Washburn called out to their men. "Hold your fire. Keep your eyes open."

When the twelve men were about ten yards away, Franny swung his BAR toward them. "That will be close enough. Do you speak English?" He inquired.

Looking angrily toward Franny, a tall thin man wearing a beret began walking forward, until Franny pointed his weapon directly at him. "Far enough I said!" Franny warned placing his finger on the trigger.

Fully comprehending Franny had no qualms about pulling the trigger, the man nodded then spoke. "I am Claude Romay, head of the local resistance. I see you have destroyed the blockhouse and its Boche inhabitants.

Good work. Now Captain, are you the man in charge?"

Capt. Washburn signaled Franny to let the man pass. After studying the man's face for a moment he replied, "I am Capt. Washburn Fourth U.S. Infantry Division. What can I do for you?"

"Tell me what you are doing in my sector, and what your plans are. Is this your entire unit?" Romay inquired.

"Let me make one thing perfectly clear. First off, I don't care whose sector this is, or who's in charge around here. I represent the invading allied forces and I'm in charge where ever I'm standing. The only person I answer to is General Eisenhower. And there is no way in hell I'll tell you what my mission is. Are we clear on that?" Capt. Washburn explained harshly.

"Well yes, I suppose I do understand." Romay answered as he eyed the German soldier. "You see we have been hunting down war criminals all night, and we are very tired. So you must excuse our bad manners. If you will just hand over that man we will be on our way then."

"I'm sorry, sir. That man has surrendered to the United States Army and he'll be given all the rights guaranteed by the Geneva Convention." Captain Washburn informed the irritated French man.

"No you don't understand. That man was part of Lt. Dietrich's SS unit. He is guilty of crimes against French citizens. It is our duty to bring them all to justice." Romay retorted angrily.

"Look Dietrich is dead as is Lt. Bowman and most of their men. We know you mean well, but he surrendered to my man so he belongs to us." Steve stated forcefully.

"So you let a mere Corporal speak for you, Captain?" Romay inquired signaling his men to come forward.

Franny fired a blast from his BAR into the dirt directly in front of Romay's men, where they stopped instantly.

"Think real hard." Anderson stated as he now aimed his BAR toward the nervous partisans.

"Look Romay, we don't want problems with your people. What the Corporal told you is one hundred percent accurate. We're not handing that man over to you, or any other French forces. He is now a POW and will be dealt with accordingly." Captain Washburn explained again angrily.

After several seconds Romay took a deep breath. "Well Captain it is starting to get dark. We need to get Moving. We will let you proceed."

"You'll let us proceed?" Franny asked indignantly. "You forget who's holding this BAR at your throat.

Smiling at Franny's total lack of respect for the French partisans Captain Washburn said. "Romay, neither you nor any other partisans will stop us from going where we choose to go. Do I make myself clear?"

"Yes, yes, I understand you have things to do. What are you going to do with him?" Romay inquired.

"He'll remain with us until we run across a Military Police unit. Then we'll turn him over to be escorted back to the cages on the beach." Captain Washburn explained, fully understanding this situation was not yet over.

"But of course. It would be the proper thing to do. But then we might be willing to pay you a price, as there are bounties on the heads of these murdering Huns." Romay replied smiling at the Captain.

Before anyone could say another word, one of the partisans fired several shots from a pistol in the direction of the German soldier. Letting out a scream he fell to the ground in a bloody heap.

"What the hell was that all about?" Harry yelled as he walked over taking a pistol away from one of the partisans.

A female voice yelled out, "Papa I could not help myself. What they have done is so horrible; I could not let another one of them go free."

Everyone quickly realized the partisan wearing the dark hood was a young woman.

"This is my daughter Charlene. My last daughter! Lt. Dietrich suspected me of running the underground in this sector. He came to my farm one night when I was away. Only Charlene and her sister Claudine were there. They beat Claudine, and then raped her repeatedly. There were ten of them. Charlene was forced to watch.

She was only fourteen at the time. When they were through, four men including your prisoner, held Claudine down to the floor, as Dietrich desecrated her body with his bayonet. It took two days of suffering before she finally died. This is Just one such case. There are many, many more." Claude Romay said as he held his sobbing daughter. Franny and Mike lowered their weapons, as everyone stood in total shock after hearing Claude Romay's gruesome story.

"I'm so sorry." Capt. Washburn said extending his hand in sympathy toward the underground leader.

After shaking hands Claude Romay took another deep breath. "There is no need to say nothing more. It is over.

We must be going and allow you men to complete your mission."

With that the group of partisans slowly turned away, walking back across the orchard. Claude Romay walked just a short distance before stopping. He looked back over at the American soldiers nodding his head. "Viva America. Good hunting and the best of luck to you. Welcome to France. Viva America"

As Romay and his daughter prepared to leave, Harry ran up beside Charlene. He handed her the pistol he had taken away.

Smiling slightly she said, "Merci."

Turning away, they followed their loyal band of partisans back through the orchard. Darkness began to settle over the embattled French countryside as the American force continued on their way to Saint Martin de-Varreville. Steve looked down at his watch which read 8:00 p.m. He could not believe how fast this day had gone.

Nor could he believe what had all taken place since they landed in France.

The sounds of battle also diminished with the growing darkness. Sporadic gunfire and occasional small explosions could be heard coming from the expanding beachhead. Abruptly, automatic weapons fire broke out about thirty yards in front of the relief column. It had the distinctive sound of a heavy German M.G. machine gun. The men quickly sought cover while scanning the area in front of them for movement. Another blast from the MG was followed by the chatter of a BAR answering the German attack. Seconds later more small arms opened fire, the night sky in front of them become alive with tracers, flying lead, and blinding muzzle flashes. To their right, a large diesel engine coughed before springing to life. A heavy machine began crashing through the underbrush on the far side of the hedgerow.

"Tanks, Tanks! Get away from the road." Captain Washburn yelled out.

Steve dove into a small drainage ditch paralleling the road. He listened intently to the clank of a heavy steel tread grinding through brush and small tree branches, as the driver maneuvered toward the road. Moments later, it was evident the tank had exited through an opening in the hedgerow. After turning slowly onto the road, the driver progressed cautiously toward their position.

The steel monster crept forward ever so slowly. Although it was not visible in the darkness, its throbbing engine and clanging treads brought terror to the men scattered through out the field.

Steve's heart was beating so rapidly and loud, he felt it could be heard all the way to Paris. A light mist began to fall as the men lay silently in their positions. They had no way to take on this deadly monster.

Capt. Washburn had to make a critical choice as the tank lumbered toward them. Either lie on the ground where he was, thus allowing his trucks and men to become cannon fodder, or make an attempt to warn them. Taking a calculated risk the tank crew might not be able to see him in the dark mist, he sprang to his feet. He ran along the edge of the hedgerow, hoping to blend in to the foliage. Small branches slapped him in the face as he ran.

Arriving at the waiting convoy, he ordered the drivers to back down the road toward the blockhouse then get off the road.

As soon as his trucks were moving, Capt. Washburn bent over to take a deep breath. Hearing footsteps approaching, he stood up peering down toward the tank. About ten of his men had followed him on his desperate run. One of them was his platoon Sergeant. "What do we do now Captain?" The Sergeant inquired as he caught his breath.

"Glad to see you joined me. Let's work our way toward the back of that damn orchard. Maybe we can get behind that damn tank and take it out. Or, if there are infantry following to the rear, we can fight them causing enough of a disturbance, where the driver of that thing will want to back up and reorganize. Let's go."

Quickly the men began searching for a safe entry into the orchard with out being seen by the tank.

The sixty ton tank rolled about four feet away from the tree Harry was using for cover. As it rumbled by, Harry was able to identify the machine as a panther tank. The machine gunner sat erect in his open hatch, while the commander was down inside the hull buttoned up. Feeling the odds were on his side, he cautiously stood up, and leapt onto the back of the crawling beast. He lay still for a second to make sure he had not been observed by the gunner. Quickly he removed several hand grenades from his pocket. As he prepared to move on the machine gunner the commanders hatch popped open. A figure arose, immediately turning to face the rear of his panther. Harry froze where he was, hoping the man in the turret would not see him.

But that was not to be. The commander began yelling while pointing toward Harry. He then fired several shots toward Harry's from a Lugar he held in his right hand.

Harry fumbled for the captured German machine gun he had placed on the steel deck, as he dropped the grenades.

The screaming commander fired two more shots just as Harry let go a solid blast from his sub-machine gun.

The tank commander slumped forward dropping his weapon.

Harry's shoulder burned as a searing pain traveled down his arm. He felt dizzy and some what nauseous as the huge tank rumbled to a stop. He knew he had to finish the job before someone came around to finish him off. As he was about to grab the grenades, he observed the machine gunner spinning the MG-42 in his direction. Scrambling to his feet Harry pulled the pin from one grenade. He jammed it down aside of the dead commander's body as he drew his bayonet. Lunging forward, Harry slammed his knife into the machine gunners throat. As the first grenade exploded Harry lost his balance. Grabbing the turret cover for stability he slammed his bayonet into the man's upper chest. Several German infantry men who had followed the tank at a distance came running forward firing at Harry. With no time to lose, he pulled the pins on his last two grenades. After dropping them down inside the tank, Harry jumped off the side. Rolling across the ground he caught the smell of diesel fuel. He knew well if the tank was leaking fuel; it would go up like a roman candle when those grenades detonated. Gaining his feet, he ran with every ounce of energy left in his legs deep into the orchard.

After the first grenade popped he dove behind a tree landing on his injured shoulder.

Seconds later the second grenade detonated followed by a massive explosion illuminating the entire area.

A fire ball rose high into the night sky as the once terrifying machine now became a funeral pyre for its crew.

About twenty-five infantry men had been following the tank. As the light exposed Harry's position they began firing in his direction. Bark ripped lose by bullets flew all around him, some of it striking him in the face.

Abruptly a grenade exploded behind the German infantry. Small arms fire opened up upon them from several directions. Several German soldiers instantly crumbled to the ground. Realizing they were caught up in a murderous crossfire, they began to withdraw.

Finally being able to move, Harry swung around the tree. He opened fire with his sub-machine gun emptying the magazine in one long blast.

As the infantry men withdrew to safety, the fire from the tank slowly died down, allowing darkness to once again overtake the battlefield.

Harry sat up against the tree letting the cool mist wash over his hot dirty face. Knowing full well this could just be a short respite before the attack renewed; he slammed a fresh magazine into his weapon.

Before he could make another move, Oscar came crawling up beside him. "How bad you hit, corporal?" "Damn, Oscar you scared the living shit out of me." Harry replied tossing a hunk of mud at him. "I don't know Oscar I haven't had the balls to look yet. But my arm hurts like hell. It actually went numb for a bit back on the tank." He explained.

Removing Harry's red flashlight from his pack, Oscar prepared to examine the wound. Pulling in real close he turned the light on.

"You have a hell of a gash. The bullet tore you open as it passed by. It never actually went all the way into your arm." Oscar reported as he ripped open a battle dressing package. "I have some sulfa a medic gave me.

I'll pour it in the wound to help keep it from getting infected." Oscar tightened the dressing securely around Harry's arm. "How's that feel?"

"Actually a lot better, Oscar. I now pronounce you Florence Nightingale. Thanks a lot. I appreciate it. Do me a favor though. Don't tell Kenrude what it looks like. That ass hole will send me packing sure as shit."

Laughing, Oscar assured Harry his secret was safe.

Hearing some one call out from the road, Harry looked over at Oscar. "What do you see out there?"

Scanning the road carefully Oscar shook his head. Again the voice cried out. "I think it's a wounded kraut calling for help. I'm not a hundred percent sure, but there isn't anyone moving around out there. Stay put, Harry, I'm going to move up a bit so I can get a better look." In a flash Oscar took off low crawling toward the road.

As Harry leaned back against the tree, he was sure he could hear someone crawling through the tall grass to the rear of the orchard. Was it Germans or Americans? He had no way of knowing, and it was to dark to see clearly.

Steve lay in the drainage trench looking out over the dark wet battlefield, wondering what to do next. He knew someplace out there Harry was laying wounded, possibly bleeding to death. What about Mike and Franny? Where were they? Were they dead? Was he all alone now? He had no idea what had happened to Capt. Washburn after he ran toward the rear to warn his truck drivers.

He questioned if the remaining Germans would regroup and attack again, or had they had enough for now.

In the dark lonely ditch, Steve thought about his next move. He was tired of the killing and dangers that lurked around every corner. There was no doubt he was surrounded by German infantry. One thing was for sure. If he didn't keep his mind attuned to everything going on around him, he was a dead man. Taking a deep breath, he cautiously pointed his Thompson out of that muddy trench.

Being so cold and wet, he struggled hard to keep his mind on the matters at hand. What he needed to do most was find his men.

Steve had no way of knowing those very same thoughts and feelings were raging through Mike Anderson's mind. He was lying behind a pile of rocks and brush, with two dead Germans not three feet away from him.

Although dead, one soldier stared eternally at Mike. It gave him a case of real bad karma. Somewhere behind him, somebody was moaning with what must have been extremely severe pain. Who was it? He wanted to know so badly, but common sense told him to stay put. The mist was getting heavier, almost covering the entire area with a thick blanket of fog. Franny sat behind a mound of wood some farmer had stacked neatly by the side of the road. He was positive Harry was dead, and possibly Steve and Brant. The battle had erupted so quickly no one had much of a chance. Franny also knew that somewhere to his right, were the remnants of Capt. Washburn's platoon who had attacked the infantry behind the tank. In the cold wet night Franny felt scared, totally alone, and very hungry. He remembered placing several Candy Bars in the side pocket of his pack. Gently withdrawing one of the bars, he unwrapped it carefully.

As he bit off the first piece, a green flare burst brilliantly in the dark night sky above the fog shrouded field of death. Franny tossed the balance of the candy bar, grabbing his BAR, readying himself for whatever action was to come.

The whistling sound of incoming mortar shells was easily identifiable. But who was doing the firing, and where were they aimed to land? That question was answered instantly as one after another, mortar rounds crashed into the battlefield, sending deadly shrapnel screaming in every direction. The barrage only lasted several minutes, but it seemed like an eternity. As the last round exploded, another flare popped in the night sky. Seconds later, a heavy German machine gun began firing from east to west. White tracer rounds made an eerie sight as they screeched through the fog laden air.

The machine gun fired four more long bursts before falling silent. No one dared move from their positions.

It was evident the Germans had this area zeroed in. Every few moments another mortar round would scream in, or the machine gun would once again rake the area. All the men tried taking quick naps when things fell silent, but it was fruitless. The continual whine of mortar shells and machine guns kept them awake and on edge. The night dragged on endlessly, as death and terror stalked the soldiers. Sometimes a manned screamed over here. Later one would scream over there. Then it was quiet again. Too quiet! Everyone felt his turn was next.

A cool gray dawn heightened their fear level, as the tired wet soldiers expected a large enemy attack at any moment. They peered into the predawn gloom, watching for any signs of enemy activity. The fog began to lift as the night relinquished its grip on the field of death.

Consequently, they were not out of the woods yet. The heaviest German mortar attack was yet to begin.

At 0600 mortar rounds began to drop at a rate of one every ten seconds for nearly twenty minutes.

It was nonstop and spread over a wide area. It was evident the German were trying to knock out the relief column headed inland.

This large barrage was followed by what the men had suspected all night, and feared the most. Through the mist came German infantry crouched over advancing slowly.

Franny realized in the light of dawn, that his position was rather poor for a gun battle. He backed away from the wood pile slowly taking cover near a pile of brush. It was not the best to stop enemy bullets, but it would give him concealment for firing. As he laid down an American voice from behind said quietly, "Keep coming buddy, we got you covered."

Franny whirled around to see a soldier signaling him to keep backing up. To his amazement, that man was wearing the 101st airborne patch.

Cautiously, Franny went the last five yards to join up with a large group of dirty, tired airborne soldiers. He was amazed to think he had spent the balance of the night, just yards away from this group of his own men.

"What a sight for sore eyes you guys are." Franny said as he took cover beside another soldier who also held a deadly BAR.

A few moments later a young second Lieutenant whispered to Franny, "Are you good to go?"

Franny nodded, "Anytime you are, sir."

"It will be on three." After a quick count the Lieutenant yelled, "Fire! Give them hell boys!"

A roar went up as every weapon the American patrol had at their disposal ripped through the morning air.

Germans began falling. Some dashed about looking for cover but were quickly overwhelmed by Capt. Washburn's men, who had circled around through the woods during the night. Others stood their ground or charged forward into the withering fire, attempting to dislodge the well camouflaged Americans.

Regrettably, their remarkable tenacity, and dedication to duty was measured out in seconds, as they fell victim to the mounting tide of American firepower.

The German assault disintegrated into panic. Those toward the rear of the attack broke, leaving their wounded comrades to fend for themselves. Several tossed their weapons in panic as they rushed headlong in retreat.

Suddenly as if someone had flipped a light switch, the battlefield went silent. Only the low moans of wounded men were audible in the morning fog.

After what seemed like an eternity, the Lieutenant commanding the paratroop unit ordered his men to move out.

Ever so slowly the paratroopers walked nervously down the road of death. Franny had never seen anything so ghastly. The massive mortar attack had shredded bodies through out the night. The ground was strewn with arms and legs, while entrails hung from branches in the hedgerows. The wounded Germans no longer moaned, as they had given themselves over to death. Everything became eerily quiet.

Slowly one by one, surviving Americans emerged from their concealment to join in the sweep of the area.

Franny first observed Woodward. Then Brant emerged from the hedgerow covered with leaves and mud.

Anderson and Abbot materialized from the orchard. He watched Steve pull himself clear of a culvert that ran directly under the road. What remained of Captain Washburn's men moved slowly out of the pre dawn shadows.

After surveying the situation for several seconds, the Captain walked over to the paratroopers extending his hand toward the lieutenant.

"I'm Captain Washburn Fourth infantry. It was good to have you join us last night. Where were you headed?"

"I'm Lt. Comstock 101st, sir. We were just trying to break through to open a road for your column. We have been in fights all up and down this damn hedgerow country since we landed. Last night we heard the commotion and figured we better check it out. So we arrived right in the middle of the damn battle. I lost three men in that mortar barrage and my right leg is not in the best of shape. I have a good size piece of shrapnel just below the knee. One of my guys bound it up, but I won't make it too far in this condition. I guess I better turn my men over to you"

"Good enough Lieutenant. I'll take good care of them. We have several trucks to the rear with litters and medical supplies. We'll get you bandaged up and send you back to the invasion hospital. There are several more wounded back in the woods that need evacuation also."

Turning to Steve the Captain asked. "What's you situation, Corporal?" Looking over the men on the road

Steve replied. "I'm missing two, Jensen and Joblanski."

"No Jensen is fine, I saw him back by one of the German trucks as we came this way, it looked like he was tending to a wounded man." Anderson explained.

"Better check it out." The Captain encouraged Steve.

The men walked back into the orchard. Near a burned out truck, they saw Harry kneeling beside a man. It was Joblanski. His left leg had been blown off at the knee.

Looking up at Steve Joblanski began to cry. "I'm sorry, Corporal. I didn't mean to have this happen. Damn I don't want to leave you guys."

Steve knelt down on one knee holding Joblanski's hand. "You're a good soldier Oscar. You were the best. But your war is over now. Look, I know this isn't easy. But you have your life. You can still make something out of all this. In fact I insist you do something really good when you get home. Do you understand?"

"You bet, corporal. I'll never let you down." Oscar replied with a smile.

"The Captain is getting the trucks up here now. You'll be back in England tomorrow. Clean sheets, pretty nurses, warm food, and for sure a bath." Everyone chuckled as Steve ran his hand over Joblanski's muddy head. "Oscar I still have one more important job for you."

"Name it, corporal." Joblanksi replied forcing another smile.

Steve reached into his jacket pocket pulling out all the dog tags he had collected from the dead. "You make sure someone from headquarters gets these. You tell them these men are scattered all over this damn hedgerow country. You tell them they came from me, Alright?"

"You got it, Kenrude." Oscar replied shoving the meal tags into his shirt pocket.

Several minutes later they heard Captain Washburn's trucks on the road. "Come on Oscar time to go." Harry informed their wounded comrade.

Everyone took hold of Joblanski, lifting him off the ground. After handing him up to the medics on the truck Oscar called out, "Hey Jensen."

Harry walked back to the truck. "What's up Joblanski?"

He tossed down a chocolate bar. "Down payment for the tourniquet you placed on my leg. I owe you a steak when we get together back in the states after the war."

Waving the candy bar at Oscar Harry called back, "With a damn big baked potato!" "You got it, corporal!" Oscar replied with a slight laugh.

After the truck carrying the wounded drove off, Steve looked at the large bandage on Harry's arm.

"You should have been on that truck. That arm looks none to good."

"its fine, Steve. The bullet just ripped the flesh open a bit. I'll be fine. You're not getting rid of me that easily.

Besides, Oscar rapped it pretty good just before you guys arrived. He did a good job. I'll check with a medic down the road. Man, don't say anything to Washburn. He'll send me packing for sure." Harry pleaded with Steve.

Nodding his head Steve handed Harry his weapon. "Glad to see you this morning. I wasn't sure who would be left after that barrage last night."

"Yeah no shit, I didn't think I would see any of you guys ever again. That was the most horrific night I have ever lived through." He responded as they approached Captain Washburn.

Once everyone was assembled, Captain Washburn looked over his ragged bunch. "Our orders were to reach Sainte Martine-de-Varreville. The last twenty-four hours have been a bitch. But we're moving on. Kenrude, Jensen, take your men and walk point. Lt. Comstock's men will cover our rear. What's left of my platoon will stay with me as reserves, Questions?"

No one said a word. The stoic soldiers stood silent until Steve motioned for them to move out. Franny and Anderson took point position, while Steve, Harry, Brant, Woodward and Abbott followed about ten yards behind.

As heavy fighting raged to the left and right, this sector of the beachhead appeared to be extremely quiet now.

Steve hoped the Germans had expended their muscle during this mornings attack, and had retreated farther toward the east. Arriving at the crossroads Anderson motioned for Steve and Harry.

"To the right is Beuzeville to the left is Saint Martin-de-Varreville. Do we still try and help out Gossman, or do you think he has given up on us?" Anderson inquired pulling out his near empty canteen.

"Take a break. We'll ask the Captain when he catches up." Steve replied kneeling down near the hedgerow for cover.

When Captain Washburn arrived Steve walked up to him. "Beuzeville is to our right. We were trying to bring help back to Lt. Gossman when we ran into the SS unit and the bunker. Is there anything we can do for them?"

"Corporal, I sure as hell wish we could. But I've lost too many men, too many trucks, and we need to make sure that main east-west road inland is open. I'm sorry, but Gossman will have to hold without our help."

Understanding the situation all to well, Steve desired to argue the point. He had made a promise to the beleaguered forces in Beuzeville, and he longed to keep his word. Nevertheless, he knew an argument with Capt. Washburn was not a good idea this particular morning.

Unfolding his map, both he and the Captain gave it a good look over. "About four miles and we should be there.

Refolding his map Steve stated boldly, "Let's hope our first contact is American and not German."

Preparing to leave the area he called out, "Let's move out. Anderson, Abbott take the point this time."

Although tired, wet and dirty, the men moved with a sense of confidence. They had survived one hell of a night, and now felt like full combat veterans.

After covering nearly a mile Anderson stopped, "Vehicles?" He whispered to Abbott "Yeah, sounds like they're coming this way real slow." Abbott responded as he turned to warn the rest of the men.

Capt. Washburn was walking with Steve and Harry when Abbott arrived. "Vehicles, we didn't see them but it sounds like more than one. We don't know if they're ours or Germans."

"Damn we need cover!" Capt Washburn said looking around. "Back, back toward the crossroads. It's our only hope if they're krauts."

As tired as the men were, they ran at an amazing speed back toward the crossroads. Some of them chose to climb over a shorter hedgerow, while others continued running with the Captain.

They had barely taken cover when Abbott came running full force down the road yelling, "Vehicles, heavy treads, sounds like tanks or half tracks."

The trucks with their precious cargo of wounded paratroopers and supplies fell back toward the block house once again.

Capt. Washburn, Steve, Harry and Franny were set up behind a large wall of rocks just beyond the crossroads intersection. They watched intently as the ground vibrated beneath them. Steve observed Anderson positioning himself on top of the hedgerow with his BAR. Frantically waving, Steve motioned him to fall back lest he give away everyone's position.

Mere seconds later, a half track with two MG-34 machine guns rounded the curve heading straight for the crossroads. Three cargo trucks filled with infantry followed, before two more half tracks, a panther tank and a kuebelwagen staff car brought up the rear.

"What do you think Captain?" Harry asked as he stared at the steel monster moving toward them.

"Not sure. Either they're headed toward Beuzeville, or they're searching for the unit we fought last night.

It could be reinforcements or a recon in force. Either way, that's way too powerful of a force for us to take on.

We need to lay low and let them pass." Captain Washburn instructed nervously considering their odds.

"Think it's a vanguard of a larger force?" Steve inquired.

"Naw I don't think so. I still think its either recon or reinforcements." The Captain replied as he placed his rifle sights on one of the half track gunners.

Unexpectedly the convoy stopped. All the gunners swiftly swung their weapons toward the west as they yelled in panic. They pointed toward a low flying British Spitfire that was paralleling the road about a hundred feet above the ground. The pilot pulled up climbing several hundred feet, than banked toward the east. There was no doubt he had spotted the convoy and was preparing to attack. All the paratroopers that had taken cover along the backside of the hedgerows, fled toward the open fields throwing themselves down in the dirt hoping to be clear of the aircrafts attack. Captain Washburn still sighted in on the half track gunner, squeezed off one round.

The man grabbed his throat as blood sprayed over his ammunition handler, then tumbled to the floor. Totally confused, the second gunner lowered his weapon as he looked over both hedgerows, as he glanced back and forth at the menacing aircraft.

Watching the British pilot begin his dive on the trapped convoy, Captain Washburn yelled, "Cover fire!"

The men jumped to their feet firing at anyone moving in the lead half track. German troops began jumping over the sides of trucks and half tracks attempting to take cover in the tangled hedgerows.

The Spitfire charged directly down the road toward the lead half track firing his twenty millimeter cannons.

With in seconds the lead machine erupted into a ball of fire tossing pieces of metal into the air. Men screamed as burning fuel washed down upon them. Just as quickly the second half track exploded, sending a massive fire ball skyward. In panic, the staff car driver killed his engine just as the panther tank began to back up. It was clear the tank operator cared little about the occupants of the staff car, as self preservation took over. He continued backing, crushing the car and driver beneath his massive sixty tons. The two officers in the back seat of the staff car jumped clear, waving their arms in protest as the giant monster continued in reverse.

After the Spitfire finished its first pass the pilot climbed once again. He turned in a tight circle beginning another run on the stricken convoy, this time back to front. The paratroopers in the field had become organized by now.

They turned facing the hedgerows with their weapons. Any time a German soldier attempted to climb over the top to escape the carnage he was shot. The same thing was happening at the crossroads. Any soldier attempting to run forward of the convoy was cut down by Franny with his BAR. The British pilot once again hammered away with his cannons setting the two troop transports on fire as he screamed over the road of death.

With ammunition left, the pilot prepared to make another attack, hoping to disable the escaping panther tank. However this time, the machine gunner had opened his turret, and was preparing to fire his MG-34 as the pilot came streaking toward the convoy. Apparently out of cannon ammunition, the pilot was now using his machine guns. There was a quick dual between the tank gunner and the aircraft, before the pilot pulled up with smoke spewing from his engine bonnet. A trail of thick black smoke trailed the damaged Spitfire, as the pilot flew west toward the channel and safety.

The tank operator continued backing away from the battle, knowing he was a sitting duck if any other aircraft wandered upon the scene. As the panther disappeared to the north, the men behind the rock pile stood up. They stared at the thick, black greasy smoke rolling skyward as flames licked at the wreckage. There did not appear to be any movement from inside the hedgerows.

"Good lord!" Franny mumbled. "Do you think anyone in there is alive?"

"Doubtful." Harry replied shaking his head, "Those poor bastards. I wonder if Hitler is happy now."

As the four men watched the fires, their men slowly reassembled around them. Steve made a quick head count finding everyone safe and sound. He knew the scenario would have been much different had it not been for the marauding British pilot.

Either the Spitfire pilot radioed other pilots in his squadron about the convoy, or the thick black smoke drew attention. Amazingly, a Spitfire and a Hurricane arrived from the west. Both pilots began circling the area giving the men at the crossroads a good once over. Every man waved, hoping to alert the pilots that they were friendly's and not targets of opportunity. Franny jumped up and down pointing down the road as if trying to inform the pilots about the escaping panther tank.

But they were not interested in Franny's antics. A lone Messerschmitt 109 streaking down from the north became the focus of their attention. The men on the ground dove for cover as the British pilots pulled up, swinging wide toward the north. The German pilot quickly realizing he was well out gunned and in deep trouble, began climbing at a high rate of speed with both fighters in pursuit. An amazing dog fight erupted in the sky above the paratroopers. Machine guns clattered, cannons popped as three well trained pilots fought for their lives in the deadly duel. With in minutes, sections of the Messerschmidt's wings were being torn from the frame by well placed cannon fire. Smoke began trailing the aircraft, as the pilot twisted and turned, struggling to keep his damaged aircraft aloft. Nevertheless, the German pilot made a horrendous mistake. He displayed the belly of his aircraft to the Hurricane pilot. Armor piercing bullets ripped the Messerschmitt from front to back.

The veteran Luftwaffe pilot dove swiftly toward the ground, directing his stricken aircraft toward the east.

The Spitfire pilot turned sharper, coming down directly behind and on top of the German fighter. With a blast from his cannons the rear stabilizer was torn from the aircraft. Out of control the Messerschmitt spun wildly to the left before crashing into a row of trees. A large explosion shook the area as debris and fire rose a good hundred feet into the air. Their job completed, the British pilots flew south, and on to their next mission.

Captain Washburn called the men together as he removed the map from his pocket. While studying the worn document he could here the sounds of heavy fighting coming from in, and around the beachhead. Men and equipment were pouring ashore at a rate unprecedented in military history. As the Captain turned toward Saint Martin-de-Vareville he could see thick black smoke rising from the crippled town. "Alright, let's just pass the town itself and head straight for the beach. That damn town is just going to slow us down. There's nothing we can accomplish there. Kenrude, send out a patrol and let's get moving."

Steve called out, "Rabinowitz, Abbott, Anderson take point. Keep you eyes and ears open. We're headed for the beach." He turned toward Captain Washburn. "What about those trucks sir?"

"They'll have to fend for themselves, Corporal. We need to move and we might have to go cross country.

We'll have to let them find their own way out of here."

Rabinowitz had barely walked a quarter mile when he observed five paratroopers walking toward him. He stopped and called out, "Damn it's good to see some more familiar faces." They were a mixture of men from first platoon, Corporal Cummings along with Broadwell from forth squad, Gunderson from second squad, and Haley and Markham from first squad.

Corporal Cummings shook hands with Rabinowitz, "Good to see you too trooper. Where are you headed?"

"The beach, Kenrude and Jenson are back down the road with a Captain Washburn who has taken charge of us. You might want to check in with them." Rabinowitz replied as Abbott and Anderson shook hands with the tired paratroopers.

"Sounds good," Cummings replied with a smile.

As the five men approached the main force, Steve and Harry shook hands with all the men. "Damn good to see you Cummings. Where the hell have you been?" Harry inquired.

"All over this damn beachhead, I was so off course when I landed I could just as easily have walked to Paris.

I picked up around ten wandering troopers over the night, and lost five during hit and miss fire fights."

Captain Washburn shook hands with each man as he welcomed them. He then turned to Cummings.

"Where did you just come from, Corporal?"

"Sorry to say sir, I lost my map during one of our battles last night. Best I can tell you, we were pretty much south east of the drop zone. We just entered this road about a half mile up though a break in the hedgerow.

We haven't seen a kraut in the last hour or so, but it's sure loud down toward the beach. We figured we would avoid the beach and maybe help out somewhere back here."

Captain Washburn nodded. "Well Corporal, we're headed toward the beach so you might as well come along.

There will be missions for all of us once we check in."

Corporal Cummings was correct. Heavy fighting supported by devastating naval bombardment could be heard coming from the east and west. Thick black smoke filled the air as the men approached SaintMartin-de-Vareville.

Captain Washburn directed his point men to circumvent the town by following the bank of a small stream that flowed to the northwest. Markham joined the point men as they moved forward. They were just west of town approaching a wide culvert that fed water under an east-west road, when the sounds of clanking treads could be heard approaching from the west. "Cover!" Abbott called out waving his arms in the air.

Everyone scrambled toward either the culvert or the adjoining hedgerow. Harry and Steve crawled slowly up toward the edge of the road in order to ascertain whose tanks were approaching.

Slowly a column of Sherman tanks came into view.

"Praise God," Harry yelled out dashing up onto the road. Steve signaled Cummings and Capt. Washburn to follow.

The lead tank stopped as everyone under Captain Washburn's command poured onto the road.

Harry walked up to the lead tank smiling as he climbed aboard. He offered his hand to the Sergeant sitting in the open hatch of the turret. "Welcome to France, Sarg. We've been softening up the bastards all night for you."

The Sergeant climbed out of the tank shaking hands with all the men. "We could have been here earlier but Omaha is a disaster. Nothing went right from the beginning. There are corpses piled all over the place. The water was actually red when we finally got to shore. That was one rough ride in. Scuttle –butt has it the brass considered pulling of the beach several times." Lighting the end of a well chewed cigar the sergeant continued. "The krauts gave us one hell of a fight, but we finally rolled over them. Glad you guys were mucking up the rear.

Can't believe would it would have been like, if all these crazy kraut bastards had joined in down by the beach."

After answering many questions the tank commander waved his cigar in the air.

"Now if you don't mind gents, we have a date in Berlin with that paper hanging son of a bitch and we don't want to be late."

"Couldn't agree with you more," Captain Washburn replied with a broad smile.

Before the lead tank could move on, a Major with several other officers arrived in a jeep. "What's holding up this procession?" The Major called out.

"I guess that would be us, sir." Captain Washburn stated saluting the tall skinny Major.

"Where are you headed, Captain." The Major inquired as he looked over the dirty paratroopers.

"The beach sir, hoping to get a bit of a rest and new orders, it's been a long damn day." Captain Washburn replied.

Nodding his head the Major once again looked over the paratroopers. "Sorry, Captain. I received orders just a few minutes ago that we need to clear a road block at Sainte-Mere-Eglise. It's holding up the entire invasion.

I might need some extra infantry, so climb aboard the tanks."

Steve shook his head in disgust, but climbed aboard the lead tank with Harry, Franny, Anderson and Woodward. The rest of the men found space on the other waiting tanks. Sliding back into his tank the Sergeant looked at Steve. "They got krauts in this Mare-Eglise place?"

"Oh yeah, they got krauts." Steve replied laughingly. "Maybe more than you would really want to deal with."

The Sergeant smiled as he pulled on his radio head set, "The more the merrier, Corporal. Alright let's move, giddy-up." He called out signaling the other tanks to move forward. The tank jerked forward moving slowly down the road. Everyone scanned the hedgerows for any sign of German snipers. Several American and British fighters screamed overhead taking the battle further inland.

Steve stood up looking toward the rear of the column. He counted three more tanks along with three half tracks filled with infantry bringing up the rear. As he sat back down he thought to himself. This must be total war American style.

As they rolled along the Sergeant turned toward Steve, "The names, Barnes, all the way from the greatest city in the world. New York. I'm going to turn that place upside down when I get back home. They won't forget Sgt. Barnes welcome home party any time soon. Hell, you're all invited. We'll have one hell of a great time. Yes sir, turn that place upside down, how about you Corporal, Where you from?"

"Minnesota, a place called Glendale. Nice farm country" Steve responded.

"Sounds nice, But the big city is my kind of place." Sgt. Barnes responded once again relighting his cigar.

Harry leaned over to Steve, "Think we should tell him about the convoy we met this morning. There might be more of them now." Steve nodded in agreement.

"Hey Sarg, you see that wooded area over there." Steve called out over the loud Detroit diesel engine.

"Yeah, I ain't blind, Corporal. Yeah I see them. Why? We got problems waiting for us?" Sgt. Barnes inquired looking nervously toward Steve.

"We ran into a German convoy on a small road that runs just west of those woods. A British Spitfire tore it up pretty good. That road is going to be blocked by burned out half tracks and trucks. I'm thinking you might have to find a break in the hedgerow, then run cross country to avoid the road block.

There was a kraut panther at the end of the convoy. I think it got away. It still might be hiding in those woods. There might be infantry left to deal with also. Some of them probably made it out of there before all hell broke lose." Steve explained.

"A panther huh, I don't like that idea." Sgt. Barnes responded as he pointed to a break in the hedgerow.

After conferring on the radio with the Major, Barnes told his driver to proceed into the open field.

One by one the rest of the convoy followed through the hedgerow. After going about a hundred yards Sgt. Barnes ordered his driver to stop.

"Where abouts are they, Corporal? Could we see their position from the top of this hedgerow?"

"I would guess so. They certainly can see us right now if they have scouts on top of those hedgerows to your left." Harry replied pointing toward the east.

"Shit." Sgt. Barnes yelled. "Get this thing moving, move, move." He screamed at his driver.

"You trying to get us all killed, Corporal? Move this damn thing." Barnes screamed again into his microphone.

"Me?" You're the one who stopped the tank, Sarg." Steve yelled back indignantly.

"Yeah whatever, Corporal, ever see one of these things take a hot hit standing still? Everyone dies, and I mean everyone! Slide off the back and get your asses of my tank. You won't survive a minute out in the open up there if we need to fight that panther." Barnes yelled angrily.

Harry laughed as Sergeant Barnes started screaming into his headset to the other tanks behind him. "Think you got him riled a bit there Stevie boy. This could get damn interesting"

"Watch for Krauts on and around that hedge row near the woods. Could be a panther out their also. Keep your damn eyes open." Sgt. Barnes yelled down into the tank.

Steve jumped back up cocking the fifty-caliber machine gun next to Sgt. Barnes, before aiming it toward the woods.

"I said get the hell off! What the hell are you doing?" Sergeant Barnes screamed at Steve as Harry took cover behind the turret.

"Just shut up and drive this contraption, Sarg. Let us worry about our sorry asses." Steve yelled at the angry Sergeant.

All four tanks rolled forward across the open field at flank speed. Small arms fire began to crackle from in and around the hedgerow nearest the woods.

Steve saw a muzzle blast from the panther tank, which was now backed into the woods on the far end of the field. The projectile landed behind the third tank with a deafening roar. "Commence firing! Get that bastard!" Sergeant Barnes yelled into his headset.

All four Sherman's fired in unison toward the hedgerow where the German infantry had taken cover.

Three rounds slammed into the hedgerow near the top sending dirt and tree branches skyward. One round slammed into a tree behind the panther tank snapping it in half. There was panic among the German infantrymen as shells found their targets. Several men still hiding in the underbrush, leapt from their concealment rushing back toward the woods.

"If you know how to use that damn thing now would be a good time to shoot, Corporal!" Sergeant Barnes yelled defiantly at Steve.

Depressing the trigger, Steve opened up on the running men. Several fell to the ground; others dove back into the hedgerow for cover. One of the soldiers jumped clear of the hedgerow, aiming a panzerfaust toward the line of tanks. Steve directed the machine gun toward the valiant soldier cutting him down, just as he fired. The anti-tank round went skyward toward the west, exploding harmlessly in the middle of the open field.

The panther gunner fired a second round, landing about fifty yards short of Sgt. Barnes Sherman.

"Where's that damn panther?" Barnes screamed scanning the woods with his binoculars. "Where the hell did he go? Son of a bitch!" he cursed.

Small arms fire occasionally rattled of the sides of the steel hulls but the panther had disappeared for the moment.

The German tank commander maneuvered deeper into the woods, attempting to avoid taking on all four Sherman's at the same time. It was apparent the tank commander understood his advantage in size and armor was wasted on four American tanks.

Suddenly the German tank broke through the underbrush attempting to position him self where only the lead tank could fire on him.

"Get that rat bastard!" Sergeant Barnes screamed at his turret gunner.

With the turret facing forward, all the gunner had to do was raise the level of the barrel before firing. But his range was off. The round landed several feet short of the maneuvering monster.

"Reload damn it, reload or we're all dead!" Barnes barked at his gun crew above the deafening roar.

The other three American tanks broke out across the field charging head on toward the steel behemoth.

Totally unprepared for such a maneuver, the German tank commander hurriedly fired a round toward the on rushing Sherman's, before turning back toward the woods.

The armor piercing round slammed into the ground several feet in front of the number three Sherman, showering the tank with mud and rocks.

"Fire," Sergeant Barnes screamed again. All four Sherman's appeared to fire at the same moment at the escaping German tank.

Steve and Harry felt the heat from the muzzle blast, as the round screamed from the barrel. Sgt. Barnes crew hit pay dirt. Their round struck the German tank near the rear tread sprocket, leaving the tank disabled just at the edge of the woods. Two other tanks had similar success. One round slammed into the turret, the other struck the barrel of the cannon shearing off a good three feet. The tank was now not only disabled, but totally defenseless.

All four American tanks rolled to a stop. Without a moments thought, every tank commander fired another volley, striking the stricken tank in several locations. A violent explosion erupted inside the panther, lifting the turret several feet into the air. A white hot sheet of flame roared from the hull of the enemy tank, as spare shells exploded ripping the dreaded beast apart.

Sergeant Barnes turned toward Steve grinning, "All in a days work. Well that's one less Hun tank we'll need to be concerned about, Corporal."

With the immediate threat out of the way, all four tanks turned their cannons and machine guns toward the German infantry remaining near the edge of the woods. With in minutes the firing stopped from both sides.

Steve and Harry both stood up scanning the area. There wasn't any type of movement or small arms fire from the hedgerow or woods. Other than the sound of idling tank engines it was dead silent.

Steve turned as he heard the half-tracks coming through the opening in the hedgerow. Their drivers stopped several yards behind the tanks. The Major walked forward toward Sergeant Barnes tank along with two infantry men for protection.

"Think we should sweep the area or should we move on, Sergeant?" The Major inquired as he looked toward the woods with a set of binoculars.

Looking down from his turret at the Major and his two bodyguards Sgt. Barnes shook his head. In a rather sarcastic tone he replied, "I think we can move on. If anyone is alive over there they aren't going to impede us one way or the other. However, sir if you're interested in starting your souvenir shopping this might be a good place to start. But I think the war is calling and we should get moving."

Sgt. Barnes opened his canteen taking a hefty swallow of warm water as the Major spun around. His face was bright red as his jaw was tightly clenched. "Is there a problem we need to deal with Sgt. Barnes?"

After wiping his mouth Sgt. Barnes added, "No sir. However I do think everyone deserves a well done on this attack, Major."

After gaining some composure the Major stated angrily, "This isn't grade school Barnes.

We don't get gold stars for good work. This is war. We're all expected to do our best. Will there be anything else?"

Fighting back a smile Sgt. Barnes responded, "No sir. Ready to move out when you are."

"Then let's get this show on the road, Sergeant." The angry Major yelled out as he turned to walk back toward his halftrack.

Placing the head set back over his jeep cap he broke out into a large belly laugh. Shaking his head Sgt. Barnes roared into the microphone. "Alright let's get this travelling circus back on the road. Next stop Saint Mere-Eglise."

"I don't think the Major was happy about your comment, Sarg." Harry said as he prepared to move out.

"Started in England, Corporal, he has a real urge to get the biggest souvenir collection from this war that he can ship back home. The man is not interested in getting bloody, just bloody rich." Sergeant Barnes responded retrieving another cigar from his pocket. "Me? All I want is a good cigar and a bottle of vintage Cognac while I rest my tired feet on Adolph's desk in that damn Reichstag."

As Sgt. Barnes passed near the burning hulk of the panther tank, what remained of three infantry men came into view. They had been smashed into the ground and torn apart from the grinding treads. All the men on top of the tank turned away from the macabre scene.

Several minutes later Sgt. Barnes found a break in the hedgerow allowing, him to pull the convoy back onto the main road. Finally they were heading straight for Sainte Mere'-Eglise.

The trip back seemed almost like a dream to Steve, compared to the problems they had encountered during their slow journey the night before.

The convoy lumbered along the road as the morning sun drifted in and out of heavy cloud cover, which blanketed the sky above the embattled French farmlands.

Once again the peace was shattered. The third tank erupted into a massive inferno, as a single German eight-eight millimeter shell slammed into the turret. Another shell slammed into the burning hulk, tipping the tank over onto its side. Everyone excitedly looked around for the German tank or artillery piece that just obliterated the American tank.

From a depression ahead camouflaged by a hedgerow, came a German tank spinning onto the road. Another enemy tank followed crossing over into a field on the far side of the road.

"Christ sake; God almighty!' Sergeant Barnes exclaimed loudly.

A third German tank burst through a low segment of the hedgerow directly in front of the first half track.

The enemy gunner fired his eighty-eight point blank into the vehicle killing everyone on board.

Several men from the second half-track ran toward the burning hulk checking for survivors. They were instantly cut down by accurate fire from the tanks machine gunner. Every American vehicle was either attempting to back down the road, or searching for a way to get into the open fields. Their best hope in the open field was to use their speed advantage to out maneuver the German tanks.

Steve was tossed against the turret landing very hard, as Sgt. Barnes crashed through a rock wall heading for an open field. The tank bounced over the rough terrain of the field, as the driver struggled intently to keep his tank out of the sights of German gunners. Explosions filled the air as German and American tanks exchanged rounds in a fast moving battle for survival.

The remaining half tracks successfully retreated back down the road to avoid the battle, and save their precious infantry from being slaughtered.

Moment's later; number four tank blew up in a violent explosion. Nearly the entire engine compartment had been ripped away. What was left of the engine lay several feet away from the tanks hull.

Sgt. Barnes yelled at the men, motioning for them to get off his tank as most of the other drivers had done before starting battle. Steve knew he was not going to stop the churning machine for them to exit. As quickly as possible, the five men rolled off the tank as the Sergeant was making a quick turn. They jumped to their feet, dashing for cover on the bank of a large drainage ditch that flowed near by. The German tank commanders were too preoccupied with the snarling American tanks, to worry about a few infantry men, so they made it to the ditch unscathed.

The Sherman carrying Abbott, Rabinowitz, Markham, Haley and Brant was churning wildly in the field as eight-eight shells exploded all around them. Huge pieces of shrapnel slammed against the tank, barely missing the five terrified men who were holding on for dear life. The driver made a quick pass near the drainage ditch, sliding the tank sideways. Rabinowitz and Brant were thrown clear of the machine. The other three men took the opportunity to dive clear off the careening monster. Quickly, they regained their feet diving for the safety of the deep depression.

Thanks to a wild skid, the driver of number two tank was able to come directly up behind one of the German panthers, bearing down on Sergeant Barnes.

The seventy-five millimeter cannon fired a blast into the rear of the enemy machine, causing it to shudder before rolling to a stop. As flames burst from the engine compartment, one of the turret hatches opened, as the crew desperately struggled to evacuate their doomed behemoth. Watching the action from the drainage ditch, Franny took quick aim with his BAR; firing off several quick bursts at the fleeing tankers. Quickly Harry and Brant joined in the fray.

None of the escaping Germans were able to get very far away from their burning tank. The two remaining German panthers now caught Sergeant Barnes in a cross fire. Their deadly rounds struck the Sherman simultaneously. As the tank rolled to a stop, it nearly leapt into the air as it exploded in a tremendous ball of flame. From the drainage ditch the men could see the body of the tough Sergeant slumped over the side of the turret. The once powerful weapon of war now became a blazing crematorium for its gallant crew.

The driver of the lone Sherman left on the battlefield charged full speed toward the depression from which the German tanks made their initial attack. One last eighty-eight shell exploded behind the retreating

Sherman, before it disappeared behind the hedgerow.

Steve studied the two German tanks sitting side by side in the field. The two tank commanders talked back and forth from their turrets. One of them pointed toward the drainage ditch where the paratroopers had taken cover.

Steve motioned for everyone to take cover in a large concrete culvert that ran under the adjacent road. However, after exchanging a few more words, the German tanks slowly began moving back toward the hedgerow. Reaching the road they stopped for a few moments before moving back toward Sainte-Mere'-Eglise.

Once the tanks were well out of sight, the men crawled up out of the drainage ditch. The rest of the men who had taken cover elsewhere came running to join them.

Looking out over the burning wreckage, they were stunned as to how fast this action had taken place. Worse yet was the cost it took in American lives.

Slowly they walked toward the Sherman of Sergeant Barnes, which was still burning around the engine compartment. A small explosion from the burning German tank caught the paratroopers of guard. They either quickly fell to the ground, or sought cover behind Sgt. Barnes battered tank.

Carefully Steve crawled up onto the hot tank, examining the charred body of Sergeant Barnes. An ironic sight caught his eye. A partially unburned cigar still remained in the Sergeants right hand, as it hung lifeless over the side of the turret.

"No doubt it would have been some party. I believe Barnes would have turned New York upside down just like he said. It would have been something to see." Harry explained as Steve jumped from the smoldering wreck.

Harry turned his attention toward the German tank, where Franny was pointing his BAR at a body on the ground, before firing a short blast. The body shook for a second then laid still, as Franny prepared to fire again.

"He wasn't dead yet, Harry. He was moaning. The son of a bitch wasn't dead yet. For Christ sake Harry, what the hell happened? What the hell went wrong?" Franny demanded in an angry voice as he looked at the dead German near his feet. "Hell this guy doesn't look like he's over sixteen years old. What the hell, man!"

"I don't know, Franny." Harry replied as he looked around the field. After looking over all the men Harry called out. "Does anyone know where Captain Washburn is? Which vehicle did he get into?"

Gunderson walked up to Steve. "I saw him direct everyone into halftracks. Then he jumped on the back of the fourth tank. I saw most the guys jump off as it entered the field. He was still holding on to the fifty-cal just prior to it getting hit. If he didn't jump off much after that, he must be dead."

"Spread out, take a look around before we get out of here just in case he's wounded." Steve directed as he walked toward the burning vehicle. Approaching the break in the hedgerow where the tanks entered the field Gunderson called out, "Over here, Kenrude."

Aside the hedgerow laid the lifeless body of Captain Washburn. His left arm was torn away at the elbow. The stub of the arm was badly burned nearly cauterizing all the blood vessels. It was apparent the arm had been amputated by a large, hot piece of shrapnel.

Markings on the ground indicated he crawled to the hedgerow after being thrown from the back of the tank.

Harry knelt down removing the Captain's map, and other essential papers from his pack. Taking a deep breath Harry looked at Steve. "Let's get the hell out of here."

Nodding his head in agreement, Steve stood silent for a moment as if in deep thought. "Alright let's hit the road.

If they needed help in Saint-Mere-Eglise, then let's see what we can do to help them out." They just entered the road when Franny called out, "Wait! Did you hear that?"

"Hear what?" Steve inquired.

"Someone just called for help in English. It was faint but I heard it." Franny explained as he looked back toward the burning half track.

Franny and Brant walked slowly toward the half-track, as everyone else stood quiet listening for another call for help.

The two men walked just a few feet when Franny stopped. "Did you hear that Brant?" "Yeah I did, sounds like it is coming from over there." Brant replied as he walked back toward the burning hulk. Quickly the men ran toward the wreckage. It was impossible for anyone to have survived the explosion and fire that consumed the demolished vehicle. The road around the half track was littered with debris, and the remains of charred bodies twisted in grotesque shapes. Steve carefully climbed on to the rear of the half track looking around the gutted interior.

"No one alive in here," He called out before jumping back down.

"Help me! Over here, Please." came a voice from the hedgerow about ten yards beyond the half-track.

Quickly the men ran toward the sound of the pleading voice. A horribly injured American soldier lay on his back looking up at them.

Steve and Harry knelt down beside the wounded man.

"Where the hell did you come from?" Harry inquired, as Steve looked over the blood soaked battle dressing on the man's abdomen. His body was covered with horrible burns and his right hand was missing.

"I was thrown from the half track when it got hit and landed several yards away. I crawled over here to get away from the tanks. The last one to leave nearly ran me over. I didn't think anyone was alive until I heard you guys. I was hoping the other half-tracks would come back. But I guess they went all the way back to the beach" Trying desperately not to admit he was in pain the soldier looked over toward Steve.

"Am I going to be alright? Can you take a look at my right arm corporal? I think something is wrong with it.

I, I can't move it. I couldn't get it to work when I tried to bandage myself. It must be broken pretty bad.

Harry was about to speak just as the man closed his eyes passing out. Steve felt the man's neck for a pulse.

"He's still alive. I think he just passed out from shock and blood loss."

Harry set up a make shift tourniquet on the man's smashed right arm to slow the bleeding. "He should have bled to death by now. Can you fix that dressing on his abdomen, Steve?"

Carefully removing the soaked battle dressing Steve looked underneath. Setting it back down over the wound he shook his head.

"Someone up there likes this guy. There's no reason he's alive. Harry there's nothing we can do for this man.

He needs a hospital and a surgeon soon, and I'm not sure that will make much of a difference anymore."

Harry nodded his head looking with pity on the young American soldier. "Yeah you're right.

There just isn't anything else we can do. But we can't just leave him here all alone in this condition either."

Franny, Brant and Anderson had been keeping watch about a quarter mile down the road in case the marauding German tanks returned. Suddenly the men came running toward them yelling, "Tank, tank!"

"Who's tank, damn it?" Harry called out.

"Don't know, couldn't see it, but heard it clanking around the bend, moving pretty good speed too." Franny replied searching for cover in the hedgerow.

Everyone quickly sought cover as the sound of the tank became louder. The men listened intently as the machine came to a stop just out of sight, then started up again slowly.

"It's going to come through the hole in the hedgerow near the big depression." Franny explained as he watched for the armored beast to come into view.

"Maybe it's the Sherman that got away coming back looking for survivors." Rabinowitz added.

"Let's hope your right. We've got nothing here to fight a damn tank." Steve responded quietly.

Rabinowitz was right. Slowly a Sherman tank rolled through the hedgerow into the battle littered field. The tank commander was standing in the open turret examining the wreckage with his binoculars.

Franny jumped out from the hedgerow. He began to yell and wave his arms frantically. The Sergeant hearing Franny's screams, directed his driver to head back toward the road. Slowly the driver inched along the hedgerow as the Sergeant nervously continued scanning the area.

The young Buck Sergeant looked down from the turret asking. "What's up trooper? "We've got a badly man injured here. We need to get him back for medical help or he's going to die. Can you help us out Sarge," Franny inquired desperately.

"Sorry pal, but this isn't an ambulance. Hell I don't even know if there's an aid station established anywhere in all of France. Where the hell do I take him? What happens if we have to fight along the way?" The frustrated Sergeant replied as he looked toward the wounded man.

A string of machine gun bullets clanked along the side of the tank causing the Sergeant to quickly slide down inside the turret. Turning, he observed the smoking German machine gun in Harry's hands.

"Are you fucking crazy? What the hell's the matter with you?" The Sergeant yelled out angrily.

Smiling, Harry pointed his weapon back toward the tank. "Think you can get out of the way a second time?"

He barked out with an angry tone.

"Look, men are dying all over this damn country and we can't help all of them. I would like to accommodate you I really would. But let's be realistic here for a minute. We just can't take a tank out of battle every time someone needs a trip to an aid station. Think about that, Corporal." The Sergeant replied keeping a nervous eye on the German machine gun in Harry's hands.

"Have it your way then, Sarg." Harry replied raising the barrel of the weapon toward the turret.

"Alright, alright, you have yourself an ambulance, Corporal. Load him up and tell me where to go, because I just don't have a clue as to where we'll find an aid station" The Sergeant called down angrily as he watched the men pick up the injured soldier.

They were about ready to lay the injured man on the back of the tank, when a half-track approached up the beach road, flying two Red Cross flags above the windshield.

Abbott ran toward the vehicle as it came to a stop. "We need your help. We have a badly injured man here that needs a surgeon in the worst way."

A second Lieutenant jumped from the passenger seat. "That's why we're here, private. We we're told there might be some men up here that need our attention.

How many you got?"

"Just one, and he's hurt real bad." Abbott informed the Lieutenant.

Quickly several medics jumped from the half-track carrying a litter and several first aid kits. As they examined the injured soldier they just shook their heads. He's bad, real bad." One medic explained to Steve as he looked under the battle dressing covering the man's abdomen.

As they carried the soldier toward the half-track he opened his eyes slightly. He called out in a faint voice.

"Corporal, I need to talk to the corporal."

The medics stopped walking for a moment as they looked back toward Steve.

"Move it damn it." Steve screamed at the two stretcher bearers.

"No wait, wait." The injured man pleaded.

The lieutenant looked toward Steve. "You better come up here' Corporal."

The young private reached out with his good arm taking hold of Steve's hand.

"You risked your lives for me. Thank you. Thanks to all of you," The private said gasping for breath in a low voice.

"Come on move it!" Steve demanded motioning for the medics to continue.

"No wait. I want you to do me a favor. Please." The young man again pleaded reaching into his shirt pocket.

The medics looked toward Steve. Begrudging Steve nodded his approval for them to wait until the soldier was ready.

The injured man handed Steve a plain silver Crucifix. "My mom gave me this before I left home. Will you see she gets it back? Tell her I was brave and did my best."

Steve handed the cross back to the injured man saying, "You can give it to her yourself when you get home.

Besides, you might need it between now and then."

"No, please take it for me. My name is Daniel Garnet. I'm from Buddtown, New Jersey. My folks are John and Helen. Only Garnet's in the phone book. Please get this to them. Please!"

As private Garnet struggled to take another breath, a gurgling sound emanated from his lungs. "You men risked everything for me. Good luck to all of you. We shall meet again some day in a different land where nobody will ever again fight another war. I assure you."

The medics placed the stretcher on the ground knowing full well the man was dying. Everyone knelt down around the stretcher as the tank crew observed from a few feet away.

"I will remember you all, God be with you. Mother, Mother!" The man desperately called out.

Drawing in one more choppy breath he took hold of Harry's hand whispering, "Remember me."

Slowly his hand slipped to the ground.

"We will, Garnet. We'll never forget you, kid." Harry responded to the dead man's final wish.

"He's gone." Harry said as he gently closed Garnet's big blue eyes.

The small group knelt quietly for several moments, all looking at the lifeless body of the young private.

"Corporal we have to…." The one medic began to say.

"Yeah go ahead. Thanks for your help." Steve responded as he stood up. Watching the medics carry the stretcher toward the back of the half-track, he quietly whispered a silent prayer.

Taking a pencil and piece of paper from his pack, Steve quickly wrote down the information private Garnet gave them about his family. Wrapping the silver cross inside the paper he placed it back inside his pack.

Slowly the tank crew walked back toward their Sherman, as the medical crew prepared to leave.

Patting Steve on the shoulder Harry took a deep breath, "Saint-Mere'-Eglise anyone?" "Yeah we best get moving." Steve responded retrieving his Thompson from Franny.

The lanky tank Sergeant stopped a few feet from his Sherman. Turning he walked back toward the paratroopers. "Not that it makes any difference I suppose, but my name is Russ Gentry. I'm glad to have met you guys."

Harry shook hands with the Sergeant introducing him self and the rest of their team. "Look, I need fuel and ammo for this crate before I can even think of heading toward Saint-Mere'-Eglise."

Looking at his watch he continued. "I'm guessing I'll need to drive all the way back toward the beach before I'm going to find supplies. Why don't you guys climb aboard and come along with me.

Maybe we can pick up more help and make a real splash when we get to Sainte-Mere'-Eglise."

Over hearing the conversation the half-track driver called out, "Hey Sarg. There's a small fueling, resupply depot being set up several miles up from the beach on the north side of the road, it will save you a ton of time over getting involved with that mess down on the beach, Shouldn't take you long at all."

"There you go, Corporal what do you say." Sgt. Gentry inquired.

Steve contemplated it for a moment turning toward Harry. "What do you think?"

"I don't know Steve. I think having this tank for fire power when we get to Saint-Mere'-Eglise makes good sense. It could make a difference in the long run." Harry responded hoping Steve would agree.

"Exactly what I was thinking," Steve replied looking over his tired men who were all nodding their heads in agreement. "That settles it. Thanks Sarg we're all headed back with you."

After everyone was on board and the half-track turned around, they drove straight toward the refueling point.

Arriving at the depot they found trucks with ammunition, weapons, and much needed food rations. Two fuel trucks were parked near a grove of trees covered with camouflage netting. Sgt. Gentry rolled his tank next to the fuel trucks, as several men prepared their equipment for fueling the thirsty Sherman. As their fuel tanks were being topped off, the crew loaded shells into the turret from the ammunition trucks.

Harry asked about exchanging the German machine gun he had been carrying a good part of the night, for a Thompson and ammunition.

The Lieutenant in charge of the ammunition trucks took Harry toward a tent set up in the grove. It was filled with every type of weapon an infantry man could use. Harry reached down picking up what appeared to be a brand new Thompson. Looking it over there appeared to be blood on the barrel and sling.

"Yeah their used, Corporal, most of those guys never made it more than a few feet onto the beach before they got it. Most of them will never need these weapons again. You can get ammo from the truck." The Lieutenant explained as he eyed the German machine gun slung over Harry's shoulder.

"What are your plans for the Kraut gun, Corporal?"

"You want the damn thing you can have it. It doesn't mean a thing to me." Harry replied handing over the weapon.

After loading up with ammunition, Harry walked over to the rest of the men who were stocking up on grenades and food.

When everyone finished resupplying, they walked over to the tank just as the fueling and ammo loading was completed.

Preparing to slide back into the turret Sgt. Gentry called out, "You guys ready to head for Saint-Mere'-Eglise."

"You know it Sarg, Ready to give us a lift?" Steve inquired smiling up at the turret.

"You bet! Hop on." The lanky Sergeant responded motioning down to his driver to take off.

The Sherman drove away from the supply depot in a cloud of dust, heading down the now familiar road.

Steve was still totally determined to complete the mission they had started out on so long ago, although now his force had shrunk considerably. Some of the familiar men they had just acquired disappeared with the retreating half-tracks. There was no telling where they were now. Nevertheless, they would do what they could just as they had been doing since they first dropped into Normandy. He looked around at the men sitting quietly on top of the bouncing tank. Harry had his eyes closed trying desperately to get some sleep.

Franny was wiping down his B.A.R. with a couple of rags he picked up in the ammo truck. The rest of the men were just holding on for dear life as the veteran driver sped forward fearlessly.

Suddenly Steve's spirits were heightened, as he watched the massive amount of trucks and other equipment making their way up from the beach. He felt confident; the allied foot hold in Normandy was finally the beginning of the end for the Nazi war machine. He was proud to be part of such a grand operation.

CHAPTER 11
GLENDALE STORM

The clanging alarm clock broke the silence of the Kenrude house at five A.M. Outside in the still morning; light dew covered every exposed surface. Through the open window Alex could hear one of his newborn calves raising a fuss with its mother. He laughed and thought; kids are kids no matter what type of species they were.

"Breakfast," Nancy said quietly. "The little guy wants to eat breakfast."

Alex smiled looking over at his wife. He still thought she was the sweetest woman he had ever known.

What a wonderful life they had shared together. Three great children, a successful farm, and all the love a man could ever really ask for. Life had been very good to them, and they were very thankful for all the blessings they had received.

"What are you smiling about?" Nancy inquired as she sat up in bed and stretched.

"You, What do you think?" Alex responded as he began to get out of bed.

"I love you to." Nancy replied as she watched her husband pull back the curtains to look outside at the new day.

"Looks like it will be another nice day." Alex commented as he left the curtains fall back. "Always so many things to do, so I suppose I should get going."

"Did you hear me Mr. Kenrude?" Nancy inquired waiting for a reply.

"Yes, Mrs. Kenrude I did. I love you too. Good Morning, Honey."

Nancy threw a pillow at her husband and laughed as she dashed from the room.

Mike stumbled awkwardly down the stairs into the hallway as Alex was heading toward the kitchen.

"Morning, son," Alex said as he rubbed Mike's bushy hair.

"Yup it is morning for sure. No doubt about that. We need to put a muzzle on that new calf. He wakes up way too early. Let's get the milking done. I'm hungry." Mike replied following Alex through the kitchen out into the damp new morning. They had their morning routine down to a science. Mike went right to work without Alex having to say a word.

Nancy was busy in the kitchen preparing breakfast for her family like any other day. Today it would be scrambled eggs, bacon, and oatmeal. Mike's favorite.

She began compiling a list in her head of all the things she wanted to accomplish during the day. The house seemed quiet this morning, almost too quiet for her liking. She remembered the hectic but fun days of three little children flying around the house, always creating some sort of disturbance. She missed those days very much, especially with Steve away at war.

She walked over to the shelf above the refrigerator to turn on the radio. It was too early in the morning for the local station to be on the air, so she played with the tuner trying to get a station from Minneapolis.

After several attempts up and down the dial, she found a station just beginning to read the morning news.

She listened intently as the announcer began with daily updates on the war fronts.

Suddenly, the door to the barn swung wide open slamming into the wall with a tremendous bang. Alex spun around looking at the open door. His wife stood in the doorway, silhouetted against the dark morning.

"What on earth is wrong with you woman?" He called out. "Are you alright? Is something wrong, Sweetheart?"

Mike walked up beside his father looking strangely toward his mother. He had never seen her look this way before. She was shaking as if she had just been terrified by someone or something.

"It's on," Is all she was able to say as she stared at her troubled husband.

"What's on?" Alex inquired approaching his wife who was wringing her hands in the blue apron she wore.

"The radio, the radio said it. Last night we invaded France." She responded. "I heard it on a Minneapolis station. They had a special report. The reporter announced thousands of men were going ashore. There was no report of exactly how things were going yet." Nancy explained as she reached out to hug Alex.

Mike shot passed both of them heading toward the house to listen to news reports on the radio.

Alex took his wife into his arms holding her tightly. "Steve is there, Alex. I don't know where but I know he's there. I feel it. I feel it in my soul." She explained as she began to cry. Alex felt it was best to just be silent, as he attempted to comfort his trembling wife. He knew if he attempted to talk right now he might also cry, as he thought about his oldest son. After several minutes he drew a deep breath, "All we can do now is pray for his safety, Honey. It's in the hands of the Lord to take care of him, and all the other men involved in this battle."

They walked together to the house where Mike was listening intently to every word the announcer was reporting.

There were few details to report, other then the United States and its allies landed on five beaches on the Norman coast of France, and heavy fighting had occurred.

He listened attentively hoping to hear some news as to whether airborne forces had been used. He wondered if Steve was in the thick of the fighting, but in a way hoped he wasn't. Nevertheless, some how he knew highly trained soldiers like the 101st airborne had to be involved some way.

Christine came into the kitchen. Seeing everyone standing together quietly, listening intently to the radio she asked in a bewildered voice, "What's happening?" What's all the commotion about?"

"Quiet!" Mike called out. "I couldn't hear what the announcer just said."

"Hear what, Michael? What happened? Will somebody tell me?" Christine yelled out angrily.

"The second front, Christine." Nancy explained as she walked up behind her daughter, wrapping her arms around her. "Our boys invaded France last night." Nancy kissed her daughter on top of her head.

"Do we know if Steve is there?" Christine asked quietly.

"No Sweetheart we don't. No body really knows anything right now. We may not know for days or even weeks if Steven was there. All we can do is pray for your brother and all the brave men, who are fighting and dying right now for our freedom. We need to ask God to bring your brother home safe and sound."

Nancy said softly.

After breakfast Alex pried Mike away from the radio so they could go about their morning chores. Mike had a terribly hard time concentrating on what he was doing. Thoughts of the massive invasion filled his mind.

At times it angered him that he could not be part of it. About midmorning Alex finished repairing the fence behind the barn. He sat down on a hay bail to take a break. Observing Mike struggling with a saw as he attempted to cut boards for the new cattle feeder, Alex called out.

"That saw sounds mighty dull, son."

"I think so." Mike responded as he laid it on a sawhorse before walking over to his Father. "We could run into town and get it sharpened at the hardware store."

"We sure could, son. But we just started a new month. We'll need to have ration coupons for gasoline the entire month. I can sharpen the saw myself. I'll teach you, Mike. It's a skill you'll always use the rest of your life." Alex explained as he walked over picking up the saw. "Yeah it's plenty dull, but we can remedy that in a few minutes."

Alex handed the saw to his son as he walked toward the work bench. Mike tossed the saw on the hay bails and stomped his foot. "I don't care about the saw. I want to hear what's being said in town. The whole world is involved, and here I sit on this damn farm doing nothing. It's not fair. Dad, I want to be part of it.

And don't give me that talk again about how working on the farm is a big part of the war effort. That's not what I want. You and mom both know it. I want to go fight this war like Steve."

Mike started walking briskly across the barn toward the back door.

"Listen here, Michael. Come back here we need to talk!" Alex called out angrily to his youngest son.

Michael did not stop. He walked out the door directly toward the road leading to Glendale. He walked about two hundred yards before stopping. His head was somewhere between anger and frustration.

He was not sure what to do about anything. After taking several deep breaths he walked over to a tree several yards off road and sat down. After sitting for several minutes he stood up slamming his fists into the tree. As he tried to calm himself he thought of the way he had treated his Father. That upset him even more.

After some serious soul searching Mike walked back toward the barn. He could hear the sound of Alex hammering nails as he worked on the new feeder. For several moments Mike stood just outside the barn door. He watched his Father measure for the next section of the pen, then write down the dimensions on a small piece of wood. As Alex went to pick up a large plank Mike walked into the barn quietly.

"Need help with that plank?" Mike asked. Startled, Alex turned to see Mike standing by the door. He could sense the frustration his youngest son was feeling. "Yup, I sure could use a hand with this. Know anyone who would like to get their hands dirty and give me a hand? Alex responded with a smile.

"Yeah, guess that would be me. Sorry." Mike said quietly. "Let's sharpen the saw. Okay?"

Nodding in agreement, Alex picked up the saw from the hay bale before walking toward the work bench.

Glendale was buzzing with news of the invasion. All over town residents congregated where ever radios were on, hoping to hear the latest war dispatches.

At the Donnelly residence, Karen was awakened by her Mother after she heard word of the invasion.

"Karen, Honey wake up." Janet said as she stroked her daughter's hair. Karen opened her eyes as she sat up in bed. "What's the matter, Mom" she inquired, studying her mother's nervous face.

"Mr. Gilbert from next door just came over. He told me the radio reported the invasion of France took place last night. He said there is not a lot of information yet, but it was a huge operation and every thing appears to be going well for our boys so far. They keep repeating the same news, so I guess they don't know much more then that I'm afraid." She informed her daughter reassuringly.

Karen was quiet for a few moments as she took in what her mother just told her. "Did they say anything about airborne troops?"

"No Honey that was about it. I asked Mr. Gilbert the same question and he said it was all pretty vague."

Janet responded looking at the photo of Steve on Karen's dresser.

"I suppose Steve is somehow involved. I mean, all the training they have done since arriving in England must have had something to do with the invasion. Don't you think, mother?" Karen inquired as she reached for her robe.

Shaking her head Janet replied, "I don't know, honey. War is a strange thing. Only God has the answers I'm afraid."

"Steve can never say much I know, but he says they are always training nonstop." Karen said calmly as she looked over at Steve's photo. Slowly Karen got out of bed, wrapping the robe around her as she walked toward the dresser. Picking up the picture frame she studied Steve's face for several moments. "I have faith in him that he will do the right things and come home to us." She stated after setting the photo back down.

"What do we do now, mom?"

"We pray sweetheart. We can pray. That's all a person can do." Karen's mother replied as they walked out of the bedroom together.

As evening fell over Glendale, storm clouds gathered in the western sky. Slowly they moved over the fields west of town becoming more menacing with every passing minute. The sky turned from a dark grey into menacing grayish green color.

The powerful west wind that had been disturbing everything not nailed down suddenly dropped off.

Not a leaf moved on trees in the Kenrude yard. Alex watched the rolling clouds intently, remembering the tornado that struck when he was a young boy. The sky that dreadful night looked exactly like it did now.

He would never forget the damage that twister had caused in Glendale.

Nancy walked out onto the porch taking a long look at the threatening sky. "My, this does not look good.

Not good at all. No wind, no breeze. Alex, I think we are in for a rough night." She declared gazing at the ever changing sky.

"Get the kids and head for the basement. I think we better be ready because this is going to pop any minute. I can feel it coming in my bones." Alex warned as he walked back toward the porch.

Without a word Nancy dashed into the house where she found Christine already in the basement. Mike was standing in the kitchen peering out the big west window.

"Come, Michael your Father wants us in the basement right away. He remembers the twister that tore up Glendale when he was a boy and thinks it will happen again tonight." Nancy explained as she took Mike by the arm, attempting to pull him toward the basement door. "Let's light some candles in case we loose power."

The wind picked up dramatically blowing dirt and anything loose across the yard. Alex raced for the house, slamming the door shut before retreating to the basement with his family.

The wind howled and blew with a tremendous force. Mike felt it was impossible a house could remain intact the way their old farm house creaked and moaned. It appeared as if at any minute the storm would rip their house from its foundation.

Rain began falling in torrents. The sound of hail slamming against windows raised a terrible noise.

Lightning flashed constantly, followed by tremendous crashes of thunder. Alex jumped up from his chair running toward the stairs.

"Where on earth are you going?" Nancy screamed at her husband.

"Stay here. I have to see what's going on. I'll be alright" He called back to his wife.

"Alex no, get back here. Alex!" She screamed to no avail as he continued up the steps into the entryway.

Opening the door he stepped out onto the porch unable to see anything through the wind driven rain.

Extremely brilliant lightening streaked across the dark Minnesota sky, followed by a rolling thunder which caused the hair on the back of his neck to stand up.

Suddenly the wind changed directions. It began blowing from the south as the temperature suddenly fell.

Alex knew there was a tornado somewhere out in that darkness. The wind began howling as if the gates of hell were opening wide.

It felt like an invisible hand was attempting to rip him from the porch. Alex decided it was best to get back down the basement. Just as he reached for the door handle, a tremendous lightning bolt lit up the eastern sky. He could see a large rotating funnel skipping across the ground. It mesmerized him for several seconds, making it impossible for him to move from the porch. Each time the lightning flashed, he watched the funnel in its macabre dance across his corn field.

It weaved back and forth as if it were playing a child's game. But this was anything but a child's game.

"Oh Lord." Alex shouted. "Dear God, don't let this storm wipe us out." He prayed out loud as he stood holding on to the screen door. He knew he belonged in the basement, but he wanted to get another look at the position of the funnel cloud before leaving. He could hear the tremendous roar of the angry cloud, but could not see it until another flash of lightning lit the sky. The whirling funnel now appeared to be closer to his farm.

"Not the farm Dear God, not the farm. It's all we have. Please not the farm." Alex cried out. He stood by the end of the porch frozen in place, trying to get just one more glimpse of the devastating funnel.

From out of the dark a large tree limb struck him from behind, sending him face first into one of the roof support beams. Tumbling to his knees he gasped for air. The huge branch had knocked the wind from his lungs. As big as he was, Alex had been completely stunned by the flying branch. For several moments he knelt on the porch, as he strained with every ounce of energy in his body to draw in a solid breath. Finally pulling himself up, he gazed back toward the funnel but he could not see it.

Still dazed, Alex grasped tightly to the post he had just slammed into. Blood ran down his face from a gash above his right eye. Knowing his life was in danger, Alex fought with every ounce of energy within him to grab for the kitchen door.

He could still hear the ominous roar of the tornado, but was unable to see anything through the driving storm.

"Good bye farm." Alex muttered as he pushed open the kitchen door on his way to the basement.

"Everyone against the east wall." Alex yelled as he ran frantically down the stairs. "Quickly, quickly."

He yelled as he grabbed Nancy by the arm pulling her toward the stone wall.

"What happened to you, you're bleeding. My God, Alex." Nancy screamed as she began to cry.

"Get down and cover up with these blankets. We're going to get hit hard." Alex exclaimed as he tried to cover his family with his outstretched arms.

For what appeared to be hours the Kenrude family huddled in the corner, praying as the monster storm roared toward their farm. The fury of the storm tore across the rural Minnesota community destroying everything in its path.

Then as if in a dream everything became eerily quiet. Alex stood up from the floor walking toward the stairs.

"I think its past. I'm going to take a look and see what's left." He explained, as he slowly climbed the wooden stairs to the main floor.

Mike stood up helping his still shaking Mother and Christine to their feet. "Come on; let's go with Dad to see how much damage there is."

His mother nodded her head in agreement as she bravely walked toward the stairs, where Alex now stood at the top with his hand on the doorknob. Cautiously he pushed the door open looking around the darkened kitchen. There did not appear to be any damage that he could immediately see. Preparing to open the porch door he took a deep breath. He expected to see his farm buildings flattened, and his livestock dead. Rain was still lightly falling as he and Mike stepped out onto the porch. They both took a quick survey of the yard. Although it was very dark, they could see the barn was intact although one door was missing. The corn crib and large storage shed were still standing. Several trees were either snapped off, or had large limbs missing.

"I think we were spared, son." Alex said placing his arm around Michael's shoulders.

"Let's wait until daylight to check everything out. It's to dark now, and with the rain we won't be able to see well or do much anyway. Let's all get some sleep; it's been a rough night." He added as the two men walked back into the house.

As dawn broke over the Glendale area it was easy to trace the track of the storm. Alex lost a small corncrib behind the barn, while having some minor damage to several other buildings. But compared to their neighbors to the north and east who lost nearly everything, their damage was minimal. They were very thankful for being spared by the powerful storm.

Alex and Mike spent the next several days offering assistance to friends who received heavy damage.

Many roofs and windows needed immediate repair or patching until new material could be acquired.

As Alex drove up in front of the Wagner farm, Mike stared out the window totally speechless. After he finished surveying the destruction he shook his head.

"Dad, do you think this is what war looks like after a big battle?"

"I suspect it does, son." Alex replied as he stared at his young son. "I guess Steve is seeing sights like this and a whole lot worse where ever he is."

Alex continued up the long driveway before Marv Wagner motioned them to stop.

"You best stop about here Alex. There are nails and debris all over the place that could ruin your tires."

Stepping from his truck Alex shook hands with Mr. Wagner. Mike looked about the yard for a moment before joining the two men.

"Thanks for coming over. We can sure use the help. I hear they're looking for old man Schmidt since last night. He ran out to close some doors on the barn and no one has seen him since." Marv informed Alex and Mike.

"That's too bad. Odds of finding him alive aren't very good any more." Alex responded shaking his head.

"Yeah his barn is gone totally. We found pieces of it just south of our house. No telling where he could be.

There's even talk about dragging Eagle Lake for his body. But that damn lake is awfully deep. If he's in there they may never find the poor guy." Mr. Wagner continued as they walked up toward the shattered house.

"Do you think that's possible?" Mike asked as he looked in the direction of the Schmidt farm.

"Anything is possible with a storm like we had last night, Michael. I suspect we will find him when we walk the fields. They looked through the rubble on his farm and in the pastures but couldn't find him.

I guess the Sheriff is going to be setting up a list of volunteers to take care of jobs like that. His wife Mary is lucky to be alive. They found her pinned under the rubble in their basement. But she'll be all right." Marv responded.

Alex just shook his head. "Well where would you like us to start here."

"Well if you want to help salvage stuff from the barn that would be great. Storm tore up the building, but just about every thing was left inside."

Alex pitched in with several other neighbors pulling what ever they could from the barn, before it was knocked down the rest of the way. Mike walked over to the storage shed behind the house where he saw Iris Wagner working.

"Can I help you with anything back here?" Mike inquired.

"Yes Michael that would be nice. I sure would appreciate some help. Wiping sweat from her forehead she looked up at him. "You know we lost a lot of belongings, and have lots of damage to buildings, but at least we're alive and unhurt. We can rebuild. Yes, Michael we can rebuild."

Mike pulled some boards off a suitcase as Iris pulled it clear of the rubble. "It's almost good as new, not even very wet. Well one more thing we'll not have to replace." She exclaimed staring at the damaged building.

"Mike, start pulling debris of the roof, so we can get at what is left underneath. But be careful so the whole thing doesn't come down on top of you."

Mike walked around the back of the shed. He gently began pulling a large section of the roof off, that was barely teetering on the back wall. "Oh damn! Dad, someone," He yelled out.

Several men came running from the barn to see what he was yelling about.

"What's up son?" Alex called out as he neared the shed.

Mike stood back a few feet from the shed pointing toward the ground. "I think I just found Mr. Schmidt."

Alex and Marv rolled the body over to see if in fact it was Donald Schmidt. The body was mutilated very badly. After several minutes Mike became light headed, as his stomach began to churn.

He ran over to the cornfield dropping down to his hands and knees as he began to vomit. Alex walked over placing his hand on his son's shoulder as he stood up. Removing a bandana from his pocket Mike wiped his face.

"Are you alright, son?" Alex inquired.

"I can't go back over there. I can't look at him again." Mike replied staring at his shaking hands. "I can help out by the barn or anywhere else. But not back over there. Okay?" "You don't have to, son. Its fine, we can head home if you want to." Alex said reassuringly.

"No I want to help. We need to help get this place cleaned up." Mike replied with a forced smile.

The neighbors worked until nearly dark before calling it a day. Walking toward their truck Alex placed his arm around his son giving him a hug. "You were brave today, Mike"

"I just want to go home and take a bath and go to bed. I don't think I can even eat anything." Mike commented as he climbed into the truck.

As night closed in on the Kenrude farm, Mike could still see the torn up body in his mind as he lay in bed. He tried hard not to think of it, but the gruesome images would not leave him alone.

Nancy stopped by her son's room before she went to bed. "Are you alright Mike? Do you want to talk about your day?"

He sat up on his bed looking toward his mother. "I suspect Steve has seen worse things already. I feel like a fool for getting sick in front of all those men."

Smiling, his mother walked over and sat down on the edge of his bed. "You have no need to feel that way, son.

What you saw would make most people sick. You are just human, Michael." She explained stroking her son's hair.

"But I wasn't strong. I didn't act like a man." Mike replied quietly.

"You're not a man yet, Michael. You're still a boy by most standards. Don't try and grow up so fast.

I know you want to be like your brother, off to war, trying to save our country and all. But in many ways Steve is still just a boy. He will grow up way past his years I'm afraid. It's alright for you to stay a boy for a while longer." Nancy said looking lovingly at her son.

She kissed him on the forehead as she stood up. "Try and get some sleep now."

After His mother left the room Mike thought about everything she had told him. Some of it felt right, and some of it made him upset.

Growing up was tough he thought, especially with a war going on. He wondered where the life of a boy ended and being a man began. However right now in the safety of his home, being a boy seemed alright. But there was no doubt he would think differently in the morning.

As days rolled by news was increasingly good coming out of France. The invasion was a big success. The troops were now moving inland massing for a break out across France. Everyone waited for the newspaper or listened to the radio to get the latest war news. However Glendale was no different from any other town in the United Sates. What everyone feared most was the sight of an olive green sedan driving up in front of their home. That meant a loved one was seriously wounded, dead, or missing in action. Just the sight of one of those cars driving through the streets of Glendale made most mothers anxious beyond words.

As the war moved across Europe and the Pacific, hope for victory and the return of their soldiers was foremost on the minds of everyone in Glendale as well as the rest of the Country.

However another battle raged inside Michael every day. He was continually torn between fulfilling his parent's desires for him, which included finishing school, and working on the farm or fulfilling his dream of running off to join the Army. He knew they would never give their blessings for him to enlist. But each day the over powering desire to fight for his country seemed to be winning the battle. It was clear to Mike, that one day he would have to come to grips with the battle within him. He knew there was no good way to fulfill that desire with out hurting his folks very seriously. That was still the major set back that kept him home on the farm.

CHAPTER 12

RELIEF TO SAINTE-MERE-EGLISE

Sgt. Gentry's Sherman tank crammed with paratroopers rumbled away from the supply depot by itself, turning back toward Sainte Mere'-Eglise. Private Garnet lay heavy on the minds of every man who heard his final words.

Steve mulled over his last words again and again. Garnet's comment about meeting in another place sent a tingle down his spine. Sure he thought about dying. He knew it was possible for any of them at any time. When your number was up that was that. They had all seen way to many good men die already. Steve knew his will to survive and return home was probably stronger than most men. His love for Karen and desire to live out the rest of his life with her was what kept him going. But in the same, he knew all to well that anything was possible in war.

The tank entered a road now clogged with vehicles headed for the interior of France. An M.P. was directing traffic at a crossroads jammed with waiting vehicles, loaded with every imaginable tool of war.

The M.P. waved Gentry's tank toward the side of the road. "Where are you headed, Sergeant. Tanks are a priority item around here."

Removing his head set Sgt. Gentry called down to the M.P.

"Saint-Mere'-Eglise, The town needs help bad. That's where these paratroopers came from."

Steve scrambled off the tank approaching the M.P. "We were sent by Captain Lewis at Sainte-Mere-Eglise to get help. When we`left the town it was being held by just a remnant of units. We have got to get some help back up there soon." Steve explained in an agitated tone.

"Calm down, Corporal. I can understand your hurry but I have orders also. Now just sit tight a few minutes."

The M.P. commanded picking up a walkie-talkie from his Jeep.

"Jolly Roger five this is Jolly Roger four-six. I have a Sherman with airborne infantry wanting to return toward Sainte-Mere'-Eglise. They have no written orders with them. What do you want me to do? Over."

The M.P. listened to the radio for a reply before adding, "Jolly Roger four-six out."

"Well, Corporal. Major Devitt will be here in just a couple minutes to talk to you. He has a column of mechanized infantry and supplies behind him moving this way right now. You'll just have to wait. His orders not mine, Corporal. I don't think you want to cross the Major if you can help it. My best advice is you just sit tight right here and be patient." Shaking his head Steve responded, "Damn. Alright. I guess we haven't much choice but to wait."

Harry and Franny jumped off the tank approaching Steve, as the M.P. moved back toward the road continuing to sorting out the outbound traffic.

"What's happening Steve," Franny inquired as he watched the steady flow of military vehicles.

"We need to wait for a Major Devitt to get here." He replied while watching a Jeep come toward them down the side of the road.

The driver came to a stop behind the Sherman. The M.P. walked over immediately and spoke to a Major seated in the passenger seat.

"Over here, Corporal." The M.P. called out waving his arm.

The three men walked over quickly as the Major slid out of the Jeep in time to receive a salute from the paratroopers.

"The M.P. tells me you were sent by Captain Lewis up at Sainte-Mere'-Eglise to get some help.

What's happening up there, Corporal?" Major Devitt inquired.

"Well sir, that was yesterday. Things could have changed a lot since then. But when we left the town, it was being held by a small group of paratroopers that could have been overwhelmed at any time. The Germans were attacking on and off in probing raids to see what kind of strength was there." Steve explained.

"Do I understand you properly, that just airborne units were holding that key town?" Major Devitt asked while removing a map case from his Jeep.

"That's correct, sir. They were tired and under manned when we left. Unless other help has arrived since we left, there's no telling what the situation might be right now. And to be honest sir, the longer we stand around here the more uncertain it may become." Harry said very professionally.

Major Devitt picked up the radio microphone from his aid directing him to change frequencies.

"Jolly Roger five-niner calling whiskey Oscar seven, do you copy? Over."

Static filled the frequency for several seconds before the reply came.

"Whiskey Oscar seven here, I read you Jolly Roger. Go ahead."

"Can you kick your boys in the butt? We've got to catch a bus. Over." Major Devitt stated in a very commanding voice.

"Jolly Roger we're about a half mile from your location. We'll be right there." The voice on the radio replied.

Tossing the microphone back toward his aid Major Devitt turned back toward the three paratroopers.

"Okay gentlemen, I just spoke to a mechanized infantry unit coming up the road. They have everything we should need to hold Sainte-Mere' Eglise. You boys lead the way with that tank. We'll follow you all the way. Tell the Sergeant commanding that Sherman to kick butt when we move out.

Understood." The Major demanded as he waved to a Jeep approaching from the west. Behind the Jeep was a long column of vehicles filled with equipment and fresh fighting infantry.

Steve felt a sudden rush of excitement race through his body. Major Devitt and his heavy equipment was exactly what he had been hoping to bring to the battle for Sainte-Mere'-Eglise.

"Thank you Major. This is just what the Doctor ordered." Harry yelled as he ran back toward the idling Sherman.

Major Devitt jumped into his Jeep and stood up. He waved to the first half-track driver. "Follow that tank all the way to Paris if that's where the son-of a- bitch takes you."

Sergeant Gentry rolled the big tank back on to the road as the three paratroopers scrambled aboard.

Rabinowitz took control of the fifty caliber machine gun directing the convoy to follow them. The lead-half track closed up tight behind the lumbering tank. A Captain riding aboard the half-track waved at him, flashing the British victory sign. Steve and Franny laughed heartily for the first time since they left England. A real sense of accomplishment was felt by both men.

In just a short time the convoy was rumbling past the hedgerows and remains of the burned out half-track. In the field to their right sat the gutted remains of the tanks from their earlier encounter with the three German armored units.

"I wonder if Capt. Washburn can see what we brought back with us." Franny questioned as he peered at the silent, body lying in the field covered by the poncho they had lain over him.

"I'm sure he can, Franny. He was one hell of a good officer. You don't find many like him I'm afraid."

Harry replied as he threw a quick salute in the direction of the field.

An English Spitfire flying low screamed over the convoy heading inland, searching for German targets still waiting to be attacked. The fighter was drawing some light antiaircraft fire from the hedgerows ahead.

Nevertheless, the pilot never veered off course or made an attempt to fire back at the German units. He kept his plane on course searching for larger enemy targets that might impede the allied advance.

As the tank rounded a curve a large explosion tore apart a hedgerow about ten yards in front of them.

"Eighty-eight shells for damn sure." Sergeant Gentry yelled from his turret.

A truck five vehicles back in the convoy was ripped apart by the next shell that made a direct hit.

Everyone was looking about trying to discover where the deadly artillery fire was coming from, as it was zeroed in on that segment of the road.

The third round landed in the field beside one of the half-tracks, showering the men inside with dirt and shrapnel.

Rabinowitz still manning the machine gun, observed a muzzle flash up ahead near a small grove of trees.

"Up by that grove to our left." He yelled at Sgt. Gentry while pointing with his left hand. Another round from the German artillery piece slammed directly aside the second half-track shredding the steel track. Everyone on board bailed out, seeking shelter in the hedgerows or a ride in one of the other vehicles.

Sergeant Gentry yelled to his driver. "Kick it in the ass. Let's get that son of a bitch before he tears this entire convoy apart, damn it!"

The next round from the well aimed artillery piece struck the helpless half-track ripping it apart. Luckily everyone had cleared away from the hapless vehicle.

Sgt. Gentry slowed his tank. "Off, everyone off damn it!" He roared at the paratroopers. Once everyone was off, Sgt. Gentry kicked his tank into overdrive pulling away from the convoy at full speed. He charged down the road toward the grove where the artillery piece was positioned. It was now going to become a deadly duel between Sgt. Gentry and the fire spotter for the German eighty-eight, to see who could out fire the other.

The gunner inside the tank was already traversing the turret to bring it to bear on the German gun emplacement. Mean while the German spotter had his crew readjusting the heavy gun so they could fire on the charging Sherman. Both men wanted to be ready when they had a clear shot. There was no doubt in anyone's mind the well trained artillery crew would lower their weapon to attempt a point blank shot into the side of the approaching Sherman. The Germans fired fist sending their lethal round completely over the tank into the hedgerow.

A second later Sgt. Gentry screamed "Fire!" as the Sherman closed distance on the German position. He knew if he gave the enemy any more time they would reload and have a clear shot at him.

His well trained gunner fired sending his round into the grove where the artillery crew was hastily loading their next projectile. The high explosive round landed directly behind the artillery piece, where the crew had piled their spare ammunition. A massive explosion rocked the grove followed by several secondary explosions, as the remaining eighty-eight rounds detonated. A large fireball rose over the area. Flames continued rolling from the grove as each additional case of spare ammunition ignited.

"We hit their God damn ammo head on. Look at her go." Sergeant Gentry yelled out shaking his fist in the air. He ordered his gunner to reload and keep the turret aimed toward the wooded area as they proceeded cautiously down the road.

Small arms fire ricochet off the side of the tank, as German infantry who were located in the grove as support for the artillery crew began attacking.

The paratroopers still on foot immediately returned fire taking on the advancing enemy infantry.

Sgt. Gentry ordered his gunner to fire directly toward the infantry as he jumped from the turret grabbing the deadly browning fifty. Several bodies flew through the air as the high explosive round detonated in the middle of the attackers.

The machine gunner on the half-track directly behind the Sherman joined Sgt. Gentry, as they fired toward the quickly retreating infantry.

Remnants of the German squad took cover deeper in the grove or in a pit behind the artillery piece.

"Let's get in there and finish those bastards off." Gunderson yelled at Steve above the roar of battle.

"We can't waste time on any small group of infantry. If there is anyone left after what we just handed them they can be mopped up later. We need to move on toward Saint-Mere'-Eglise."

Steve replied peering around the front of the half-track to see what was happening in the grove.

Just a few sporadic shots came from the pit behind the battered artillery emplacement. Sgt. Gentry sent one more cannon shell toward the pit for good measure. After the round exploded the paratroopers rushed toward the tank retaking their positions.

Except for the roar of the fire around the artillery piece the grove appeared quiet.

Sergeant Gentry ordered his driver to continue rolling down the road at a much slower speed. He did not want to be caught of guard again.

Steve pointed to several bodies lying on the ground just outside the tree line. Scanning the artillery piece with his binoculars, Steve was happy to see it would not be usable to anyone else. The barrel was ripped from the carriage and the breach block had been torn off.

"I'm guessing they did not get the breach closed on the gun when all that ammo went off. The shell in the chamber must have detonated in the fire. It's finished." Sgt Gentry reported with a smile.

Franny and Harry nodded their satisfaction with the Sergeants description of the battle field.

"Alright then. Let's kick this thing in the ass and get moving." Harry yelled out to Sergeant Gentry.

"Are you sure, Corporal?" Sgt. Gentry called down from the turret. "Might be more Kraut batteries along the road."

Harry and Steve both shook their heads. "No. Kick this thing in the ass." Harry called back.

As Sgt. Gentry picked up speed the convoy quickly closed in behind the rumbling tank. "Anything else I can do for you?" Sergeant Gentry yelled down to Harry.

"Yeah A hot meal, a soft bed, and a bath would be very nice about now." He called back examining his filthy, bloody uniform.

Removing the map from his shirt Steve studied it carefully. He knew they were only about six miles from town and closing fast with every turn of the tanks treads. He glanced over his shoulder looking at the convoy following close behind. It was a beautiful sight. The men had accomplished their mission against overwhelming German resistance. They were bringing all the help that could be mustered to relieve the beleaguered paratroopers. He prayed that is wasn't too late for them.

The cost of the mission had been way too high. Steve felt a huge pain in his heart as he thought about the men that died over the last twenty-four hours. He had never experienced this kind of grief before. It was a grief he knew would not go away any time soon. The memory of the young private they had fought so hard to save raced back into his mind. His last words calling out for his mother chilled Steve to the bone.

His train of thought was broken when Franny yelled out. "Smoke up ahead. Looks like it's coming from town."

Harry and Steve turned peering over the turret in the direction of Saint-Mere'-Eglise. Franny jumped up behind the tanks heavy machine gun preparing to fire in case any enemy infantry showed their faces.

The column came to a stop about a quarter mile from the edge of town. Other then the black smoke billowing off to the north, no other movement was detected by anyone.

"What do you think, Harry?" Steve inquired scanning the area over and over.

"I just don't know what to think, Stevie boy. It just seems way to quiet." Harry responded nervously.

The sun was staring to set as dusk settled over the embattled French town. Steve jumped off the tank motioning Abbott, Rabinowitz and Woodward to follow him. "Harry, you stay with the rest of the men. If you hear all hell break lose, come a running."

Nodding his head Harry motioned for the rest of the men to follow him into a low ditch along side the road.

"Maybe we don't hold the town anymore, Steve. You would think someone would have seen us and sent a runner out to welcome us." Harry said quietly to Steve as he prepared to take up his position.

"I thought of that my self. But we'll see what's happening in short order," Steve replied motioning his men forward.

About a dozen men along with a Captain McHenry from the convoy assembled with Harry in the ditch.

Franny climbed back on top of the tank near the machine gun. Borrowing Sgt. Gentry's binoculars he followed Steve's approach into the quiet town.

"It seems awful damn quiet to me, Corporal. Shouldn't there be some sort of a welcoming committee for such a glorious relief column? I hope this isn't a trap with the Krauts just waiting to open up on us as we approach." Captain McHenry whispered as his cold gray eyes burrowed in on Steve.

The three men took cover behind a wooden fence near the first house on the north side of the road. Abbott covered the road as Rabinowitz kept an eye on the second floor windows in the house. Steve pondered the situation for a couple of seconds.

"What do you think, Steve?" Rabinowitz whispered wiping sweat from his brow.

"Well we know the Krauts had heavy forces in the area when we landed. There was a pitched battle in the town before we took control. I just don't know what to make of this right now." Steve replied trying to appear in control of his jittering nerves.

Sergeant Gentry jumped off the tank joining the men on the road. "Let's move forward and be ready for anything. We can't stay out here as it gets dark. We're just sitting ducks."

Nodding his head in agreement the Captain stated, "Yeah, I totally agree. Let's move out slowly. I'll have some of my infantry take up positions on both sides of the road. Corporal, you can take your men and move up with your point people."

"With all do respect Captain, I think that might be a real bad decision. You just arrived and want to mix it up with the Krauts. But we've been fighting for nearly two days now. We know how the Krauts operate.

If this is a trap they'll mow us down like corn stalks as we near the town. We need to give Kenrude a chance to figure this out." Harry replied abruptly.

Angered by Harry's response Captain McHenry glared at him for several seconds before Franny spoke up.

"Look Captain, the Corporal is right. We've been through this all damn day. Let Kenrude figure it out before we have to start digging mass graves."

"Fine we'll give him a few more minutes, but no more than that." The impatient officer responded.

They all watched as Steve and Rabinowitz swiftly darted away from the fence toward the first house. A common sigh of relief rose from the ditch when the men arrived safely. Abbott followed as Steve quickly dashed toward the burned out hulk of a German truck parked about ten yards inside the town.

Seconds later several figures walked out of a building about a half block in front of Steve. Rabinowitz and Abbott took careful aim as the men approached Steve's position. Both men were primed to shoot if anything went wrong. One of the figures walked directly toward Steve's position stopping about five feet away. After several nervous seconds the man called out in a very nervous voice. "Flash!"

Taking a sigh of relief Steve answered, "Thunder."

The man screamed to his partner. "I'll be damned! They're ours. Yeah, yeah by God in heaven they're ours."

He danced a little jig before running over giving Steve and Rabinowitz a giant bear hug. He then ran toward the tank yelling every foot of the way. Several shots rang out from snipers hiding in the near by fields. But they were unable to hit or deter the jubilant soldier.

"That's one crazy son of a bitch." Franny exclaimed grabbing the man as he stumbled forward the last few feet totally out of breath.

"Now that's more like it!" The man exclaimed examining the vehicles and infantry from the convoy.

"Oh yeah now we can give them hell!" He yelled.

Captain Mc Henry first patted Harry on the back, "Thanks for taking me on a few minutes ago. You guys definitely know the score." He then proceeded to shake hands with the out of breath paratrooper.

"Where do you want us son?"

"Come on in come on in to our little village. Damn if you're not the most beautiful sight I've ever seen.

Come on move this convoy into town. We've been holding on waiting for you guys. We've taken a kick in the shorts from the krauts but we have held on, Captain. They must not have had what they needed to dislodge us or we'd all be dead by now. "The private reported taking a swallow of water from a canteen Brant handed him. Damn I could kiss every one of you ugly creeps."

"Alright private. So the entire town is in your hands right now?" The Captain asked the bedraggled soldier.

"Well sir, we hold the town. But those kraut bastards sneak a sniper in every once in a while and fire on us from second story windows or a roof until we hunt him down. Mortars too. They drop them in every so often to let us know they're still around. We've been waiting for the eighty-eight barrages to start, but luckily they haven't used them yet. Anything else?" The man inquired.

Shaking his head no Captain McHenry signaled for his convoy to finally enter Saint- Mere'-Eflise.

Turning toward Sergeant Gentry the Captain called out. "Take us in, Sergeant."

Slowly the Sherman tank rolled into town followed by the infantry men and the rest of the vehicles.

They were greeted by a proud, dirty, bunch of paratroopers as they rolled down the cluttered streets right in to the town square. A loud cheer went up from the tired men as they gathered around the vehicles, shaking hands with the fresh infantry. A sheer sense of pride overwhelmed Steve as he looked over the weary band of men he knew so well. They had held out beyond anything they could have ever imagined.

Their mission had been successfully accomplished, "Keep the road open and hold until relieved."

Captain McHenry jumped down from the lead half-track shaking hands with the paratroopers as he made his way forward. "Who's in charge here?" He asked a Sergeant that was standing in front of the tank.

"I am." Captain Lewis replied making his way through the excited paratroopers.

The two officers shook hands. "I'm Captain McHenry sent here by Major Devitt to resupply you, and reinforce this position. This town is to be held at all costs. It's the only good east-west road heading up from the beach. We can't afford to let Jerry shut it down. Where would you like my men and equipment? We have medical supplies, ammo and rations in the trucks. We can get them unloaded as soon as you tell us where you want it. We also have one Doctor and three corpsmen with us that can set up a decent aid station. We lost one truck along the way because of a kraut eighty-eight. Other then that, we are intact and ready to join you in defense of this town."

Captain Lewis removed his helmet running his hands through his dirty hair. "Alright. That sounds almost too good to be true. It has been a long twenty-four plus hours. My men are dog tired and in need of some rest and rations. They hit us pretty hard last night. We held them back from our defensive line but we took an awful lot of casualties doing it. Without your help, I'm all too sure we could never hold tonight under another such attack. Lieutenant Krueger will show your men where to unload the supplies and where our aid station is set up. Staff Sergeant Kranston can place your men where they're needed to bolster our perimeter before it gets much darker. We could use some of those fifties on roof tops and we could use the tank as an artillery piece for now."

Captain McHenry agreed without question. He quickly explained to his men the procedures outlined by Captain Lewis.

Steve, Harry and their other ten men stood near the tank as the two officers' conversed. They felt very tired but happy. With everything working against them in a hostile country, they succeeded in getting help back to their men.

Captain Lewis walked over and shook hands with each of them. "Well done gentlemen. We had no way of knowing whether you got through or were all killed." Turning toward Steve the Captain continued.

"I see you picked up some help along the way."

"Yes sir. But we also lost some good men. This has not been a walk in the park by any stretch of the imagination." Steve responded humbly.

"And Corporal Jensen it's good to see you again. Glad you made it." Captain Lewis stated patting Harry on the shoulder.

"Alright then, men. Get some rest and something to eat. It may be another tough night around here."

Captain Lewis directed the tired paratroopers before he turned to walk off.

After Captain Lewis had departed, Captain McHenry approached the twelve paratroopers. He shook hands with each of them. "Damn Paratroopers! I wouldn't fight without all the armor I could muster and you guys fight with what you can carry or scrounge. You guys are something else. Get some rest. You sure as hell deserve it."

He stated proudly as he walked off with Staff Sergeant Kranston.

The six half-tracks were parked in various areas around town. The fifty-caliber machine-guns were placed on roof top positions covering the main approaches into the important little town. As total darkness fell, the fresh infantry units were in prearranged positions established by the paratroopers for defense.

Captain Lewis arrived back at his command post that now occupied what had been the town bakery.

Quickly he Cleared space in the crowded building for Captain McHenry to set up his command post. After discussing a relief schedule for the night, Capt. Lewis left to inspect the new defenses.

As Captain Lewis approached one of the damaged buildings he heard voices. Stepping in he found the twelve paratroopers. They were just finishing up a meal of cold rations.

"How was dinner?" He inquired as he safely lit a cigarette.

"Cold but tasty?" Franny replied licking his spoon.

"Where do you want us tonight, Captain?" Harry inquired leaning forward from an old wooden chair.

"You men have done enough for today. You all look very tired. Just get some sleep here for a while.

If we need you we know where to find you." Captain Lewis responded as he turned to leave.

"No sir. We can cover a position wherever you think defenses may be light. We can take turns napping while it's quiet." Steve answered picking up his Thompson from the floor. "We've all talked about it and agreed, sir."

"Well we could use a few more men to bolster the east road coming into town. We have a half-track parked near the road in a burned out shop. The fifty cal. is on the roof overhead. You could help cover any where along there." Captain Lewis explained as he took a note book from his pocket making a quick notation.

"Thanks, sir. We'll pick up some ammo and head over there." Harry replied saluting the thankful Captain.

The men picked up ammo from the fresh supply that was still being unload from the trucks.

Quietly they made their way across the square where Sgt. Gentry's tank and Captain McHenry's half-tracks were still parked. Men had been placed on rooftops manning the fifty caliber machine guns that had been stripped from most of the half-tracks. They scanned the sky and fields around the town for any sign of enemy activity.

As the men approached the east end of town they observed the half track parked in the burned out business display room. Several men stood near by keeping a sharp eye on the east access road.

A sergeant walked out from the building to greet them. "Aren't you the men who escorted us out here?"

"Sure are. Where do you need us Sarg," Harry replied.

"Well for now we're sitting in good shape. Everything appears to be pretty quiet right now. My men are spread all along the edge of town. Go grab some sleep near the half-track inside that building; it's also my command center.

I'll wake you in a couple of hours to relieve some of the other men, or in case the krauts try to move in on us."

The Sergeant explained as he peered up into the black sky.

"That sounds good, Sarg. We sure could use some shut eye for a little while." Steve replied following the Sergeant back into the dark building.

After removing his pack, Harry walked into a back room of the shop where several other paratroopers were sacked out. He sat down on the floor, leaned against the wall and closed his heavy eyes.

Steve and Franny also removed their packs, setting them aside of Harry's.

"Well I think I am going to scoot underneath the half-track. I'll be out of the way so I can get some sleep."

Steve said to Franny running his hands over his unshaven face.

"Alright, Steve. I'm going to just crawl over in the corner across the room with the rest of the guys and sack out there. I think Harry beat us both to it. Good night, Steve." Franny added as he walked across the large room.

Steve crawled under the half-track. He took a deep breath as he closed his eyes. Surprisingly he was actually able to relax somewhat. However sleep did not come easy. He found himself tensing at the smallest noises.

Each time he was awakened his mind began to process everything that happened since they first bailed out of their aircraft. He wondered if the aircraft crew were dead, POW'S or safely back in England. That plane was in tough shape. Worse yet, they still had to fly back through the flak field on their way home.

He thought about the battles he had been in, the men he saw die, and the farm back home.

Happy memories of the farm and Karen helped him to relax a bit more as they forced out the ugly visions of war.

He was sure once the entire front was stabilized, the airborne units would be pulled out of combat for rest and refit. There were so many letters to write and so much to say. Some where off in the distance, artillery batteries were exchanging blows. As the guns roared and the shells exploded they made the floor gently vibrate. The vibration against his tired muscles felt like a well earned massage. He closed his heavy eyes slowly drifting off to sleep.

The night was extremely dark as heavy clouds covered the moon and stars. Every soldier manning the perimeter was extremely tense. Just the slightest unexplained sounds were thought to be advancing Germans.

From time to time entire segments of the perimeter opened fire on make believe targets. About two o'clock in the morning aircraft could be heard to the east of Sainte-Mere'-Eglise.

Every soldier on guard duty, especially those on roofs desperately scanned the skies for some sign of the approaching aircraft. Above the sleeping paratroopers crews manning the fifty calibers became increasingly tense, as the roar

of aircraft engines became louder by the passing second.

Every man wondered if they were German bombers coming after them, or were they American bombers returning from a night mission over occupied territory. Tension mounted as the drone of engines came closer and closer with no way of knowing who they were.

Between broken clouds a short distance away, blue flame emanating from engine exhaust ports could be seen flickering in the dark night sky.

The aircraft were flying at an extremely high altitude, which convinced every one they were indeed heavy bombers, but whose? That was the question every one kept asking. There were no antiaircraft weapons around Sainte-Mere'-Eglise capable of reaching bombers at that altitude.

If they were enemy bombers the men knew the pilots had nothing to fear tonight.

Answers to all their questions regarding the bombers were answered in short order, as the quiet night was shattered by the whistle of falling bombs. The German Heinkel bombers unleashed their loads on the American positions around Sainte-Mere'-Eglise with exacting accuracy.

"Take cover!" The Sergeant yelled as bombs came screaming down to earth.

Men scrambled for cover as the first stick of bombs slammed against the earth, shaking the already damaged structures, filling the streets with additional rubble.

Screams pierced the darkness as men were struck by jagged flying shrapnel. There did not seem to be any safe place to dive for cover.

Harry jumped up quickly, racing from the back room to take cover in a stairwell across the road.

Steve jerked his head up as he heard the first bombs detonate just outside the city. The air was filled with dust, making it very difficult to breath under the half-track. He could hear the fifty caliber machine guns hammering away at the aircraft even though they were well out of range.

With a blinding flash the half-track above Steve exploded in a fireball. He screamed as he felt terrible pain pierce through his legs. Flames roared through out the half track filling the room with thick black smoke.

As Steve tried desperately to slide out, he observed flames on the floor working its way toward him. He realized the fuel tank had ruptured during the explosion, spilling the flammable liquid onto the floor.

Although in tremendous pain, Steve knew he had to move quickly or be incinerated by the ever advancing flames. Gathering all the strength inside him, Steve slid out from under the half-track.

The room was dark with thick acrid smoke. Nevertheless, light from the flames helped Steve orientate himself enough to see the opening in the wall facing the street. He tried desperately to stand up, but instantly fell back to the floor as his legs would not hold him. Dragging himself along the floor he looked back at the fire raging in the half-track. He could see the charred body of a man hanging over the side.

Gradually, although in tremendous pain, Steve slid closer toward the street and fresh air. He stopped for a minute running his hand over his left leg. He felt shards of mettle sticking from his thigh. His hand was totally covered with warm sticky blood.

As the pain became more excruciating, Steve felt as if he were going to pass out, although he knew he had to get out of the building or die. He remembered the words of private Garnet as he lay dying on the dusty road. "We will meet again. Remember me."

He wondered now if the final words spoken by the dying man were about to come true. His strength was nearly gone; he couldn't slide his body anymore. He watched the raging fire close rapidly as timbers from the roof collapsed around him. Steve closed his eyes waiting for the horrible end.

Silently he prayed that death would come quick, so he would die before the flames reached him.

Gasping for air once more, Steve decided he could not quit, he had to survive. With great effort he began dragging his body across the floor, as more of the building collapsed around him spreading the advancing flames. Half conscious and loosing strength rapidly, he thought he heard Franny's voice. He was not sure if it was real or his mind playing tricks on him, as smoke rapidly choked out his oxygen supply.

Amazingly, someone grabbed him by the shirt yelling loudly. "I found him, Harry I got him!"

His mind was not playing tricks on him. It was Franny pulling him away from the onrushing flames.

Once they reached the safety of the street and fresh air Franny looked down at Steve, "How ya doing, Corporal? You gave us a pretty good scare. We couldn't find you at first."

Steve reached up grabbing Franny's arm but was unable to talk.

"Take it easy Steve. Just try and breathe. You sucked in a lot of smoke back there." Franny explained as he looked over Steve's injured legs.

After taking in several breaths of fresh air Steve looked up at Franny. "Harry. Where's Harry? Is he okay?

What about the rest of the men?

"Yeah, yeah, Harry's fine. We're all fine Stevie boy. Harry and Rabinowitz ran to get a medic. They should be back shortly. The rest of the guys are helping other injured men. We're alright, Corporal just relax.

In fact here comes Harry and Rabinowitz with a medic right now." Franny replied waving toward Harry and the medic. The men knelt down around Steve. Attending to Steve's legs the medic asked, "How you feeling, Corporal?"

"Like I've been kicked by a mule." Steve responded slurring his words.

"Do you know where you're at?" The medic inquired as he finished pouring sulfa on Steve's wounds.

"Yeah, Sainte-Mere'-Eglise." He replied.

"That's good. Can you tell me what day it is?" The medic inquired.

"Either June 7th or 8th. What time is it?" Steve answered attempting to look at the shattered watch on his left wrist.

The medic smiled. "That's close enough, Corporal." After administering a shot of morphine the medic looked down at Steve.

"Don't you give up on us Corporal, you've lost a lot of blood and your legs are messed up. But you'll be alright. I gave you something for pain so you might pass out shortly. Anything else I can help you with?"

"I can't walk. I tried but I fell down. Will I walk again?" Steve nervously inquired.

"Oh yeah. You just went down because of shock and loss of blood. Your legs may not be as pretty as they once were, but you'll walk just fine." The medic replied motioning for Rabinowitz to bring the stretcher closer.

Steve closed his eyes drifting into unconsciousness as Rabinowitz and Brant carried him to the aid station.

Harry placed Franny in charge of the men before running off to the aid station to be with Steve.

Now that the air attack had softened up the defenses, everyone prepared for what they expected would be a major German offensive to retake the important town.

"Hurry, give me some suction over here. Damn, come on hurry. Christ what a mess." A Doctor yelled from a surgery table in the aid station in Sainte-Mere'-Eglise. "We're loosing him come on clamp that bleeder." He called out to his assistant. Frantically the Doctor worked on the soldier for a few more moments then stopped. Removing his gloves the doctor angrily tossed them on the floor. Shaking his head he stared down at the lifeless body. "Such a waste, such a waste. We shouldn't have lost him."

After recomposing himself he walked over to Rabinowitz and Brant, who were still holding on to Steve's Stretcher. "What have we got here?" The Doctor inquired.

"Bad leg injuries, Doc! He's really tore up. Some pretty good pieces of shrapnel still sticking out of his legs. You got to help him Doc." Brant pleaded with the over worked doctor.

"We will son. Place him on the table marked number two." The Doctor replied taking up his station on the right side of the table. Carefully he and a corpsman began removing the hastily applied field dressings from Steve's legs.

Entering the aid station Harry walked up to Rabinowitz. "Where is he?"

"Over there on table two. The Doctor is working on him right now." Rabinowitz replied watching every move the doctor made.

Steve fought desperately to open his eyes but they did not seem to work. He could feel someone touching him as he attempted to listen to the muffled voices overhead.

"Alright." The doctor said to his corpsman. "We have a hell of a mess here. I've seen worse, but at least there is no need to consider amputation. We're going to sew him up, and then securely bandaged the wounds best we can, and then move him on. We don't have time to go after all that damn shrapnel here."

Forcing his eyes open Steve was immediately blinded by the lights above his table.

The Doctor looked down at him. "Well Corporal, your legs are a mess but they are fixable. We will do what we can for you here then send you back to England for more surgery."

"But they don't work. My legs. They don't work. I tried to stand and they wouldn't hold me. The medic told me it was because of shock. Was he telling me the truth?" Steve inquired frantically.

"Was he hit anywhere else?" The doctor inquired of the three paratroopers.

"I don't think so, sir. But we really didn't look either." Harry responded.

"Alright let's take a look around. Can you help me roll him over onto his side?" The Doctor asked Harry and Brant.

As the two men held Steve on his left side the doctor examined Steve's back and head.

"Okay, roll him back." The doctor instructed the men. "I don't see any injury to your back, Corporal. I think the medic was right. You lost a lot of blood, and you suffered some very serious injuries to your legs. The mind can do strange things when a traumatic injury occurs. Now we're going to sedate you somewhat. I don't have enough medication to completely knock you out. But we'll do our best for you, Corporal. Now, if you men want to say your goodbyes do it quickly, I have more wounded to care for."

"Looks like you're going back home, Stevie boy. You got the million dollar wound." Harry said as he tried to force a smile.

"Is everyone else alright?" Steve asked as he grasped Harry's arm.

"Yeah we're all fine Steve. Look, we have to get out of here so the doctor can work on you. We need to get back and help out. We'll see you in the morning. You just take it easy now and let them take care of you." Harry said reassuringly to his best friend. The aid station continued to be a bustle of activity as more wounded soldiers were being delivered every few minutes.

"Yeah, Corporal we better get out of her. This damn place is getting crowded." Brant commented as he quickly shook hands.

After Rabinowitz shook hands with Steve they followed Harry to the door.

Captain Lewis came walking up to the aid station just as Harry and Brant were walking out.

"How bad is Kenrude?" The Captain inquired.

"His legs are full of shrapnel and pretty torn up. He lost a lot of blood and is feeling pretty week, but other then that I think he'll be all right." Harry reassured the worried Captain.

"We took a lot of casualties from those damn bombers, but more injuries then deaths the way it looks.

No matter though, it puts our unit in tough shape. It doesn't look like a counter attack is underway at this point in time. However, it could still come so we need to be ready. Are you boys heading back to the east end of town?"

Captain Lewis inquired as he watched the constant flow of wounded men entering the aid station.

"Yes sir. We were on our way when you walked up. Brant replied.

"Good. That's good. I'm going to check on Kenrude then I'll be back out." Captain Lewis stated as he walked to the aid station door.

Approaching table number two the doctor turned to face Captain Lewis.

"Look Captain, I have a lot of patients to work on. You will need to talk to this man later!" The doctor insisted pointing toward the door. And that's an order from me. Understood Sir," The doctor stated in a demanding voice, as he stood by a make shift curtain around the operating area.

"Understood." Captain Lewis replied to the harried doctor.

The doctor turned back toward the surgical table asking a corpsman to help apply a new set of gloves.

"Are you in a lot of pain Corporal," The doctor inquired as he looked at a large piece of shrapnel sticking out of Steve's right thigh.

"No not to bad." He bravely replied.

"Liar!" The Doctor responded as he examined Steve's left knee. "Here's the deal, Corporal. We're out of some medical supplies like Novocain, and we don't have the sedatives here like a hospital. We don't even have much morphine left. I don't know what the hell we're going to do when we run out of that. So we're going to give you about half the dosage you should get. Like I said, we're taking out the big pieces best we can. The rest will have to be removed later.

In England they can x-ray your legs and find the rest of the shrapnel. Understand." "Sounds alright." Steve replied with a slight smile.

"Good, we are just about finished here except for the large piece in your thigh. We really should take that piece out." The Doctor explained as he reached for a large forceps from the surgical tray.

As he began to pull it out, Steve twisted his body moaning loudly. Quickly the corpsman picked up a hypodermic needle handing it to the doctor.

"We're going to give you another small shot of morphine. It will help as we work." The doctor gently stuck the needle into Steve's arm closely observing his eyes.

After closing his eyes, the doctor picked up the forceps quickly removing the shrapnel from his thigh. With that completed, two corpsmen wrapped his legs with gauze and ace bandages. Steve drifted in and out of consciousness as the men worked. After the doctor inspected their work, he ripped his gloves off and yelled, "Next case. Let's keep it going."

Steve was moved from the surgery table to a spot on the floor near two corpsmen, who were keeping watch on the wounded soldiers after leaving surgery.

Although Steve was in moderate pain, he drifted in and out of sleep through out the night. Every soldier in Sainte-Mere'-Eglise was on full alert expecting the worst. There were several probing attacks by German infantry but nothing that seemed to be coordinated, or indicators of a much larger attacks in progress.

Some adjustments to the defenses were made during the night, to assure every angle of approach to the town was covered.

Both men manning the fifty-caliber machine gun on the roof perished during the bombing raid. Surprisingly the weapon had survived.

After some heavy cleaning and minor repairs it was back in working order. The men relocated it across the street on top of a large two story building. This allowed the new gunners a much better view of the approaches to the town.

Just as dawn broke, the largest attack took place once more on the east side of town. The strike started with a quick mortar barrage, followed by an assault of about fifty men. The attackers worked in squad patterns

One squad laid down covering fire, while the other unit advanced quickly firing as they moved.

When the first squad moved within about twenty yards of town, the machine gunners opened up along with Franny and his B.A.R.

They cut down all but four of the attackers. Quickly the Germans answered with mortar fire, attempting to take out the machine gun position. They were successful as their second round dropped right on top of the sand bagged position. With the fifty caliber gone, the balance of the German infantry raced forward tossing grenades and firing as they ran. Several of them reached buildings on the edge of town where they dove inside for cover. The remaining enemy charged headlong into the American positions attempting to over run them. After brutal hand to hand combat that was costly to the American defenders the attack ended. Now the problem was to find and eliminate the German attackers who penetrated their defenses. Instantly the town square became a no mans land as well camouflaged Germans sniped at anybody that moved. It took until about midmorning for the balance of the enemy attackers to be hunted down and eliminated.

After the town was once again secured, Harry took who ever could be freed up over to the aid station to check on Steve. They found him lying on a stretcher near the door as they entered. A corpsman had just finished changing the bandages on his legs.

"How you doing, Stevie boy?" Harry asked trying to force a smile.

"I guess alright. They only took out the large pieces and stitched up some of the wounds. I guess the rest will come out once I get to England. They have been operating all night on guys coming in here. Just trying to do what they can." Steve replied looking up at his friends.

About the same time Captain Lewis arrived to make a check of the aid station. He spoke to and shook hands with each man. Walking up to Steve he smiled and said, "Well Corporal, looks like we're going to get you on a truck shortly for a ride to the beach. Once they finish with you in England, you'll head back home for a well deserved rest. Your war is probably over. Once you're healed they most likely will have you training new paratroopers.

Good luck Kenrude. I wish we had more men like you."

"Lucky guy." Woodward said smiling down at Steve.

Steve scowled as he tried sitting up to look eye to eye with his Captain. "No, Sir. Not home. Not yet. I know I have to go to England for surgery and recovery. But Captain, you can't let them send me home. Please not yet. I want to come back as soon as I am able to. Captain, you have to do something to keep me from going state side. Please, Sir." Steve pleaded respectfully.

After helping Steve lay back down Harry looked him in the eye. “Steve your ticket is punched. You earned it.

You can go home to see your family and Karen.”

“I know that all sounds great, Harry. But I want to finish what we started. I want to help finish the war here, not in some backwater base training green recruits how not to get their asses blown off.” Captain please help me out, I don’t want to be sent back home.” Steve countered.

Captain Lewis sighed heavily looking down at Steve. “Some of the boys in this room are going home for sure.

They will de discharged after leaving the hospital.

Some guys know their wounds aren’t bad enough to be sent home and they’ll be back like it or not.

But you actually have a choice, Corporal. But if coming back to this God forsaken war is what you want, I can work it out. I’ll go sign an order sending one copy with you, and a second copy in your medical jacket. I have misgivings about doing this but it’s your choice. Good luck Kenrude.”

The Captain shook hands with Steve before going to his command post to change his transfer orders.

One of the corpsmen walked over to Steve’s stretcher. After looking over the chart he placed it on Steve’s chest.

“Okay Corporal. We have a truck outside we’re loading with wounded, and you are next to go.”

Steve turned toward the men and smiled. “Well I guess its clean sheets, pretty nurses, and hot food for the next few weeks. I’ll see you guys as soon as I can. Take care of each other, and some how find your way back to the unit. You know I wouldn’t have wanted to go through any of this without you guys.”

Franny brushed a tear from his eyes trying to regain his composure. “You know Steve I would have never made it this far with out you. We need you back as soon as possible. You’re always welcome back in France.”

Everyone laughed as the corpsmen prepared to pick up Steve’s stretcher.

“Well maybe the krauts don’t see it that way. But remember, all of us are going to drink a bottle of cognac at Hitler’s grave when this is all over. Damn straight, that’s what we’re going to do when this is all over.” Franny exclaimed confidently.

"Where the hell are you going to find a bottle of cognac in Berlin after we bomb the shit out of that place, Doogan?" Harry inquired hitting Franny on the back of his helmet.

"Don't quite know right now, Harry. But hell, there has to be a liquor store around there some place that will survive, or maybe from Adolph's private stock. Who knows? But if it can be found, Francis Doogan the third will come up with it." Franny retorted quickly. The men walked out of the aid station watching Steve's stretcher being gently placed on the truck.

Harry walked over taking Steve's hand. "Get better, Stevie boy. We can't win this war with out you. Hell I don't know if I can make it with out you. To be honest and a bit selfish Steve, I was hoping you would come back. You're the best."

Steve smiled. "Jensen you best not let anything happen to you while I'm gone. No stupid heroics. You understand?"

Harry nodded his head. "Promise."

As Steve was the last stretcher on the truck, a medic crawled aboard before the tailgate was closed; he placed Steve's new orders into his file.

Harry walked up to the driver. "Look pal, you've got our buddy in there. You better take care of him and get him to the beach in one piece. Alright?"

"Hey look, I didn't volunteer for this mission but I'll get these guys there in one piece, and bring back what ever supplies they give me. See you guys later." The driver replied before jumping into the cab and firing up the large six by six Studebaker built truck.

Slowly the small convoy rolled west out of town onto the main road, which was now filled with hundreds of vehicles coming up from the English Channel.

It only took the driver about fifty minutes to arrive at the medical loading station on the beach. Although the drive was uneventful, fighting could be heard all around them. The crash of the big navel guns reverberating off the sand dunes was deafening.

Besides the roar of the naval guns, Steve could here the sounds of a massive army building strength, preparing to break out of its pocket and bring death to the Third Reich. Trucks grunted and groaned as they hauled heavy loads of equipment through the deep beach sand. Generators could be heard humming in every direction, supplying electrical power to all the headquarters and traffic control units located around the busy beach. It was a huge operation directing and supplying an invading army of this size.

The tailgate dropped as two young soldiers picked up Steve's stretcher, gently pulled him off the back of the truck. As the men walked the short distance to the waiting landing craft Steve looked around. He was awed by the amount of activity and sights that were part of Omaha beach.

There were burned out vehicles sitting on the beach where they had been hit or shoved to the side by massive caterpillars. Graves registration workers knelt by a row of bodies that washed ashore over night from the sunken wreckage.

Military Police directed traffic onto new hastily built access roads leading inland.

Everyone involved was attempting to efficiently move the large number of vehicles arriving by the minute on landing ships, filled with the tools of war.

Once all the wounded men were safely and securely loaded on the landing craft the ramp rose up from the beach. The Coxswain backed the Higgins boat through the rough surf before slowly turning toward the fleet.

The ride through the rough surf and surging waves was anything but smooth, as the flat bottom boat rose and fell on every swell.

In about fifteen minutes the Coxswain maneuvered the landing craft up against the hospital ships loading dock.

Looking up from his position in the landing craft, he could see the tall white ship towering above him.

A crane onboard lowered a platform into the landing craft. Six stretchers at a time were loaded onto the platform before it was raised up to the ships main deck. Orderly's stood by, quickly moving them to a ward and placing them in bed. Steve looked around the ward from his bed, and was instantly taken back by the amount of wounded men. Many were much worse off than he was. It was evident they had lost arms and legs or had severe abdominal or head injuries.

"Pretty sad sight if you ask me." The man in the bunk next to Steve said quietly.

"Oscar McBride is the name. Who might you be?" he inquired.

Although Steve did not feel like making small conversation he turned to the man replying.

"Kenrude, Steve Kenrude."

Both men were quiet for a moment as they watched the nurses fill the last bunk in their ward.

"Where did you get hit?" Steve inquired nervously.

"Get hit! Hell I never saw any combat other then jumping from that damn burning plane. Then my chute was ripped by some shrapnel and I couldn't control the damn thing. Came down over an abandoned farm and hit the barn roof. My chute caught on something and tears the rest of the way, and off the edge of the roof I go. Broke my right leg pretty good and cracked some ribs. I laid there for two days before anyone came along. Two damn days! We drop a thousand troopers over that country and it takes two days for someone to stumble on to me. But I did see two Krauts patrolling along the road. I didn't shoot at them, although I probably could have hit them both with my Tommy gun. I didn't know if there were more behind them and I didn't have a speck of cover. They could have made Swiss cheese out of me. I just lay there still as I could, hopping they wouldn't see me.

I tried to crawl once toward a couple of old hay bales but the pain was to much and my leg didn't work very good."

"Yeah not taking on those two Krauts was probably a good idea, Oscar. At least you're alive and should heal up alright." Steve replied watching several nurses walk through the ward.

"I want to go back, Kenrude. No way am I going home to tell everyone I didn't see any action. I know my Mother would like that. But I need to go back. Know what I mean? So how are your legs?"

I saw the nurse look at them when they laid you down." Oscar inquired.

"A lot of shrapnel. I got the stuff sticking out all over the place. They took some out at the aid station, before bandaging me up. Hospital in England is going to take out the rest of it." Steve replied pulling back the blanket back to show Oscar his legs.

Over a loud speaker came an announcement for the staff. All the wounded were aboard and preparations were being made in order to get under way. It seemed like just a few minutes before the ship began turning west in the direction of England.

Through out the short voyage Steve and Oscar kept up a pretty good conversation regarding the war, home, and the pretty young nurses working on the ship. There were several air raid warnings while in route, that terrified most men on board the massive ship. They all hoped Germans pilots would comply with the Geneva Convention and avoid attacking a hospital ship. Both warnings were short. As the all clear was sounded, a collective cheer rose through out the ward.

As the ship arrived safely in Southampton it was immediately tied up to the pier. The crew was very busy as they prepared to unload their wounded soldiers.

Oscar looked over at Steve. "What unit were you with Kenrude? I was just a quick fill in for a guy that got hurt on a training mission. Maybe when we get back into action I can get assigned to your outfit."

"Yeah would love to have you Oscar. We have a good bunch of guys. Think you would fit in fine.

I'm with C-Company, second battalion, 502nd. When you get out of the hospital see what you can do."

Steve explained, smiling at Oscar who reminded him a bit of Franny.

The unloading process began immediately operating with complete precision. A nurse walked through the ward placing a string with a tag attached to it around the neck of every man. Placing the string around Steve's neck the young nurse smiled. "There you go Corporal Kenrude. Now you won't get lost in the hustle and bustle as we unload. You should be off the ship shortly. You have a bit of a ride to your hospital. So take it easy. Good luck soldier."

Before Steve could respond, she turned and walked off in a hurry to place more tags on waiting patients.

"Guess we're not headed to the same hospital, Oscar. These look like they're color-coded. I was hoping we could stick together." Steve stated as he read the information on the card. "Kind of figured since we both had leg injuries we would be in the same hospital. Maybe they're giving you the bridal sweet."

"Man I hate that last name. You can not believe the jokes I get because of it." Oscar replied with a laugh.

Both men were still laughing when two corpsmen approached. One of the men looked over Steve's card.

"Well I hate to break up your conversation guys but it's time to go, Corporal."

Working as a team they quickly moved Steve onto a stretcher.

As they prepared to walk off Oscar shook Steve's hand. "Good luck, Kenrude. Be seeing you in Germany."

"Sounds good, Oscar. Take care and get that leg back in shape." Steve replied as the corpsmen carried him away.

The ship was being unloaded with the crane, and through a large door on the side of the ship that lead directly onto a very busy pier. Ambulances and buses painted white with large red crosses lined the parking area.

Once Steve was off the ship, he was carried to a bus that was modified to carry stretchers instead of seated passengers.

The corpsmen loaded the bus quickly handing all the files to a young British Nurse.

She quickly went through the bus comparing tags to the files she was carrying. "Well that makes twelve we can go then." She called out to an older gentleman sitting behind the wheel.

Instantly the bus began to snake its way through the heavy traffic and parked vehicles clogging the large pier. Although Steve was anxious once again to see the English countryside, he was unable to stay awake.

Within minutes he was sound asleep.

The old bus turned north from Southampton heading toward the hospital at Guilford. Traffic on the roads was heavy with military convoys shuttling vehicles and supplies toward ports of embarkation for France.

Several times the bus had to pull nearly off the road allowing trucks with extended loads to pass by.

The hospital was located at the edge of town in a large two story building.

Small homes with perfectly manicured gardens lined the road up to the hospital. It was evident the structure had once been some sort of warehouse that was converted to a military hospital.

As the bus came to a stop, American and British nurses climbed on board. They read each man's tag before assigning two corpsmen to unload them. The unloading of the bus was done in near record time.

Steve was quickly taken to a ward consisting of about fifty beds. When he was transferred to the bed a doctor arrived to read the file a nurse left on his nightstand.

"Well, Corporal how are you feeling? Do you have much pain?" He inquired as he unwrapped one of the dressings on Steve's left leg.

"I feel pretty good. As far as pain goes they have been giving me a shot every three to four hours. It helps to keeps the pain tolerable. So where do we go from here?" Steve inquired.

"Simply this Corporal! I come on duty as relief surgeon in an hour. You are my first case of the night. We'll start with some x-rays so we know where to find the shrapnel. Then we will put you out and go after all that junk. We should get most of the metal out of your legs. There will be smaller slivers that are impossible to remove. They get imbedded in some of the muscle tissue making it totally unfeasible to remove them. Some pieces nearer the skin will work their way to the surface in time. We will then close up your wounds, and clean up some stitching work from the aid station. Then you will be bandaged and begin the healing process. Any questions Corporal?"

"No that about covers it." Steve replied.

"Very well then." The doctor added before moving down the line to another new arrival. About two hours later two corpsmen arrived pushing a gurney. A nurse with them looked over Steve's chart.

"Are you ready for surgery, Corporal?"

"As ready as I can be." Steve replied.

The corpsmen transferred Steve to a gurney before rolling him to an x-ray room. They took so many x-rays of his legs he lost count. With the x-rays completed they rolled him to the operating room. The room was bustling with activity as nurses and surgical staff made preparations for his surgery.

The doctor entered the room with a nurse trailing him, still tying his gown from behind. He looked over several of the x-rays intently before speaking. "Well Corporal are you ready? It looks like we have a bit of work to do here. You are case number one for the night with several more to follow, so let's get moving shall we."

The doctor walked away from the x-rays then stood beside Steve. "You'll be good as knew when we are done. Nothing to worry about."

Steve smiled as a mask was placed over his face. With the surgical staff gathering around the table, Steve felt a rush of oxygen through the mask. He became very drowsy, drifting off to a deep sleep.

The ward was very quiet with all the lights dimmed as Steve slowly cracked open his eyes. He looked down at his throbbing legs to see they were both wrapped in new wide white bandages. He tried to remove the oxygen mask with his left hand.

"No you don't, Corporal." A woman's voice called out from his right. "You leave that mask right where it is until I take it off. Understood?"

Opening his eyes wider Steve turned to the right observing a nurse standing beside him.

"Are you in a lot of pain?" She inquired.

Steve just shook his head no.

"Let's check your vitals and see how you're doing. I'm Nurse Smith. I'll be your nurse through out the night." After checking his vital signs and bandages she removed a hypodermic needle from her pocket.

"We want you to sleep so I'm going to give you something that will pretty much knock you out for a while, Corporal." She rubbed a spot on his arm with a cotton ball soaked in alcohol then gave him a quick injection.

Slowly sleep overcame Steve as the pain in his legs began to dissipate.

Awakening, the sun was shining through the large south windows. The oxygen mask was gone and for the first time in days he felt rather rested.

An older doctor walked up to Steve's bunk removing the chart from the end of the bed. "Well the surgery went well for you I see by your chart. Most of the shrapnel was good size so they were able to get at it easily."

"So how am I? When do I get out of here?" Steve inquired.

"Well let's not jump to fast here, Corporal. Doctor Abner had to sew up one large muscle up as it was torn rather bad. I guess you'll be here about a month or so. We want the muscle to heal before you leave here.

But you shall be just fine. By the way I am Doctor Calloway."

"Nice to meet you Doctor Callaway. So the end of July I can get back to my unit?" Steve inquired.

"Back! You want to go back there and fight those damn German's! Corporal, I can sign the paper work sending you home for a well-deserved leave. A nice break to see family, friends and relax a bit."

The Doctor explained with a frown on his face.

"No way doc." Steve replied. "I'm going right back to my unit. That's it period. Captain Lewis signed an order before I left France, directing I be returned to my unit as soon as I am healthy enough."

"Well yes I saw that directive. But I am the doctor, it is my duty to decide whether a man is fit both physically and mentally to return to combat. That's the way it is, Corporal."

Doctor Callaway looked down at the floor for several moments. "However, unless something else comes up I can not for see right now, yes the end of July you should be able to return if that's what you choose to do, Corporal."

Shaking his head in disgust Doctor Callaway placed the chart back on the night stand, walking off down the ward mumbling incoherently.

Days dragged on as Steve lay in the hospital with thoughts of Harry and Franny in combat somewhere in France. He passed the time writing letters to Karen and his family. They were hard to write, as he was not sure what to tell them. He knew they could never understand what he had seen or been through. Nor could they ever understand the death and horrors he had witnessed.

After he had been in the hospital about two and a half weeks he was scheduled to be moved to an ambulatory recovery unit near London. Twenty men were moved along with Steve on a rainy Tuesday morning.

The recovery unit was basically a tent city made up of twenty-five large hospital tents each housing thirty men.

A small dispensary, mess halls and several other administrative Quonset huts made up the recovery unit.

All the men in this unit were able to get around on their own, but were not quite ready to return to combat yet.

Being so close to London brought back earlier memories of Marjorie and good times they had before going off to Normandy. He felt sad when he thought about Marjorie's death and all she had gone through.

It was almost as if all that had happened in another life time. So much had changed in such a short time since landing in Normandy. He pondered the deaths of Sgt. Winslow, Willie, Wade Rollins and so many more good young men. He wondered if Juarez and McGruder were still in England, or whether they had been sent stateside to recuperate. They had both been wounded very badly.

As Steve went for a stroll through the camp one evening, he came upon a doctor near the dispensary "Can I ask you a question?" Steve inquired of the tired looking doctor.

"Sure, Corporal. What's on your mind?"

"Two friends of mine were wounded just shortly before I got it. If I tell you their names could you find out where they're at?

"I don't know, Corporal that's a tough request. You know how many wounded men have come through here since the invasion. Tell you what, give me there names. I have a friend over in a large hospital South of London. They keep most of the transfer records there. Let me talk to him and see what I can find out." The doctor replied handing Steve a pencil and paper. "Also write your name, tent, and bunk number so I know where to find you if I get some information on your friends."

After writing down all the information Steve handed the paper back to the doctor. "I understand this is a large request but I would appreciate what ever you can do."

Smiling the doctor placed the paper into his pocket before returning to the dispensary. A few days later Steve lay on his bunk reading a news paper when a man entered the tent yelling out, "Kenrude you son of a bitch."

Steve sat up observing a paratrooper he knew from Camp Toccoa standing in the doorway.

"Karl Drussing! Damn it's good to see a familiar face." Steve called out standing up from his bunk.

"Where the hell did you come from? Last time I saw you I figured you were done with the Army as sick as you were."

The two men gave each other a big hug and shook hands.

"Yeah me to, Kenrude. That yellow jaundice and fever really was a son of a bitch. Doctors were not even sure where it came from. The bastards sent me home. But when I was better they agreed to bring me back, fatten me up and let me finish training. I missed the invasion because I got my ass hurt in a damn practice jump over on the west coast of this crazy island. But I'm doing well so they made me a runner. Oh, damn I almost forgot. Doctor Brewster handed me this note to deliver to you.

Saw the name on it and figured there could only be one Steve Kenrude." Karl said as he slapped the paper into Steve's hand.

Steve couldn't help chuckling at Karl as he opened the note. It read, "Billy Juarez did well in Surgery. He is here in tent twenty-eight. Josh McGruder's hand was in tough shape. He needed a lot of surgery. Still in hospital near Southampton but will be fine."

"Hot damn!" Steve yelled out.

"Good news I take it." Karl inquired.

"Yeah. The doctor found some information on two guys from our unit that had pretty bad injuries. Guy by the name of Juarez is here right now down in tent Twenty-eight. The other guy is still in the hospital but will be fine. I knew they were tough paratroopers." Steve said slapping his hands together.

"Well damn that's good news, Kenrude. I think we ought to take a walk down to twenty-eight and visit your buddy." Karl replied motioning Steve to follow him.

Arriving at the tent, Steve saw Juarez standing out front tossing a softball underhand to another soldier.

"You'll never make the Dodgers tossing a ball like that Juarez!" Steve called out.

Spinning around Juarez ran over giving Steve a huge hug. "Hey Corporal, what the hell you doing here?"

"Well a couple Kraut bombers tried to use my legs as pin cushions. But I'm ready to head back as soon as they clear me. What about you?" Steve inquired smiling.

"My shoulder feels good. They told me about another week or so and I should be ready to go. The bullet went straight through without hitting anything. I can't wait to get back with you guys." Juarez explained handing his glove and ball to the other soldier.

"You know what this just plain calls for a drink." Karl said with a large grin on his face.

"A drink! Where do you think we'll get any booze around here? Or do I not want to know?" Steve replied as he and Juarez followed Karl down a row of tents.

"As I said, Steve I'm a runner. You do some favors for certain people and they do favor's back. And sometimes I get paid well for special favors I handle." Karl chuckled.

The three men walked a few minutes to a row of steel huts beyond a sign that plainly stated, "Cadre Only."

"Home sweet home, Stevie boy." Karl said turning into the next hut. He walked up to his bunk, pulled out a footlocker removing a pint bottle from under his clothes. With a quick twist he removed the cap, raised the bottle and said. "To victory." After taking a large swallow he handed the bottle to Juarez.

"Damn straight. To victory!" He added before taking a quick shot.

Smiling Steve raised the bottle, looked at the two men repeating. "To victory."

"Come on Kenrude, this is good stuff. Who knows it might even be a month old. You need to take a better shot then that." Karl exclaimed handing the bottle back to Steve. Steve took another good size drink from the bottle, coughed and said. "Smooth. Yeah this stuff might just be a month old." He handed the bottle back to Juarez who refused before passing it back to Drussing.

After taking another small drink himself, Karl placed the cap on the bottle shoving it back into the footlocker. "Rationing you know. There is a war on."

The three warriors laughed before walking out of the hut, turning in the direction of the hospital tents.

"What unit are you with, Steve? I want to get into the war. I can't stay here. When I was injured I was taken out of my unit. I need a home. I need guys I can trust. Last thing I want is to end up in a reserve unit with guys you can't trust. You know what I mean, Steve? What do you think if I try for you're out fit?" Karl asked as they strolled toward the mess tent.

"We're with Charlie Company, second battalion, 502 parachute infantry regiment. We're assigned to the 101st. No slackers there believe me. Tough bunch and they fought well, Karl. Sure would be good to have you aboard. Hey remember Harry Jensen? He's still with us. Well at least he was fine when I left."

Steve explained as his stomach suddenly felt rather queasy. He knew all to well something could have easily happened to Harry, and he had no way of knowing about it. "Sure I remember Harry. Sounds like someplace I would like to hang my hat. Sergeant Winslow and Captain Fontaine still running the outfit?" Karl asked.

"Sergeant Winslow died during the jump. The Captain I'm not sure about. We were dumped all over Normandy. I never saw the Captain before I left." Steve explained.

"He's not bullshitting you, Drussing. All the training we did, all the planning they went through was for nothing.

It was a mess, but little by little we made it work." Juarez clarified.

As the three men entered the mess tent Karl turned toward Steve. "I'm going over to the repo-depot tomorrow. See if I can get myself assigned. There's a Lieutenant there that would like to see me out of here and kind of owes me a favor."

"Repo-Depot?" Steve inquired.

"It's Short for replacement depot. Guys go there and get assigned to fill in units that need replacements. We have one here at the camp.

They're going to move it to France once the battle moves inland. I'm going there first thing in the morning to see what I can do." Karl commented as he picked up a tray and coffee cup.

Steve smiled patting Karl on the back. "I hope you know what the hell you're doing. You got a pretty sweet gig here. But if they give you the assignment welcome aboard.

About noon the next day Karl came running into the mess tent. He dropped down on the bench aside of Steve.

"I got it, Steve. I'm going to be with Charlie Company. Was a peace of cake."

After shaking hands Steve asked." When do you ship out?"

"Believe this, tomorrow at 0800 from the repo-depot. Way it sounds then to a port and across the channel by ship to France. It could take up to a week to get there, unless." Karl stopped in midsentence.

"Unless what?" Steve inquired.

"Some of the airborne units may be coming back to rest and regroup here in England. Others are going to new rest camps near the beach. If your unit comes back first, then I would meet up with them in Newbury." Karl explained with a big smile.

"Damn Newbury sounds great. Almost sounds like home to me. Any word on when or if they're coming for sure?" Steve inquired.

"No nothing for sure, but soon I guess. Some of the units lost a lot of men and are in need of huge refits.

You miss them a bunch I take it?" Karl said looking intently at Steve.

"Yeah I do. I miss them a lot. Especially Harry. I'll keep my ears open around here for their return. If I'm still in Merry Ole England when they return, I'll get to Newbury one way or the other." Steve replied.

The following morning Steve and Juarez went to the repo-dept to see Karl off. "Give my best to Harry and the guys when you get there, Karl. Let them know I will be back in no time."

"Count on it, Steve." Karl replied listening to the Sergeant ordering the men to get loaded.

After the men shook hands Karl tossed his barracks bag onto the truck and climbed aboard. "Look out Adolph!" Karl yelled as the truck rolled out of the repo-depot. Steve was sad to see him go; Karl had been like a long lost family member from the past. Although there were a lot of great guys in the recovery camp, Steve was thankful Juarez lived just a few tents away. Without having someone close by that shared his experiences, Steve felt he would have gone stark raving mad.

Letters began arriving from Karen and his family. Each one raised his spirits tremendously. He enjoyed reading about the farm and what Mike and Christine were up to along with the latest news from Glendale.

He always saved Karen's letters for last, reading them slowly over and over. He savored every word she wrote, especially her dreams for their future after the war. Knowing that Karen still felt the same way about everything, made him feel exceptionally happy.

Steve was called to the medical building midway through the next week. Arriving, he took his place at the end of a long line behind a very tall Sergeant with a southern accent.

"Well corporal guess we have recovered enough to send us back to the war. Guess I'm ready as I'll ever be.

I'm getting pretty tired of this damn place." He commented to Steve as he shuffled forward.

"Yeah me too." Steve replied. "I'm ready to get back to my unit and finish up this damn war"

The Sergeant nodded his head. "Well now Corporal, I all don't think this war is going to go for too much longer. After all, George Patton is on the move now that we broke out of the coastal areas. My plan is to get into the fourth armored and ride with George all the way to Berlin."

The two men carried on a conversation all the way to the front of the building. When it became Steve's turn, he entered the exam room. He was directed by a clerk over to a small desk.

"Corporal Steven Kenrude reporting."

"Okay, Kenrude." The clerk said flipping through the pages in his file. "You have been discharged and are ready to move over to the repo-depot. Here is your paper work. Go pack your stuff and move over to the depot right away. We need your bunk for new men coming in today."

The clerk slammed a rubber stamp down on several pages before handing over the file.

Anticipating the move, Steve packed his bag first thing every morning the last four days. After a few good byes to the men in the tent,

Steve grabbed his bag. Before leaving he walked over to tent twenty-eight. Juarez was as excited as a June bride.

"What's with you?" Steve inquired as he entered the tent.

"I just got my medical clearance, Corporal. Fit for action! I should be joining you and the boys sometime real soon." Juarez explained waving the paper in the air.

"Fantastic, Billy. I need a good grenade thrower when we get back in action." Steve replied shaking hands with his good friend.

After making the short walk to the repo-dept Steve followed the signs to a building marked, "Administration."

Entering the door marked, "New replacements." Steve observed a corporal sitting behind a large wooden desk. Before he could do or say anything the clerk called out, "Over here Corporal."

Steve walked over to the desk handing his file to the man. "Corporal Steven Kenrude reporting as directed."

"Okay, Kenrude have a seat as I look this all over. Lets see 502nd parachute infantry regiment, C-Company.

They just returned from France last week and have been encamped at Newbury. We'll transport you over there in the morning. You're assigned to tent A-2 for the night. We'll roll you out about 0800 for the trip. Be ready and on time." The corporal explained making several notations in Steve's file.

"That sounds great." Steve replied as he picked up his barracks bag and file.

"Have any Lugers in there, Corporal?" The clerk inquired pointing toward the barracks bag.

"What?" Steve asked.

"Lugers, souvenirs, Kraut stuff you might want to sell. I can get you top dollar for anything you want to liquidate. I have a great market for any Kruat stuff. Especially lugers!" The Corporal replied with a big smile on his face.

It took every ounce of restraint Steve could muster from reaching across the desk, and grabbing the smiling

Corporal by the neck and smacking him.

"Why don't you volunteer for combat? You can pick up all the souvenirs you want. Or are you just plain scared?" Steve replied in an angry voice.

The Corporal began to laugh leaning back in his chair. "Corporal Anthony Baxter at the front? Now there's a laugh. No Kenrude, I plan to stay with this gig for the duration. After all, once the front moves away from the beach we'll be moving to France. Probably sleep in an old Chateau every night, and drink French Bordeaux with my dinner.

And believe me, I'll have all the Kraut stuff I can handle delivered right to me." The Corporal shook his head and laughed. "Scared! Hell no. I just know how to work the system, Kenrude." He looked at Steve for a moment before yelling, "Next." Angrily, Steve kicked the chair over before heading toward the door marked exit. Arriving at tent A-2, he found several other soldiers inside from the 503rd and the 506th parachute infantry regiments, which were also returning to duty tomorrow. The men spent the balance of the day talking and sharing their experiences of D-Day.

The following morning dawned cold and dreary with intermittent light showers. After eating breakfast Steve laid on his bunk awaiting orders to board the trucks. After his encounter with Corporal Baxter, he wanted out of the repo-depo as quickly as possible. It took everything inside of him from smashing Baxter's face with a right hook. But Newbury sounded much better than a brig.

He was anxious to see Harry and Franny. He prayed they made it back alive. For a minute he wondered how he would feel if he arrived at Newbury all excited, then found out they were dead.

Immediately he tossed that thought from his head as someone outside began calling out names to report for transfer on the double. Steve's was the fourth name called. He picked up his bag and jogged over to the waiting trucks.

Once all the tucks were loaded, they rolled out of the repo-depot in convoy fashion. Steve's truck drove just a short distance to a train station. The train for Newbury was preparing to depart when the trucks arrived.

The conductor rallied the men into the last car so they could keep on schedule.

As the train approached Newbury station Steve recognized many of the areas where they had trained all those long months before the invasion.

The station platform at Newbury was crowded with civilians and soldiers coming and going. Military trucks were lined up on every road around the depot.

Leaving the train Steve walked up to a Sergeant who appeared to be directing the flow of military traffic.

"Where to, Corporal?" He inquired as he observed troops preparing to load onto the train leaving for London.

"Charlie Company, second battalion 502nd." Steve called out above all the ruckus.

The Sergeant nodded his head while pointed toward a row of trucks. "Jump onto any of the trucks parked by the white curb. They'll be heading out shortly."

Steve climbed aboard the first truck where five new replacements were sitting. They all looked so young. It did not seem possible for them to be in the army, much less a parachute regiment.

"You guys headed for the 502nd? Any of you assigned to second battalion? "Steve inquired.

"Yes, Corporal I am." One recruit replied fumbling with his paper work.

"Does it have a company designation on your orders?" Steve inquired as he reached out to look over the man's freshly signed orders.

Seeing no company designation Steve returned the orders." What's your name private?" "Eddington, Max Eddington. All the way from Northwood, Iowa, Corporal." The soldier stated proudly.

"Well we're all here from somewhere, Max. Iowa you say. Ever get to Minnesota?" Steve inquired.

"All the time. My grandparents live just south of St. Paul. We have a farm just across the border in Iowa so

we visit there a lot." Private Eddington responded nodding his head.

"I live about seventy miles north-west of St. Paul. If you're interested, I can put in a good word and get you assigned to C-Company if we still need replacements when we get there." Steve explained to the nervous private.

"Yeah sure. I'd like that. Thanks, Corporal. I won't let you down." Max answered reassuringly.

"Besides, we have another Corporal in the unit from Iowa. You two could probably swap stories from time to time. He's a pretty good guy to get to know." Steve explained as he anxiously waited to see Harry himself.

"Moving out!" The truck driver yelled as he slipped the transmission into first gear rolling out of the station.

Steve couldn't help but smile as the truck rolled through the gate at the airfield. It really felt like he was home again. But he could not stop wondering if Harry and Franny were still alive. He knew very well that he would have an answer to his question in the next few minutes. At the 502nd building Steve and Max jumped off the truck. They walked inside to the busy assignment desk.

"Corporal Kenrude reporting back from the hospital," Steve told the Lieutenant as he handed over his file.

"Alright, glad to have you back, Kenrude. I'm sure C-Company will be excited to see you. Take care and good luck. Next man!" The Lieutenant called out.

"Sir this is a friend of mine newly assigned to second battalion 502nd. Private Max Eddington is his name.

Any chance we can get him into C-Company?" Steve inquired.

The Lieutenant took Eddington's orders and read through them quickly. Picking up a clip board he went down a list of names he had on several sheets. "Lets see. Eddington you say. Okay here you are. Yeah he's still unassigned. You want him you got him, Kenrude. Charlie Company still needs a few more men to bring it up to fighting strength. I see Juarez should be back in a few days also. So yeah he's all yours."

"Thank you sir," Steve said smartly as he went to attention saluting the capable officer. After the Lieutenant returned their salute Steve turned to Max. "Well grab your bag, Iowa and follow me."

The walk to C-Company took about ten minutes. Approaching the Company orderly room, Steve saw Franny coming out of the door reading a sheet of paper he was carrying. "Don't you ever watch where the hell you're going, private?" Steve yelled out.

Franny looked up excitedly from his paper, "Holy shit! Son of a bitch! Damn Corporal where the hell did you come from?" The two men gave each other a big hug as they slapped each other on the back several times. "Man it's good to see you, Kenrude. No one told us you were coming back yet.

"What are you doing over here with us Franny? No more gliders left for you to wreck?" Steve asked the very accurate BAR man.

"Hell no, Steve there are plenty of gliders left. But Harry pulled some strings and got me and Woodward reassigned back to regular paratrooper status, so we could be assigned to Charlie Company. No way were we going to fight the rest of this damn war without you guys." Franny explained.

"Wow that's great. Glad Harry was able to pull that off." Steve replied with a big smile.

"Come on let's go. Harry is going to be damn happy to see you." Franny replied picking up Steve's barracks bag.

"So how is the old boy doing?" Steve inquired.

"Oh hell he's fine. His wound is healed up. He's fine as shit. He has some new guys on the rifle range right now. They should be back shortly. Go inside and get checked in, then get your sorry ass over to the tents. Everyone is waiting to see you." Franny said slapping Steve on the shoulder again.

"Are we short in my squad yet, Franny?" Steve inquired.

"Hell yeah, we took a lot of casualties, Steve. We still need men in all four squads. Is that another of your hand picked replacements behind you?" Franny asked stretching out his hand to Max.

"Francis Doogan the third at your service. Best B.A.R. man in the whole stinking army. Call me Franny."

"Max Eddington, glad to meet you," Max replied as the two men shook hands. "Just call him Iowa, Franny. I gave him a new name like it or not." Steve said as he poked at Max.

"You mentioned hand picked recruits. Did Karl Drussing get assigned?" Steve inquired. "Yeah he arrived in France just before we loaded up to come back. Said you recruited him. Harry took him into second squad. He remembered Drussing from back in Camp Toccoa and was more than willing to take him." Franny explained.

"Great. Well Franny we'll get checked in and see you over in the company area shortly. Don't lose my bag. Say did captain Fontaine make it?" Steve nervously inquired.

"Yeah he sure did Steve. We got back with him two days after you left. He was sorry to hear about what happened to you. However, he is now Major Fontaine the Battalion Exec. Officer. We also have a new Captain you're about to meet. His name is Wesco. He seems like a good guy. Fontaine recommended him. Our new company Sergeant is a go getter by the name of Clarkson. They haven't replaced Sergeant

Winslow yet, so Clarkson is doing double duty with his First Sergeant Job until they appoint someone. He's no Winslow, but hell he'll do." Franny reported quietly looking over his shoulder to make sure nobody was listening. Steve nodded his head then walked into the orderly room with Max.

Sergeant Clarkson was standing by the situation board. "Can I help you men?" He inquired.

"Corporal Kenrude reporting back from the hospital," Steve responded.

"Yes, Great, I had a memo you were returning today. And you are?" Sergeant Clarkson asked looking over Steve's shoulder at Max.

Quickly Steve jumped into the conversation. "This is Private Max Eddington. New man just assigned. I would like to have him assigned to my squad if possible, Sarg."

Taking the paper work from Max he looked it over. "Ever handled a B.A.R, Eddington?

Would you be willing to learn? We have a great instructor that can teach you. Maybe you ran into him on your way in. Private Doogan. His bark is worse than his bite, but he's the best I know of." Sergeant Clarkson explained.

"I have fired one a few times, Sarg. I would be willing to take on the job." Max answered excitedly.

"Good. He's all yours, Kenrude. Captain Wesco is going to assign you guys a platoon Sergeant this week.

Until then I have those duties. Any questions or need anything just contact me." The Sergeant told Steve placing their paper work into his file cabinet.

"Understood Sergeant," Steve responded.

The two men walked the short distance to the platoon area. As Steve approached their tent a roar went up from a tent across the walkway. Harry and Franny had crowded all the guys from the platoon into one tent to surprise him. They all came charging out screaming and congratulating him on his return. They all took turns shaking hands and hugging him. The last person to approach him was Harry. The two men threw their arms around each other and hugged for a few seconds.

"Man it's good to see you, Steve. You look great. How do you feel? How are your legs? Ready to work and train these new fools? Damn I missed you, Stevie boy." Harry said slapping Steve on the shoulder.

"You're a sight for sore eyes, Harry. You have no idea how much I missed you and the guys. This is just like old times again.

I'm fine, my legs are fine and I'm ready to work." Steve replied as he looked around at the old faces and the many new replacements. "Well I haven't done a lot of running yet, Harry. But that will come. It looks like we have a lot of work cut out for us."

"Oh Yeah! But thanks for sending Drussing our way. He's a great guy. Hey Drussing get over here."

Harry called out.

Karl walked up shaking hands with Steve. "Good to see you again, Kenrude. Thanks for giving me the straight facts on these guys. This is a great unit."

Steve smiled and said; "Well when we do the inspections, I know which foot locker to search."

"Nothing but G.I issue, Corporal, Mr. Jensen here squared me away on that right away. But hell, that's fine with me. I swore the stuff off. Just like an altar boy from now on. And besides that, now I got me a home."

Karl replied as he laughed looking over at Harry.

Steve reached out grabbing hold of Max's arm. "Harry this is Max Eddington. He's assigned to my squad.

He'll be my new BAR man once Franny trains him. Actually you two are practically neighbors. He lives in Northwood, Iowa just across the border from Minnesota. So we're all kind of like neighbors."

Harry laughed and said; "Hell no. We look at Iowa as another country. You Minnesotans are foreigners to us.

Glad to meet you Eddington."

After the two men shook hands Harry turned to Steve very seriously. "We have a lot of new guys. We need to get them working as a team with the veterans real quick. The trust factor is not the same as when we left for Normandy. The old guys need to learn they can depend on the new men when the going gets tough.

Right now they're kind of standoffish. They need to learn some serious trust. The Captain is going to give us a Platoon Sergeant any day. Hopefully then we can get to work."

Steve nodded in agreement as the two men walked into his tent.

The next couple of days were spent getting the last of the new replacements, including Billy Juarez who was excited to be back with his company.

Saturday morning Captain Wesco called a company formation.

"For those of you who have not met me yet I'm Captain Wesco. I was the exc. officer of Alpha Company during the invasion. So I know what the hell is going on and I know what needs to be done.

First off we need to assign some new positions." After reading off the changes for first platoon he came to second platoon. "Replacing Sergeant Winslow will be Corporal Kenrude."

Steve stood in total disbelief with the announcement. A huge cheer went up from the platoon.

"Assistant platoon leader will be Jensen. First squad leader will be Crawford, Second squad leader will be Greenburg, Squad three will be Corporal Fineday and fourth squad will remain Corporal Cummings."

As the Captain went on to third and fourth platoon assignments Steve barely heard a word he said. He could not believe he was being given such a job of authority.

After the formation Sgt. Clarkson handed men their new rank patches. "Get them sewn on as soon as possible.

That means today or tomorrow. Monday training kicks in for earnest and things are going to get tough. We have a lot of new men to train before we are called back up. And that could be at any time. We need to be ready. Congratulations Kenrude, you'll do well. Any questions just ask me."

There was no need to question anything Sgt. Clarkson had just explained. It was simple and to the point.

Steve was very happy with the assignments that were made. There could have been no one else except Harry to be assistant platoon leader. He was the consummate warrior and a natural leader whether he wanted to admit it or not. Jake Crawford had been through training with the original group and was a good soldier.

Stan Greenburg joined second squad just prior to the invasion. He worked hard and was always about business. Steve enjoyed having him in his squad. John Fineday was replacing Bill Smith who was killed during the jump on D-Day. He was a very likeable man. Being a Native American from Michigan he had great tracking skills. Although a quiet person, Steve knew he could count on him to lead third squad. Dave

Cummings was still in charge of fourth squad. He was a big man who delighted in defeating anyone around at arm wrestling.

He had been wounded on D-Day during a knife fight but refused medical treatment. Steve turned to Harry. "Dismiss the men, but have the squad leaders meet us by the supply tent. We need to discuss some things right up front."

As Steve walked over to speak with Captain Wesco, Harry yelled out, "Corporals Fineday, Cummings, Greenburg and Crawford meet Sergeant Kenrude and my self behind the supply tent in ten minutes.

Everyone else, dismissed!"

The six men sat on benches behind the supply tent for over an hour discussing issues that were foremost on Steve's mind. Both men told their squad leaders what would be expected of them, and how they desired them to operate. All the men left the meeting with a good feeling.

The balance of the weekend was pretty laid back. Work details were divided among the men allowing each of them a chance to visit Newburg. However no one was allowed a pass to visit London.

Steve and Harry did a lot of planning and met with other platoon leaders to get ideas and compare notes.

On Sunday afternoon Steve took time to write letters home to Karen and his family. He was excited to announce his promotion to Sergeant and all the other changes to the platoon. Finishing his letters he lay down on his bunk and thought about all that needed to be accomplished, and the awesome responsibility that had been placed on his shoulders. He was happy Harry would be his assistant, as he trusted no one more. No matter who was platoon leader or assistant, things would have been just as good. They were a team plain and simple.

Harry strolled into the tent looking down at Steve. "Well the beer was cold, Stevie boy. You should have come along. The men behaved well and I did not see one fight. Well not with our men anyway."

Steve chuckled. "No I just wanted to write some letters and relax a bit. I want to be ready for tomorrow." Steve answered as he unlaced his boots before dropping them to the floor. "We are ready. We know what needs to be done, and we can tell the new guys what we learned over in Normandy. They'll need to learn and learn fast. No screwing around and absolutely no excuses from anyone.

We are ready, Steve. We both know it." Harry demanded slapping Steve on the head as he walked over to his bunk. "See you in the morning."

Steve smiled as he pulled his sleeping bag over him. "Yeah, see you in the morning."

The camp was unusually quiet as the men returned from pass. They all made for their tents to get as much sleep as possible before Monday morning rolled around.

Steve was not able to fall asleep right away. His mind was tormented about taking all the new untested men into battle. It seemed ludicrous to think that way, since everyone who jumped into France had been green and untested and they did well. But now he knew the horrors of combat, and what can happen to new men when tested under fire the first time. The task came down to getting the veterans from Normandy to accept the replacements, and teach them all they had learned. Rebuilding the platoon into a quality fighting unit had to be the main priority starting Monday morning. He was sure they would be called back into the war very shortly. There would be no second chances after that.

CHAPTER 13

MIKE'S BIG DECISION

Nancy Kenrude sat by the kitchen table listening to the news on the radio. Alex and Mike were out cutting hay in the meadow, and Christine left early with Karen to do Red Cross work in town.

Everything was so quiet she could hardly stand it. Picking up the last letter they received from Steve before he went off to Normandy. She reread the now familiar lines he had written. It never mattered how many times she read the letter. She always stopped short of wanting to read the last half page. He had honestly written regarding his thoughts of surviving in combat. He pulled no punches and was straight to the point. She could tell her son was scared, but ready to do what was demanded of him. His last line literally tore her heart in two. "I have always loved and respected all of you. If it is God's will that I must die, please remember we will meet again. Love always. Steve."

Tears rolled down her cheeks as she thought about her first born son fighting this brutal war. She tried to picture him fighting and killing, but shook her head to remove the thought from her mind. It was something no mother ever wanted to imagine. She sat wondering where Steve could be right now. Was her son alive or dead? This was all so cruel.

Sounds of the creaking hay wagon diverted her thoughts away from the war and her son. She walked to the door to watch Alex direct the horses to a spot under the hay loft door in front of the barn.

Mike jumped off the wagon, unhitched the horses before leading them to the coral aside the barn for water.

"Let's take a break before we unload this thing." Alex called out as he walked toward the house.

Nancy pushed the screen door open as he approached. "How's it going out there?" "Well if we could get more gas for that tractor it would sure help. But the kid sure works his butt off. He makes things go a lot easier and doesn't complain." Alex responded as he washed layers of dirt and sweat from his face.

Mike walked in smiling at his Mother. "Any news on the radio, Mom"

"No not really. Just that progress is being made in Normandy. They continue to explain how the huge hedgerows are slowing their progress. Sounds like its pretty tough going." She responded running her fingers through Mike's thick sweaty hair.

"Sure wish we could hear something about Steve's unit. But I guess it may be a while before we get any letters from him. I guess it would be tough to write letters in combat and tougher to find a place to mail them." Alex commented as he walked toward the coffeepot on the stove.

"Today's mail should be here shortly. We can hope for a letter." Nancy said looking out toward the mailbox.

"Someone is coming down the road real slow in a black car." Nancy stated as she watched the car turn into their driveway and roll to a stop in front of their porch.

"Why it's Reverend Martin and Hank Morris. This can't be good." Nancy said as she sat down slowly.

Alex charged out the door meeting the two men near the car. Mike stood frozen in place by the sink unable to move.

Nancy could see Alex nodding his head then direct the two men toward the house.

"No not Steve, please not my Steven. No, no, please no." Nancy cried out.

Alex rushed over and knelt down beside the chair taking his sobbing wife into his arms. "He's' alive Sweetheart. He was wounded seriously but not life threatening the way it sounds."

Nancy looked up to Reverend Martin, "Tell me what it says. Tell me what the damn telegram says. Read it all."

Revered Martin handed the telegram to Nancy and said, "Well just that Steve was wounded and his wounds are serious but not life threatening, like Alex told you. Steve's being treated in a hospital in England. But we don't know what thy mean by serious. That's all Nancy. I wish I could tell you more but I can't."

After Nancy finished reading the yellow document she handed it to Mike who was now standing beside her. He looked it over and said, "When will we hear more about him?" Hank Morris took a deep breathe before replying. "The Government has such a hard time just keeping up with notifications. I guess you may have to wait for Steve to write and tell you more. There are a lot of boys in both theaters getting wounded and killed. It all just takes so much time."

Mike nodded handing the telegram back to his Mother. "Are you headed back to Glendale from here?"

Mike inquired of the Mayor.

"Yes we are, Michael. What do you need? Can we give you a lift somewhere?" He asked.

"Christine and Karen are at the Red Cross Center in town. I don't want them to hear about this from just anyone. Can you drop me off there?" Mike asked very politely.

"Yes we can, Mike. That's a good idea. We can go with you, if you like." Reverend Martin replied.

"Thanks, but I can do it. Is that Okay with you, Dad?" Mike questioned looking at his grieving parents.

Alex smiled as best he could toward his youngest son. "That's fine, Michael. I think that is a great idea.

I'm just going to stay here with your Mother. I'm proud of you, son."

Mike nodded and forced a smile before following the Mayor out toward the car.

"If there's anything else we can do for you just let us know. We all know how hard this is for everyone." Reverend Martin added before following Michael and Hank Morris to the car. As the car came to a stop behind the Red Cross center, Reverend Martin again asked Michael if he wanted their help, but he still refused. Mike thanked them for the ride. Exiting the car he walked to the glass door containing a large Red Cross.

Entering the building the first person he ran into was Karen's Mother.

"Well Michael what a surprise. Things were pretty slow over at the feed mill today, so I came over to help over here. I just saw you get out of Hank Morris's car. Is there something wrong, Michael?" She inquired as she nervously studied his face.

"It's Steve." Mike said quietly.

"Oh God no. He's not…." Janet started with a shaky voice. But before she could finish Mike cut her off.

"He was wounded. He's in a hospital somewhere in England. The telegram says the wounds are serious but not life threatening." Mike explained as she placed her arms around him.

"Is that all it says? The telegram does not give you an indication of what his injuries are?" She whispered to Mike.

"No nothing like that. It just said not life threatening. I came here to tell the girls." He replied.

"Well thank God, Thank God. Do you want me to help tell Karen and Christine? That won't be easy, Michael." She responded wiping her wet face on her apron.

"Yes. That would be great. I don't know if I can do it by myself. I thought I would be able to. But now I'm not so sure." He responded to Mrs. Donnelly with a quivering bottom lip.

Janet stepped back, took a deep breath then said. "I will get the girls and bring them outside, meet us at the flower garden near the fountain.

Mike agreed and walked out the door trying hard to be strong, so he could tell the girls without breaking down. He knew they would both take this very hard.

As Janet escorted them out to the flower garden, Mike's eyes locked onto Karen.

It was evident she suspected something bad had happened when she saw him.

She stopped short of the garden placing her hands over her face and began to cry. "Oh my God, Steve."

She said in a broken voice.

"What happened?" Christine yelled out grabbing the front of her brother's shirt.

Before Mrs. Donnelly could do or say anything Karen collapsed onto the grass. Several women from the Red Cross group came running to see what was happening. They knelt down by Karen to assist Janet.

"Tell me, Michael. What happened? Tell me!" Christine was screaming as she began pounding her fists on Michael's chest.

He grabbed hold off Christine by pulling her into him. "He's alive, Christine. He's alive! But he's been wounded. He's in a hospital somewhere in England."

"Is he going to live? Will he be all right, Michael?" Christine cried out.

"The telegram says the injuries are serious but not life threatening. That's all we know." He replied holding on to his shaking sister as he watched Karen sit up slowly. "Come on over here and help me, Chris."

They walked over to Karen kneeling down beside her. She was shaking and looking wide eyed at Mike. "Is he…." Karen began.

"No he's alive, and in a hospital in England. We don't know where. The telegram said the wounds were serious but not life threatening. That's all we know, Karen." Mike reached out taking her hands. "You know Steve.

He's stubborn, as the day is long. He's a fighter. He'll be fine."

Karen nodded slowly looking first at Christine then her Mother. "I can't loose him. I can't."

"Now, now, Sweetheart. Mike said his injuries are not life threatening so you don't need to think about losing him." Her mother said reassuringly. "Now stand up Honey and I'll take you home."

Slowly Karen stood up with a little help from Christine as her legs were still shaking.

"He comes home then, right? I read some place that after a serious injury most of the guys get to come home. I mean, he does not have to go back and fight again." Karen insisted of Mike.

"Karen we don't have the answer to any of that. The telegram didn't say. We all hope he comes home too. We all do." Mike replied. But in his heart he knew Steve would return to his unit and back to the war if it were at all possible.

Karen and her Mother started slowly toward their car. "Can we give you a ride back to the farm?"

Janet asked Christine and Mike.

"Nonsense." Mrs. Brown called out. "I just live a half mile from their farm. It does not make sense to use your ration coupons to drive out there and back."

Mike and Christine agreed with Mrs. Brown who had always been a good neighbor to them.

"Well all right then." Janet replied. "We'll see you two later on then. Have your Mother give me a call this evening."

Mrs. Brown drove slowly out of town toward the Kenrude farm with out saying much at first. As she rounded the big bend in the road near her house she said, "My, that girl is really in love with your brother.

It's tough having your loved one go off to war and never know what's happening to them or where they are. I remember world war one with my husband. There were lots of sleepless nights. Just lying awake wondering and worrying. You can imagine so many bad things. We were lucky here in Glendale, although we did lose some very nice young men during that war. But this war is so big. I'm afraid we may loose many more of our boys before this is over."

Mike nodded in agreement as he looked over at Christine who was desperately fighting back her tears.

As the car stopped in front of the Kenrude porch, Christine climbed out of the back seat running straight for the house.

"Thanks for the ride home, Mrs. Brown." Mike said forcing a small smile.

"Any time Michael, try and be strong for your folks. They need a lot of support with Steven off in this war. They depend on you more then you will ever know." Mrs. Brown stated as Mike stepped from the car.

About a week and a half-passed before Karen and the Kenrude family received their first letter from Steve. He explained he had received shrapnel injuries to his legs during a bombing raid, and that the surgeons did a fantastic job so the only lasting effects would be some scarring.

Karen was not able to keep her feelings secret about Steve returning to his unit instead of coming home. She wrote several letters chastising him for his decision. But in the end she chose to tear them up before mailing them. It was nearly impossible for her to express the feelings inside her without getting angry. She felt betrayed. For the first time in their relationship she was totally upset with Steve. When Christine called to set up a date to work in the Red Cross Center she declined. She told Christine she was just sick and tired of the war and wanted nothing more to do with the war effort.

Mrs. Donnelly waited outside church on Sunday in an effort to speak with Alex and Nancy regarding their children.

Alex stepped from the church first, as Nancy stopped to speak with Reverend Martin for a moment.

"Good morning, Alex. Wasn't it a wonderful service today? Reverend Martin really hit home with his sermon."

Janet pointed out attempting to make small talk until Nancy came outside.

"Yes it was a fine service. And it looks like it will be another fine summer day too. I think I'll convince that son of mine to take a walk down to the lake and see what we can catch." Alex replied just as his wife walked out the door.

"Well good morning, Nancy." Janet said to her best friend while fumbling with her purse. "I sure would like to talk with the two of you, if you can spare some time."

"We always have time for you, Honey. What's the matter? You look simply worried. Is there anything wrong with Karen?" Nancy inquired placing her arm around Janet's waist. Alex directed them across the street to the small Café and said, "Why don't we sit down and talk about this over coffee."

After the waitress walked off Janet looked down at her cup, "I don't know how to talk to Karen about Steve. She is so upset. She really feels like he turned his back on her when he turned down the option to come home. I tried to explain to her about his strong feeling of commitment to finish what he starts. That was the wrong thing to say. She questioned me whether his commitment to her and their relationship wasn't more important. I know Steve loves Karen very much and I know Karen loves him. But I'm so worried she is second guessing their relationship and Steve's love for her. If only he had come home for a short visit."

Alex and Nancy were quiet for several moments as they contemplated Janet's words and feelings regarding her daughter. After all, other than Steve, no one knew Karen better than her mother.

"I know Steven. I don't think his decision not to come home in anyway meant a change of mind toward their relationship. In the letters we have received from him he talks about Harry, Franny and the rest of the men he has fought with. He talks about wanting to get back to them and finish the war. I think there's a bonding that takes place between men in a situation like that none of us are capable of understanding. I guess we would have to walk a mile in their shoes before we could ever comprehend it. And would any of us really want to experience what those boys have had to endure? I can understand how Karen feels cheated. Nancy and I were both wishing he had come home too. My hope was that he could get reassigned stateside and train new men to go fight. We were upset. But we had to realize Steve knew what was best for him." Alex explained in a reassuring tone.

Nancy reached across the table taking hold of Janet's hand. "Honey, I was mad as hell at God for sending my son to war and letting him get wounded. And I was mad as hell when my son turned down a trip home, choosing instead to return to the killing and ugliness of war.

But I have been praying for understanding of God's will. I keep thinking maybe this might have been the last chance to ever see my baby again. Next time he may come home in a box. That's hell to live with every day, every damn day! It gnaws at me constantly. It keeps me awake at night. Karen is not alone with her grief, fears, and anger. But we need to get past it for Steve's sake. How would we live with ourselves knowing our last thoughts of him were anger, if we found out a minute later he was killed. It's not fair in anyway for any of us."

Nancy explained as tears whelmed in her eyes. "And I pray every day that this horrible war will end soon, so I don't have to see another son go off to fight."

Janet squeezed Nancy's hand tight while choking back her tears. "I can not even imagine the anguish you go through each day. Nancy, I love Steve also. It scares me every day thinking he might not come home alive. Some days it's impossible to listen to the war news."

"Would you like us to talk with Karen? I don't know if it can make any difference but we sure can try. We don't want to loose Karen as part of our family either." Alex replied. "You know what scares me the most, Alex. If Karen would just give up on them and write that poor boy a Dear John letter. With all he has to contend with how in God's name would he deal with that so far from home. And we all know he loves Karen deeply. Yes, I was thinking if Karen could sit down with Nancy for a heart to heart talk it might make a difference. Maybe even have Christine there might help. Those girls have become so very close." Janet replied wiping tears from her eyes.

Alex looked out the window observing Mike and Christine standing by their car. "Well the kids are through helping Reverend Martin, so I suppose we should get going."

"I'll call Karen and setup a time for Christine and I to talk with her. I think she just needs some reassurance. She also needs to know she is not alone. Our feelings were crushed when Steve decided not to come home. This will all work out." Nancy explained as she stood up from the table.

A few days later Nancy and Christine picked up Karen. They drove to the park where they sat and talked for several hours. Karen began to mellow, as she listened to Nancy and Christine vocalize their frustrations and hurt regarding Steve's decision. Karen explained she would never have written a Dear John letter to Steve. She just felt so alone and wanted to be with him for just a short time. As Nancy dropped Karen back home, she knew they had crossed a threshold and everyone was now doing much better.

However, Mike wrestled even more with his desires to be involved with the war. Listening to the news every day, it was clear the war in Europe could not go on for another year. He longed to be involved and fight for his country. His best friend Benny Atchison was going to Minneapolis to enlist.

Benny like Mike wanted to join the army when school let out for the year. His Mother argued with him to finish high school first but Benny was determined to go. The two boys met down by Eagle Lake the first week of August to discuss Benny's plan.

"So you really are going to Minneapolis to enlist next week?" Mike asked his best friend. "Yeah, sure am. Mom finally gave up arguing. She knows I'm going one way or the other. So finally she told me to do what I thought was right for me. I know if Dad were still alive he wouldn't let me go.

But I have to do this, Mike. Are you going to come with me? We look eighteen! The recruiters in Minneapolis talk to hundreds of guys a day. They won't even think of asking. I know you want to go, Mike." Benny stated staring intently at his friend.

"I want to. I really do. But my Mom and Dad will be so mad they may never get over it. I just don't know if I can do that. How would I explain going to Minneapolis?" Mike quizzed Benny.

"That's simple, Mike. Tell your folks you want to go to the State Fair with me in two weeks on the bus. We just get off in Minneapolis, enlist, go to Snelling and we are on our way." Benny replied.

"Yeah but when we don't come home they'll look for us. When Dad finds out he'll tell the recruiter we lied about our age and it'll be over. Even if Dad would sign for me Mom would never let it happen. Not in a million years." Mike explained feeling torn between going with Benny and staying home.

"Well Mike, I'll talk to you a couple days before I go. If you want to join me just let me know. But either way I'm going to enlist." Benny told Mike firmly.

The next week and a half were very tough on Mike. His mind was pulling him in two very different directions. Just for safety sake he told his parents that he would like to go to the Fair with Benny on the bus. He told them they might stay over a night with Benny's cousin. Alex told him that was fine, but explained he could not afford to give him any money. Mike agreed, telling him he had saved enough over the last year to cover everything. At least now if he did decide to enlist the story was set.

Three days before they were to catch the bus the boys met again by the lake. "Well Mike, have you thought about going with me on Monday?" Benny asked desperately hoping he would say yes.

"I guess so. I've given it a lot of thought. It really is what I want to do. I guess I will have to deal with my parents later." Mike replied still having mixed feelings about his decision.

"Good, I'll pick you up with my Moms' car the day before. You can spend the night at my house.

That way we can get to the bus stop early. How does that sound?" Benny inquired.

Surprisingly, it sounded like a great plan. Mike felt even more comfortable with the decision he had made. Sunday night he jumped into the car with Benny carrying a small bag with some clothing.

As Benny backed the car on to the road Mike took a long look at the farm. He figured it might be a long time before he would see it again, if ever. Monday morning the boys were at the stop about fifteen minutes before the bus arrived. By now both boys were totally excited and ready to carry out their plan.

Once they were on the bus, Benny explained to Mike about a change in their plans. "I found out you can go right to Fort Snelling to enlist and everything goes much quicker. We can be out of the Fort and on our way to the training base by Wednesday. This bus actually makes a stop at the Fort. What do you think about that?"

Mike nodded his head in agreement and smiled. "I like it. We can be on our way before the folks figure out what's going on. Maybe they'll let me stay then." He replied, although still feeling somewhat sick about deceiving his parents.

The bus stopped across the street from the induction center about two hours after leaving Glendale.

There was a small line in front of the enlistment office. Quietly they took their place in line. The wait was about forty-five minutes before they entered the office. By this time there was a very long line behind them. They figured every recruiter would move fast asking very few questions. Hastily they filled out the forms they were handed, delivering them back to a Corporal at the front desk. He looked everything over, before rubber stamping some of the forms before tossing them in a basket. He handed each of them a file directing them to follow the yellow line on the floor. In no time their physical was completed, along with all the additional forms. By late afternoon they finished all required tests and interviews. Along with about thirty other men they were ushered into a large room. A tall Captain entered the room smiling. After looking them over he directed them to raise their right hand. He had them repeat the oath of allegiance to the United States. When they finished he smiled again.

"Congratulations men. You are now property of the U.S. Army; it's too late to back out. We'll put you up over night in a barracks. Tomorrow you'll leave for Basic Training at Fort Leonard Wood Missouri. Now just follow my Sergeant."

Mike was having a difficult time realizing he had followed through and was actually in the Army.

What were his folks going to think of him? He had lied and totally deceived them. Would they ever be able to forgive him or trust him again? He wondered if his parents would try to stop the enlistment since he lied about his age.

Hurting Christine bothered him most. She became so close to him since Steve left. He knew she would be extremely angry with him. No matter, it was a dead issue now. He was in the Army. It turned out to be a long restless night with little sleep for him.

After a quick breakfast at 0530 the men loaded on a bus bound for Fort Leonard Wood. Mike sat down by a window with Benny aside of him.

"Well here we go, Mike." Benny exclaimed with a huge smile on his face.

Mike simply nodded his head without a response. After looking out the window for several minutes he turned back toward Benny. "I know this sounds really bad. But I'm not sure I did the right thing.

I guess I'll just have to live with it." Letting out a big sigh Mike looked out the window again for a moment before turning back toward Benny. "Hell, this is what I wanted for so long, Benny. It's my life and my folks will just have to live with my decision."

Benny smiled at Mike. "We did make the right choice. Your folks will have to understand you did what you needed to do. In the end they'll be proud of you. I know my mom will be proud of me."

Mike nodded in agreement, but in his heart he doubted they would be proud of him. Slowly he drifted off to sleep.

When the bus arrived at Fort Leonard Wood, the men were hustled off and directed into lines for hair cuts, clothing issue, and more paper work.

As night fell over the Fort the lights went out in the barracks. Mike felt somewhat homesick. However he felt very satisfied with his decision. There was no doubt there would be a terrible argument with his Father when he found out. He was sure by now his folks were wondering why they had not arrived back from the fair, and would be worried. It made him nauseous when he thought about how much they would worry, and how terribly he had deceived them.

Wednesday morning Alex poured a cup of coffee before walking to the kitchen door. He looked around the yard scratching his head.

Nancy poured herself a cup of coffee before joining her husband at the door. "What are you thinking, Alex?"

"Well I kind of wish Mike would have come home last night. But then I guess we worked him pretty hard this summer. Two days at the fair having fun is all right I guess. It will give him a chance to blow off some steam before school begins. You know there are some things I need at the hardware store. Think I'll run into Glendale later this afternoon. The bus comes in around three-thirty on Wednesdays.

So I'll just pick up the kid and bring him home instead of Benny making the trip out here.

"That sounds fine, Alex. I'll make a big supper tonight because I know Mike did not have a lot of money to buy food." Nancy replied as she finished her coffee.

Alex stood by the drug store talking with several men from town when the bus arrived. He watched several people step off the bus but no Benny or Mike. When the driver stepped off to unload baggage Alex approached him.

"Didn't you have two boys to bring back from Minneapolis on this run? They would be seventeen years old, both about six feet, one with dark brown hair the other kind of sandy brown." Alex questioned the driver.

"No sir, I only picked up four passengers in Minneapolis. I walked into the terminal myself to pick up paper work for my next stop. I didn't see your boys or anyone else inside the terminal. Sorry." The driver replied.

Alex stood on the corner totally baffled as to what happened to the boys. It was not like Mike to be this late for anything. He drove his truck over to the Atchison residence. He observed Mary working in her flowerbeds. Parking the truck across the road Alex paused for a moment, figuring out how he would ask her about their boys. He did not want to scare her if he could help it.

Slowly he exited the cab walking over to the Atchison home.

"Good afternoon, Mary." He started. "Your flowerbeds sure were colorful this summer. We enjoyed them every time we drove past."

Mary stood up shaking dirt from her hands. "Why thank you Alex. What can I do for you this afternoon?" She inquired looking at Alex some what perplexed.

"Well I was wondering if you heard from Benny as to why he and Mike haven't come back from the State Fair yet." Alex inquired.

"State Fair? What are you talking about? I lost an argument with Benny several weeks ago. He took the bus for Minneapolis to enlist in the Army. He knew he couldn't do it here in town because the recruiter knows all the boys' ages. So he figured he could enlist in Minneapolis and get away with it.

Now I know it was probably wrong for me to have let him go. I wanted no part of it and refused to sign for him. Nevertheless, I told him if they took him and it was what he wanted; he had my blessing as he's as bullhead as his Father was. And, well with the war on I guess being patriotic and wanting to defend your country isn't such a bad thing." Mary explained smiling at Alex.

He felt a knot tightening in his stomach as the blood drained from his face.

"Alex are you alright, do you need to sit down? You look down right pale." Mary inquired as she led him by the arm to the porch. "Alex do you want some water?"

For several minutes he was not sure what to say. He just sat there looking at Mary. "Was Mike with him when he left?" Alex asked not really wanting to hear the answer.

"Why Mike spent the night here on Sunday. I didn't think he was going with Benny. I thought he just came over to spend time with Benny before he left. You know those two have been friends since first grade. You think Michael went with Benny? Oh dear! And he told you they were going to the Fair?

Alex I don't know what to say." Mary declared as she also sat down. "What is Nancy going to say when she finds out, oh dear, poor Nancy."

Slowly Alex stood up. After a moment he stepped off the porch walking toward his truck with Mary following behind. "I can't believe Michael would do something like this. He talked about enlisting many times, but I thought we had this whole Army thing taken care of. What the hell am I going to tell my wife?" Alex asked while opening the door to his truck. He looked straight at Mary repeating. "What the hell am I going to tell my wife? This is going to kill her."

Alex drove exceptionally slow on the trip back home. He was trying to put together the right words to tell his wife. He knew she was in the kitchen right now, preparing the big supper she had spoken about earlier this morning. Still being in shock he struggled to come up with an easy way to tell her. He knew in the long run there would be no easy way.

Christine was standing by the kitchen door when Alex pulled up in the truck. She came walking out with a puzzled look on her face. "Where's Mike? Wasn't he on the bus?" She questioned.

Alex put his arms around her giving her a hug. "Why don't you come in the house, I'll explain everything to you and your Mother." He replied to his daughter.

As the two walked in Nancy was just placing a hot apple pie on the counter. “I figured we better start using those apples in the cellar. There’s going to be another big crop this year.” Nancy said smiling. “Where is that Vagabond son of mine?” She asked looking out the door behind her husband.

“I think you might want to sit down before I tell you.” Alex replied looking thoughtfully at his wife.

The smile instantly disappeared from Nancy’s’ face. It was replaced immediately with a very worried look. “What’s happened to Michael, Alex? Where is my son?”

Alex pulled out a chair from the table sitting down directly in front of Nancy taking her hands. “He’s all right, Honey. When he and Benny did not get off the bus I drove over to see Mary. Seems Mary and Benny have been going around for some time about the Army.

She finally gave Benny her approval to try enlisting in Minneapolis since he was under age. She would not sign for him here in Glendale. I suspect Michael went with him.”

“Oh my dear God!” Nancy cried out. Placing her apron over her eyes she began to weep. “No not two sons. No! Alex we need to stop this. We need to let them know he’s under age. We need to bring our son home, today!” She cried out.

Christine stood by her Mother in total shock. She was totally motionless as tears ran down her cheeks.

“I don’t think there is anything we can do today, Sweetheart. Tomorrow I’ll drive into town and speak with the recruiter to see what’s possible. I’ll find out where he’s at and see about bring him home.” Alex explained attempting to be reassuring.

Finally Christine was able to speak. “I didn’t think Mike would do this, Dad. But he wanted to enlist badly. We have talked about it for a long time. I just thought he would some how convince you to sign for him.”

“No way would that have happened, Christine. He needed to finish high school first!” Alex argued in a stern voice.

“What happens when you bring him home? He’s going to be embarrassed and resentful. Maybe you need to try and understand Mike. He really wants this. I don’t want him to be in the Army either. I worry enough about Steve. But I understand Mike very well. And I know he'll resent you for bringing him back home." Christine explained defiantly.

"He lied to us, Christine. He totally deceived us with his story about going to the fair. He needs to face some sort of punishment for that kind of behavior. I will not allow my son to treat us this way." Alex countered glaring at his daughter.

Christine ran up the stairs to her room throwing herself down on her bed. Her emotions were torn. She was angry at Mike for deceiving her, but yet she somehow understood why he made the decision.

The Kenrude house was a very somber place the rest of the evening. Nancy and Christine attempted to comfort each other while Alex took out his frustrations on a broken gate in the barn.

Thursday morning Nancy went about breakfast as usual just a whole lot slower, as she would gaze out the window from time to time. Christine was trying to avoid any conversation as she placed dishes on the table. It seemed strange to be setting just three places.

After finishing morning chores Alex came into the house to wash his hands. He walked over to his worried looking wife, giving her a kiss on the cheek.

"Soon as we're done with breakfast I'm heading into town to see that damn recruiter. We're going to get the situation rectified and bring Michael home." Alex declared as he hugged his wife.

Nancy looked up at her strong husband. "I don't know Alex. Is that the right thing to do?"

Alex took a step back with a puzzled look on his face. "What do you mean?"

"What Christine said last night makes a lot of sense, I've thought about it all night. I wish he would have finished school first. Maybe the war would have been over by that time. And yes, I wish he would have talked to us before he made such a bold decision. But Alex, if we go after Michael and force him to come home, I'm afraid he will resent us for a long time. We may even lose him in another way."

"What do you mean?" Alex questioned not sure what his wife was talking about.

Yes, I agree it was wrong for him to deceive us. He will have to live with that for a long time. But if we force him to come home, he may just run of somewhere else where we may never find him. I think we should wait until we get a letter from him. He will write to explain everything

I'm sure of it. Then we'll know where he's stationed, we can go there to speak with him. Alex can you consider that?" Nancy asked placing her hands on her husband's chest.

He looked out the window then back toward his wife. "If that is what you want I can wait. Maybe there is something to all of that. I don't know right now. I just don't know." Alex responded.

About two weeks went by before they received their first letter from Mike. He was very apologetic for his actions especially for lying to them. He sought their forgiveness while asking for their understanding as to why he needed to enlist. He wrote about how much he missed them, the farm, and apologized to Alex for leaving all the work to him this busy time of the year. However he also described how happy he was. He explained how being in the army made him feel alive and worthwhile, and he was proud to be doing his part for the war effort. The last thing he wrote was asking them not to have his enlistment over turned.

Mike continued sending letters every week describing all his experiences and the new friends he was making. His parents answered every one of them, but always avoided the issue of his actions when he left home.

Near the end of September Alex came to Nancy with a request. "I've given this a tremendous amount of thought. I still am upset with Michael and how he deceived us. Some times I want to walk into the recruiter's office when I'm in town and tell him the whole story.

But I have avoided doing that even though I think it's the right thing to do. It's time now we talk with Michael. We need to speak face to face and hash this whole thing out once and forever, or I'll never get past these feelings I have. Would you take a bus trip with me to Missouri to see our son?"

Nancy nodded as tears filled here eyes. "I would love to go with you. I would love to see my son very much."

Parking their truck at the Donnelly's, Karen drove them to the bus depot. "I know this is going to be hard for you both. But Michael is just like Steve. Hard headed and totally determined to do what he thinks is right. I know I had a tough time with Steve's decision, but I love him with all my heart. I understand better now why he made the choice he did." Karen explained to Alex and Nancy.

Alex nodded as he watched the bus pull up to the curb. "Thanks, Karen. I don't know if it makes this entire situation any better. But these are strange times, and maybe, just maybe the rules have to be bent a little. I'm not so sure about that yet. But I'm working on it."

Karen hugged both of them before they boarded the bus. She could feel their absolute pain. But she also felt this trip just might clear the waters a bit, allowing all of them to find some peace and acceptance.

Nancy kissed Karen on the cheek before turning to join Alex who was climbing aboard the bus for a long ride to Missouri.

The bus took them to St. Louis where they found a room in a hotel. The next morning they caught a military bus that delivered them directly to the front gate of the fort.

Alex handed a sentry the letter they received from the Base Commander allowing them to enter the Fort to visit their son.

Alex and Nancy were totally taken back by the sprawling base with all the activities taking place.

They were impressed by all the marching men they saw, as well as the tanks, trucks and towed artillery pieces being moving about the fort.

Arriving at the training station they were ushered into a recreation center filled with pool and ping-pong tables, comfortable chairs, card tables and stacks of magazines.

A handsome well built Sergeant came into the room. "I'm Sergeant Broadmore your son's drill instructor. I was asked to welcome you to Fort Leonard Wood and answer any questions you may have."

Alex shook hands with Sergeant Broadmore. After a moment of silence he asked. "How is Michael doing? Is he handling Army life all right?"

"Your son is doing very well. He has taken to Army life splendidly. I made him a squad leader so he can help out some of the guys who don't catch on as quickly. To be honest, I wish we had another thousand like your son. He'll be a great soldier. Actually with time and experience he'll make a great leader." The Sergeant replied smiling reassuringly. "How soon can we see, Michael?" Nancy inquired.

"He should be here any minute. I had him change uniforms before he came over here, as he was a bit dirty. I'll be in the office over there in the corner. If you have any questions for me please do not hesitate to call." Sergeant Broadmore explained before walking back over to the small office.

Seconds later the door on the far side of the day room opened. Mike hesitantly walked into the room before Nancy ran forward throwing her arms around her son, trying desperately not to cry. Alex walked up to Mike, extending his arm to shake hands. "Nice to see you both," Mike exclaimed as he held his Mother.

"Nice to see you too son, it looks like the Army agrees with you. You look taller and definitely look like you're eating well." Alex responded looking his son up and down. "Yes sir, they feed us well, and they work it right back off." Mike replied with a slight smile.

Alex and Nancy laughed lightly at Mike's comment.

Mike took his Mother by the hand walking her over to some chairs and sat down. "Look, I know what I did was not right. I should not have lied to you. But I knew you would never sign for me so I could enlist. When Benny came to me with his plan, it was just something I wanted to do so badly. So here I am. I know you can have me discharged for being under age. But I'm asking you not to do that. I really love the Army and I want to stay here. Please give that some consideration."

Nancy held her son's hand looking into his eyes. "You really do want to do this don't you?"

"Yes, Mom I do. I'll finish high school when I get out or maybe even here if I decide to stay in after the war. But this is all I have dreamed about and this is the life I want." Mike replied looking at both his Mother and Father.

"We could have had you discharged right away, son. But your Mother begged me to wait until we heard from you. She wanted to see what you had to say. So we waited and every letter you sent was more positive then the one before. It was my decision to come down and see you face to face. I guess I'm not sure what this was supposed to prove.

We needed hear your side of the story face to face and whether or not you still felt you made the right decision. The most important thing for both of us is to know you're really happy. And that's about it. I can manage the farm. Christine says she will help where she can.

So I guess this is your call, Michael." Alex said in a compassionate voice.

After looking at his mother Mike smiled. "This is what I want. Again I am sorry for lying to you and upsetting all of you. But I'm happier then I have been in a long time, Dad. You remember what I was going through all summer. I love you all and will never let you down again. I promise. But like I said, I really love army life and I want to stay in." Mike explained.

"You could never let us down, son. You're too much of a man for that." Nancy said smiling at her handsome son.

"Well then that's about it. We found what we came for I guess, as long as you're happy and fully believe the Army is totally right for you. We will accept your decision although we don't totally agree with it, or how you went about it." Alex replied as he stood up to shake hands with Mike.

"Thank you. Thank you for everything. I love you both." Mike responded with a huge smile on his face.

Nancy gave Mike another hug. "You know where your home is. It will always be there for you as will your family. Take care of yourself and don't do anything foolish."

"I know I hurt Christine as well. How is she doing with all of this?" Mike questioned his father.

With a smile on his face he replied. "To tell you the truth son, the night we found out about all of this Christine defended you. She didn't necessarily like the way you went about things. But she stood up for you. If it would not have been for her we probably would have forced you home right away. You owe your little sister a big thank you."

Mike smiled as he looked at his parents. "Well I would like to spend more time with you but we're getting ready for a big field march. I have a couple of guys in my squad that need help getting their packs ready, so I should be getting back to the barracks."

After kissing his mother on the cheek and shaking hands with his father Mike turned and left the room.

Sergeant Broadmore walked over from the office. "Do either of you have any questions? Anything you need from me or the army?"

"Just train him well and do your best with him." Nancy answered smiling at the Sergeant. The following morning Alex and Nancy boarded the bus for the long ride back to Glendale.

They were both relieved after their visit with Mike. They knew they made the right decision to leave him in the Army. He was happy and that was pretty much all a parent could ask for in such a dangerous world they now lived in.

Returning home they explained to Christine how happy Michael was. They told her about their conversation and how positive they felt about leaving him there. Although Christine shared her parents fears she was happy they made no attempt to force Mike out of the army.

CHAPTER 14

COMBAT TO THE BREAKING POINT

Training began in earnest Monday morning as the men were rolled from their bunks at 0430. They began with a three mile run with full packs before a grueling round of calisthenics for a half hour. They reshouldered their packs before running another mile back to the Company area for breakfast. Some veterans complained about the strenuous schedule they were forced to endure. But to a man, each of them knew they had to stay in shape to contend with combat demands of an airborne soldier. There was little doubt in any one's mind; Eisenhower's command center would be once again calling upon them for their specialized talents in the near future.

Steve and Harry worked diligently molding their veterans and replacements into a tough cohesive combat unit. After about a week of intensive work the veterans began accepting and working with the new men. They came to realize their very lives depended on the battle worthiness of every man in the unit.

Max Eddington took to the BAR as if he had handled it for a long time. He enjoyed working with Franny on the range, learning the many ways to make his weapon more efficient in combat.

Max clung to every word Franny told him about his experiences in Normandy with his weapon.

Anderson joined in the training from time to time, explaining how the BAR could turn the tide of battle in small unit actions. Max quickly became an expert with his new piece of equipment.

Charlie Company made long marches with heavy packs, to simulate battle field conditions paratroopers could face in open country. It was necessary for the new men to experience the rigors of carrying all the equipment needed for a regimental parachute team to survive in battle. Many new men questioned the sense of carrying some of the cargo they were now required to jump with. They had not trained with such heavy loaded packs in jump school.

The veterans explained how the extra equipment might have saved many more lives during the Normandy campaign.

The British Citizenry didn't seem to mind the airborne yanks as much as they had before the invasion. In some of the small villages they passed through, town folks would come out and greet them while cheering them on.

Nevertheless, problems arose the first time the men were allowed weekend passes to London. Many of them proceeded to get drunk and blow off excess stress. This nearly always would result in problems with the Military Police or worse, the London Authorities. Although Captain Wesco understood very well the traumas every man faced in Normandy, he ended the weekend passes to London.

He attempted to be sympathetic when dealing with minor infractions, but kept a heavy hand dealing with serious breaches of Military Conduct. Those cases he would turn over to the Provost Marshall for Courts Marshall Proceedings. He felt it was imperative each man understand discipline was the hallmark of survival in battle.

Luckily second platoon had very few discipline problems. When a couple of paratroopers from fourth squad were arrested for drunken and disorderly conduct, Steve pulled their local passes assigning them extra duty for two straight weekends. Both men learned the lesson well. From that point forward, no men from second platoon were discipline problems while on leave.

As August turned into September the cool crispness of fall filled the air. Since day light began to get shorter, many training missions went well into the dark evening hours; little did they know this would pay huge dividends come December, when they would fight in the bitter cold of the Ardennes.

Steve and Harry were impressed with the progress and efficiency of their platoon. On several occasions Captain Wesco referred to second platoon as the tip of his spear. One particular night jump hampered by cold rain and gusty winds, second platoon was the only unit able to assemble and complete their mission ahead of schedule. However that did not happen without some major difficulties. With gusty winds and heavy cloud cover, drop targets were obscured. Pilots dropped some members of second platoon in the wrong location. However well learned experiences from the Normandy Campaign worked to their advantage. The two platoon leaders laboriously collected their scattered force, carried out a three mile forced march in the dark and attacked their positions with accuracy.

Every man paid close attention to the progress of the war as it rolled across the continent. Rumors ran rampant through Charlie Company concerning when and where they would be going. But as each rumored date arrived, nothing happened. Captain Wesco did his best to control rumors and scuttlebutt as it was tough on morale and daily training schedules. September tenth they repeated a training mission for a second time concerning the securing of multiple bridges in conjunction with a large ground movement. This set rumors flying they were preparing to work with General George Patton's Third Army, to be his spearhead in crossing the Rhine river into Germany.

In spite of all the rumors, September fifteenth Major Fontaine assembled his battalion giving them the real run down on the mission they were about to embark upon. They were not going to work with General Patton.

Instead they would be under command of British Field Marshall Bernard Law Montgomery, operating in a risky plan code named, Market Garden.

The Market portion of the plan was to parachute an entire airborne army consisting of British and American paratroopers behind enemy lines into Holland. They would seize five bridges along the main north south highway ending at the city of Arnhem. They were to hold the bridges at all costs for the Garden portion of the operation, which consisted of a heavy armored column racing north to break through German defenses. The main American targets were the bridges over the Wilhelmina Canal near Zon and the Willems Canal near Veghel.

Allied intelligence estimated there were just small German garrisons in both towns that could be easily overcome. Capturing these two bridges was an intricate part of a much larger plan the men were not aware of. If all went as planned, this attack would give the allies a back door to the heavy industrial Ruhr Valley of Germany. The problem was every ground maneuver; every jump had to take place on a precise schedule.

Every man studied sand tables of the areas that were updated daily from aircraft photo reconnaissance. It gave them a good idea of what the terrain was like where they were to land, and types of obstacles German engineers had placed near the bridges.

The attack was set for the morning of September seventeenth.

Dawn was still hours away as C-47 Dakotas loaded with paratroopers lifted off from runways in England. Steve had memories of June sixth raging in his mind. He remembered the deadly flak, exploding planes, screaming injured men and being hopelessly lost in Normandy. He prayed hard that this mission would not end up the same way.

Captain Wesco sitting across the aisle from Steve pulled back his sleeve examining his watch for a moment. "About ten minutes Kenrude." he yelled out above the drone of the aircraft.

Steve nodded looking toward Harry who was seated next to him. "Well I think we did our best with them. We'll know shortly."

"They'll do well, Steve. They're a good bunch." He responded. After looking around the aircraft at their nervous men he yelled out. "Get ready. About eight minutes to drop." There were some light flak bursts as the flight of C-47's closed in on the landing zones. It was not as heavy or as accurate at it was on D-Day when they approached Normandy.

A few minutes later the jumpmaster pulled the door open as he called out. "Stand up, hook up!"

The men stood up attaching their static lines to a cable running the length of the aircraft.

"Everyone check the man in front of you. Make sure everything is the way it is supposed to be."

Steve called out over the roar of engines and rushing wind. He was well aware the men knew the procedures they were to follow, but he felt better reminding them one last time. He could sense the nervousness among the men waiting to make their first combat jump. It was easy to understand their frame of mind. He also knew the veterans wanted to get out of that huge floating target and return to solid ground. Smiling lightly he knew each man in his platoon would do their jobs.

The green light popped on over the door a second later. "Go, go." The jumpmaster yelled as he literally shoved the first man in line out the door.

Without hesitation the rest of the men approached the door jumping into the early morning sky.

When Steve's chute opened he could see the second bridge and the town of Veghel. There was some light small arms fire coming up at them from surprised German defenders. Although this was a dangerous mission, Steve couldn't help smiling a little knowing they were on target, and the German defenders were totally caught off guard. Hitting the ground Steve lost his footing. He dropped to the ground rolling across the wet grass once before regaining his feet. Immediately he removed his harness, raised his left arm skyward and began yelling, "Assemble on me. Quickly let's get moving."

He could hear firing coming from the bridge between defenders and paratroopers who landed to close.

Harry landed about thirty yards from Steve. He came running from his right with a large group of men. "Looks good, Stevie boy, looks real good, we better move fast to help out our guys."

Steve nodded in agreement as he stared at the assembled force. "Let's go. Move out." He yelled as they began a moderate run toward the bridge.

Sporadic fire was coming from the canal bank near the bridge, as a heavy German M.G. machine gun hammered away south of them toward Zon.

"Harry, take two squads along the tree line. Squads three and four follow me. Move out."

Steve directed as they moved in on their target.

German resistance around the bridge faded fast, as they were totally overwhelmed by well prepared paratroopers. Within twenty minutes of landing the bridge was secured.

Steve assembled the squad leaders on the north end of the bridge, "What's your status?"

"First squad all accounted for no casualties, Sarg." Corporal Crawford reported.

"Second squad accounted for. I have two men with minor wounds. Both can stay in the fight, Steve." Corporal Greenburg stated with a smile.

"Third Squad all accounted for. One man hit pretty bad, Sarg. I don't think he's going to make it.

A medic is with him right now." Corporal Fineday reported placing a fresh magazine into his Thompson.

"Fourth squad all accounted for, Steve. One man dead one wounded slightly but he can fight. He's sitting with the medics over by the trees getting bandaged." Corporal Cummings reported as he removed his canteen from his belt.

"That's good. Good job men. Fineday take your squad, patrol out to the north about two hundred yards toward Veghel. Stays lose don't get engaged in any heavy fighting for now. Back out if the need occurs. Harry, take squads two and four. Assemble near the trees be ready to move out for Zon if the need arises. Crawford, hold this damn bridge until the convoy arrives." Steve directed his squad leaders as he observed Captain Wesco approaching the bridge with a company of men behind him.

"All right, All right, Great job." The Captain stated pulling a map from his pocket. He studied it quickly before placing it back inside.

Sergeant, Clarkson assembled the rest of Charlie Company by Kenrude's men. "Dog Company will hold this bridge until British 30th Corps arrives. Kenrude get your men together and follow us. Both A and B Companies should be ahead of us. We should link up with them down the road. Let's move, Kenrude your platoon out front." Captain Wesco directed as he scanned the area ahead.

Steve signaled Harry to join them on the road. "Send a runner to get Fineday back here on the double. Squad two I want you on point, but I want Franny, Brant, Woodward and Eddington in the lead. I want those BAR's out front and ready for action."

Franny smiled, "At your service, Sarg, just like old times."

After the four men took off Corporal Greenburg directed his squad to follow at a short distance. The balance of Charlie Company followed in two columns north toward Zon. Captain Wesco was walking with Steve and Sergeant Abrahms from first platoon with the radio operator to his right.

"Captain," The radio operator called out handing over the receiver.

Captain Wesco took the receiver. "This is blue dog, over." He was silent for a few seconds before calling out, "Damn it, Son-of-a-bitch!" He handed the receiver back to his radio operator. "The damn Krauts blew the bridge at Zon." He looked at his radio operator yelling, "Get me battalion on that damn thing fast."

When Major Fontaine came on the radio Captain Wesco informed him of the situation. Finishing his conversation he turned to look behind the company.

"Major is calling for engineers with bridging equipment. God only knows how far back south they are toward Eindhoven. Word is that big armored column that was supposed to rule the day is tangled up in the rear. We may be in for a long damn day. All we can do now is take up positions near the bridge and prepare for counter attacks."

As the paratroopers continued moving north toward the blown bridge, British fighter aircraft roared overhead firing their machine guns at German targets where ever they appeared.

Shaking his head Captain Wesco stated loudly, "Well at least we can count on the British Air Force to do their part to keep this operation rolling. We should have known Montgomery couldn't fight his way out of a damn wet paper bag." Everyone hearing him busted out laughing.

Both A and B companies were digging in along the canal bank when Charlie Company arrived. There was no enemy fire coming from the opposite bank as British fighter pilots were seeing to that. Captain Wesco went ahead to talk with the commanders from A and B companies. When he returned he called the platoon Sergeants together.

"Charlie Company will dig in to the left of A Company. When Easy Company gets here they'll dig in to our rear as a reserve unit. They can move forward to cover any company requiring help. Dog Company will have to stay on the bridge at Veghel for the time being. Once the engineers arrive and have a bridge up, we'll move to the city of Einhoven and secure it. Questions?" The Captain inquired looking over his men.

As no one had questions the platoon Sergeants moved out to get their men dug in along the canal.

It was apparent operations command was highly upset about the delay in getting the bridging equipment up to where it was needed.

By late afternoon trucks filled with heavy equipment began moving up to the battered bridge. They carried all the material engineers would need to construct a pontoon bridge. During the night small German units attempted probing attacks from the north. Each time they probed, forward observers called in coordinates to mortar teams. After a heavy barrage the enemy units either retreated or were destroyed.

Prior to dawn Captain Wesco assembled his platoon Sergeants once again. "Get your men ready.

At 0630 A-Company will start across followed by B-Company and then Easy Company. We will bring up the rear.

A heavy artillery barrage will commence at 0600 and continue until we are across the bridge and ready to move.

What ever the artillery does not destroy we'll eliminate and then move on into Einhoven. That's it gentlemen. Good luck."

Exactly at 0600 a heavy barrage of artillery and mortars began raining down on German positions between the river and Einhoven. The ground and air shook as tons of high explosives crashed to the ground.

Exactly at 0630 A-Company began their dash across the pontoon bridge, followed in turn by the other companies as spelled out in the briefing. When Charlie Company arrived at the bridge Steve led second platoon across assembling the men where Sergeant Clarkson directed him.

Fighter aircraft once more streaked overhead providing much appreciated support for the paratroopers. The battalion began moving toward Einhoven at a brisk pace. There was some light resistance along the way that was easily overwhelmed and destroyed, either by paratroopers, artillery or fighter aircraft.

Entering Einhoven, German infantry put up slight resistance as coordinated mortar and artillery fire took a devastating toll on their forces. They barely secured the city when the British Guards Armored Division, the vanguard of General Horrock's 30th Corp rolled up the road from the south, finally linking up with them. The armored spearhead passed through Einhoven on their way to secure the Wilhelmina Canal Bridge near Zon.

With Einhoven secured Captain Wesco arrived in the Charlie Company area. He walked to each Platoon congratulating the men for an outstanding job. Later he took all the platoon Sergeants into a garage where he set up his headquarters.

Placing a map on a make shift table he reported. "The Germans near Zon have been counter attacking all day on our flank and into our rear areas. We need to push them back and form a defensive line. It is imperative this road stay open with every vehicle getting north."

He pointed with a stick at his map. "We'll push the Krauts back out of Zon and then hold our positions. The defensive line will connect Zon, Einhoven, and St. Odenrode then over to Veghel, which is still held by the Krauts. We jump off at 0600 in the morning. Alpha and Charlie Companies will lead. Bravo and Easy Companies along with first battalion will stretch out the line. I'm hoping to get Dog Company back sometime tomorrow. We'll hold them in reserve. Any questions,"

Sgt. Abrahms from first platoon raised his hand. "Sir once we push the Krauts back how long do we hold the line?"

"That's a good question, Sergeant. I don't know yet. I suspect a short while. Once I hear I'll pass the word on. If there are no more questions get some sleep, something to eat, and have your men ready in the morning. We assemble the company near the church at 0530." Captain Wesco directed as he folded up the large map placing it back into his waterproof case.

Steve and Harry walked back to the small storage building where second platoon was waiting. They laid out the plan for morning encouraging their men to get some sleep.

Franny came over to Steve after they finished their explanation. "Do you think there'll be heavy fighting, Steve?"

"I don't' know, Franny. We don't know what we're up against just yet. I suspect the Germans are not too happy with us cutting through the middle of Holland. They certainly will try to break our line of communication and destroy what ever they can on the highway. I figure we'll hit them pretty hard and they will fall back into prepared defensive positions. Maybe there'll be just marauding infantry units cut off from their command by our attack. No one knows." Steve explained as he opened a can or rations. "Why what's up, Franny?" Harry inquired.

"Well it's all kind of strange. We jump in here on top of them and they don't come out and fight, it feels kind of funny. Not something we're used to with the Krauts. Know what I mean?" He replied.

"Yeah that makes good sense, Franny. But no one seems to know right now what the score is. Some rumors state a good part of the Kraut forces here in Holland packed up and left a few weeks ago.

Another rumor I heard says they got rid of all the dead weight they were carrying, before pulling back the tough units to regroup.

Guess we'll see what happens in the next few days. Go get some sleep and have that BAR ready in the morning." Harry said smiling. At 0530 the company assembled by the church. Major Fontaine was there with Captain Wesco and several other officers. When they finished conferring Major Fontaine signaled for Alpha Company to begin moving out. Captain Wesco directed Charlie Company to move out following Alpha toward the assault on Zon.

German mortar and artillery began dropping shells around the approaching paratroopers. American artillery and mortars answered the call with their projectiles in a deadly dual.

There was a large wooded area in the Charlie Company sector just over a small rise.

The men formed a skirmish line along the top of the rise then awaited orders. Steve looked into the woods with his binoculars as Sergeant Abrahms came over and lay down beside him.

"What do you think, Kenrude?" He inquired nervously. "Nothing has seemed right since we arrived."

Steve looked over at Sgt. Abrahms. "Yeah I know what you mean. We discussed it for a while last night. But as far as the woods go we don't have much choice. We're going to have to clear it. I suspect they have at least one damn M.G. set up waiting for us. If we move over this rise they'll cut us to ribbons before we can get down that hill. We need mortar fire on them before we move and covering fire from third platoon machine guns as we head out." Steve replied sounding like he was a long time expert in warfare.

Harry peered over coordinates he had written on their map that morning. He called over one of the men from first squad. "Take this back to the radio team. Have them call for mortar fire on the circled coordinates to begin in about....How does fifteen minutes sound, Steve?"

Both Steve and Sergeant Abrams agreed as they watched the tree line for any signs of enemy movement.

"Alright," Harry responded as he turned back to his runner. "Fifteen minutes no more, no less, got that!"

The soldier shook his head in agreement before dashing off.

"I'll have Sergeant Bellows over in third platoon ready to fire when we move out." Sergeant Abrams stated before he took off down the line.

Steve and Harry kept an eye on their watches. Right on the money, a heavy barrage of mortar fire began falling into the wooded area. Third platoon opened up with their machine guns spraying the woods with deadly projectiles.

When the barrage lifted the men immediately jumped up charging forward toward the German position.

Amazingly a significant amount of small arms fire erupted from every large tree, log, or pile of brush. First platoon reached the edge of the woods first. They began laboriously working their way forward. Second platoon strung out to the right, stopped when they reached the tree line.

"Grenades," Steve yelled.

The men pitched grenades into the underbrush then ducked back down before they exploded.

"Let's go!" Harry yelled out signaling the men to begin their assault.

Slowly the company began moving into the heavy underbrush. There were mangled bodies of dead

Germans everywhere, the mortars and machine guns had been very effective. But now it was time to hunt out each remaining German defender and kill them. Small battles were taking place in many areas as pockets of resistance were pain stakingly eliminated.

All of a sudden a German heavy M.G. machine gun began firing. There were several screams as the patient gunner found his targets.

"Where is that damn thing?" Harry yelled.

Jake Crawford yelled back. "It looks like a heavy emplacement to my right. I can see several logs horizontal across the ground. They're stacked about three high."

"Yeah, Yeah I see it." Harry yelled out. "Eddington to your right about ten yards give them some BAR fire."

Max and Franny began spraying rounds into the log emplacement. Several men tossed grenades that either missed their target or bounced back off the logs.

Two men from fourth squad charged forward after the grenades exploded. They were instantly cut down by the German machine gunner.

"Wish we had a damn bazooka right about now." Harry yelled as several machine gun rounds struck the tree above him.

Several more grenades were tossed at the position. One of them exploded on the make shift roof of the bunker. The machine gun stopped firing. Max jumped up rushing forward toward the fortified enemy position.

"Iowa, what the hell are you doing?" Steve screamed as the M.G. commenced firing. Max jumped into a pile of brush just to the left of the emplacement. He rolled over pointing his BAR in the direction of the enemy gun.

"I don't think they saw him.' Franny exclaimed, "Doesn't look like he was hit. He's crawling toward them."

A German soldier stood near the door of the bunker preparing to toss a grenade in the direction of Max, but was cut down by fire from the entire American line. The grenade fell just outside the log emplacement where it detonated.

As soon as the grenade exploded, Max jumped up running the last few yards toward the German position. He tossed a grenade into the deep pit before dropping to the ground. This time the M.G. stopped permanently. Max jumped up firing a quick burst from his weapon into the flaming gun pit.

The rest of the men resumed moving forward. Franny ran past the now destroyed emplacement spraying his BAR into the underbrush.

Steve approached Max who was sitting on the ground by the pit as the battle moved on beyond him.

"You Okay, Eddington?" Steve inquired observing Max's trembling hands.

"Yeah Sarg, I'm fine." Max replied looking up toward Steve brushing dirt from his face. "That was a hell of a stunt, Iowa. You lucked out this time. I would be careful about doing that too much. But you did a hell of a job, Eddington." Steve complimented rapping the top of Max's helmet with his knuckles. He made a mental note to place Max in for an accommodation for his actions when they returned to base.

Remnants of the German resistance were now in full retreat toward Zon. Some of the retreating forces were caught in a murderous cross fire between advancing Americans and German defenders inside Zon.

In order to save themselves, some of the retreating Germans attempted to turn back toward the safety of the tree line. However that too became a death trap, as advancing paratroopers realized the woods was clear all the way to the edge of town. Any enemy soldier attempting to take shelter in the tree line was instantly wiped out by small arms fire.

As the fighting ended, everyone held their positions inside the tree line until receiving further orders.

Harry began working up a casualty list from their squad leaders as Steve adjusted the platoon's defensive position.

Arriving at first squad's position he sought out Cpl. Crawford. "Send one of your men back to see if he can contact anyone from headquarters. Give them our position and find out what they want us to do next." Steve whispered as he watched for a German counter attack.

Harry came looking for Steve with an update on casualties. "Steve, Fourth squad two dead one wounded. Third squad one dead four wounded only one seriously. Second squad two dead no wounded. First squad one dead two wounded."

"Damn!" Steve replied. That was too many for this operation, are medics taking care of them?" Steve inquired.

"Yeah, now that the firing stopped the walking wounded are making their way back on their own."

Harry replied pulling his canteen out.

Corporal Crawford's man arrived back sooner than they expected. He knelt down by Steve and Harry. "We are to dig in across our positions and hold this line until further notice." The young private reported trying to catch his breath.

"Okay. Let's pass the word to the company." Steve ordered as he signaling for Sergeant Abrahms to come over.

"What's up, Kenrude? Got word from the old man on what he wants us to do?" Abrahms inquired.

"Yes, we are to dig in along this line and hold until further notice. Looks like it could rain so we might want to get dug in quick and get some ponchos over our holes for protection. Steve explained to the first platoon sergeant.

"Dig in! Hell Zon is mostly deserted. I think we could take it by nightfall if we plan our attack right.

"What do you think, Kenrude? It would be a lot warmer and dryer occupying those buildings instead of sitting here in muddy fox holes all night long." Abrahms replied impatiently.

"Are you crazy?" Harry blurted out. "We got orders to stay put from the old man. Have you lost your mind?"

Abrahms glared at Harry, "Well I think we can do it if we try. Besides, I think headquarters would be damn happy if we showed some initiative for once and just took it."

"How many dead you got right now?" Steve inquired.

"Ten dead about a half dozen slightly wounded." Abrahms replied almost sarcastically. "How many more do you want dead by nightfall? Get your head together Abrahms, and tell your men to dig in, damn it." Steve replied angrily.

"And what the hell do you mean by show some initiative for a change?" Harry questioned Sgt. Abrahms.

After glaring at Harry for a moment Abrahms went back to first platoon, passing along orders to dig in and be prepared for a counter attack.

During the night German snipers fired random shots into American positions without hitting anyone. But it kept the paratroopers awake, making for a long, cold, nerve wracking, wet night.

On the morning of the twentieth German mortar rounds began raining down on the American positions for nearly fifteen minutes. As soon as the barrage lifted German infantry from inside Zon began a counter attack toward the woods. A light machine gun had been placed in a window over night that helped cover the attack. The paratroopers fiercely repelled the assault with everything they had including hand to hand combat.

A forward observer for the American artillery also moved up, spending most of the night about fifteen feet off the ground in a large crook of a tree.

As the attack began, he immediately called in the coordinates for the building with the machine gun. He continued calling out additional firing assignments to help repel the attack. The first rounds fell in front of Zon right in the midst of the charging German infantry. The third round landed directly on the roof of the building containing the machine gun silencing the weapon. Artillery batteries kept up their barrage for about five minutes, laying waste to a good part of Zon and the German defenders within. The counter attack ended abruptly, as artillery and small arms fire from the well dug in paratroopers made the area between Zon and the woods a death trap.

As the attack faded out, only an occasional sniper round was fired at the dug in paratroopers. Rain began falling about midday continuing through out the long night. Although everyone used ponchos, shelter halves and tree boughs to water proof their fox holes, the steady rain found its way in. By morning most men had nearly six inches of water and mud in their holes. Sitting or lying down was simply out of the question.

September twenty first a large American attack toward the town of Schijndel jumped off by units of the 506th parachute infantry regiment. The battle lasted through the twenty first and well into the twenty second, forcing the Germans to fall back from their positions in Veghel and Zon.

The men of Charlie Company were finally able to occupy buildings in and around Zon that were still habitable after the enemy pulled out. It took days to dry out all their equipment and wet clothing. Second battalion was assigned the task of holding Zon and patrolling areas to the east of town. The fall weather became increasingly wet and cold. In order to stay warm men collected kindling from destroyed buildings or broke up anything wood to burn in stoves or open fires. With little to do, and the German Army no longer an immediate threat, the men wrote letters, played cards, and read whatever they could get their hands on. Replacements arrived from the repo-depots in France to fill in some of the vacancies left by dead or wounded paratroopers.

On the rainy morning of November twenty-eighth Captain Wesco called a meeting of his platoon Sergeants. Steve and Harry pulled their ponchos over their heads and walked the short distance to the Command Post. When all the platoon leaders arrived Captain Wesco came from a back room with Sergeant Clarkson. He looked over the dirty, unshaven, cold men and felt nothing but pride for them.

"I called you men here for some good news. We are to pack up and be ready to move out around 1200. Our replacements are here and will take over the positions. So go get your men ready.

Once the trucks have unloaded all the supplies and equipment for our replacements, we'll board them for the ride out of here, any questions or problems?"

Steve raised his hand about the same time everyone else did.

"Well, Kenrude you beat the others by a second so what's your question?" Captain Wesco inquired.

"Where are we going, sir? It would be nice to give the men some sort of an idea where we're headed." Steve inquired.

"That's a very good question. Actually I should have told you outright. We're headed to France for a rest, refit and training, exactly where I do not know right now. Also, I don't know if Allied Command has another mission in store for us at this time. However I can tell you we're being placed in reserve for the time being." Now you know as much as we do.

Any more questions," Captain Wesco asked. Every one stood quiet but happy.

Arriving back with his men Steve laid out the plan. A cheer went up as the men immediately put together the meager belongings they had with them.

About 1200 Charlie Company made their way through the rain and muddy roads to the waiting trucks. Although the ride was cold, everyone knew warm dry tents, hot food and clean clothes awaited them in France.

The rehabilitation camp was located near the town of Vire at the base of the Cherbourg peninsula.

Who ever designed this camp must have set up the base at Newbury, as they were both nearly identical. The men immediately went to work setting up teams for intercompany base ball games and many other activities. It was evident the men had lots of steam to blow off after two long hard months in Holland.

Steve and Harry looked over the new replacements they were getting from the Repo-depo. They were excited to see Josh McGruder returning from the hospital. Also on the list were Andy Jameson and Oscar McBride. They both were seriously injured in England prior to D-Day. It was good to have the three men back in the platoon.

One of Steve's first jobs was to write an accommodation for Max Eddington's bravery in taking out the pill box in Holland, he recommended him for the bronze star. After reading the citation Major Fontaine signed off on it immediately. He then instructed Steve to recommend the bronze star for Harry, Franny, Phil Brant, Larry Woodward and Mike Anderson for their actions during D-Day operations. Harry was also to be awarded the Purple Heart for the injury to his arm.

One of the biggest problems they had to contend with was the constant rumors and scuttlebutt. The paratrooper's moral rose and fell as each new rumor raced through the camp. Especially when a rumor was given credence by someone considered privy to that type of information. The rumors covered every subject including heading back to the states, to being transferred to the Pacific for some special secret mission.

Nevertheless, the men were excited about receiving regular mail deliveries and packages from home. They also enjoyed having a roof over their heads along with hot food, hot showers, clean clothes and weekly movies. Watching movies was great therapy, as the men were able to laugh and watch Hollywood's hottest divas strut their stuff on the big screen. On several occasions the men were given passes to Cherbourg. Although a good part of the city was still in ruins, it was still a place for the men to go on leave. At least the men were able to get out, have a drink, talk to a pretty girl and have a good time. As always sleep was a big item occupying everyone's spare time. Every paratrooper was pretty worn out from the cold, wet conditions they had been living in.

Nearly every day some one asked the proverbial question as to when they were going to be called back into action, or if they were just going to finish up the war where they were. The platoon leaders continued giving the same responses. "No one knows but Allied Command and they aren't saying anything."

Of course everyone enjoyed following the progress of General George Patton. They cheered every time he won another battle or raced over another large section of France. The German border was quickly coming into view. Slowly they were finally closing in on the Third Reich. Many men felt another huge campaign for airborne troops would most likely never happen, as Germany appeared close to collapse.

Conversely, no one could have guessed what the German High Command was planning for mid December. All across Europe the weather was colder than normal. Belgium was experiencing the harshest winter in forty years. Snow in the Ardennes Forest was being measured in feet, as strong, bitterly cold winds blew the light snow into massive drifts. Temperatures dropped down well below freezing creating deadly wind chills.

December sixteenth began like any other day in the rest camp, a good hot breakfast, followed by some type of training. But as the day progressed, a new rumor raced through the camp at lightening speed. Stories abounded of a massive German offensive some where in Belgium. Scuttlebutt was that entire American units were being over run or destroyed before they could react. Complete units were in wholesale retreat.

Many men were throwing their equipment away so they could move faster. Not very many men completely believed what they heard. Especially when it was rumored the massive armored column was heading for Antwerp, in an attempt to divide the allied armies. This rumor was just too unbelievable. Most men felt scuttlebutt was proving to be way off base. Even at Allied Headquarters in Verdun, it was nearly impossible to piece together what was actually happening.

Confusion and lack of communication equipment were causing horrible losses at the front. There were many individual efforts, or small group actions that were hampering the mighty German Panzers but it was not enough.

By midday calls from Allied Command began reaching reserve units in France. They were ordered to the front immediately. Cooks, supply workers, and clerks were rousted from their jobs. Anyone who could carry a gun was needed to stem the tide of this German onslaught. Most of the units were poorly equipped to fight a battle in the frozen snow covered forests. There was little or no winter clothing to issue the fighting men as they prepared to move out. Winter boots necessary to protect men's feet from trench foot were no where to be found. All spare winter clothing was sitting in warehouses in England. Most of the men preparing to move into the harsh winter battle left camp wearing summer uniforms. But that was not the worst of it. Spare weapons and ammunition were in short supply. Some replacements arriving from the repo-depot had not been assigned a weapon since arriving. Their first opportunity to obtain any type of weapon was when they arrived at the front. Retreating soldiers were glad to hand over their weapons and ammunition to anyone crazy enough to fight the German onslaught.

As the 101st airborne was considered to be a tough elite fighting force, they were one of the first units to assemble and leave for Belgium.

Morning of the seventeenth the 502nd moved from Vire to the new front that was changing by the hour, as German units roamed nearly at will.

The 101st crossed into Belgium on the eighteenth moving north at full speed. As paratroopers reached the front, they were immediately sent to the Belgium town of Bastogne. This was a key transportation hub where five major roads converged at one point. The Germans desperately needed these roads to effectively continue their assault. The order to the men of the 101st was to hold Bastogne at all costs. If it fell, certainly Antwerp would easily be reached by rapidly moving German armor.

The well disciplined paratroopers were shocked by the long columns of retreating infantry taking every piece of equipment with them. Officers tried to convince the retreating hordes to turn back and fight with them. Nevertheless, they kept pushing south as fast as they could go.

As the trucks rolled into Bastogne a defensive plan was already being set into motion by their commanders. It wasn't massive and it wasn't multi layered. It wasn't much more than a reinforced skirmish line. Second battalion was sent to the north of Bastogne to cover the highway leading north toward Houffalize. Major Fontaine met with his Company Commanders as soon as the trucks were unloaded. He discussed placement of their companies to ensure the defensive line was covered to the best of their ability. Charlie Company was ordered to dig in on the west side of the all important highway. Captain Wesco went with his platoon Sergeants pointing out the best defensive positions, then marking them on his map. Steve and Harry went from squad to squad instilling in their men the importance of getting their holes as deep as possible, then camouflaging them with tree branches. This was no simple task as the ground was completely frozen. Many men chose to dig long flat trenches where they could lie down and fight so they did not have to dig as deep. In too many cases this turned out to be a bad decision. When the German's began throwing huge artillery barrages at them, they could not curl up down in a deeper hole for protection. Neither did the long flat holes offer as much protection from the elements. Soon everyone was digging deeper holes for their own protection.

Sergeant Clarkson made sure the platoon leaders did not dig a hole together. He hoped if one platoon leader was killed, the other man would be ready to take command on his own. That night the first of many German attacks moved down the road toward Bastogne. The forward observer dug in with Charlie Company, called in the coordinates for an artillery strike on the enemy force. Shells rained down right on target striking several vehicles setting them a blaze. It was evident the German were not willing to drive forward in the dark through such a massive artillery barrage. They quickly turned around making a hasty retreat. The night continued to be unnerving for the men. They could hear German tanks and trucks moving about the dark forest. On and off through out the night, German soldiers would yell and scream, or fire random shots to keep the Americans on their toes. It was a long sleepless night.

When dawn broke over the frozen battle ground Steve and Harry walked the platoon to make sure all the men were in good shape. They ordered several men to add to or rebuild their fortifications.

Suddenly the air was alive with screams of incoming artillery shells.

"Incoming!" Steve yelled as he dove for the nearest foxhole.

German eighty-eight shells rained down on their position for nearly a half-hour. A good percentage of the incoming rounds struck treetops creating air bursts. These explosions sent a deadly combination of steel, heavy tree limbs and sharp splinters down on the semi-exposed paratroopers.

Once the barrage lifted Steve crawled out of the hole he was in. He thanked the two men who dug the big hole for allowing him to share it with them. Harry came out of a hole several yards away shaking his head.

"Man that was just plain tough, Steve, I didn't think it would ever end."

Cautiously more men exited their shallow bunkers. They were all discussing the massive bombardment when the next barrage came screaming in. By now Steve was close enough to the hole he dug with Karl Drussing. He dove inside from the left as Karl dove in from the right. They both screamed out as they slammed their helmets together.

This barrage was not localized as the first one was. It rained down all along the Battalion line. Some men not affected by the first attack had wandered to far away from their holes. Luckily only one man was killed but five were seriously wounded. Everyone learned quickly not to stroll to far from their holes when a barrage lifted. Enemy artillery officers counted on the replacements to feel a need to stretch their legs after being cramped up in their holes. After finishing a barrage they would wait a few minutes before sending another salvo hoping to catch them in the open.

Night barrages were the worst. The enemy would rain down high explosives for an hour or more following up with infantry probing raids. It was impossible for the men to sleep or even rest.

Word came down the line on the twentieth that Bastogne was now completely surrounded by S.S armored units. All forms of resupply for the entrapped paratroopers were now cut off.

It now became a test of wills between the two armies. The outlook for the cold paratroopers was anything but stellar. They had no heat, no warm food or clothing, dwindling supplies, and their best friend was a frozen hole in the ground. Making matters worse, their numbers dwindled every day as men were killed or seriously wounded by the continual artillery and mortar barrages. If they lost this test of wills against the Germans their chances were not much better. They would either be marched off to harsh prisoner of war camps or be shot. Rumors were already flying about American prisoners being slaughtered by S.S. units in a field near a town called Malmedy. All the platoon leaders worked incessantly trying to keep their men poised for the next attack, while down playing the numbing cold that was beginning to take a toll on their abilities and spirits.

There were already too many cases of frostbite and trench foot. Morale dropped further as rations were cut in half. Food was beginning to run scarce.

Ammunition and hand grenade shortages were also becoming a reality.

BAR operators were told to fire short bursts and to verify their target before shooting. During the late night hours of December twentieth a German S.S. unit wearing white coveralls attacked in force along the Charlie Company line. Their assault was preceded by a heavy artillery and mortar barrage that lasted the best part of an hour. Franny was the first to see several figures moving toward their location. He opened fire with his BAR cutting down two of the attackers. Amazingly it appeared as if the entire field across the road rose up. Hundreds of German infantry clad in white, stormed across the road firing as they charged through the deep snow.

The men of Charlie Company opened fire with everything they had available. A machine gun from third platoon was situated perfectly allowing it to participate in the battle. Above the terrible roar of battle, screams of dying and wounded men could be heard from both sides of the fight. Five battle hardened S.S. soldiers breached the line, after wiping out several fox holes killing the American defenders. They attempted to roam from fox hole to fox hole shooting at the occupants. After bloody hand to hand combat all five were eventually killed.

These well-trained S.S. infantry arrived with a plan. The first wave was to destroy Charlie Companies portion of the perimeter. That would open up a gap large enough to allow a second line to drive straight for Bastogne. Once the second assault moved past the trenches, tanks would roll up and down the defensive line crushing any resistance from the battalion.

As the fighting intensified Steve grabbed the forward observer yelling. "Call it in damn it, Call it in on our position or we'll all be killed."

The observer looked at Steve replying, "What do you want, Sergeant?"

Steve grabbed the hand set from the shaking radio operator calling back to the artillery officer. "This is Kenrude, Charlie Company, Second battalion. Drop anything you have on our position or we're through and drop it now! From the road to the tree line let it go! Be quick about it or we loose this entire sector!" He threw the hand set at the scared private before running toward his hole as the barrage began to fall.

Artillery and mortars began firing almost immediately. Their first rounds landed between the road and the dug in paratroopers, right in the middle of the advancing enemy force. They were caught in the open with Charlie Company pouring fire on them from the wood line. The well planned attack suddenly turned into disarray.

Some SS infantry attempted to retreat back across the road to safety. Others continued charging forward into the teeth of the American fire, still intent on breaching the defensive line. After about a ten minute barrage the American artillery attack ended, leaving numerous white clad attackers near the American pits.

Attempting to finish off the last attackers Sergeant Clarkson helped cover the line near Max Eddington with several other second platoon men. Max stood up firing point blank at a group of charging S.S.

"Get down, damn it get down!" Sergeant Clarkson screamed at Max as he fired his BAR at the onrushing Germans. Ignoring the directive Max kept firing from his standing position. A bright flash was followed by a spray of hot metal as a German grenade exploded a few feet in front of Max. The feisty Iowan flew back several feet still firing before falling to the ground mortally wounded.

Harry was just coming to the aid of the men when he saw Max get hit by the exploding grenade.

"You son of a bitches," Harry screamed as he ran forward firing his Thompson. He continued firing until the bolt slammed shut against an empty chamber. He tossed the smoking weapon to the ground picking up Max's BAR, just as Sergeant Clarkson took a fatal hit to his face falling backwards.

Harry charged over the top of the log and dirt emplacement firing the BAR in short bursts at the attacking S.S. Infantry. In seconds only one German was left alive. He spun around attempting to avoid the deadly BAR. Angrily Harry pulled the trigger one more time but the weapon failed to fire. He was out of ammunition. Instinctively the German attempted to bring his machine gun up to fire at Harry who was charging toward him with the empty weapon. Spinning the empty weapon around Harry used the heavy stock of the BAR as a club. He struck the S.S. soldier across the right arm snapping his wrist. The man yelled in pain dropping his machine gun. Harry raised the empty weapon into the air swinging it downward striking the injured man in the chest. The enemy soldier struggled on his feet for a second before falling to his knees. Throwing the BAR away, Harry pulled his bayonet from its scabbard. Grabbing the man around the head with his left arm Harry plunged the bayonet into his throat three times. As Harry let go of the dead soldier, he fell backwards turning the snow where he laid crimson red.

Immediately Harry scooped up the empty BAR and his Thompson, as he ran back toward the safety of the perimeter. Jumping over the log emplacement he observed Steve and a medic kneeling beside Max.

The medic was working feverishly while muttering something Harry could not understand. But he knew it wasn't good. Kneeling down he looked at Max. "You hang in there Iowa. We can't afford to lose a good man like you."

Trying hard to force a smile Max responded. "When you see General Patton, you tell him Max Eddington did his best and wasn't afraid to die. You tell him. You tell him that."

Steve looked down at the dying man. "You can tell him yourself when you see him, Iowa."

Max smiled slightly then gasped for air once more before he died.

"Damn it! Damn it to hell!" The medic yelled as he watched Max pass away. "There was so much damage, Sarg. There was nothing I could do." The medic reported as he stared at Steve. "I know." Steve said nodding his head. "You did your best, that's all you could do." Harry stood up. He looked at Max for a moment before walking over to Sergeant Clarkson's body.

"He's had it, Sarg" The medic said observing Harry roll the body over.

"Yeah, I know." Harry replied. "Do you have a jeep back on the road we can load these guys on so we can get them out of here?"

"Sure do. We have a small wooden trailer behind it that will work fine." The medic replied as he finished putting his medical kit back together."

Several volunteers loaded Max, Sergeant Clarkson and several other bodies on the make shift trailer.

They all stood quietly as they watched the medic drive slowly towards Bastogne.

Dawn was a welcome relief along the small defensive line. Everyone took time to rearrange their fox holes after the long night of fighting. Platoon leaders reassigned men along the line, filling in holes left by the dead and wounded.

German pressure continued on all sides of the encircled Americans at Bastogne. On December twenty-first everyone's moral was greatly enhanced, as cargo planes dropped large quantities of supplies inside the tenuous perimeter. Promptly ammunition, rations, medical supplies and a smattering of winter clothing was handed out to the worn out paratroopers.

The next morning General von Luttwitz, Commander of the German forces sent a message to General McAuliffe, commander of the 101st asking him to surrender his forces to save their lives. General McAuliffe replied with a one-word response to the enemies' request. On a large envelope he wrote the word, "NUTS."

The story spread like wild fire through out the 101st, emboldening the men to resist and fight even harder then they already had.

Several times during the day Franny stood on top of a log emplacement yelling out toward the German perimeter. "NUTS! Did you get that? Nuts, to you sons a bitches!" By the twenty-fourth half the city of Bastogne lay in complete ruins as casualties mounted daily.

German artillery and mortars continued pounding around the clock attempting to break the paratroopers will to hold and force a surrender of the vital transportation hub.

Nevertheless, every enemy assault on the perimeter was repulsed by heavy fighting, denying the battle hardened S.S. units access to the important roads they desperately needed.

On Christmas Eve Oscar McBride was struck by a sniper as he helped Steve repair one of their pits damaged in the last artillery attack. A nearby medic rushed to Oscar's side. Looking up at Steve the medic shook his head. "It' bad he needs a doctor quick." Steve and Brant helped slip him onto a stretcher, than carried him to a waiting Jeep. Just as the driver was to take off Oscar raised his hand. "Kenrude stay with me." Captain Wasco who was near by heard the request.

"Go ahead Kenrude. A few hours away from the line would do you good. Jensen can handle it."

Steve jumped into the Jeep for the short ride to Bastogne. The driver stopped near what was left of a stone church. Several corpsmen came running over grabbing Oscar's stretcher. They took him down into the church basement where a make shift hospital had been set up. One of the doctors directed the corpsmen over to his table. Immediately the skilled surgeon went to work. It was clear to Steve the surgeon was fighting a losing battle. Ten minutes later the doctor stood back, motioning the waiting corpsman to remove Oscar's lifeless body from the surgical table.

Shaking his head Steve turned to go. The medic who treated Oscar grabbed him by the arm. "Hey Kenrude, why don't you hang tight here a while, It's warm and you can get a little grub and some hot coffee. Besides, I'm not ready to head back yet. I need to get supplies." "Alright, grab me when you're ready." Steve replied removing his helmet.

After pouring a cup of hot coffee he walked farther into the basement. Cots filled with wounded men lined the walls. One man called out to Steve. "Hey, sergeant, is that really hot coffee?"

"Yeah it is." Steve responded.

"Man that would taste great right about now. Can you get me a cup?"

Smiling Steve responded, "Heck you can have this one. I don't think my body appreciates anything warm anymore."

Knelling down to hand the man his cup Steve was taken back.

"Yeah you're going to have to help me a bit." The soldier explained as he sat up.

The soldiers left arm was gone at the elbow. His right hand had been amputated at the wrist.

Fighting back tears Steve placed the cup up to the man's mouth.

After taking a drink the man smiled. "Man it's been days since I had some hot Jo. Thanks sergeant."

He helped the man finish the entire cup. When the cup was empty the man laid back down.

"That did the trick. I think I can sleep now. Thanks again Sarg."

Steve had just taken a few steps when he heard a woman's voice cry out. It came from an area of the basement divided off by some blankets. Curious, Steve entered the make shift room. There were about a dozen men observing several nuns assisting a young woman giving birth. When the baby was born, the nuns simply wrapped it in part of an American military blanket before placing it in the woman's arms. The newborn cried slightly before the mother pulled it in closer to her.

A blonde solder from the 101st walked forward gently touching the baby on top of its head. He then picked up a box from the floor. After retrieving several pieces of GI script from his pocket he tossed them in the box. He then passed the box to the next G.I. Each man in turn contributed something to the box. By the time it came to Steve he had already removed several script notes, and a French Frank he found someplace back in France from his pocket. After dropping his money in the box he handed it to one of the nuns.

"Merci." She said softly accepting the box for the woman.

As the men slowly prepared to leave, one G.I. removed a green scarf from around his neck. No doubt it had been a gift from a loved one back home. He folded it neatly before placing it on the bed aside of the woman. Another man dug into his pack, placing a pint bottle of Cognac he most likely pilfered from an abandoned house atop the scarf. A third soldier pulled a box of K-rations from his pack, placing it aside the bottle of booze. Many men at Bastogne would have killed for that box of rations. Tonight, that soldier out in the bitter cold would probably go hungry he thought. Steve wanted to contribute something to the growing pile but he had left his pack in his fox hole. Suddenly he remembered the small chocolate bar he had in his shirt pocket. Placing it aside the scarf the woman smiled, “Schokolade! Danke!”

Settling back into the Jeep Steve thought about everything he had just witnessed in the church basement. There had not been any wise men or gifts of gold, Frankincense or myrrh. Just a ragged scarf, a stolen bottle of booze, some GI Rations and a candy bar. But to Steve these were real treasures, given by men who did not even own the clothes they were wearing.

In fact, some of them may not even live to see the light of Christmas day. Looking up toward the sky Steve could see a break in the heavy clouds. Several stars twinkled momentarily before they were once again covered by ashen grey clouds. It reminded him of the star leading those poor shepherds to the place where Jesus lay in that manger. However tonight, there was no peace on earth. In fact, men were dying all around him as German artillery smashed in the Belgium forest. The baby that had just been born would probably not make much of a difference on the world, if it even survived this war. But tonight, Christmas Eve watching a new life begin, surrounded by so much death was a sign of hope for those brave weary soldiers. And for all the cold freezing men at Bastogne surviving in fox holes, that was just about good enough.

Rumors abounded on Christmas Day that American forces could break through the siege at any time. Most of the men refused to believe the rumors as they had heard them all so many times. Christmas day was bitterly cold. No one caught up in the embattled city felt much like celebrating.

At dawn on the twenty-sixth the leaden skies covering the Ardennes over the past ten days finally broke. American and British fighters swooped down from the blue skies striking at anything German. Despite the aerial assaults, several determined enemy counter attacks were launched against the northern sector of the perimeter. Around 1700 as the cold night was beginning to settle in, three tanks broke through the woods approaching the American lines.

There was much confusion and disbelief at first as to what was really taking place, until a Captain in the first tank yelled they were American fourth armored. After midnight tanks from the 53rd. armored Infantry also broke through into the perimeter. Thus the bloody siege of Bastogne was finally over.

Every man along the perimeter crawled from their holes screaming and yelling. Although stiff and sore from the cold, several men attempted to run out and greet those beautiful tanks. They jumped on the first Sherman giving the Captain a huge hug. The highway was now open allowing reinforcements, supplies, artillery, and much needed armor to roll into the beleaguered Bastogne encirclement. Although security along the main highway was tenuous, two hundred and sixty of the most seriously injured soldiers were evacuated in twenty-two ambulances and ten trucks. The siege had cost the 101st one thousand six hundred and forty one casualties.

As green replacement forces flowed into Bastogne, many were immediately assigned to fill vacancies among the battle hardened airborne units. Charlie Company was no exception. Harry worked diligently with the replacements as Steve hastened to rebuild his shattered defensive positions.

Enough men were assigned to Charlie Company allowing them to construct a secondary line of resistance that could also be designated as a mobile reserve.

Despite the allies growing presence, Berlin insisted Bastogne be taken at all costs. Accordingly, on December thirtieth General von Luttwitz counter attacked in force along the sector occupied by a reinforced second battalion. The attack hit at the juncture of Charlie and Baker Companies with second platoon right in the thick of the fighting.

American tanks and artillery now well entrenched inside the perimeter repulsed the desperate attack.

British and American fighters dove from the clearing skies wrecking havoc on any German armored units taking to the open roads. The desperate battle lasted most of the day. By dusk depleted German forces began retreating without having penetrated the American lines.

Once the fighting ended Steve and Harry worked their way down second platoon checking on their men. Sergeant Hammond from Baker Company's fourth platoon met them where the companies joined.

"We took a lot of casualties." Sergeant Hammond said watching the medics working among the many wounded men being pulled from the bunkers.

Steve nodded in agreement removing his helmet to wipe his dirty face. "Yeah, we did to. We we'll need to move some men from our secondary line forward to fill in the gaps before night fall."

"Yeah, I'll take care of it, Steve." Harry said as he turned signaling for Corporal Crawford.

Steve walked a short distance with Sergeant Hammond before stopping when they heard a wounded soldier screaming at a medic.

"It's one of the replacements." Sergeant Hammond explained shaking his head. "I've been surprised one of our own men didn't shoot the son of a bitch before this. Everything we have gone through and this piss ant has been whining constantly since he arrived.

The two men walked over to the complaining soldier. Steve looked down watching a medic bandaging up several shrapnel wounds on the man's back, buttocks and legs. "That's the best I can do for now." The medic explained looking up at Sergeant Hammond. "He'll need to be evacuated to a hospital. Some of the shrapnel is pretty deep."

Rolling over onto his side the soldier complained loudly. "Look you idiot, you need to give me something more for this pain. I can't handle it. Sergeant, make him give me something."

The medic looked up at the two Sergeants. "Look we're short on morphine and pain killers.

There are other men who need help too. I just can't afford to give him anymore."

Steve looked down at the wounded man for a second. Smiling, he knelt down beside him. "I thought that voice sounded familiar. Corporal Baxter from the repo-depot, how did you end up here? Find any souvenirs yet?"

Steve inquired coldly of the wounded man.

"He doesn't need to find any, Sergeant. I'll give him one he can hang onto for a long time." A

young Lieutenant called out approaching from the Baker Company lines.

Steve stood and saluted as he looked inquisitively at the Lieutenant. "What do you mean, sir?"

I had Corporal Baxter feeding ammo to my fifty-caliber man. When the Krauts came, he left his position high tailing it out of the gun emplacement. When the fifty ran out of ammo the gunner was killed trying to reach for another can of ammo. We took casualties because we lost that machine gun. I'll see to it he is charged with desertion under fire. He can hang onto the Courts Marshall papers as a permanent souvenir." The lieutenant looked toward the medic, "Get him out of here, I don't want these incredibly brave men to hear this whining son of a bitch."

Steve helped the medic pull Corporal Baxter to his feet. "You'll need to walk a ways under your own power. Let's go, Baxter." The medic informed the crying soldier.

Just as they began to walk off Steve called out, "Wait a minute!" Removing the bayonet from his belt, he cut the corporal insignias from Baxter's sleeves. Handing them to Sergeant Hammond Steve looked Baxter eye to eye. "You don't deserve to wear them. I hope you can deal with the sight of a firing squad better then you could the Germans." Before Baxter could respond Steve told the Medic to leave.

The 502nd continued fighting in the snow and cold Ardennes, taking more casualties as they fought gallantly to reduce the salient caused by the initial German attack of December sixteenth. They repeatedly assaulted retreating enemy forces until the end of January. With the Germans in full retreat the 101st took up defensive positions along the Moder River.

On February twenty-fifth the weakened 101st was replaced on the line before being transferred to Mourmelon, France for rehabilitation. Harry checked off their men as they loaded on the open trucks for the long ride out of the combat zone. As the men waited in line to load, Steve took a long hard look at his men. They were visibly tired and worn out. Most, if not all suffered from frost bite, trench foot and battle fatigue. All of them, including Steve, had lost weight and were under nourished.

He was proud of his men, of what they had accomplished and the iron wills they proudly displayed. Even now there was no complaining as they stood in the cold waiting to board the trucks.

Karl Drussing stepped out of line to speak with Steve. "Kenrude, if I would have known in advance what we were going to go through, I might have had second thoughts about leaving that cushy job back in England. But you know. I wouldn't trade what I experienced these last two months for anything. We took one hell of a beating day in and day out. But the best the Krauts had couldn't over run us. We did something big here, Steve. People will remember what we did here for a long time. I'm proud to have been a part of it."

Steve shook hands with Karl as he looked him over. The smiling eyes Steve remembered so well from England were sunken and dull. The boyish face was replaced with the look of a rugged, unshaven, dirty man many years past his age. His lips were cracked and bleeding from the incredible cold. There was no doubt the hardships endured by every man of the 101st had taken a tremendous toll on them.

The difference was even more noticeable once they were settled into the refit station in France. Arguments, fights as well as complete disregard for military protocol ran rampant through out the company. Captain Wesco worked hard dealing with the men's problems. He understood all to well that most of the combat veterans of the 101st were plain burned out. They needed rest, but they also needed good physical workouts to burn up their frustrations and anger.

New replacements began arriving to fill the many vacancies that existed. Some of the replacements were returning veterans from D-Day and Holland that were just released from the hospital. They were eager to get back with their buddies which helped morale improve immensely.

Sergeant Randall who was wounded in the D-Day jump from Easy Company was assigned immediately to replace Sergeant Clarkson.

Sgt. Randall was liked by the men. He was not only fair but a natural leader, whose foremost desire was to rebuild Charlie Company into a top notch fighting company. Much to the disgust of Franny, he was promoted to Corporal. He took over fourth squad to replace Corporal Cummings who was listed as missing in action since December twentieth. All the veterans wondered what happened to Dave Cummings. He left his squad to confer with Steve about removing a wounded man and was never heard from again. They had served with him since jump school. Cummings had proven himself as a good leader and an all around tough soldier. It was hard to believe he could have been overwhelmed without a major struggle.

Steve and Harry were very happy about the assignment. They knew Franny was the best man for the job despite his protestations. However Franny was reluctant to hand over his beloved BAR. He loved the weapon and even more enjoyed being the go to guy when extra fire power was needed. But squad leaders were not allowed to carry the weapon. He would have to find a new BAR man for his squad. Steve enjoyed ceremoniously presenting Franny his freshly rebuilt Thompson machine gun as his personal weapon.

For the first time since arriving back from England, Steve was not only tired physically, but also of mind and spirit. He spent much more time thinking about home, Karen and Glendale then he ever had before. After hearing about Mike's run away and enlistment last summer, Steve prayed hard for the war to end before Mike could get into it. However Steve's prayers were not answered. The second week they were in France he received a letter from Mike. He had had just arrived in France with an armored reconnaissance unit. They were temporarily being in Reserve near Orleans.

Steve talked Captain Wesco into authorizing him a two day pass to visit his brother. Arriving at the sprawling base Steve found the encampment for Mike's company. He began the tough task of hunting down his younger brother. He found him replacing an antenna on top of a half-track. "Does your Mother know what the hell you're doing?" Steve called up to Mike.

Startled by the sound of his brother's voice Mike nearly fell off the ladder. The two brothers hugged one another before shaking hands. Steve could not get over how much Mike had grown and filled out. Mike could not get over how much his older brother aged since leaving home. His gray complexion and sunken eyes revealed the truth about a young man that had seen too much war.

"I couldn't believe you ran off and enlisted the way you did." Steve said glaring at Mike. "Look Steve. That issue is not open for discussion. I did what I had to do for me. Please let's not waste time getting into a discussion over it." Mike requested.

After a moment of silence Mike forced a small smile. "Hey, you look pretty good Steve for what you guys went through up at Bastogne. Mom and Dad were sure worried during that whole mess." Mike added.

"Yeah I guess they were. The first letters I read from them in months was when we finally returned to France. Yeah, there is no way I can ever tell them everything that happened up there. Actually I don't think most people would believe what we all went through, so how about you Mike? In letters I received from Mom after you left home she stated you wanted to be airborne. What happened?"

"I did sign up for airborne training. But when we arrived several officers told us the war would be long over before we finished training.

They gave us a chance to move on to something else if we wanted to. I'd met a guy back at Leonard Wood that was part of this recon unit. He told me before I left for jump school they were getting ready to ship out for Europe. So I did some quick leg work. I got back to Leonard Wood and sure as hell they needed two guys to replace a couple of goof off's that went A.W.O.L. I convinced Captain Forester that I could do the job. So he took me and here I am."

Steve shook his head. "I could still kick your ass but I guess that wouldn't solve a thing." Mike laughed slapping his brother on the arm. "First off who says you could kick my ass, and secondly we're both in this together so we best save our anger for the krauts."

Both men laughed as Steve nodded in agreement. "Well little brother I'm not going to bullshit you.

It's great to see you again. It really is. So any word on when you're moving out, or which army you are going to be assigned to?" Steve inquired.

"Well, we were ordered to prepare to move out in the next 48 hours. We all want to be assigned to Patton. Word is he needs another good armored recon unit so he can keep his forces moving forward. Believe me Steve, we may be green, but we're probably the best trained, best equipped, new recon unit on the continent. But who knows. We'll know for sure in the next 48 hours. How about you, Steve? Any idea of where you're going next?" Mike inquired.

"Well I'm thinking we're going to move out soon. When I asked for the pass to see you they gave me these dates. Captain said it was the only time I could go. So I'm guessing we'll be back on the line some time soon." Steve replied not letting Mike know it gave him a sick feeling in his stomach.

The day Steve left Mike walked him to the truck that was going to haul him back to Mourmelon.

"Take care of yourself, Mike. Don't take any unnecessary chances. I know you came here to see combat, but this war is almost over. Don't get yourself killed over some foolishness." Steve stated boldly as they shook hands.

"I'll be careful, Steve. You do the same." Mike responded smiling reassuringly at his big brother.

Not sure what else to say to his younger brother Steve jumped on the back of the truck. "See you in Berlin?" Mike called out.

"Hell yeah," Steve replied. "Franny says we're going to drink a bottle of cognac over Hitler's grave so you might as well join us. I swear Doogan could find a bottle in the middle of a cow pasture."

"You got a date, Steve. I'll be there." Mike replied as the truck began rolling out of the parking lot.

Arriving back at Mourmelon the tempo of training had picked up tremendously. It was obvious to the men they were headed back to the front soon.

Most of the veteran paratroopers hoped they would be sent back to England or maybe even state side. They figured with all the new replacements and fresh units arriving weekly, their war was over. However, Allied Command wanted experienced combat soldiers to be in reserve for units still actively pursuing retreating German forces.

The fear of another enemy offensive such as Bastogne kept everyone at Allied Command on their toes.

While awaiting orders Steve received a letter from Mike. He got his wish. His recon unit was assigned to Patton's third Army. By now his little brother was inside Germany fighting the war.

March thirty-first the 502nd moved out from France. Their assignment was to be in position on April fourth in the Ruhr Valley to cut the 97th Infantry Division loose. The collapse of the Third Reich was coming fast and furious now as events were taking place with blinding speed. The 502nd again moved to a new position on April twenty-seventh in the Memmingen Region, where they took up the task of policing the Kaufbeurnen-Saulgrub-Wertach-Kempten zone.

The first day in camp Capt. Wesco ordered Charlie Company to patrol east of their encampment.

About two miles out Sgt. Randall stopped in the middle of the road looking about the wooded area.

As second platoon was in the lead Steve and Harry both walked up to Sgt. Randall.

"Problems, Sarg." Harry inquired.

"Do you smell that Jensen? What the hell is that? It appears to be coming from the south through those woods.

"Yeah everyone has commented on it." Steve replied gazing over the woods with his binoculars.

I don't see anything, Sarg. Do you want us to work our way through the woods and check it out?"

"Yeah maybe, something is wrong, Kenrude. Do you hear that?" Sgt. Randall inquired "Hear what?" Harry responded. "It's quiet as a cemetery."

"That's just it, Jensen. It's spring. I grew up on a farm just like you guys did. Those woods should be alive with birds, frogs and all kinds of little critters. Something's not right. Jensen get back down the road tell the other platoon leaders to take a break along the road and be ready to back us. Tell them second platoon is going to patrol through the woods." Sgt. Randall ordered Second platoon spread out preparing to enter the strange wooded area.

The woods were eerily quiet, but the odor became more offensive the deeper second platoon moved south. Corporal Fineday called out, Sarg. I can see some sort of tower about fifty yards ahead. Looks like a fence near by. There's movement on the far side of the fence.

Stopping the platoon Sgt. Randall ordered Franny to take three men from his squad and check it out.

They were gone just a short time when Gunderson returned in a hurry.

"Damn. You got to see this. You won't believe it, Sarg."

"What is it, Gunderson?" Steve inquired.

"Damned if I know corporal, but I think we just stumbled onto hell. Come on you need to see it." Gunderson explained as he began walking south.

Sgt. Randall directed the men to continue until they all came to a stop by a massive electrified fence about twelve feet high. Behind the fence were men in black and white striped ragged clothing. Most of them appeared to be near starvation. Emaciated, fly covered, naked bodies lay everywhere.

One of the men approached the fence. He looked over the Soldiers for a moment before he spoke.

"What's he saying?" Sgt. Randall inquired.

"It's Yiddish." Rabinowitz explained excitedly.

"Can you talk to him?" Harry asked.

"Hell yeah, I know Yiddish fairly well. I came from a pretty strict Jewish family. My grandmother made sure we could speak it. In my neighborhood you either spoke Yiddish or you just kept your mouth shut." Rabinowitz replied as he neared the fence.

The two men talked for several minutes before Rabinowitz turned back toward Sgt. Randall. "They're all Jews, Sarg. The man's name is David. He's a Romanian. Says this was some sort of a work camp. He said the Krauts brought them here from all over Europe. We got some French, Czechs, Dutch, Romanians you name it. Sounds like the krauts high tailed it out of here about two days ago. They have no food or water. They don't know what to do."

"Ask him if there is anyone in charge we can deal with." Sgt. Randall asked.

"Don't have to, Sarg. He says the camp had a type of council up until two days ago. The Krauts shot all of them before they left. Since then no one has wanted to step forward. They're all scared as hell. When they saw us coming through the woods they figured we were here to finish them off."

"What the hell!" Sgt. Randall said shaking his head. After a moment of thought he called out, "Fineday get over here."

When Fineday approached Sgt. Randall turned to him. "You can run like a damn elk. Run back to camp and find the Captain. Tell him what we got here. Bring food, water, medics and what ever the hell else you think we need."

Dropping his pack and weapon Fineday took off like a flash.

"Jensen, tell the rest of the company to come on in here. Let's check around the area but no one, and I mean no one opens this damn gate! Greenburg do you speak Yiddish?" "Enough to get me by, sir," He responded as he walked up beside Rabinowitz.

"Good, you guys keep four men with you to secure that gate. If any of those people approach the gate just keep telling them help is on the way. Everyone else spread out to check the area.

They had barely begun moving around the camp when an S.S sergeant riding a large white horse came thundering down a trail. Several first squad men attempted to stop the charging animal with out success. The rider pulled a pistol from his belt and began firing toward them. Angered at the escaping soldiers defiance, Markham cut loose with his BAR

The horse tumbled to the ground throwing its rider into the air. The Sergeant hit the ground, rolling twice before rebounding directly onto his feet. He continued holding the weapon by his side as he observed the nearly twenty men surrounding him. Blood flowed from a large cut on his cheek as he breathed heavily.

Terrified, he began swinging the weapon from side to side threatening everyone in the circle.

Markham stepped forward pointing his BAR at the soldier. In broken German Markham stated, Drop your weapon or die!"

Taking another look around the circle of paratroopers he dropped his pistol.

Rabinowitz came forward holding his bayonet. "You a big Jew killer Hans, you want to take on a Jew that has a weapon man to man, here's your chance."

Tossing his bayonet at the Sergeant's feet, he quickly pulled Brant's bayonet from its scabbard.

"Pick it up Hans, you and me, master race against Jew. Come on damn it, pick it up you worthless piece of shit!" Rabinowitz yelled pacing back and forth.

After looking around the circle the S.S. Sergeant grabbed the bayonet. He laughed as he tossed the weapon from hand to hand. "Jew, only good Jew is dead Jew." He yelled out in broken English spitting blood toward Rabinowitz.

"Come on asshole let's see what you got." Rabinowitz yelled stepping toward the laughing Sergeant.

Before the men could make contact a shot rang out. The bullet struck the S.S. Sergeant in the side of the head. He fell to his knees before tumbling over to his side.

Everyone excitedly looked around to see where the shot came from.

Major Fontaine walked into the circle of men carrying a German Mauser.

"We've lost enough men. I'm not loosing another good man over something like this." He walked up to Rabinowitz looking him in the eye. "Son, I understand why you wanted to kill this bastard. But do you think it would have changed what happened in that camp? Do you think an eye for an eye would resolve that issue? Do you feel your God of Abraham would think better of you?"

Hanging his head Rabinowitz handed Brant back his bayonet, looking up at the Captain he quietly responded, "Sorry sir."

Captain Fontaine threw the empty Mauser to the ground calling out. "Will some one please put that damn horse out of its misery?"

Quickly Markham pumped two rounds into the horses head.

Placing his arm around Rabinowitz Captain Fontaine said reassuringly. "No need to apologize, son. I probably would have done the same thing had I been in your shoes. It's understandable. Now, grab your bayonet and let's get the hell out of here."

Walking back up to the gate Captain Fontaine approached Sgt. Randall, "No one in and no one out until the medics get here. Let them figure out what they feel is the right thing to do. Col. Bushman along with his command will be here shortly to take charge. When you're cleared come on back to camp."

No one who witnessed the atrocity slept well that night. Rabinowitz and Greenburg spent a good part of the evening at the make shift chapel reciting prayers for the dead they had been taught as children.

No one was upset about moving away from this encampment, as everything about it felt sick and unholy after dealing with the death camp.

May first they moved once more establishing headquarters in the Miesbach area relieving the fourth Infantry Division.

Their final move in the war came May seventh when they arrived at Berchtesgaden. That was the day hostilities were officially declared over. The men were excited, relieved, and ready to blow off some pent up steam. A gigantic party was thrown, with booze and food they found in buildings formally occupied by high ranking Nazi officials, and city officials, unwilling to cooperate with the American military government.

Franny walked up to Steve and Harry as they were finishing some cheese and crackers they liberated from an unoccupied house. "Well men, it's not cognac and it's not actually Hitler's grave. But it is brandy from the bastard's private stock." Franny stated looking up at the mountain where the remains of Hitler's eagle's nest stood.

Continuing Franny stated, "Well the war is over, and it's time for the drink just like we talked about for so long."

"Yes it is Francis, so why don't you pop the cork on that thing and let's get started." Harry demanded throwing a towel at Franny.

"Francis? What the hell is that shit? I hate that name. Keep that up and you not only don't get a shot off this bottle, but I might ask for a second front be opened up on your sorry ass." Franny said holding the bottle behind his back.

Steve laughed. "Just open the damn thing, Doogan we're wasting time here."

Just as Franny started opening the bottle they heard some one yell. "Does anyone know where Sergeant Kenrude might be found?"

"Don't they know this damn war is over?" Harry yelled back.

One of the new men from second squad walked into the courtyard where the three men were seated.

There was no doubt he was half drunk.

"What do you need private." Steve inquired of the man.

"Drussing and some guy I don't know are looking for you Sarg." He replied.

"Who the hell is the guy with Drussing, and what the hell does he want? And this better be good as you are interfering with a pretty high level meeting here." Steve replied with a smile.

"I don't know who he is. All I know is he's wearing a Third Army patch and says you invited him for a drink with your buddies when the war was over." The man replied almost comically.

There was no doubt in Steve's mind it was Mike. He was the only man in the Third Army he had invited for a drink to celebrate the end of the war.

"Franny hold off on opening that bottle for a few minutes." Steve said as he turned toward the drunken private. Go get Drussing and the other guy and bring them here, and do it fast."

The private turned and ran down the alley he originally came from.

In a few minutes Drussing and Mike walked up the alley toward the courtyard.

Steve stood up walking over to Mike giving him a big hug. "So you did make it into Patton's army after all."

"Hell yeah we did. And let me tell you we kicked ass on some kraut units trying to dodge some of our bigger armored guys' right up till the end. We tried to give them a chance to surrender, but they weren't having any part of that. It got just plain ugly a few times. But it's over now. So this must be the place where we conduct the big ceremony?" Mike said with a smile.

Steve grabbed Mike by the shirt pulling him across the courtyard.

"Harry, Franny I want you to meet my little brother Mike." Steve said proudly.

Harry stood up shaking hands with Mike. "It's finally nice to meet you, Mike. Feels like I've known you for a lot of years. Your brother has told me all about you."

"Like wise." Franny said shaking hands with Mike. "Your brother and I have chewed a lot of dirt together over the past year, nice to meet you."

Karl looked at Franny. "Are we going to open that damn thing or are we waiting for it to age until the next war starts.

"Patience, patience, Mr. Drussing, after all I have two more besides this one. So why rush into anything." Franny replied slowly starting to work the cork lose.

When the cork popped everyone cheered.

Franny jumped up on top of a chair. "Well here we are, some how we all survived this damn war.

Our next order of business is to go home and put our lives back together again. But we can never ever forget the guys that died. Max Eddington, Sergeant Winslow, Wade Rollins, Davenport and all the rest. Man we just lost way too many good men to mention." Franny stated very reverently.

"Willie. We can't forget Willie." Harry added to the list.

Franny nodded his head in agreement. "Yeah Willie, He was a good man. To all of them and those we didn't know may they rest in peace where ever they lay." Franny said as he took the first swallow from the bottle before handing it to Harry.

"Amen," Is all Harry said as he took a swallow before handing the bottle to Steve.

Steve looked at Franny and Harry. "And to those of us who survived. May we always stay close and never let the world forget what we did here." He took a swallow before handing the bottle to Karl.

He looked at the other four men. "I just thank God it's finally over." After he took a drink he handed the bottle to Mike.

Although Mike had not seen as much action as the others, he had killed the enemy and seen many good men die. He already came to the realization there was no glory in war. He lifted the bottle as he looked toward Steve. "Let's pray no one will ever have to experience anything like this ever again." He took a swallow before returning the bottle to Franny.

"Amen." Karl replied giving Mike a small pat on the back.

Franny set the bottle on the table. Walking over to storage shed behind the small patio where they were seated, he removed two more bottles he had stashed inside a cardboard box.

Karl and Steve popped the corks on those bottles. The men sat down slowly drinking the confiscated liquor while they quietly talked about the war, home, and the rest of their lives.

In the morning every squad leader had a terrible time getting their platoons assembled for morning formation. Some of the men were missing and could not be accounted for. Everyone suspected some of the men were sleeping where they passed out the night before. Others were with women they met during the night, sleeping soundly in warm beds between real sheets. No one could blame them for missing formation. By ten o'clock everyone was present, although most of them were dealing with hefty hang over's. During the next few weeks the days grew exceptionally long. After being in combat or intensive training for so long the men found it increasingly hard to deal with the boredom. Some of the men took daily swims in the lake nearby, or rowed around it in boats they confiscated from nearby cabins. Officers worked extremely hard to pick up athletic equipment so they could involve men in sports contests. They had enough engineer units present to carve out decent playing fields or construct any equipment that was required. Many of the games were high spirited, drawing good attendance from the weary soldiers.

Nightly movies were available to everyone as several out door theaters were erected. Every man took time to figure out exactly how many points they had, so they could estimate how soon they would be rotated home.

Steve checked each morning to see how many men from his platoon were being shipped home. As each man left Steve became exceedingly anxious to pack his bags and leave Europe forever.

May twentieth Steve and Harry received their notices to report to the camp transfer station for processing out. Leaving the building they ran into Franny who came walking down the sidewalk whistling a tune.

"Franny I figured we would all get our notices at the same time. Sorry to see you aren't going on this rotation." Harry said to a smiling Franny.

"That would be Sergeant Doogan to you in the future, Mr. Jensen." Franny responded with a smile.

"What the hell Franny, you're staying in?" Steve inquired looking totally surprised. "Yeah, hell why not, I look around at all these new guys and I think someone is going to have to show them the ropes and train them. Looks like you lovers are all headed home to be sad sacks, so I just figured what the hell." Franny exclaimed. "Hell I like the Army. I can't think of anything back there in civilian life I really want to do. I think this is the life for me"

Harry shook his head in disbelief. "Well you really surprised me, Franny. I wish you all the best.

Stay the hell out of the Pacific if you can. You've seen enough war, buddy."

"Naw, they can't send me to the Pacific. I got that in writing. I'll be here for a while training new men. Then it's back state side to be an instructor at Benning and the good life. I'm looking forward to it." Franny responded looking very happy.

Two days later Harry, Steve and Brandt were on a train platform ready to load when an exhausted Franny came running up to them.

"Thought I was going to miss saying good bye to you guys there for a while. The Captain had a few projects he wanted done." He explained while extending his hand to his best friends.

The four men shook hands then looked at each other silently for several seconds. "Sometimes I can't believe it's over, and who knows when we'll ever see each other again. Sometimes this entire war feels like it was all just a horrible dream. When I get home it will be gone forever." Steve stated looking at his three buddies.

Harry nodded his head in agreement. "You guys were the greatest. I'll never have any friends in my life that can replace you guys. Thanks for being there so damn often. "After a moment of silence Harry continued. "Hey tell you what, New Years Eve. 1946, Des Moines Iowa. I'll find a hotel and we can drink until we fall down drunk. What do you say?"

Steve smiled. "Damn straight, Karen and I will be there."

Franny laughed. "Who knows where the hell this damn Army is going to send me. But I damn guarantee I'll be in Des Moines New Years Eve. 1946."

Brandt assured Harry he would also be there. Everyone shook hands one more time as the conductor yelled, "All aboard!"

Franny didn't say another word. He watched as his best friends took their place in line. Slowly he turned to walk away. After taking a few steps he stopped. Turning back toward the train he called out, "Take care you sad sacks!"

The guys waved one more time before climbing aboard.

Slowly the train pulled out of the rail station on its way to the port of LeHavre, France, where troop ships waited to take the victorious soldiers of the American Army back to their loved ones and civilian life.

CHAPTER 15

THE LONG TRIP HOME

Thousands of excited men packed the railings of the Liberty Ship Samuel Evans as tugs gently nudged the vessel clear of the dock in LeHavre. No cruise ship ever had a more joyous group of passengers as did this Liberty Ship, as it sailed clear of the crowded harbor. Everyone shook hands, hugged one another and spoke in boisterous conversations as if they just finished a five star vacation.

Tired of all the craziness Steve walked toward the rear of the ship. He leaned against the railing watching the coast of France slowly disappear behind in the morning fog. Harry soon arrived shaking his head. "You would swear to God everyone on board this ship was just plain drunk."

Laughing Steve turned to watch the crowd for a moment, "Drunk with happiness old friend. They're alive. They made it. They're going home. What more could a man ask for?"

Turning back toward the rear of the ship they watched the coast of France peek in and out of the fog as they sailed toward the south coast of England.

"What the hell did we all do, Stevie boy? Huh. I mean, look at how we arrived, what happened in between, how many men we watched die. Man, what the hell Steve." He stated watching the dark forbidding waters of the English Channel turned into a bright froth by the churning props of the big ship.

"Yeah, Harry I have been thinking some of the same things. We sure as hell defeated Germany. That goes without saying. But the man power and material we went through staggers the imagination. And now just like that it was all over. How do things like this happen in the first place? Doesn't anyone sit down and consider the cost from everyone involved before taking on such a reckless adventure?"

Steve inquired looking over toward his good friend.

"Awe man, things like this have been going on forever. They just get bigger and bigger. But then, who would have ever thought about how cruel anyone could be to do what they did to the Jews. What was that all about?" Harry replied shaking his head.

Watching a British Destroyer sail by in route to LeHavre Steve responded. "Well I guess we'll never fully understand it Harry. I think we can just be lucky to have survived it, and now we get to spend the rest of our lives with our loved ones."

As Steve finished speaking Phil Brant joined them along the railing. "Thinking about jumping in and swimming back to France? Do you miss it already?"

Both men laughed as Harry gave Phil a good shove toward the railing.

"No we're just trying to figure out how to make those props turn faster so we can get to New York one day earlier." Harry joked.

This trip across the Atlantic was completely different from their voyage to England. There were no convoys, no sub alerts and no fears of being sunk in the cold gray North Atlantic. From time to time they would see a cargo ship sailing by; otherwise the vast Atlantic Ocean was empty.

The trip home was to take six days. There were some activities for the men to partake in, but for the most part everyone was on their own. None of the activities included any thing on deck for three entire days, as the North Atlantic was at its worst. Huge waves rocked the vessel forcing the Ships Captain and M.P.'s to make all out door areas off limits. With so many sea sick sailors this certainly was not a voyage to remember. The only activities left to the men were sleeping, reading or hot poker games. The bowels of the ship once again smelled awful from vomit and plugged up toilets. Searching for fresh air became a challenge for many a man.

As the Samuel Evan finally sailed along side Staten Island into Lower Bay the decks were crowded from bow to stern. One man called out, "There's my home. Staten Island. Good old Staten Island I love you."

The men were mostly quiet until the ship passed under the Verrazano Bridge. With the Statue of Liberty in sight the men began to yell and dance about on the deck. Some cried, others hugged their buddies saying over and over, "We're home, we're finally home." Steve, Harry and Phil found a spot along the railing well before the ship neared New York. They had a ring side seat as Lady Liberty passed by the port side. They could see lower Manhattan sparkle in the midday sun.

Crowds along the water front cheered and waved to their returning hero's. Everyone on deck waved back, cheering on the boisterous well wishers.

After two tugs shoved the Liberty Ship into place at the pier, an announcement came over the speaker system.

"Let me have your attention. We will be unloading in about fifteen minutes. There are two trains waiting on the pier. Both are going to Fort Dix where you will be processed out. Please be patient, we will get you all off as soon as we possibly can."

About an hour after docking the trains rolled down the pier to screams of welcome home from hundreds of waving people. It did not take long for the three combat veterans to fall asleep in the comfortable rail car.

They were all suddenly awakened by a Porter strolling through the car calling out, "Fort Dix next stop."

Trucks and busses lined the platform as the train came to a stop. Sergeants with clip boards sorted out the men directing them to the proper vehicles.

Steve and Harry were assigned to a barracks containing all non-commissioned officers. Brant was assigned to a barracks with privates just across the road.

Processing out was a much slower procedure than processing into the Army. For several days the men laid around with little or nothing to do.

Steve walked over to the orderly room to speak to an officer about getting a quick leave, to deliver the cross Private Garnett asked them to return to his mother.

After listening to Steve's story the young Lieutenant in charge was nearly in tears. He immediately signed two passes so Steve and Harry could delver the cross.

Harry was able to borrow a car from one of the cooks for the short drive over to Buddtown.

Arriving in the small town Harry stopped at the first gas station he saw. Steve went to the phone booth to search for the Garnet's address. True to their son's word, there was only one listing for a Garnet. The station attendant explained to them how to find the house. Finishing his directions Steve handed the man a quarter.

"Hey, that's not necessary soldier. After all, it's all of us who owe you for your service." Steve just smiled as he walked back toward the car.

Moments later they rolled up to the small well kept brick house. Harry rang the door bell than stood back. An attractive red haired woman opened the door.

"Can I help you soldiers?" She inquired with a puzzled look on her face.

Taking a deep breath Harry asked, "Were you related to a private Daniel Garnet?"

"Why yes. He was my younger brother. Did you know him? Please come in." She stated directing them into the living room.

The house reminded Steve of his parent's home back in Glendale. Everything was neat and orderly, with shelves along the side wall full of family photos.

Standing near the kitchen was a couple about the same age as his parents.

"Mom, Dad, these men were friends of Daniels" The young woman explained as she motioned for them to sit down.

After everyone was seated Daniel's father spoke. "I'm John, this is my wife Helen and you already met our daughter Brenda. So how well did you know our son?"

Smiling Steve replied, "First off I'm Sgt. Steve Kenrude and this is my friend Sgt. Harry Jensen."

Before he could say another word Brenda leaned forward. "You gentlemen are airborne. Daniel was infantry. How did you meet him?"

"We met Daniel on D-plus one several miles up the beach on the road to Sainte-Mere-Eglise. There was a battle involving tanks, infantry and paratroopers." Harry began than looked toward Steve.

Clearing his throat Steve continued. "Well, the hedgerow country was horrible. There wasn't room for maneuvering, or at times room for much of anything. So there was lots of confusion. Explosions, tanks whirling around in an open field, small arms fire, machine guns it was a tough battle. Everyone fought as a team to drive out the Germans." After taking a deep breath he continued. "There were heavy casualties on both sides. Daniel was wounded badly. We were going to deliver him to a medical station down near the beach when a half-track arrived with medics and equipment. He had lost so much blood there was just nothing they could do for him."

"Was our son brave?" Mr. Garnet inquired as he held hands with his wife.

"Yes he was." Harry replied. "He was the best."

"Did he suffer badly before he passed?" Helen Garnet inquired of Steve.

"Actually he didn't appear to be in much pain at all. He talked all the while before he died. "Steve explained as he removed the small silver cross from his uniform jacket. "Daniel gave this to me. He asked if we could return it to you." He explained handing the cross to Daniel's mother.

Tears rolled down her cheeks as she clutched the cross in her right hand. "Daniel is home." She said quietly as she wept.

After several minutes of silence Brenda asked, "Do you know where Daniel is buried?" Harry shook his head. "We don't know for sure, but we heard rumors a big cemetery was going to be established somewhere above the beachhead. I'm guessing someone at Fort Dix should be able to get you that information."

John Garnet smiled reassuringly, "Thank you boys, for being such a good friend to our son. Knowing Daniel did not die alone and that he was in piece makes a big difference to our family. You have brought much closure to this house. We would appreciate it very much if you would stay for dinner."

Harry quickly poked Steve. "Remember we need to be back for that special formation in a couple of hours."

Nodding his head in agreement Steve smiled at the family. "Harry is right. Our passes were only good for a few hours, and we need to make the formation, other wise we'll be A.W.O.L. so we must get moving."

Brenda smiled, "Military protocol?"

"Exactly, it will be nice when we can get away from all those rules and regulations." Harry replied as they all stood up.

"Will you be at the Fort long? Could we get together some other time?" Brenda inquired as she led the two men to the door.

"It's really hard to say. Things are happening so fast. They really want us there so we can be processed quickly." Harry replied with a smile.

"Well alright then. It was so nice meeting you men." Brenda responded.

After exchanging a round of hugs the men departed. As Harry drove off he looked over at Steve. "I don't know about you but I had to get out of there. I kept thinking how my parents would react if two guys showed up at their front door like we did. It was plain killing me."

"I know Harry. I almost wished I would have mailed the cross to them. But I'm glad we delivered it. I think it gave them more peace, and somewhat better understanding of how their son died." Steve replied as Harry turned on to the highway leading back to the fort. A few days later the men finally began processing out. Once they started, the process actually went rather quickly.

The last part of processing was to receive their final pay and their travel documents home. Phil excitedly informed his buddies they were all going to be on the same train heading west. Steve was excited about that as it gave him several more days to be with his two friends.

They traveled by bus to Lakewood where they boarded the train. Settling into their seats Phil looked over at his buddies.

"Can you believe this? We're actually going home. It's like a dream. I kept waiting for the Army to pull the rug out from under us and say, Ha-ha, gotcha!"

Harry laughed. "Now that sounds more like the Army that I got to love and almost understand. Franny reenlisting! I'm still baffled by that move."

Steve had to laugh as Phil just shook his head.

As the train pulled out Harry yelled, "Iowa here I come, Hot Damn!"

The train made several stops along the east coast, before it finally broke out of the congestion rolling into America's heartland. At nearly every stop soldiers departed the train, usually into the arms of waiting families. Some times blaring bands playing patriotic music added to the commotion.

Everyone left on the train jammed windows at each stop to partake in the festivities.

Slowly Steve began to dread the thought of Chicago as the train moved farther west. He knew that would be the splitting point with Harry. Although he longed to see Karen and rejoin his family, he felt sick over leaving his best friend behind. They had been through more than anyone could ever understand.

Steve never imagined he could become this close to anyone besides his family. He looked over at Harry and Phil who were sound asleep. For a crazy moment he wished they were still over in Europe. But he also knew eventually one or all of them would have been killed or maimed for life. Ultimately their luck had to run out sooner than later. Closing his eyes Steve joined his friends in a deep sleep.

They all jumped as the conductor called out, "Chicago next stop, next stop Chicago. The Windy city, next stops folks."

Harry looked over at Steve. "Well buddy looks like we've reached the end of the line." Steve choked back his emotions and smiled. "It's been a hell of a ride, Sgt. Jensen."

Harry laughed as he looked out the window. "It sure was Stevie boy. I couldn't have done it with out you."

As the train came to a stop they all stood up. Steve first shook hands with Phil. "Take care of yourself Phil, and don't fall off any mountains out there in Colorado. It has been a pleasure serving with you."

Phil laughed for a second then became very serious, "You were the best, Steve. You always looked out for us no matter what. Thanks for all you did to bring me home. I'll see you on New Years Eve next year in Des Moines."

The two men hugged quickly before Steve picked up his bag. Harry followed Steve to the platform.

"I guess this is good bye, Stevie boy. Take care of yourself and be good to Karen." After a moment of silence Harry continued. "I'll never understand war, Steve. But you have been the best friend, best confidant and best all around soldier. Thanks for everything."

Seriously fighting back tears Steve nodded. "Harry without having you by my side I don't know what that damn war would have been like. It sure would have been a lot worse without you. Promise me we'll stay in touch. And damn it, you best show up for my wedding."

Laughing Harry shook hands one more time, "Neither wild horses or Franny with his BAR could keep me away from that celebration. And when I get to that point, I'm counting on you as my best man."

Harry jumped back onto the rolling train after the conductor threatened to leave without him.

Steve waved as the train continued rolling out of the station. Harry leaned ever farther out the door one last time screaming, "Airborne forever, Stevie boy."

Steve watched until Harry disappeared inside the car. Suddenly he felt all alone in the world. His sidekick since Fort Snelling was gone. The one person he counted on for the last three years through unbelievable horrors and strife was gone. No one not even Karen could ever fill that void in his heart.

Slowly Steve walked down the platform toward the area he was to catch the train for Minneapolis.

About ten minutes later his train pulled into the station. Although Steve hoped to sit alone the train was full. Another returning soldier from St. Paul sat down beside Steve.

In the end, Steve was happy the soldier sat by him. They shared many stories about their experiences.

As the train neared Minneapolis Steve began to feel restless. Although he couldn't wait to see Karen, another part of him wanted to jump from the train and run, where to he did not know. But suddenly he was afraid to go home. He felt awkward and out of place. No one in Glendale could understand what he had been through. He wondered if he would feel like a square peg in a round hole when he walked into his parent's home.

When he last passed through this depot he was young and innocent, heading off toward a huge adventure with Harry at his side, he could have never imagined the horrors and carnage that awaited him in Europe. Now everyone he learned to depend upon for those three long years had gone their own ways.

There was little doubt he had changed dramatically. He had killed, while learning not to mourn deaths of those around him to heavily. After all, it was just part of war. But could he now separate himself from what he had become, to the man he truly wanted to be for Karen. In fact, would Karen even be able to accept him now.

He was jolted back into reality as everyone around him began to stand up. They were stopped at the Great Northern Train Station in Minneapolis.

Grabbing his bag, Steve said goodbye to the soldier who accompanied him from Chicago. He walked toward the bus terminal searching for the one that would take him home to Glendale.

After boarding the nearly full bus a woman about the age of his mother sat down beside him.

"Welcome home soldier, job well done." She stated with a huge smile on her face. "My boy Tommy arrived home a few days ago. I feel so much better now that the war in Europe is over."

Steve smiled trying to figure out what to say. "Where did your son serve?" he finally inquired.

"He was in North Africa, Sicily and then France. He doesn't talk much about it though." She replied with a frown on her face.

"Give him time. He went through a lot. Just give him time." Steve reassured the woman. They spoke on and off until she departed the bus at Litchfield, Minnesota. Now Steve was about fifty miles from home. His stomach was tied in knots as sweat poured down his back. He never remembered being this nervous before, scared yes, as he remembered the long flight from England to France on D-Day.

Finally the country side began looking familiar. He could recite names of lakes and rivers as they whizzed by. Small towns such as Cokato, Atwater and Grove City, with their high water towers, and busy grain elevators were memories from the past. A little while later he saw the sign, "Glendale five miles."

He felt his heart rate climb dramatically as he thought of home and Karen. Now it felt like the best thing in the world. All his fears, all his misgivings had suddenly disappeared. All he wanted to do now was hold Karen tightly in his arms.

Finally he could see the water tower as they rounded the bend in the highway. The driver slowed as he entered the city limits. Steve looked from side to side as the bus made its way to the drug store bus stop. It didn't appear much had changed in town while he was away.

Looking through the windshield he could see quite a crowd near the drug store. He made out Christine standing in the road pointing at the bus as she jumped up and down. He had to laugh as he watched Mayor Morris pull her out of the street so she wouldn't get hit by the bus.

Looking out the window he now saw his folks along with Karen and Janet Donnelly waving at him. Jumping from his seat, he raced up the aisle. The driver barely had the door open as Steve bounded down the three steps to the sidewalk below.

He grabbed Christine giving her a huge hug as she whispered in his ear. "I missed you so damn much, big brother. Welcome home."

After releasing his little sister Steve looked her over. "You are absolutely beautiful. You've grown so much. I missed you too."

He then shook hands with his father before Nancy grabbed him with all her strength. She sobbed nearly uncontrollably as she held him in her arms.

"It's alright mom. Everything is fine now. "He told his mother before kissing her on the cheek. I made it mom. I'm finally home."

He intentionally grabbed Janet next keeping Karen for last.

Janet hugged her future son-in-law. "Welcome home son. We've been waiting for this day for a long time. Now go to Karen."

He walked up to Karen taking both her hands. "You are gorgeous. I can not believe how much you have changed. He then took her in his arms and held her tightly as they kissed. "Don't ever leave me again, Steve. I love you so much." She whispered.

"I'm home. This is where I belong. I'll never leave you again, I promise." He reassured her. After they finished talking Mayor Morris welcomed Steve home. He had kept the promise he made after his son was killed at Pearl Harbor. He would see every boy from Glendale leave for the war, and he would be there to welcome them all home again.

After all the well wishers welcomed Steve home, the crowd dissipated. His father walked up to him.

"Well, son, are you ready to head home?"

"Home that really sounds great, Dad. Just one request, can Karen and Janet come along." Steve inquired as he stood with his arm around Karen's waist.

"Absolutely, after all their part of the family too," Alex responded with a big smile.

As Alex drove into the yard Steve could see the changes the storm had made on the property. But it didn't matter he was home.

After dinner Karen and Steve went for a walk down to Eagle Lake. He took Karen's hand helping her climb out on to the big rocks like they had done so many times before when they were in high school.

"You know there were times I never thought I would see you again." Steve explained.

Karen placed her fingers on Steve's lips, "Sush, nothing about the war, nothing about any of that. Not now. I just want to pick up where we left off. There is time for all the rest latter on, Alright with you?"

As a tear rolled down Steve's cheek he nodded his head. He took Karen in his arms placing her head against his chest.

Karen was right. Tonight nothing mattered. They were finally together again. All his fears were gone. All his dreams for their future were beginning to unfold. He was holding Karen once more. God had truly answered all his prayers.

EPILOGUE

Harry kept his promise to host a 1946 New Years Eve celebration in Des Moines. He and Marylyn rented a large meeting room at the Royal Hotel, stocking it with booze, hors d oeuvres and plenty of decorations. Steve and Karen worked diligently finding their comrades and getting invitations out.

The party was a big success. Attendees included Franny, Mike Anderson, Josh McGruder, Phil Brant, Karl Drussing, Oscar Joblinski, Billy Juarez, Ben Rabinowitz, Harvey Greenburg, Russ Abbott, Major Fontaine and their wives. Several others sent messages of appreciation but were not able to attend.

As the war ended the survivors went home. Those that were killed were ether buried in the D-day Cemetery in France or the allied Cemetery in Luxemburg.

Most of the survivors remained in touch celebrating holidays, birthdays and many numerous happy and some times sad occasions. However as with all things time takes its toll. So what happened to the men from Charlie Company?"

* Corporal Dave Cummings went missing at Bastogne was never found.
* Major Fontaine remained in the army serving in both Korea and Vietnam. After retiring from the Army in 1967 he then worked as an import-export broker until 1978. He passed away from a heart attack in 1990.

* Mike Anderson returned to South Carolina where he joined his brother-in-law in a successful seafood business. He passed away in 2000 from cancer.
* Russ Abbott returned to Pennsylvania. He took advantage of the G.I. bill graduating from college with a degree in business management. He worked for several national firms before retiring in 1990. He passed away in 2002.
* Josh McGruder After being discharged he went to school on the G.I. bill graduating with a degree in psychology. He worked in private practice his entire career. Josh passed away in 2003.
* Larry Woodward returned to Kansas. For no explained reason he committed suicide in 1947.
* Phil Brant returned to Colorado where he became a police officer. He was killed in the line of duty in 1976.
* Karl Drussing returned to Oklahoma where he worked in the family business operating a wholesale food distributing company. He was killed by a drunk driver in 1996.
* Roy Markham Returned to Michigan where he worked in an auto assembly plant. After retirement he became a Deacon in his church. He passed away in 2010.
* Billy Juarez returned to New Mexico. He tried out for several major league baseball teams but was never able to get signed. He played amateur ball for three years before giving up the game. He then worked as a correctional officer for the state prison system. He wrote three novels, several short stories and one children's book before passing away in 2009.
* Oscar Joblinski returned to Illinois after receiving his artificial leg. He attended college on the G.I. Bill graduating with a degree in Education. He taught elementary school for thirty-five years. He spent much of his free time working with handicapped children. Oscar always remembered Steve telling him to do something good when he got home. Oscar passed away in 2010.
* Ben Rabinowitz returned to New York where he studied to become a Rabbi. He moved his family to Israel in 1963. He was killed in a terrorist bombing in 1978.
* Father O'Healy who spoke with Steve the morning of June 5th survived the war in Europe to be killed in Korea 1952.
* Danny Kettle killed in action June 6th 1944 buried in France

* Walter Jameson killed in action June 6th 1944 buried in France.
* Sgt. Clarkson killed at Bastogne buried in Allied cemetery in Luxemburg.
* Max Eddington killed at Bastogne buried in Allied cemetery in Luxemburg.
* Oscar McBride killed at Bastogne buried in Allied cemetery in Luxemburg.
* Harvey Greenburg returned to New Jersey. He drove a cab in Newark for ten years before becoming part owner in the company. He passed away in 2008.
* Francis Martin Doogan III (Franny) He ended up serving in Korea and Vietnam. Franny retired at the rank of Sergeant Major to the state of Florida. He served two terms in the Florida legislature before retiring to write. He wrote two novels and one book on his war experiences along with many columns for their local paper. He passed away in 2009.
* Harry Jensen returned to the farm in Clearview, Iowa. Along with his brother-in-law and father they turned the farm into a major beef operation. Like many airborne veterans Harry was called back into the Army for two years during the Korean War. Harry and his wife Marylyn loved spending time with Steve and Karen when ever possible.
* Harry passed away while touring battle sites in France and Germany one last time in 2011.
* Alex Kenrude farmed with his sons until retiring. He never traveled very far from home. He passed away in 1980.
* Nancy Kenrude enjoyed her grand children and helping out Karen anyway she could. Nancy passed away in 1983.
* Mike Kenrude remained in Germany until 1947. His unit continued chasing down rogue German forces that refused to surrender properly. They confiscated untold tons of war material they discovered all over Germany. He planned to make a career of the army but was discharged in 1949 after being seriously injured in an accident. He came back to Glendale married his wife Glenda. They had there children. He became a partner in Kenrude Farms Inc. Mike passed away in 2011.
* Christine Kenrude became a nurse in a large metropolitan hospital in Minneapolis. She married an attorney and had four

children. Her family loved spending weekends in Glendale. She was still alive as of this writing.

* Janet Donnelly loved helping Karen and playing with her two grandchildren. She helped prepare all the paper work to incorporate Kenrude Farms. She passed away from cancer in 1965.
* Karen Kenrude (Donnelly) Enjoyed helping out on the farm while raising two children, Jessica and Christopher. She took an active part in PTA and their church. She once again had a tough time when Steve was called back to the army during the Korean War for two years. She loved to travel with Steve and the Jensen's. She is still alive as of this writing living in a retirement center.
* Steve Kenrude returned to Minnesota to marry his high school sweetheart, Karen. They had two children. Steve was called back to the Army during the Korean War for two years due to his airborne expertise. Upon returning he and Alex purchased the old Donnelly farm and the Miller farm. With over 500 acres they incorporated their operation into Kenrude Farms Inc. Mike also became a partner when he was discharged from the Army. Steve passed away sitting on his front porch in 2012.
* Mayor Hank Morris ran unsuccessfully for state legislature twice. He remained mayor of Glendale until 1966. He passed away from lung cancer in 1970.
* Sister Carmella who spoke with Steve in the church at Beuzeville visited him once more during a trip back to Minnesota in 1969. She stayed on the farm for several days before returning to the Monastery. She was murdered doing missionary work in Tanzania in 1974.
* Capt. McHenry who led the relief column into Sainte- Mere-Eglise was killed in action November 1944. Buried in France.
* Capt. Lewis who was fighting to hold on to Saint-Mere-Eglise retired from the army in 1977 after serving in both Korea and Vietnam. He passed away in 2000.
* Corporal Baxter the soldier who ran during the battle of Bastogne served five years in Leavenworth Military prison. He disappeared after being released from prison.
* Lt. Winslow was killed on D-Day is buried in France.

* Archie Davenport killed on D-Day buried in France.
* Cpl. Bill Smith killed in Holland buried in France.
* Willie Davis killed in Normandy Campaign, buried in France.
* Lt. Daniels killed during Normandy Campaign buried in San Francisco. His family brought his remains home in 1956.
* Dave Willis killed during Normandy Campaign buried in France.
* Jim Edwards killed in Normandy Campaign, buried in France.
* Capt. Washburn killed in Normandy Campaign buried in Arlington. His family brought his remains home in 1960.
* Max Eddington killed at Bastogne, buried in allied cemetery in Luxemburg.
* Daniel Garnet killed in Normandy Campaign, buried in New Jersey. With the help of their local community his family returned his remains in 1948.